PENGUIN BOOKS

Private Members

Leonie Fox is a former magazine journalist. She lives in Kent.

Private Members

LEONIE FOX

PENGUIN BOOKS

PENGUIN BOOKS

Published by the Penguin Group
Penguin Books Ltd, 80 Strand, London WC2R ORL, England
Penguin Group (USA) Inc., 375 Hudson Street, New York, New York 10014, USA
Penguin Group (Canada), 90 Eglinton Avenue East, Suite 700, Toronto, Ontario, Canada M4P 2Y3
(a division of Pearson Penguin Canada Inc.)
Penguin Ireland, 25 St Stephen's Green, Dublin 2, Ireland
(a division of Penguin Books Ltd)
Penguin Group (Australia), 250 Camberwell Road, Camberwell, Victoria 3124, Australia
(a division of Pearson Australia Group Pty Ltd)
Penguin Books India Pvt Ltd, 11 Community Centre, Panchsheel Park, New Delhi – 110 017, India
Penguin Group (NZ), 67 Apollo Drive, Rosedale, North Shore 0632, New Zealand
(a division of Pearson New Zealand Ltd)
Penguin Books (South Africa) (Pty) Ltd, 24 Sturdee Avenue, Rosebank, Johannesburg 2196, South Africa

Penguin Books Ltd, Registered Offices: 80 Strand, London WC2R ORL, England

www.penguin.com

First published in Penguin Books 2007

1

Set in 12.5/14.75 pt Monotype Garamond
Typeset by Rowland Phototypesetting Ltd, Bury St Edmunds, Suffolk
Printed in England by Clays Ltd, St Ives plc

ISBN: 978-0-141-02806-4

Acknowledgements

A huge thank you to Mari Evans and all at Penguin for their comments and support.

One

Stifling a yawn, Keeley Finnegan pushed her sunglasses up into her hair and squinted across the eighteenth green. 'About fucking time,' she muttered as a gaggle of match-stick figures trooped into view. She glanced at the Cartier watch encircling her slender wrist and couldn't help smiling as the sun's rays caught the baguette-cut diamonds, making them sparkle and dance. 'Three hours it's taken them to get round this stupid course,' she said, resuming her frown. 'Meanwhile, *we're* all stuck out here, dying of heat exhaustion – not to mention boredom.'

'Oh it's not over yet, darling,' said Marianne, the oldest member of the group by nearly two decades. 'Not by a long shot ... if you'll pardon the pun.' She ran a well-manicured hand over her elegant platinum chignon, smoothing imaginary stray hairs. 'There are thirty teams taking part in the tournament; this is simply the leading pair.'

'Which means,' said Laura, who was married to a pro golfer and therefore knew her eagles from her birdies – even if, like Keeley, she did find the game unspeakably dull – 'that there are another couple of hours of play left at least. Then there's the prize-giving ceremony; that'll take a good hour. *And* the charity auction, of course. I'd be surprised if we sat down to eat before, ooh, eight o'clock at the earliest.'

Keeley sighed crossly. 'I can't believe Fabrizio talked me into this. I can think of a thousand other things I'd rather be doing.'

Spotting an opening gambit, Cindy McAllister, who had contributed precious little to the conversation in the past hour (though not for want of trying), seized the opportunity with both hands. 'I guess you're spoilt for choice, huh, honey?' she said, patting Keeley's knee in a way she hoped wouldn't be deemed too intimate. 'There's so much to see and do in Delchester; the city's practically drowning in culture – that's part of the reason I was so excited about relocating here.' She cleared her throat, suddenly feeling nervous. 'I hear the Haymarket Gallery is running a fabulous Toulouse-Lautrec exhibition. I was wondering if any of you gals fancied making an afternoon of it. We could have lunch afterwards, maybe wander through Chinatown . . .'

There was a brief – but pointed – silence before finally Marianne spoke. 'I'm afraid we're not great culture vultures, Cindy,' she said, managing to sound apologetic and patronizing at the same time. 'We don't really *do* galleries, do we, girls?'

'Ugh, all those dusty old paintings,' said Keeley with a stagy shudder. 'They give me the creeps.'

Cindy bit her lip to mask her disappointment. 'No? How about ballet?' she said brightly, keen to demonstrate her good taste and broad range of interests. 'There's a Frederick Ashton season on at the Royal Exchange. The *Sunday Times* critic described it as a "must see".'

Laura shook her head, knowing how the gesture caused her corkscrew curls to bob attractively. 'I hate ballet,' she said with a startling degree of vitriol. 'Those stick-thin dancers make me feel so fat and ugly.'

'Yes, but all those men in tights, darling,' said Marianne. 'It's always useful to see what credentials a man's packing before you get him into bed. Don't you agree, Cindy?'

'Oh, uh, sure,' said Cindy, trying to sound as if she were used to broaching such matters over a glass of champagne on a Saturday afternoon. Then, in a desperate attempt to raise the tone: 'So, why don't you tell me exactly what it is you like to do?'

'Shop, shop and shop some more,' said Keeley in a deadpan tone. She cocked her head and batted her eyelashes coyly – a gesture that made her look much younger than her twenty-seven years. 'Fabrizio has promised to buy me a diamond if his team wins the tournament.'

'Oh, the joys of dating a premiership footballer,' said Laura sarcastically. 'Tell me, Keeley, how *are* your Italian lessons coming along?'

Keeley wrinkled her freckled nose. 'I've given them up; I'm rubbish at learning. I was always bottom of the class at school; my teachers told me I'd end up on the checkouts if I wasn't careful.' She ran a finger over the face of her £20,000 watch and added in a soft voice: 'But I showed them.'

Keeley had been dating Fabrizio da Luca, Delchester United's top striker, for four months. They'd met at St Benedict's Country Club & Spa, which was where Keeley found all her boyfriends. In fact, it wouldn't be too much of an exaggeration to say it was the sole reason for her membership.

'How on earth do you and Fabrizio communicate when

you don't speak a word of Italian and *he* speaks less English than a four-year-old?' asked Marianne.

'Oh, I let Fab's wallet do the talking,' said Keeley matter-of-factly. She let out a filthy laugh. '*And* his dick.' She leaned forward conspiratorially. 'You know what these continentals are like. He keeps wanting to do me up the arse.'

'No!' squealed Marianne and Laura in unison.

Behind her Prada sunglasses, Cindy rolled her eyes. This was going to be a very long afternoon.

At that moment, a young Latino waiter, clad in white cotton trousers and a matching Nehru jacket, emerged from the clubhouse. He moved smoothly round the women's table, topping up glasses with Dom Perignon. As he leaned over Cindy's shoulder, he couldn't help admiring the striking redhead and the way her Diane von Furstenberg wrap dress clung to her figure, showing off her slim waist and magnificent cleavage to perfection.

Marianne noticed the waiter noticing Cindy and was instantly on the defensive. Extending a honey-coloured arm, she reached behind her and, without any preamble, languidly stroked her hand across the waiter's crotch, causing an immediate and visible stiffening. The waiter's eyebrows shot up, but his champagne-pouring hand didn't wobble.

'Nice to see you again, Enrique,' Marianne purred as she unhanded the waiter. 'I did so enjoy our last . . .' she paused and ran her tongue slowly round her peony-painted lips '. . . encounter. We must do it again some-time. Why don't you call me?'

The waiter smiled lazily. 'Certainly, Mrs Kennedy. It

would be my pleasure,' he said in heavily accented English. 'Now, if you ladies will excuse me.' He gave a small bow and, lowering the champagne bottle to mask his swollen manhood, retreated into the clubhouse.

Keeley shot Marianne a sharp look. 'Tell me you're not?'

Her friend thrust out her chin and smiled smugly. 'I'm afraid I am, darling.'

Keeley sighed. 'I don't know how you do it, I really don't. I just hope I've got half as much energy when I get to your age.'

Laura turned to Cindy, who couldn't quite believe the flagrant act of indecency she had just witnessed. 'You'll have to excuse Marianne. To say she's got a wandering eye is something of an understatement.'

Marianne sniffed haughtily. 'And I make no apology for it. I may not be young, but I'm certainly free and single – and I happen to be very highly sexed.'

Cindy smiled weakly, acutely aware that she mustn't evince the smallest sign of disapproval. A native Californian, she had arrived in Cheshire just four short weeks ago and was still struggling to find her feet in this unfamiliar milieu. Being, as she was, an inveterate social climber, the one condition Cindy hated more than any other was feeling like an outsider. She would do anything (well, almost anything) to belong – and, more than that, to be at the heart of the action; to be the sparkling pivot round which everyone else revolved, like planets round the sun. The instant she had laid eyes on these three – Marianne, Laura and Keeley – giggling over Sunday lunch in the club's sumptuous Ladies' Lounge, while other women shot them looks of disapproval tinged with envy, Cindy knew that this was the clique she wanted (correction: *needed*) to belong to if she were going to make her mark at St Benedict's.

Set in 200 acres of prime Cheshire parkland, St Benedict's was one of England's most exclusive country clubs. It lay some eight miles west of Delchester, in the village of Kirkhulme, which was notable for possessing more millionaires per square mile than anywhere else in the country. With a two-year waiting list (though this was regularly waived in the case of celebrities and aristocrats), the club's invitation-only memberships were as highly sought after as bottles of 1961 Château Latour. Dominating the landscape was St Benedict's famous Grade II-listed art deco clubhouse. Built on the crest of a hill and approached by a long rhododendron-lined drive, the vast white building enjoyed sweeping views of the eighteen-hole golf course, which had played host to numerous championships in its illustrious 110-year history, including two Ryder Cups and ten British Opens.

The annual pro-celebrity golf tournament was the highlight of St Benedict's summer calendar. Launched in 1972, the event had raised millions of pounds for children's charities, and each year the list of players grew more impressive. Today's competition featured no fewer than ten world-ranked golfers, two soap stars, a veteran TV presenter, an international recording artist, an Olympic rower and three premiership footballers – including Fabrizio da Luca, whose powerful physique and smouldering Mediterranean looks made him the ladies' choice.

Not surprisingly, the tournament attracted hundreds of spectators, many of whom positioned themselves on the course, faithfully following their favourite player from hole to hole, cameras and autograph books at the ready. Others, like our little quartet, preferred the Manolo-friendly environs of the VIP seating area outside the clubhouse, where champagne flowed and vast cream linen parasols offered some relief from the searing July sun.

Marianne frowned. Not that you would have noticed – four-monthly Botox injections kept her forehead as smooth and plump as a teenager's. For several minutes now she had been aware of the distant – but nonetheless irritating – sound of an engine revving, and it seemed to be getting closer. Marianne was very sensitive to noise. Tea-slurping, birdsong and the wilful cracking of finger bones set her teeth on edge; the churning of a washing machine made her physically nauseous; gum-chewing drove her to distraction. A month earlier, the sound of a dripping overflow had kept her awake all night; so had the plumber who came to fix it.

Twisting round in her chair, she surveyed the stretch of undulating parkland, edged with banks of azaleas and well-regimented flowerbeds, which lay on the east side of the clubhouse. 'Where in God's name is that noise coming from?' she said tetchily. 'I can feel one of my heads coming on. I shall have to take an aspirin if it doesn't stop soon.'

A moment later, the mystery was solved as a golf buggy came bouncing over the crest of a man-made hillock.

Hunched over the wheel was a mahogany-skinned twenty-something with an artfully tangled mane of hip-length hair and a manic glint in her eye. Judging by the way she kept casting worried looks over her shoulder, she was fleeing from something – or rather some*one*. After driving straight through a flowerbed, crushing a row of lovingly cultivated Himalayan blue poppies and a rare hybrid tea rose, the blonde floored the accelerator, pushing the buggy to its maximum speed of 20mph.

Suddenly, a second buggy came hurtling into view. Its driver was also deeply tanned and blonde (with a few coffee-coloured streaks thrown in for dramatic effect). This buggy appeared to be chasing the first and, as she drew closer to her quarry, driver number two could be heard screeching a string of unintelligible insults.

Pursuing both buggies on foot was a middle-aged man, perspiring heavily in his regulation Barbour wax jacket, which he refused to remove, even in the warmest weather. Bob Daley was St Benedict's head groundsman. It was his job to maintain the club's eight putting greens, six tennis courts (four grass and two clay), crown green bowling lawn, 17,000-square-foot greenhouse that provided the 180,000 flowers for planting every year – and the jewel in the crown: the Peter Alliss-designed championship golf course with its computer-controlled pressurized irrigation system. With the gap between him and the buggies widening by the second, Bob quickly gave up the chase, shaking his fist at the departing vehicles before collapsing to his knees, his fifty-eight years clearly having got the better of him.

'Those carts are going awful fast,' said Cindy – who,

having struggled to find any common ground with her companions thus far, was glad of the distraction. 'I wonder what's going on.'

The women watched in amusement as the buggies zigzagged across the clubhouse's rolling gardens, their tyres throwing up fat divots of newly laid turf. 'You know, I'm sure that's Destiny out in front,' said Keeley, repositioning her teak recliner for a better view. 'I'd recognize those minging hair extensions anywhere. I keep telling her they make her look cheap, but will she listen?'

'Who's Destiny?' asked Cindy.

Keeley raised a perfectly shaped eyebrow. 'Destiny Morris. You must have heard of her.'

'Uh, no, I don't think so. I'm sure I'd remember an unusual name like Destiny.'

Keeley looked at the American woman aghast. 'Destiny Morris is only *the* most famous glamour model this country has ever produced.'

Marianne made a snorting noise. 'Which, let's face it, isn't saying very much.'

Keeley frowned, but didn't have the courage to contradict the older woman. 'Destiny's latest calendar outsold her nearest rival's two to one,' she told Cindy. She paused. 'Actually, she's one of my very best friends.'

'Really? Wow, that's great,' said Cindy unconvincingly. 'Has Destiny had much experience driving those carts? Only her steering seems a little shaky.'

The women watched as the model's buggy veered sharply to the left, decapitating a low-lying topiary peacock. In the distance, Bob Daley started keening. 'It certainly doesn't look like it,' said Marianne.

'So who's that chasing her?' asked Laura, shading her eyes with a hand as she strained to identify the second buggy's occupant.

Keeley smiled tightly. 'I'll give you three guesses.'

By now, other VIP guests had noticed the rapidly advancing buggies. An elderly woman nursing a Shih Tzu at the next table shook her head despairingly and remarked to her companion: 'St Benedict's used to be such an exclusive establishment. See what happens when you let the riff-raff in?'

Keeley's eyes narrowed. 'Aren't dogs banned from the clubhouse?' she said in a loud voice. She glared at the dog. 'They don't call 'em *Shit*-zus for nothing, you know. If I get doggy doo-doo on my new Gina sandals, *somebody's* going to find themselves barred for life.'

The dog owner opened her mouth to fire back a retort, but before she could speak her friend grabbed her arm. 'Oh my goodness, Marjorie, the lunatic girl's heading straight for us!'

She was right. In the tight confines of the two-man buggy, Destiny Morris was struggling to maintain her course, hindered as she was by her gargantuan 32F breasts, which were apparently trying to fight their way out of her three-sizes-too-small vest top. The look on her face was one of grim determination as she tried to steer the buggy away from the dozen or so tables ranged outside the clubhouse. Meanwhile, Destiny's pursuer had slowed her buggy to a crawl, apparently waiting to see what would happen next.

Spotting a disaster in the making, Enrique thrust a tray of martinis into the hands of his nearest colleague and started running towards the buggy, keen to avert any incident that might affect his customers' tipping generosity. 'You must stop!' he bellowed.

'I'm trying to!' Destiny shrieked, as her foot pumped the pedals in vain. 'Which one's the brake? I haven't passed my driving test yet.'

The waiter skidded to a halt. 'Try the handbrake; it's in between the seats,' he yelled. 'You must hurry, or people are going to get hurt.'

'Enrique is terribly macho; you wouldn't believe how dominant he is in bed,' said Marianne, shuddering as she relived some earlier act of depravity. Behind her back, Laura and Cindy exchanged wry looks.

Meanwhile, the buggy continued on its collision course. Enrique manfully stood his ground, but behind him there was mayhem as the VIPs took to their heels. Chairs were sent toppling, champagne bottles were shattered, canapés were mashed into the lawn. Keeley, Laura, Marianne and Cindy joined the stampede, grabbing their designer handbags and fleeing to the safety of the clubhouse. Realizing that self-sacrifice was pointless, Enrique was hot on their heels.

Seconds later, Destiny's buggy clipped one of the heavy wrought-iron tables, sending it crashing to the ground. The impact seemed to shock the model into action because she turned her steering wheel sharply to the left, just in time to avoid mowing down the Shih Tzu, who had given his mistress the slip and was lapping up spilled caviar from a broken Conran dish. As the dazed spectators regrouped around the wreckage of their tables, Destiny's buggy trundled on, now heading directly for the golf course. The second buggy followed close behind, its driver's face locked in a bitter smile.

Over at the eighteenth green, Laura's husband, Sam Bentley (world ranking: 52), was preparing to take the shot that could win him and his team mate – soap sex kitten Annalise Terry – the tournament, and his name etched on the coveted cut-crystal rose-bowl trophy for the third time in as many years. Adjusting his grip on his putter, Sam surveyed the short distance between golf ball and hole, trying to focus in the way his sports psychologist had trained him. He was just about to take the shot when a spectator's mobile phone started to ring, shattering his concentration. Immediately, Sam spun round and glared at the miscreant until he produced his phone from his backpack and shut off the call, grimacing apologetically. This may be a charity tournament, but Sam played each and every game as if it were the Ryder Cup final. Suddenly aware of the BBC North West camera trained on him, Sam's scowl turned into a smile. 'I hope you didn't just hang up on your wife, mate. I'd hate to be responsible for the break-up of someone's marriage,' he quipped, prompting a ripple of laughter among the spectators.

Once the tittering had died down, Sam refocused, blocking out every sight and sound around him – everything but the five-foot stretch of turf that lay between him and victory. Oblivious to the distant drone of a brace of golf buggies, he assumed his set-up stance: legs shoulder-width apart, weight centred over the balls of his feet, forearms tensed. Around him, the crowd held its collective breath. Sam was certain the tournament was his; only an idiot would fluff a five-foot putt. At the very second Sam's club left the ground, he heard a loud shriek from Abi, his caddie. The next thing he knew, the crowd of spectators clustered round the green had scattered and he was lying face down on the closely trimmed turf, felled by a painful rugby tackle from one of the course stewards. 'You fucking idiot!' said Sam struggling to his feet and wiping his nostrils free of dirt. 'You've just ruined my shot.'

'Sorry, Mr Bentley, it was the buggies, sir,' said the red-faced steward. 'I was trying to protect you. It looked as if they were heading straight for you.'

'Don't be ridiculous,' Sam snapped. 'Buggies are banned during tournaments. The club brought in a ruling last year.'

'I'm well aware of that, sir – but two of our members appear to have torn up the rulebook.'

Sam followed the steward's pointing finger and watched in disbelief while a pair of buggies, painted in the maroon-and-gold livery of St Benedict's, hurtled across the green, forcing players and caddies to flee in every direction. 'What the fuck . . .' he said as the lead buggy flattened the flag marking the eighteenth hole before careering through the avenue of pine trees that separated the green from the fairway beyond. Realizing where the real story lay, the most agile member of the BBC North West camera crew grabbed a hand-held and took off in pursuit.

Back at the clubhouse, the women had relocated to the Moorish-style roof terrace, which afforded excellent views of the unfolding drama below. 'This sure is turning into a strange afternoon,' remarked Cindy as she settled on a mosaic bench. 'So c'mon, guys, put me out of my misery. Who *is* the chick in the second cart – and what's her beef with Destiny?'

Laura settled beside Cindy. She was warming to the vivacious Californian, and it wouldn't do any harm to forge an alliance with a fellow golfer's wife. In fact, it could prove eminently useful – here, at last, was someone who'd understand what she had to put up with. Everyone thought Sam and Laura had the perfect marriage; few understood precisely how difficult, demanding and downright temperamental professional sportsmen could be. Laura linked her arm through Cindy's. 'It's another well-known glamour model – Shannon Stewart. Believe it or not, she and Destiny used to be best friends.'

'Until Shannon waltzed off with Destiny's fiancé.' Keeley pursed her lips. 'And if that wasn't humiliating enough, poor Des only discovered she was being two-timed when Shannon 'fessed up, live on *Richard & Judy*. The little slapper had an autobiography to promote, and I suppose she thought that shagging her best friend's boyfriend and then shooting her mouth off about it was a sure-fire way to drum up interest in her pathetic little memoir.'

'She was right too,' added Laura. 'The tabloids had a field day with the story and Shannon's book flew off the shelves.'

'Poor Destiny,' sympathized Cindy. 'Is Shannon still dating this son of a bitch?'

'Uh-uh.' Keeley shook her head. 'Dean Hurley was just a means to an end. The minute his star started to fall, Shannon dumped him.'

'You mean he was a celebrity too?'

Laura shrugged. 'After a fashion. Dean won the first series of British *Pop Idol*. He had a couple of top-ten hits, but then his album flopped and the record company dropped him like a hot brick. At the height of his fame, he made the cover of *Heat* magazine; these days, he'd be lucky to get on the guest list at the British Legion.'

'This all happened last year and Destiny and Shannon have been sworn enemies ever since,' continued Keeley. 'Des does her best to give Shannon a wide berth, but it's pretty difficult, especially when they're both members at St Benedict's.' She gave a theatrical sigh. 'Fuck knows what this latest spat's about. Anyway, Destiny's an absolute angel. We'll have to introduce you two.' She gazed out across the fairway, where Destiny's buggy was racing up a bunker-strewn hill. 'That's if Shannon doesn't get hold of her first.'

Keeley needn't have worried, for the model had hatched a cunning plan. With Shannon hot on her tail, Destiny drove straight into the nearest bunker and immediately engaged her newly discovered handbrake. Seeing her rival apparently stranded, Shannon sped to the edge of the bunker. 'I've got you now, you munter!' she cackled gleefully.

Two seconds later, Destiny floored her accelerator. She had timed it just right. As the buggy's fat wheels spun, they sent up a five-foot plume of sand, which poured straight through the open roof of Shannon's vehicle, covering the model from head to foot.

As Shannon's anguished howls filtered up to the roof terrace, Keeley jumped to her feet. 'Go, Destiny!' she shouted, pumping the air with her fist. Even Marianne was impressed.

'Credit where credit's due,' she conceded. 'The girl's not as stupid she looks.'

By now, a large crowd – including a number of tournament competitors – had gathered round the bunker, lured by the titillating prospect of two famous models locked in gladiatorial combat. Meanwhile, a four-strong posse of suited security guards attempted to fight its way through to the front, whilst murmuring unheard commands through their wireless earpieces. But before they could reach the bunker, Destiny had released her handbrake and accelerated sharply away, treating Shannon to a second sand shower. Coughing and spluttering furiously, the model shook her head vigorously and took off in pursuit. 'You're going to pay for this, Destiny Morris!' she screamed as she followed her quarry's meandering progress up the viciously sloping fairway.

As she neared the crest of the hill, Destiny glanced over her shoulder and, seeing the look of dogged defiance in Shannon's eyes, wondered if her pursuer was ever going to admit defeat. By the time she was facing forward again, the buggy had begun its descent and was plunging straight towards the large, kidney-shaped water hazard guarding the seventeenth hole. Horrified, Destiny slammed on her brakes, causing the buggy to slew sideways as it slid down the hill. Behind her, Shannon's eyes lit up. 'Gotcha!' she whispered.

Much to Destiny's relief, the buggy finally skidded to a halt two feet away from the edge of the lake. With a pounding heart and a dry mouth, she turned round to see Shannon sitting on her bumper. The model was wearing a peculiar twisted smile as she revved her engine threateningly. 'I think it's time for a dip,' she snarled. Before Destiny had a chance to release her seatbelt, Shannon's buggy leaped forward, shunting her rival straight through the tall reeds that lined the banks of the lake. Destiny screamed and covered her eyes as her buggy toppled into the murky water, where its engine quickly puttered and died.

First on the scene was the breathless BBC North West cameraman, who fleetingly considered going to Destiny's aid, but then thought better of it. Positioning the camera on his shoulder, he flipped off the lens cap and began filming as the shocked model half clambered, half fell out of the driver's seat and into the water. Next to him on the bank, Shannon watched triumphantly as Destiny burst into tears.

'You stupid bitch, you could have killed me!' wailed the waterlogged model as she plucked slimy strands of pondweed from her Dolce & Gabbana miniskirt.

Shannon laughed cruelly. 'I did say you'd live to regret it if you fucked with me.'

'All I did was make an appointment at the same spray-tanning salon,' hiccuped Destiny. 'Anyway, you needn't worry, I won't be going back there in a hurry – not when they've turned me the same vile shade of satsuma as you.'

Shannon let out a loud screech. Jumping out of the buggy, she kicked off her three-inch heels and – much to the amusement of the rapidly swelling group of onlookers

– began wading into the lake. 'I'm gonna make you wish you'd never set eyes on me,' she spat, kicking a spray of water into Destiny's face.

'Oh for God's sake, get a life. Haven't you got better things to do than make my life a misery?'

'You're a fine one to talk. Who was it who got me uninvited from the MOBO Awards after-party because she couldn't stand the competition?' Without waiting for a reply, Shannon lunged at Destiny, grabbing two handfuls of her long hair.

'Let go of me, you maniac!' Destiny cried as she drove her fist straight into Shannon's solar plexus. Momentarily winded, Shannon released her grip and bent over double, clutching her stomach.

'Look what you've done to my extensions,' squealed Destiny as she saw a ragged skein of blonde hair floating on the surface of the lake. 'I paid a fortune for those; that's real human hair, you know.'

'I've done you a favour,' gasped Shannon. 'With that ridiculous mane and those revolting fake tits, you look like the bastard child of Barbie and My Little Pony.'

At this, Destiny launched herself at Shannon, sending her toppling into the water. As the two women grappled in the shallows, trading slaps and insults, their skimpy tops quickly became see-through, prompting much cheering and wolf-whistling from the male spectators assembled on the bank.

Watching at a discreet distance, Sam Bentley couldn't help feeling aroused at the sight of two scantily clad and indisputably gorgeous women wrestling with such passion. Abi noticed too. 'Is that a wood in your pocket, Sam?' she said, giving him a sly nudge.

The golfer grinned as he playfully patted Abi's pert rump. 'Just you wait till later,' he whispered in her ear. 'I'm going to show you a boner like you've never seen before.'

Back on the roof terrace, Laura and her coterie were busy tucking into scones with clotted cream, their appetites whetted by the afternoon's unexpected drama. After four glasses of champagne, even Cindy was starting to relax. 'I gotta say, I wasn't expecting the tournament to be quite as much fun as this,' she admitted. 'I thought you Brits were supposed to be reserved.'

'Reserved? You've got to be kidding,' said Marianne with an arch smile. 'You wouldn't believe what goes on behind closed doors at St Benedict's.' She gestured towards the lake, where security guards had forcibly separated the two models and were now dragging them, long limbs flailing, out of the water. 'Trust me, darling, this is just the tip of the iceberg.'

Two

Jeff Goodbody unwrapped a package of fifty-pence pieces and let them drop noisily into the cash register. It was Sunday – the second busiest day of the week at St Benedict's – and soon the club shop would be bustling with customers. As head golf pro, overseeing the shop was just one of Jeff's many responsibilities. It wasn't the most glamorous part of his job, but it did provide a useful front for a second, more illicit, merchandising business.

As he reached for a bag of notes, Jeff glanced over to the shop's clothing section, where his two young assistants, Ace and Dylan, were unpacking a new consignment of designer knitwear.

'Hey, boss, have you seen these?' said Ace, holding up a Pringle V-neck with a pink-and-purple diamond motif. 'Pretty cool, huh? I've put one aside for myself.'

Jeff made a face. 'Pink's a bit gay, isn't it?'

'Nah, mate. Pink's not gay; pink's metrosexual,' said Ace, spreading the sweater across his chest. 'I reckon I'd be a real lady killer in this.' He flashed a cocky smile. 'Not that I need any help in that department.'

Dylan, who was barely out of his teens, let out a long sigh. 'I wish I had half your luck with women,' he said disconsolately. 'They all tell me I'm sweet, but none of them want to fuck me.'

Ace clapped him on the back. 'Tell you what, mate.

I'm seeing Astrid tonight. I'll ask her if she's got any friends that fancy educating a young boy in the ways of the world.'

At this, Jeff's ears pricked up. 'Astrid? You mean that hot little masseuse – legs up to her armpits and tits like Exocet missiles?'

Ace grinned. 'That's the one – and you know what goers these Swedish birds are. Let's just say my fitness levels have improved no end in the three weeks since our eyes met across a Lancashire hotpot in the staff canteen.' His smile grew even broader. 'You'll never guess what she suggested the other night as we were lying in bed.'

'What?' said Dylan eagerly.

'A *threesome.*'

Dylan gulped. '*I'm* not doing anything tonight.'

'Sorry, mate, you've got the wrong end of the stick. She meant me and two birds.'

Jeff shook his head. 'You are one lucky fucker, Ace.' He was about to request more details of Astrid's sexual predilections when the shop door began to rattle. He turned to see a man peering through the glass.

Ace mugged at Jeff. 'Can't he read? The sign on the door says we don't open till ten on Sundays.'

Jeff started moving towards the door. 'That's no customer; that's the new lad.'

Ace looked at Dylan. 'What new lad?'

A few moments later, Jeff was doing the introductions. 'This is Harry Hunter. He's going to be helping us out part-time till the end of the summer.'

Ace eyed Harry suspiciously, taking in his neatly pressed chinos and Oakley golf shoes, which looked as if they'd just been taken out of the box. 'Pleased to meet you, mate. Are you PGA accredited?'

'Er, no. But I'm a pretty useful amateur.'

'What's your handicap?'

'Eighteen.'

'Hmmm . . . not bad,' Ace grudgingly conceded.

Dylan extended a hand towards the new recruit. 'Hey, Harry. I'm Dylan. Have you ever worked in a golf shop before?'

Harry smiled. 'Nope.'

'Any sort of shop?' Ace asked.

'Nope.'

'So what was it you were doing before?'

'Motorcycle courier.'

'*Motorcycle courier?*' Ace's tone was sneering. 'You're going to need a bit of training up then.'

'Come on now, lads,' said Jeff briskly. 'Harry's only just walked through the door. Let's not give him the third degree. Dylan, why don't you take him to the back and show him where the stockroom and the bogs are, while Ace finishes hanging up those sweaters?'

'Sure, boss,' said Dylan, who was always eager to please.

As soon as the others were out of earshot, Ace sidled up to Jeff. 'How did *he* get a job like this with no experience? You should've told me you were recruiting. I know fellas who'd give their right gonad to work in this place.'

Jeff ran a hand through his thinning hair. 'Trust me, if it was up to me, he wouldn't be here.'

Ace grimaced. 'Uh?'

'He's the general manager's godson. Lanchester hired

him. I didn't have any say in the matter. I only found out about it yesterday.'

Ace made a hissing noise. 'That fucking tosspot. This place ran perfectly smoothly until he came along, and now he keeps sticking his nose in where it's not wanted. It's not good, man, not good at all.'

Anthony Lanchester had been St Benedict's general manager for less than a month, but had already succeeded in making himself hugely unpopular. Aside from his willingness to berate the staff for petty infractions (five o'clock shadows, gum-chewing on duty, failure to wear regulation footwear), Lanchester also had an unfortunate speech impediment, which caused him to spray showers of spittle from a gap between his front teeth. His predecessor, who'd run St Benedict's for twenty-two long and successful years, had possessed an altogether different management style. Officially known as *laissez-faire*, it was perhaps more accurately described as 'turning a blind eye'.

Jeff placed a reassuring hand on his assistant's shoulder. 'Don't worry, we'll keep Harry busy in the stockroom, out of harm's way. In any case, Lanchester's promised me that he's only going to be here for a couple of months max, just until he's gained a bit of retail experience. But, as long as he *is* here, we're going to have to be very discreet about our little operation.'

Ace nodded firmly. 'Absolutely, boss. You can rely on me and Dylan.'

'Speaking of which, we're expecting a delivery this afternoon. I'm running a ladies' golf clinic from twelve till four, so you'll have to deal with it – okay?'

'No probs.'

Jeff dropped his voice. 'We're shifting so much gear, the Baron's cutting the wholesale price by five per cent from next month.'

'Hey, that's good. Are we going to drop our prices too?'

'What – and eat into our profit margins? No way. In fact, I'm thinking about putting our prices *up*. I'm sure high-rolling customers like ours can accommodate a little inflation.'

No doubt the Professional Golfers' Association would have been horrified to learn that one of their members had been dealing drugs out of his club shop for years. Jeff could lay his hands on pretty much anything his customers requested, but cocaine had always been his mainstay. He'd started out small – a lone operator with his contraband locked away in a petty-cash box under the counter – dealing first to friends; and later, friends of friends. But, as word spread, Jeff's empire expanded until, for reasons of practicality, it became necessary to cut his two young colleagues in on the deal. Together, Jeff, Ace and Dylan reaped a good living from their illegal activities, but they were just the middle men. It was the individual above them in the supply chain – the so-called Baron – who was making the serious money.

As Jeff and Ace continued their preparations front of shop, Dylan was giving Harry a guided tour of the well-organized stockroom. 'It's pretty straightforward,' he said, gesturing to the ranks of shelves. 'As you can see, everything's labelled: golf balls there, tees down below, clubs at the back, and so on. The boss runs a pretty tight ship, and there's nothing he hates more than a half-empty display, so you'll need to keep replenishing stock through-out the day.'

Harry surveyed the shelves dispassionately. 'And what's in there?' he said, extending a foot and nudging a battered cardboard box, which was wedged below the bottom shelf.

Dylan held up a warning hand. 'Whatever you do, do not touch any of that stuff. That's our private stash.'

Harry frowned. 'Do you mind if I take a look?'

Dylan shrugged. 'I guess not.' He bent down and hauled the box out from under the shelf, folding back the flaps to reveal a stack of sportswear. 'These are damaged goods,' he said, by way of explanation. 'So the boss lets us keep them.'

'Damaged?' said Harry, picking up a pink-and-purple Pringle sweater, still encased in its cellophane wrapper. 'But this one hasn't even been opened.'

'Yeah, well, when I say *damaged*, I mean surplus to requirements – if you get my drift.'

Harry broke into a smile. 'Oh yeah, right, gotcha. One of the perks of the job, eh?'

Dylan nodded. 'You know what, Harry, for a bloke with no retail experience, you certainly catch on quick.'

By the time the club shop opened its doors half an hour later, there was already a small queue of punters outside, eager to book golf lessons, try out the latest equipment and peruse the extensive range of casualwear. Despite Ace's misgivings about Harry, he was grateful for the extra pair of hands and impressed with the newcomer's willingness to learn. It was during the lunchtime lull, as the three men enjoyed a game of *boules*, using golf balls and a strip of AstroTurf borrowed from the window display, that a five-foot eleven-inch blonde wandered into the shop.

'Hello, boys,' she said, stepping over a golf ball. 'Not interrupting anything, am I?'

Despite himself, Harry couldn't help staring. The woman, who was dressed in a short, tight-fitting white dress that left little to the imagination, was strikingly beautiful. What's more, her Amazonian build, razor-sharp cheekbones and ice-blonde mane of hair lent her a tantalizing air of superiority. But before he could gather his thoughts sufficiently to offer her some assistance Ace had moved to the woman's side, grabbed her about the rump and proceeded to give her a slow, and very noisy, open-mouthed kiss. At the same time, Dylan dropped to his knees and began gathering up the golf balls, using the opportunity to sneak a peek up the woman's dress. Embarrassed, Harry turned to a display of overpriced golf novelties and pretended to be inspecting a teddy bear dressed in a Burberry check cap and plus fours.

When Ace finally came up for air, several minutes later, the first thing he saw was Dylan crouching on the floor beside him, head craned upwards. 'Get up off the floor, mate,' he said, shaking his head despairingly.

Dylan grinned as he rose to his feet, fists filled with golf balls. 'Hi, Astrid.'

'Hi, sweetie,' she said, patting him on the head as if he were a pet Pekinese.

'Why don't you go and make us all a cup of tea, eh?'

said Ace, using his thumb to gesture towards the back room.

'Okay,' said Dylan, setting the golf balls down on the counter. 'How do you take yours, Astrid?'

The masseuse shook her head. 'Not for me, thanks. I can't stay long; I'm on my lunch hour.'

'Awww,' said Ace as he traced the contours of Astrid's arse with his hand. 'I guess I'm just going to have to save myself for later.'

Astrid bit her lip. 'Actually, that's what I came to tell you. I'm going to have to blow you out tonight.'

Ace's face fell. 'You're kidding.'

'Sorry, Ace. I've got to do the late shift. One of the other therapists has gone home sick and they've asked me to cover for her.'

'Can't you tell them you've already made plans?'

'I *could* – but they've offered to pay me double time.' She reached out to stroke Ace's hair. 'I'll make it up to you, I promise.' She pressed her lips to his ear. 'I've spoken to my friend Eleanor. She says she'd love to have some fun with us. She's a yoga teacher and she's *verrry* flexible. Her crouching scorpion pose will bring tears to your eyes.'

Ace let out a lewd chuckle. 'Sounds interesting.'

Suddenly a customer appeared at the door. Instantly, Ace and Astrid sprang apart. It was Sam Bentley. Tall and broad-shouldered with a powerful physical presence, he seemed to suck all the air out of the room. Harry, who'd been lurking behind a display of putters, began walking towards him.

'Good afternoon, sir. Can I be of any assistance?'

Ace elbowed him aside. 'No, you're all right, mate. I'll take care of Mr Bentley.' He looked at Astrid. 'Would you excuse us for a moment?'

'Oh no, please . . . I don't mind waiting my turn. You must finish seeing to this young lady first,' said Sam, unashamedly looking Astrid up and down, taking in the coltish legs and the ample breasts straining against the buttons of her uniform.

The masseuse smiled. 'It's okay, I was just leaving.'

Sam narrowed his eyes sexily. 'Don't I know you?'

Now it was Astrid's turn to give *him* the once over. 'I work in the spa, but I'm pretty sure you've never come to me for treatment. I don't usually forget a face.'

Sam held her gaze. 'And what sort of treatment do you specialize in?'

'Swedish massage.'

'Really?' The golfer reached a hand over his shoulder and began rubbing an imaginary ache in his deltoid. 'You know, I could do with a good pummelling. I'm feeling quite stiff after the tournament yesterday.'

'Well then, you must book an appointment. I'm sure I'd have you loosened up in no time. Just ask for Astrid.'

'I will,' said Sam. 'I definitely will.'

'I look forward to it,' said Astrid neutrally. She raised a hand in farewell. 'I'll catch up with you guys later.'

Sam sprang to the door, opened it, then stood, half blocking the exit, so that Astrid had to squeeze past him to exit, the tips of her breasts grazing his muscular chest as she did so.

Ace watched them, trying not to let his irritation show. 'Right,' he said, rubbing his hands together. 'Do you want to pop into the office with me, Mr Bentley, and we can sort out that bit of business?'

'Sure,' said Sam, letting the rucksack he was carrying drop from his shoulder.

Harry watched as the two men walked towards the door at the rear of the shop. En route, they passed Dylan, who was carrying two steaming mugs of tea. 'Afternoon, Mr Bentley,' he said cheerily. 'Congratulations on winning the tournament. I followed you every step of the way.'

'Yeah, I saw you in the crowd,' Sam replied. 'I appreciate your support.'

Dylan smiled. 'No problem.' He walked over to Harry and handed him one of the mugs. 'Here you are – get that down you.' He took a noisy slurp from his own mug. 'So, how have you enjoyed your first morning?'

'It's been good, really good. I hope I haven't got in your way too much.'

'Not at all. We've been glad of the help, to be honest.'

Harry nodded towards the STAFF ONLY sign at the back of the shop. 'I thought punters weren't allowed in the office.'

Dylan winked. 'Yeah, but we make an exception for Sam Bentley. He's one of our best customers.'

Harry bent down and picked up a stray golf ball. 'So what's this bit of business then?'

Dylan shifted from foot to foot awkwardly. 'Uh, I'm not exactly sure. We had a new delivery of Nike golf gloves yesterday – we haven't had a chance to unpack them yet. I expect Ace is giving Sam a sneak preview.'

Harry stroked his chin thoughtfully. 'Does Jeff know about this?'

'Course he does – Jeff's known Sam for years. Don't worry, mate, it's all kosher.'

'Can I ask you something else?'

'Fire away.'

'Why is Ace called Ace?'

'Cos the lucky bugger always comes up trumps – or at least he does as far as women are concerned.' Dylan set his mug down on the counter and lifted his hands to his chest, cupping a pair of imaginary breasts. 'Did you see the norks on Astrid?'

'It was hard to miss them,' said Harry, grinning. 'I must say, I wouldn't mind a brisk rub down with her myself.'

Dylan snickered. Something told him Harry was going to fit in just fine at St Benedict's.

Astrid couldn't help feeling guilty as she hurried back to the spa. She was fond of Ace, and she didn't like lying to him. Still, she comforted herself, it was only a white lie. She *was* working late – except not quite in the way Ace imagined. The fact was, Astrid's spa duties extended far beyond Swedish massage. Before, after – and even, on occasion, *during* – her regular shifts, she administered her own, rather unique, brand of treatment to private clients. What's more, a monthly backhander to the senior receptionist was all it took to ensure her extracurricular activities remained a secret from the management.

Earlier that day, Astrid had received a last-minute booking from a regular client – one far too lucrative to turn away. The minute her scheduled shift was over, she started making the necessary preparations, which began with a visit to the spa's staffroom. After removing a small polycarbonate suitcase from her locker, she wheeled it back to her treatment room, which was situated at the end of a long corridor and separated from the other therapists' rooms by a heavy glass fire door, making it virtually soundproof. Then she started to unpack, placing each item on a stainless-steel trolley, which had been cleared of its usual cargo of massage oils. First came a wooden paddle made of birchwood, its surface drilled with small holes to reduce air resistance. It was joined by a standard riding crop – the sort that could be purchased at any tack shop. A pair of custom-made iron wrist fetters and matching ankle cuffs emerged, followed by a leather head-harness, incorporating a built-in blindfold, and a gag, engineered from a rubber ball threaded on a length of rope. Then came a set of five whips, which she arranged in order of intensity. First, a deerskin flogger, whose soft lashes were wondrously sensual to those who appreciated such things. The second was fashioned from horsehair, which warmed the flesh nicely. The third was a heavy-duty strop, designed to shower the skin with leather kisses. The fourth was made of rubber and small enough to fit in the palm of a hand. Its lashes were short and thin – perfect for close-up work. The fifth was a traditional South African bullwhip, with a solid-core rubber shaft and a braided leather tail that was almost as long as Astrid herself. With the tools of her trade assembled, all Astrid had to do was place a soft, clean towel on the treatment couch and swap her orthopaedic sandals for a pair of black patent-leather stilettos with a punishing five-inch heel.

*

The Right Honourable Hugh de Montfort had been the member of parliament in the safe Conservative seat of Kirkhulme for as long as anyone could remember. Driven and obsessive, he was famed for two things: his stalwart defence of the pro-hunting lobby and his magnificent waxed moustache. Now in his late fifties and married with two grown-up sons, he had been visiting Astrid – or Mistress Valkyrie, as she was also known – once a fortnight for the past year. As usual, the masseuse greeted him in reception and ushered him to her treatment room, taking care to lock the door behind them. Hugh set down his briefcase and looked at her expectantly.

All at once, Astrid's beautiful face twisted into a mask of disgust. 'What have I told you about staring?' she growled through gritted teeth.

Instantly, Hugh's eyes fell to the floor. 'I'm sorry, mistress,' he grovelled. 'It won't happen again.'

'It had better not – or you will receive a punishment of the severest order.'

Hugh bit his lip and stared hard at his polished brogues.

Astrid prodded his briefcase with her toe. 'Have you brought something to change into?'

'Yes, mistress.'

'Then get on with it, you loathsome little worm. Mistress Valkyrie's time is extremely precious.'

As Hugh shuffled off behind the hospital-style screen, briefcase in hand, Astrid took the opportunity to slip a close-fitting black leather gauntlet on to her right hand, before taking up position beside the trolley. A few minutes later, Hugh emerged. He was completely naked, save for a large nappy, fashioned from a white hand towel and secured by two kilt pins. The wodge of fabric between his legs caused him to waddle as he made his way towards the treatment couch.

Astrid snapped her fingers impatiently. 'Hurry,' she barked. 'Get your pathetic arse on this couch.'

'Yes, mistress,' said Hugh, hurling himself on to the couch with gusto. 'How do you want me, mistress?'

'On your back,' Astrid declared, a cruel smile forming on her pink-frosted lips. She reached for the wrist restraints and slipped them over Hugh's hands, locking them securely. He whimpered in delight as she attached each one to the steel bar that surrounded the trolley so that his arms were effectively pinned to his sides. 'Now, you snivelling specimen of manhood, I want you to recount each and every one of your misdemeanours from the past fortnight. And be warned . . .' she took a step closer and flexed her gauntleted fist threateningly '. . . I shall know if you're holding out on me.'

Hugh took a deep breath. 'I exaggerated my expenses claim this month.'

Astrid tutted. '*And?*'

'I slept with my junior researcher. Again.'

Astrid took hold of one end of Hugh's moustache and tweaked it hard. The MP winced but didn't cry out. 'Anything else?'

'I told one of my disabled constituents there was nothing I could do to stop her mobility allowance being cut.' The MP paused. 'I lied.'

'Dear, oh dear, oh dear,' said Astrid as her fingers closed round the leather handle of the deerskin flogger. 'I can see I'm going to have my work cut out this evening.'

Three

The first time Cindy set eyes on Jackson West, she was watering the Chinese wisteria that sprouted from a terracotta trough on the second-floor balcony. Her husband, Kieran, employed a gardener to maintain the acre of lush landscaping that surrounded their five-bedroom home in the exclusive Kirkhulme enclave of Queen's Crescent. The wisteria, however, was Cindy's pet project. It had been top of her shopping list when she arrived in England as a newlywed and saw the mock-Georgian monstrosity Kieran called home. It wasn't that Cedar Lodge was ugly so much as soulless, and Cindy was hoping the wisteria – if and when the darned thing ever flowered – would help bring the house to life, while going some way towards masking the pristine brickwork that betrayed its late-twentieth-century origins. Aesthetics were very important to Cindy, and she'd always preferred period real estate. Back in southern California, she'd been the proud owner of a pink stucco *casa* with a pretty courtyard garden and stunning views of the Santa Ynez mountains. A textbook example of 1920s Spanish colonial-revival architecture, the house had provided the perfect showcase for her talents. And, as one of Santa Barbara's most sought-after interior designers, she had used her considerable influence to negotiate a hefty discount on everything, from the hand-painted Mexican tile fireplace to the modernist light fittings.

Cindy had certainly come a long way from the Fresno trailer park where she'd spent her childhood. After graduating *magna cum laude* from LA's prestigious School of Interior Design, she'd set up her own business at the tender age of twenty-four. Her eclectic style, which juxtaposed time periods, ethnicities, materials and artistic traditions, quickly marked her out as something of a maverick and earned her frequent mentions in glossy style bibles, as well as an honourable mention in *Architectural Digest*'s annual 'Ones to Watch' list. But it was a commission to make over a Republican senator's holiday home – in which she daringly combined Asian *objets d'art*, 1940s Biedermeier furnishings and Modernist black-and-white photography – that earned Cindy the front cover of *Elle Decor* and sealed her reputation. By her mid-twenties, she had a raft of wealthy clients who admired and appreciated her daredevil nature and her no-nonsense personality. Being extraordinarily photogenic helped, of course, though this wasn't something Cindy liked to acknowledge. She preferred to think she had got where she was thanks to a combination of talent, determination and plain old-fashioned hard work. As the years went by, Cindy notched up a string of lucrative and high-profile commissions, so that by the time she was twenty-nine, her life was just about perfect. Her bank balance was healthy, her home was beautiful, her friends were influential and she was highly respected in her chosen career. And then she did what she always swore she'd never do. She gave it all up. For a man.

She met Kieran McAllister at the Ocean Meadows Country Club in Santa Barbara, where he was competing in a charity pro-am. The British golfer had swung into the big league the previous year after winning the Dutch Open. Keen to raise his profile and earn some serious cash, Kieran had launched himself on the US professional circuit, where he was now in his second season. However, it wasn't his sporting prowess that caught Cindy's eye as she watched him stride across the fairway, golf club slung casually across his shoulder as if he were enjoying a Sunday morning friendly with the lads, but rather his piercing blue eyes and the easy way he laughed and joked with his teenage caddie.

Afterwards, the two had both been guests at a lavish champagne reception in the clubhouse, where Kieran, who had finished in fourth place, was much in demand. Across the room, meanwhile, Cindy found herself trapped in a spectacularly dull conversation with the golf club's vice-chairman. Their paths seemed destined never to cross, but then a woman standing next to Cindy, a whiny-voiced young media mogul's daughter, so skinny she looked as if she could travel by fax, dropped her champagne glass on the ceramic hearth tiles surrounding the grandiose fireplace, screaming ridiculously as the glass shattered and cold liquid splashed her toes.

Hearing the commotion, Kieran glanced towards the fireplace. Then he saw Cindy, still in conversation with the vice-chairman. At that moment, she happened to glance up and their eyes locked together. Kieran smiled at her, and Cindy smiled back, aware that she was blushing. In that second it seemed as if they were the only two people in the room, but then a white-coated waiter with a tray of canapés stepped into Cindy's line of vision and the moment was broken. By the time the waiter moved on, Kieran had disappeared, having been press-ganged into signing autographs by an over-excitable PR woman. But Cindy had made a lasting impression on him. How could she not have? She was the most beautiful woman in the room. Bowled over by the almond-eyed redhead in the tight-fitting chocolate lace sheath, Kieran made it his business to discover her identity. And when he discovered that she was one of the prizes at the charity auction – or, to be precise, she had pledged to design a room (materials not included) for the winning bidder – the golfer was determined to win her services at any cost. Later, at the auction, a nervous Cindy had watched from the sidelines as the bidding started at $1,000. It quickly rose in $250 increments and one by one the bidders dropped out, until finally it was just Kieran and the club's vice-chairman going head to head. And when the MC's gavel finally went down, Cindy was thrilled to discover it was the hot young golfer who had secured her services for the princely sum of $18,000. She'd been dismayed when Kieran rushed off to a press conference straight after the auction, without even coming over to introduce himself. But the following day he sent flowers to her hotel room together with a note, explaining that he was living in a rented condo in Malibu and asking if he could forego the room design in exchange for a date.

Four months later, Kieran proposed to Cindy, going down on one knee at the eighteenth hole of the La Quinta Country Club in Palm Springs, where he was competing in the Bob Hope Chrysler Classic. Cindy practically choked in her haste to say 'yes', much to the delight of the assembled spectators, who whooped and cheered their approval. They married in Malibu the following summer – and, given the couple's sizeable joint income, the wedding was a predictably lavish affair. The ceremony took place outdoors, on a bluff overlooking the Pacific Ocean, and afterwards the eighty or so guests – among them a three-strong reporting team from *American Bride* magazine – retired to a vast white marquee, decorated in Cindy's trademark eclectic style. At the end of the evening, as the couple stood hand in hand on the bluff enjoying the $20,000 firework display they'd laid on for their guests, Cindy had to pinch herself to believe this was really happening to a scrappy piece of poor white trash like her.

After lengthy discussions, the couple had decided to settle in England. Both were keen to start a family and they agreed that the Cheshire countryside – where Kieran still owned a house, just a stone's throw from the prestigious St Benedict's Country Club & Spa – offered the best and safest environment to raise their future brood. The sky was grey and overcast when they arrived at Delchester airport after a blissful three-week honeymoon in Bali. It had taken them ages to find a cab and, when they did, the driver had insisted on taking every corner at breakneck speed. When they arrived in Queen's Crescent, Cindy had stepped out of the cab, desperately jetlagged and shivering in her thin camisole top. She tried to hide her dismay as she surveyed her new home's self-conscious Palladian-style portico and ghastly lead-light double glazing. 'Let me show you around,' Kieran said as he threw open the front door, excited as a schoolboy. He paused. 'But there's one thing I've got to do first.' Bending down, he scooped her into his arms. 'Welcome to Blighty, Mrs McAllister.' Despite her dismay at the house, Cindy laughed in delight as her new husband carried her over the threshold.

Inside, the rooms lay cold and unwelcoming and a faint smell of mothballs hung in the air. Nonetheless, Cindy couldn't help being impressed by the billiards room, state-of-the-art gymnasium, triple garage and outdoor jacuzzi. Few people realize just how wealthy pro golfers are – even the ones who aren't household names. The previous season, Kieran had raked in half a million through prize money alone. Added to that, a lucrative sportswear contract, and he could afford a very comfortable standard of living indeed. What's more, Kirkhulme was an upmarket area, as Cindy had discovered from her exhaustive internet research. With a millionaire on every street corner, it was the ideal place to relaunch her career. She just hoped this quaint Cheshire village was ready for her daring design style.

All but one of the twenty houses in Queen's Crescent had been built in the 1980s – havens for the desperately unimaginative soccer stars and manufacturing millionaires who flocked to the then newly fashionable village in search of peace, tranquillity and off-road parking. To Cindy's eyes, the houses were frighteningly similar; all mock-Georgian, each with a 4x4 in the driveway and some object featured like a museum piece in the living-room window: a bulbous lamp, a china ornament, a vase of stiff-necked lilies. But the house at the south end of the Crescent, directly next door to Cedar Lodge, dated from a much earlier era.

Coldcliffe Hall had intrigued and enchanted Cindy from the moment she saw it. A particularly elaborate specimen of Victorian Gothic, the house seemed to disregard authentic proportions, focusing instead on exaggerated architectural eccentricities, from quatrefoil windows and flying buttresses to leering gargoyles, a pair of slender turrets and even a working bell tower. Set in a double-size plot, it was surrounded by sweeping lawns, which included an aviary, rose garden, generously proportioned outdoor swimming pool and, at the very centre, an ornate fountain, whose water gushed from the stony mouth of a falling Icarus. Both the house and gardens exuded a faint but discernible air of neglect, which only served to heighten their sense of mystery. One of the tall stained-glass windows was cracked from top to bottom, a small section of the wooden gingerbread trim was missing from the gable end and the leafy vine, which sprawled over the vaulted entrance porch, had clearly gone unpruned for some considerable time.

On her first night in England, as she and her new husband drank Shiraz in their vast kitchen, Cindy had casually enquired after her new neighbours. 'The people at number eighteen are friendly enough,' said Kieran. 'He's a dentist and she's something in finance. They've got twins, a girl and boy – darling little things.' He leaned across the table. 'Hopefully we'll be able to provide them with some playmates one of these days.'

Cindy smiled. 'But not for a couple of years at least, honey; that's what we agreed. I've got to get the business up and running first.'

Laughing, Kieran reached for the wine bottle. 'You're

the boss, but I reckon the sooner we get started on this family of ours, the better.'

'Hmmm, we'll have to see about that,' Cindy said, pursing her lips in mock disapproval. 'And the folks on the other side, in the amazing Gothic mansion, do they have kids too?'

'Ah, Coldcliffe Hall; that belongs to Jackson West. As far as I know he lives alone.' Kieran took a slug of wine. 'I don't suppose the name means anything to you, does it?'

Cindy thought for a moment, then shook her head. 'Uh-uh.'

'If you were a fan of Formula One, you'd be dead chuffed at the prospect of living next door to him.'

'Oh?' said Cindy eagerly. 'So he's a famous racing driver?'

Kieran shook his head. 'Notorious more like. A few years ago he was one of Britain's brightest racing talents, but his career came to a grinding halt when he crashed into a wall at the Belgian Grand Prix.'

'How awful – was he badly hurt?'

'From what I recall, he only sustained minor injuries from the impact itself. But a fuel line must have broken because the car went up in flames. It was almost a minute before the marshals managed to extinguish the blaze and pull him clear.'

Cindy shuddered. 'I'm amazed he survived. How old was he?'

'Late twenties I think. He was a real looker too. A bit of a ladies' man by all accounts, although I couldn't give you the details; you know me – I never read the gossip columns. But after the accident he retired from racing

41

and turned into a recluse, literally overnight. He didn't go out, didn't give interviews . . . nothing. He was living in London and then I think he left the country for a while. Then a few months after I went to the States, I heard that he'd moved to Kirkhulme.'

'So you've never met him?'

'Nope.' Kieran reached an arm across the polished oak table and began stroking Cindy's milky forearm with his fingertips. 'Anyway, babe, why are we wasting time talking about some fucked-up ex-racing driver? Why don't we finish this bottle of wine and get an early night? I'm dying to christen that four-poster.'

So Cindy forgot about Jackson West, at least for a while. But as the days turned into weeks and she still hadn't caught a glimpse of her mysterious new neighbour, she began to wonder if he wasn't awfully lonely, holed up in his Gothic pile. He had plenty of visitors – a daily housekeeper; the whey-faced pool boy, whose white van threw up a shower of gravel as it skidded to a halt outside the house; a weekly grocery delivery and regular supplies of wine and beer from the local vintner. Cindy watched them all come and go. But where were his friends and family, she wondered – and where, more intriguingly, was the man himself? She thought about dropping by unannounced, just to say hello and let him know Cedar Lodge was now occupied, after standing empty for more than a year. But something told her that a man like Jackson West would hardly appreciate a cold call. So she did nothing, and hoped for a chance encounter. And then, a few days after the pro-celebrity golf tournament at St Benedict's, Cindy's wish was granted.

Many times, she had stepped onto the large balcony that led from the master bedroom suite and gazed out at Coldcliffe Hall, silently admiring the Victorian architect's handiwork. From the edge of the balcony she had a bird's-eye view of the mansion's north elevation and the garden below. But that balmy August evening, she was too engrossed in twining the Chinese wisteria's tender new stems around the wooden trellis screwed to the brickwork to notice any movement next door. It was only when she heard a long, low sigh from somewhere below that she stood up straight and peered over the balustrade.

He was walking in the rose garden – a dark-haired man of average height and slender build, dressed in well-fitting jeans and a black shirt. Dusk was closing in and the man's face was turned away from Cindy, but his shoulders were hunched, lending him an air of melancholy. As she watched, he stooped down and picked up a fallen rose petal, stroking its velvety surface before pressing it to his nose. She waited until he'd placed it carefully – almost reverentially – back on the ground before she called out to him.

'Excuse me, Mr West?' she said, her voice sounding thin and high-pitched. The man started and spun round, eyes straining in the gloom. Cindy waved. 'Up here, on the balcony.' Tilting his head back, Jackson West locked eyes with Cindy. Now that he was facing her full on, she could make out a long keloid scar, which sliced his face in two on the diagonal. She laughed nervously. 'I'm sorry, I didn't mean to startle you. I was out here watering the wisteria and I saw you taking the night air.' Suddenly aware that she was gabbling, Cindy paused to clear her throat. 'I'm Cindy McAllister. Kieran and I – that is, my husband and I – moved in a few weeks back. I've been meaning to come over and introduce myself.'

After a small pause, Jackson smiled tightly and raised an arm in greeting. 'Pleased to meet you,' he said, although he didn't sound pleased at all. He turned and glanced back at the house. 'I'm terribly sorry,' he said softly, 'I think I can hear my phone.' Abruptly, he turned on his heel and started back to the house, walking at first and then breaking into a jog. Cindy cocked her head, listening for the sound of ringing. The night was silent.

Four

Harry Hunter glanced at the vast enamel wall clock and sighed. He felt like a naughty schoolboy summoned to see the headmaster. As he waited, he wandered around the room, inspecting his surroundings. Inside the general manager's office, a conspicuous and vaguely disquieting order reigned. There was a bank of filing cabinets, all colour-coded, ranged opposite an imposing antique desk that was bare, save for a limited edition Mont Blanc lying atop a pristine blotter. On the green baize pinboard, a smug no-smoking sign was prominently displayed, and next to it a wipe-clean calendar with various appointments marked in neat capitals. Harry's eye was caught by a framed photograph hanging on the wall beside the light switch. It showed a portly dame in a flowered dress, her ankles bulging unattractively over dainty mules. As he stooped down to inspect it more closely, the door was thrust open. Harry yelped as the sharp edge of its wooden architrave struck him square in the temple.

'Oh gosh, I *am* sorry,' said Anthony Lanchester, wincing in sympathy. 'My secretary said you were waiting in my office, but I didn't think you'd be standing right behind the door.'

'I was just admiring this photo,' said Harry, rubbing the side of his head.

'Ah yes, that's Mrs Lanchester. Wonderful woman.

Couldn't live without her. You know what they say, "Behind every great man . . ."'

'Quite,' said Harry, surreptitiously checking his fingers for blood. He glanced at the clock. 'Listen, I've only got fifteen minutes of my lunch hour left, so shall we get down to business?'

'Of course, old chap,' said Lanchester. 'Do take a seat.' He walked over to the desk and sank into his leather-covered executive chair. 'I'm terribly sorry I'm late. I was called away unexpectedly to sort out a bit of bother in the spa. There could've been quite an ugly scene if I hadn't taken control of the situation.'

'Sounds nasty,' said Harry as he sat down in the high-backed chair opposite the manager's desk.

Lanchester made a face. 'Oh it was. The customer in question was quite hysterical.' He tapped the side of his nose. 'Keep it under your hat, old chap, but we've had a couple of thefts from the ladies' changing room.'

'What, somebody's been breaking into the lockers?'

'No, no. Some silly creatures don't bother to use the lockers. They just leave their belongings on a hook or a bench. We had a Gucci blouse go last week, and today it was a pair of Ralph Lauren jeans.'

'Blimey, that could be pretty embarrassing for the club.'

Lanchester nodded. 'Legally, of course, we're not liable for any losses. But nobody likes to see a damsel in distress, least of all me. So on both occasions I apologized profusely and gave the ladies in question five hundred pounds worth of complimentary vouchers for the spa. That seemed to appease them.'

Harry frowned. 'Don't you think you should call in the police?'

'Goodness no,' Lanchester said quickly. 'The last thing the club needs is any whiff of scandal; it's not good for business.'

Sensing an opportunity, Harry leaned forward eagerly. 'Perhaps I could help you.'

'I should think you've got enough on your plate already, haven't you?'

'Yes, but I'm only in the shop part-time. I'd be happy to spend some time in the spa.' Harry paused. 'For an additional fee.'

'It's a tempting proposition, old chap, but I'm not sure the budget will stretch to it.'

'I tell you what. How about I make a few discreet enquiries, in my own time, and if I succeed in identifying the culprit, you could pay me a bonus — equivalent to, say, five times my weekly rate?'

Lanchester shook his head. 'It's still too much, but I appreciate the off—'

'Four times?'

'Double. That's the most I can do.'

Harry reached across the table to shake his employer's hand. 'Done.' His eyes flitted to the clock again. 'Listen, Mr Lanchester, if I don't get back to that shop soon, Jeff's going to send out a search party.'

'Of course. Let's get down to business then.' Lanchester opened his desk drawer and removed a hardback notebook. He turned to a clean page and uncapped his Mont Blanc. 'So,' he said, looking at the younger man expectantly. 'What have you got for me?'

*

Since his first week as general manager, Anthony Lanchester had been on a one-man crusade to stamp out drug use at St Benedict's. What his patrons did in their own homes was up to them – but he was damned if they were going to bring their filthy habits on to *his* turf. He'd done what he could, putting up polite notices stating the club's zero tolerance policy when it came to illegal substances, but still the cleaners continued to find traces of white powder on cistern lids, tell-tale foil wraps in dustbins and even the odd syringe. In an ideal world, Lanchester would have installed CCTV cameras in every toilet cubicle, gazebo and changing facility, but such a measure would be hugely expensive. What's more, St Benedict's had a long and proud tradition of privacy, and members would desert in their droves if they thought their every move was being monitored. So Lanchester made a bold decision: he would strike at the heart of the problem – at the dealers themselves.

Having offered a certain very well-informed member of the maintenance department a financial incentive, Lanchester was able to confirm what he already suspected: that a wide variety of drugs was readily available at the club. If his source was to be believed, the golf shop was the main outlet, but before he could confront the culprits, Lanchester needed proof. What's more, he was keen to deal with the problem swiftly and discreetly, in a way that would cause minimum embarrassment to both club and patrons – which was where policeman-turned-private investigator Harry Hunter came in.

'Okay,' said Harry, crossing one leg over the other and clasping his hands round his knee. 'As a result of my covert investigations, I can confirm that dubious practices are indeed occurring in the golf shop – with the full knowledge, and indeed *participation*, of the club's head golf pro.'

Lanchester punched the air in delight. 'I knew it!' he said triumphantly. 'The first time I met Jeff Goodbody I thought to myself, "There's a man who can't be trusted." It's all in the eyes, you see – and his are like a cobra's, constantly flicking from side to side.' He made a beckoning gesture with his hands. 'So come on then, let me have it.'

Harry smiled smugly. 'They're stealing from the shop.'

Lanchester screwed up his face. 'Excuse me?'

Harry nodded. 'It's true – Dylan told me everything. There's a cardboard box in the stockroom – I can take photographs if you like – stuffed with designer sportswear. They must be pilfering, ooh, at least one item each a week.'

Lanchester looked at Harry disbelievingly. 'Is that it?'

'I beg your pardon?'

'You've been working undercover in that shop for nearly two weeks and that's the sum total of your findings?'

Harry shifted awkwardly in his chair. 'Erm, yes, actually, I'm afraid it is.'

Lanchester brought his palm down on the table. 'Let me get one thing clear. I don't give two hoots about a few nicked pullovers,' he hissed, sending a spray of spittle shooting between the gap in his front teeth and on to the blotter, where it was rapidly absorbed. 'The drugs are the only thing I'm interested in. I thought I'd made that perfectly clear. I need to know which members of staff are dealing drugs out of that shop and who's supplying them.'

Harry was starting to feel nervous, as well he might. He'd exaggerated a little when Lanchester had questioned him about his experience and qualifications. He *was* a former policeman, that much was true – though not a very good one, which was why he'd never risen above the rank of constable. But he certainly wasn't a surveillance expert, as he'd led the general manager to believe. He'd only been a private investigator for eighteen months, during which time the bulk of his work had consisted of bog-standard debt recovery and process serving. He took a deep breath. 'Well, don't you worry about it, Mr Lanchester, I'm on the case. But you must appreciate that this investigation is going to take time. They're a close-knit group in that golf shop and it could take weeks – months even – to build up their trust.'

'But I haven't got months. You're supposed to be a surveillance expert; can't you install some hidden cameras?'

Harry swallowed hard. There were two reasons why he didn't want to follow his employer's suggestion. Firstly, he didn't possess any such equipment, nor could he afford to purchase it. Secondly, he wanted Lanchester to keep him on the payroll for as long as possible – and hidden cameras would be able to do his job in half the time. 'I wouldn't advise it,' he said, shaking his head. 'You're on very dodgy ground with cameras. If it went to court, you could be accused of violating your employees' right to privacy.'

The general manager frowned. 'Are you sure about that?'

Harry gave him a reproachful stare. 'I do know the law, Mr Lanchester. I *am* a former member of Her Majesty's constabulary, after all.'

'Yes, yes, I appreciate that,' said Lanchester irritably. He rested his elbows on the desk and surveyed Harry with a look of squinty-eyed concentration. After a minute or two he spoke. 'I'll give you three more weeks, Mr Hunter.' He brought his hand down on the table for a second time. 'And then I want to see some results.'

In St Benedict's vast state-of-the-art kitchen, another staff member was up to no good. Seamus O'Gorman had worked as a sous chef in the club's Michelin-starred restaurant for the past two months. During his fourth week of employment, he'd been enjoying a drink in the village pub after work when a stranger had approached him. The stranger was Christopher Delamain, owner of The Pumphouse, Kirkhulme's most exclusive brasserie. Before executive chef Xavier Gainsbourg took up residency at St Benedict's, The Pumphouse had been stuffed with high-rolling locals five evenings a week, and Christopher was making money hand over fist. Then, almost overnight, his customers had abandoned him – and it was all thanks to the fiery Frenchman and his flaming Michelin star. But Christopher wasn't about to let his business go to the dogs, and so he'd hit upon a plan. It hadn't been difficult to broker a deal with Seamus, whose wages were modest, and both parties were now reaping the rewards.

That afternoon, Seamus and Christopher had sched-uled a rendezvous in the grounds of St Benedict's, beneath one of the towering oak trees that screened the club from the world beyond. It was the tail end of lunchtime service and, in the hustle and bustle of the kitchen, it was easy enough for Seamus to go AWOL after pretending he'd cut his finger while dismembering a Barbary duck. 'I've got to get a plaster from the first-aid kit,' he told his nearest colleague. 'I won't be long.'

As he hurried past the porters' station and out through the back door, Seamus wasn't empty-handed. Rolled up in his apron was a waxed package containing half a pound of freshly prepared pâté de foie gras. And that wasn't all . . . in the pocket of his checked trousers lay a scrap of paper, on which was scrawled the recipe for Xavier's legendary Grand Marnier soufflé, a dish whose velvety texture and intense citrus aroma could – and frequently did – make women groan in ecstasy.

No words were exchanged beneath the oak; there was no need. Seamus handed over the pâté and the piece of paper and swiftly pocketed the handful of notes he received in return. The transaction complete, he hurried back to the kitchen before he was missed. He needn't have worried, for Xavier's attention was elsewhere. A few moments earlier, Charlie, one of the kitchen porters, had inadvertently thrown away a dish of goose gizzards, which Xavier had been intending to use as the basis for a piquant sauce. Now, it's no secret that the vast majority of professional chefs are dysfunctional, masochistic control freaks with egos the size of small principalities – and Gainsbourg was no exception. The tiniest thing was capable of sending him into a frenzy – tardy staff, sauces that separated, frying pans stacked in non-ascending order – and topping his list of irritants was the unnecessary wastage of food.

By the time Seamus re-entered the kitchen, Xavier had Charlie under one arm in a headlock. In the chef's other hand was a palette knife, which he was holding over the open grill. Flames were licking the edges of the knife, heating the metal to a temperature that would burn a man's flesh on contact, branding him for life.

'You have huge potential, Charlie, and I would like to see you progress in this kitchen,' Xavier was saying, 'but the only way you're going to stop making silly mistakes is if I teach you a lesson that you will never forget. You can see the logic in that, can't you?'

Charlie gulped. 'Yes, Chef.'

The Frenchman removed the palette knife from the flames and spat on it so it sizzled. 'Somebody stuff a rag in his mouth,' he said. Seamus, who was enjoying seeing the teenage porter squirm, picked up the greasiest, slimiest dishcloth he could find and wedged it in his colleague's mouth. 'Hold out your right arm,' Xavier commanded. Slowly, the porter did as he was told. His arm was visibly shaking. 'Now remember,' the chef said, his voice softer now, 'this is going to hurt me more than it hurts you.' The porter squeezed his eyes tight shut as the palette knife advanced towards his arm. It was less than two inches from his flesh when suddenly Xavier released him from the headlock.

'Well done, young man!' the chef cried, as he tossed the red-hot knife into the sink. 'You're made of strong stuff. You will go far in this business.' Charlie pulled the dishcloth from his mouth and fell to his knees, retching. Xavier patted him on the shoulder and went to the stove to check on his celeriac rösti.

Despite the taste of fish heads in his mouth, Charlie was smiling as he made his way back to his station, pleased to have survived Xavier's test of nerves. Some of his colleagues murmured congratulations as he passed, but not Seamus. The scheming sous couldn't help feeling disappointed. He would have enjoyed hearing the young porter scream.

Now that they were coming to the end of service, the flood of orders had slowed to a trickle, but still the line cooks moved at lightning speed. They were by turns aggressive, as they slammed oven doors and tossed sauté ingredients, then graceful, as they assembled each plate by hand, expertly arranging *al dente* vegetables with their fingers before squirting the plate with coloured lines of liquid from a plastic bottle, like artists signing a painting.

Xavier insisted on scrutinizing each and every plate in person as it left the pass. He eyed a pork loin and glared at Will, the taciturn grill cook, whose forearms were laced with old burn marks. 'Your port wine *jus* is separating. The plate's too hot. Replate it – and quickly, before the meat gets cold.' Xavier's eyes flitted to another dish, a pigeon breast, served with a blackcurrant sauce. He stuck his finger in the sauce and grimaced. 'It's too sweet – it needs a dash of vinegar,' he barked at the line cook responsible. 'And the pigeon,' he said, holding up a slice of breast. 'Too pink. Give it another thirty seconds.'

At that moment a barely touched bowl of porcini soup was returned from the dining room, borne aloft by Jeremy, the maître d'. Xavier scowled. 'What's the problem?'

'The customer says these porcini are chewy,' Jeremy explained.

Five cooks descended on the bowl, spoons in hand. Each selected a mushroom and chewed it meditatively. 'It's true, they are a little tough,' conceded Xavier. 'But that's nature's fault, not ours.' Nevertheless, he ordered a new bowl of soup to be served. 'When you give this to the customer, kindly tell him he's a fucking imbecile,' Xavier said as he handed it to Jeremy.

'Very good, Chef,' said the maître d' with a straight face. When he reappeared a few minutes later, he was carrying another return from the same table – this time, a whole roast sea bass with cherry tomatoes and salsa verde.

Xavier threw up his hands in disgust. 'What now?'

'She says it's dry,' Jeremy announced. Immediately, the cooks assaulted the dish, tearing off flakes of fish with their hands.

'Dry?' Xavier wailed. 'This sea bass is perfectly moist.' He turned to his colleagues, who nodded their heads furiously. Xavier threw his hands in the air. 'For fuck's sake, find out their names. From now on, they're barred.'

'Very good, Chef.' Jeremy turned on his heel.

Xavier held out a hand. 'Wait. What are they drinking?'

'A Château la Fleur-Pétrus, 1999.'

Xavier let out a groan. The wine retailed at £185 a bottle. 'Forget it,' he said. 'Get her another sea bass, but first let me piss in the salsa verde.'

By the end of his eleven-hour shift, Xavier was exhausted. His sweat-drenched hair rose to a greased peak like a baked Alaska and his tired eyes were tiny raisins in his handsome, doughy face, but still his heart was thumping and his mind was racing. For Xavier, cooking was a drug. A fourth-generation chef, he thrived in the unique atmosphere of a bustling restaurant kitchen – the brutal efficiency, the militaristic hierarchy, the terrifying precision, all laced with a tension so palpable you could cut the air with a filleting knife. Winning his Michelin star had been one of the proudest moments of Xavier's life, surpassed by one experience alone: his wedding day.

The Frenchman met Abi Hennessey, as she was then, on his very first day at St Benedict's. He'd come out of the kitchen during evening service to schmooze his new patrons and his eye had been drawn to the striking caddie, sitting alone at the restaurant bar. When he saw the young woman lift a cigarette to her lips, his hand had sprung instinctively to the brass lighter in the pocket of his chef's coat. Having made his excuses to the portly *bon viveur* who was in raptures over the roasted sea scallops starter, Xavier was at the bar in three quick strides. 'Allow me,' he said smoothly, extending the lighter towards Abi's cigarette. With a smile and the merest hint of a blush, she bowed her head to the flame, and by the time Xavier walked away, less than five minutes later, the lighter had been joined in his pocket by a complimentary matchbook with Abi's phone number scrawled across the back. Six months later, after a whirlwind romance, they'd tied the knot on a sun-kissed St Lucia beach. Theirs was a passionate relationship, and they rowed on an almost weekly basis – but, even after two years of marriage, Xavier still got excited at the prospect of returning home to his wife.

Before he could leave, however, the chef was compelled to perform his usual obsessive round of chores. First, he sharpened his knives, ready for the morning, his jaw set in concentration as he drew each blade across the diamond-coated steel. Then he went to the stack of clean laundry that had been delivered earlier that day, and rifled through it until he found the set of whites that had 'Xavier Gainsbourg, Executive Chef' stitched in Tuscan blue across the breast pocket. He draped the uniform over a wooden hanger, which he hung in a corner of the porters' station so the steam from the washing up would melt the fold lines overnight. His final task was to check that all the food prep had been done for the corporate brunch, which was being served in one of the club's private rooms the following morning. He went to the walk-in cold store and yanked open the door. Inside, row upon row of airtight containers were neatly stacked, each one labelled and dated. Xavier scanned the floor-to-ceiling shelves, mentally checking off ingredients: eggs, smoked salmon, blinis, black pudding. He frowned and checked the cooked meats shelf again. There were only three rounds of pâté de fois gras, where there should have been four. He'd made it himself that very morning, lovingly incorporating his blend of herbs – the details of which were a closely guarded secret. Xavier rubbed his chin thoughtfully. It wasn't the first time he'd noticed food missing from the walk-in. Last week, a half-litre tub of black cherry and kir compote had disappeared – and two weeks before that, a bottle of his special salad dressing. Now, as he closed the door of the walk-in, Xavier could feel his good mood evaporating. He was facing a horrible truth – a thief was abroad in *his* kitchen. But who? It was a question that would weigh heavy on his mind for the rest of the evening.

Five

Fabrizio da Luca slipped a hand into his jacket pocket and fingered the small box, gift-wrapped in thick silver paper, which nestled beside the keys to his Porsche. He opened his mouth to speak and then hesitated, mentally going over what he wanted to say. Even after a month of lessons with a private tutor, paid for by the football club, his English was still weak – and the words, when they eventually came out, were faltering.

'I said I would buy you a diamond if my team won the, the . . . how you say?' He sighed in frustration and turned to his Delchester United team mate Ryan Stoker.

'Golf tournament,' supplied Ryan.

Fabrizio nodded. 'Golf tour-na-ment,' he repeated in a painful staccato.

Keeley reached across the table and patted her lover's hand. 'But you didn't win, did you, sweetheart? Sam Bentley won, the way he always wins everything.' She giggled. 'Although Destiny and Shannon certainly did their best to sabotage his game.'

'I don't know what those stupid models thought they were playing at,' Ryan muttered. 'They nearly ruined the whole day. I'm amazed the club hasn't withdrawn their memberships.' Seeing Fabrizio's puzzled look, he quickly repeated the words in Italian.

'St Benedict's would never do that,' said Keeley smugly. 'Shannon and Destiny are too good for business.'

'Because they're the best-known pairs of tits in Britain, you mean?' said Ryan sarcastically.

'I *mean* because they're a pair of absolute stunners.' Keeley flicked the ends of her recently highlighted hair over her shoulders and leaned closer to the two foot-ballers. 'You know, I reckon half the male membership of St Benedict's only joined so they could drool over all the pretty girls wafting around the place – and, God knows, there are plenty of them.'

Ryan folded his arms across his chest and surveyed her thoughtfully. 'And what about you, Keeley? Why did *you* join St Benedict's? I mean, let's face it, you hate golf, you refuse to play tennis, you say swimming makes your hair go frizzy.'

Keeley sighed. Ryan could be very trying; he and she always seemed to rub each other up the wrong way. Unfortunately, his linguistic skills meant his presence on her dates with Fabrizio was practically a necessity. The goalkeeper spoke excellent Italian, thanks to two seasons with a *Serie B* side Keeley could never remember the name of. She gave him a scathing look. 'I like to use the spa,' she retorted. 'It's wonderfully relaxing.'

Ryan shook his head disbelievingly. 'You mean you like all the rich suckers,' he said, making a subtle gesture in Fabrizio's direction, 'who are too nice to recognize a gold-digger when they see one, even when she walks all over them with her three-hundred-quid designer shoes.'

Keeley glared at Ryan. 'I refuse to dignify that comment with a reply.'

'You mean you don't want to admit I'm right.'

Fabrizio looked from one to the other, unable to follow the conversation. 'What is going on?' he said. 'Are you two having a row?'

'Of course we're not having a row – just a lively debate about membership etiquette,' said Keeley tightly. 'Anyway, sweetheart, what was it you were saying before Ryan so rudely interrupted us . . . something about a diamond?'

Fabrizio cleared his throat. 'I said that I would buy you a diamond if I won the –'

Keeley snapped her fingers impatiently. 'Yes, yes, I've heard that bit already. I haven't got all day; I've got a massage appointment in half an hour.'

'I think she wants you to cut to the chase, Fab,' Ryan said dryly.

'What is this "cut to the chase"?'

'It means get to the point, mate.'

'Ah yes, the point,' said Fabrizio. He reached into his pocket and produced the box with a flourish. 'This is the point.'

Keeley's heart leaped in her chest. A present! She adored presents. Especially ones that came in small, velvet-lined boxes. She shot a glance around St Benedict's wood-panelled Chukka Bar to see if they were being observed. Club members were used to having celebrities in their midst, but Fabrizio was a big star, thanks to his heroics on the pitch, and their little party had caused quite a stir when they'd arrived for brunch.

'I didn't win the t-t-tour-na-ment, but I still thought you, you . . .'

Keeley rolled her eyes. Sometimes she really did feel as if she were going out with a halfwit.

Fabrizio said something in Italian.

'Deserved?' Ryan translated, turning the word into a question, as if he were challenging his friend's judgement.

'Yes . . . I still thought you *deserved* a gift. You have looked after me so well since I came to England and I want you to know I am grate-grate—'

'Grateful,' snapped Keeley.

Fabrizio nodded and placed the box on the table beside Keeley's half-eaten eggs Benedict. She paused for a second – just long enough for the woman at the next table to get a good eyeful – before pouncing on the box and tearing off the wrapping, not even bothering to remove the little gift card from its envelope. When she opened the box, she saw that it contained a white-gold diamond solitaire pendant. She forced a smile, aware that the woman at the next table would be judging her reaction and quite possibly reporting it back to her friends and relatives, or even – and the thought of this gave her quite a frisson – to a tabloid newspaper. She removed the necklace from its crushed-velvet mount and subjected it to closer scrutiny. The heart-shaped diamond wasn't very big – a quarter of a carat at most, she judged – and the setting was clumsy. Fabrizio probably expected her to have anal sex with him for this. Well, Keeley told herself, he could think again. This piece of tat wasn't worth a blowjob.

'Do you like it?' the footballer asked eagerly.

'It's certainly unusual,' Keeley conceded as she dangled the pendant disdainfully from a forefinger. 'Where did you get it? A catalogue shop?'

'What is this cat-a-log?'

'They sell mass-produced stuff,' said Ryan. 'Some people think they're a bit, um, tacky.'

Fabrizio's face crumpled. 'You don' like it, Keeley? I bought it in a *leetle* shop in Delchester. I still have the, the . . .' He gabbled some words in Italian.

'Receipt,' said Ryan. 'He says he's got the receipt, if you want to take it back and swap it for something else.

Keeley considered the options. She only wore jewellery from certain stores – namely Tiffany, Cartier and Asprey & Garrard – so, she could either take back the hideous article in question and ask for the cash instead, or say she liked it and then pretend to lose it, before selling it surreptitiously on eBay. Having decided that asking for the cash was too mercenary, even by her own exceptionally mercenary standards, Keeley plumped for the latter.

'*Nooo*,' she gushed. 'Don't be ridiculous, Fab, I absolutely love it.' She stood up and leaned across Ryan's lap, offering her mouth to Fabrizio. 'Don't mind me,' the goalie muttered as they snogged unselfconsciously. 'I am only the interpreter, after all.'

After the waiter had cleared their brunch plates and served a round of cappuccinos, the trio discussed their plans for the rest of the day. 'What are you two going to do while I'm in the spa?' Keeley enquired.

'We've got a bit of business to attend to in the club shop and then we thought we'd have a game of tennis,' said Ryan.

Keeley perked up. 'Drugs business you mean? Could you pick up a little something for me while you're there?'

Ryan's eyes flitted around the room. 'Keep your voice down,' he hissed.

Keeley gave him a withering look. '*Everyone* knows you can buy drugs in the shop. It's part of the reason people join St Benedict's, for heaven's sake.'

'I know that, Kee – but our manager wouldn't be too happy if the papers found out his star player liked to indulge every now and then.' Ryan nodded towards the woman at the next table, who was now pretending to be engrossed in a copy of the *Sunday Telegraph*. 'Walls have ears, and all that.'

'Oh. Yes. Sorry,' said Keeley, suitably chastened. 'I wasn't thinking.'

'What do you want then?'

'A gram of coke. Destiny and I are going to a nightclub opening on Tuesday and we want to be at our sparkling best.'

Fabrizio knitted his thick black eyebrows. 'You talk too quickly, Keeley. I cannot understand what you are saying.'

'You'll have to cram in some more English lessons then, won't you?' she said briskly.

'But then I would have less time to see you, and I would not like that at all.' He reached across the table and took her hand. 'Can I see you later, after your massage? We could go for a long walk and then I will take you home and cook you my special linguine alle vongole.'

'Maybe,' Keeley said off-handedly. 'I'll have to see how I feel after my massage.' She glanced at her watch. 'Speaking of which, I'd better get going. I'll call you later.'

'Okey-dokey,' said Fabrizio, smiling broadly at his mastery of English slang.

As Keeley stood up, Ryan got up too, saying he needed to take a piss. When they were out in the hallway, he gripped her upper arm and said quietly, 'You know, Keeley, you really are a 24-carat bitch. If you were *my* girlfriend, I'd put that necklace round your neck and pull it tight until you stopped breathing.'

Keeley yanked her arm away angrily. 'If you were my boyfriend, Ryan, strangulation would be a merciful release.'

Keeley sighed deeply as she surrendered to the strong hands of the massage therapist. 'I can't tell you how good that feels, Astrid,' she murmured. 'I've had such a stressful week.'

'Yes, I can see that; you're *verrry* tense today,' the therapist remarked as she kneaded her client's shoulders. 'Let me work these knots out for you.' For the next fifteen minutes, Astrid rubbed, squeezed and pummelled in silence; meanwhile Keeley mentally replayed the brunch date with Fabrizio. The man was gorgeous, that was undeniable, but just lately he'd become clingy and adoring – and that had never been part of her plan. What's more, the language barrier was starting to get on her nerves. Fabrizio's accent was so thick, it was hard to understand what he was saying half the time, and she wasn't sure how much longer they could rely on Ryan to act as interpreter. Still, she told herself, the Italian would do until someone with better taste in jewellery came along. St Benedict's was swarming with rich men and she knew it was only a matter of time before another one stumbled into her web.

Keeley Finnegan wasn't just high maintenance; she was

a professional freeloader. A former fashion model, she no longer had a job to speak of and her only source of income came from selling designer accessories on eBay. Some of the items had been given to her as gifts; other things she picked up in car-boot sales and second-hand shops. She knew the sort of things that sold well – and, more importantly, she knew a bargain when she saw one. Other than that, she relied on the generosity of the boy-friend *du jour* to put food in her stomach and clothes on her back. It wasn't that she couldn't fend for herself; it was just that she didn't need to. And if you didn't *need* to do something, why bother? At least, that was Keeley's philo-sophy. There was no secret to bagging a rich man, she told her friends – just so long as you didn't have any illusions about marrying them. There was no guy in the world who would turn down regular blowjobs with a pretty girl and entertaining company with no strings attached. In ex-change, Keeley got to eat in nice restaurants, drink expen-sive champagne, drive a fancy sports car (that's if its owner wasn't too finicky about letting her borrow it) and take exotic holidays, with spending money thrown in.

Keeley and Fabrizio had met on the tennis court – or, at least, *he'd* been on the tennis court, playing with Ryan, and she'd been sitting on a bench, topping up her tan and enjoying the sight of two incredibly fit (in every sense of the word) specimens showing off for her benefit. She had no interest in sport and didn't have the faintest idea the pair were footballers. After the game, the men had approached her, as she'd known they would, and invited her to meet them in the bar later that afternoon. Naturally, Keeley had jumped at the chance.

In the beginning she'd got a huge buzz from the fact that Fabrizio was not only rich, but famous too. However, after just a few months, the novelty was starting to wear off – there was too much competition for one thing. Whenever they went to nightclubs and bars, other women thrust themselves at the footballer, stuffing their phone numbers into his pockets as if she weren't even there. It was incredibly humiliating. With a deep sigh, Keeley closed her eyes and let her mind drift. She was just debating whether or not golf lessons would improve her chances of meeting a new lover when she became conscious that Astrid's hands were moving slowly southwards. She opened her eyes, suddenly alert.

'Is it okay if I move the towel so I can massage your glutes?' Astrid enquired matter-of-factly.

Her client's reply was the same as usual. 'Hmmm, that would be nice.'

Keeley had a well-rounded bottom that was firm and smooth like a luscious, perfectly ripe peach. As Astrid removed the towel covering her client's buttocks, her tongue flickered over her lips in anticipation. Turning to the trolley beside her, she selected a bottle of massage oil richly scented with jasmine and bergamot. She poured a generous measure into her hands and warmed it between her palms. Then, without saying a word, she drew a lubricated index finger slowly down the cleft in Keeley's butt, gently stimulating her anus. Keeley gasped in delight and squeezed her eyes tight shut.

'Oh, Miss Finnegan, I can see you're going to need a lot of work in this area,' Astrid declared in a teasing voice. She turned her attention to Keeley's buttocks, squeezing and pummelling them until the skin turned pink. As she worked, strands of her silky hair grazed the backs of Keeley's thighs, causing a delicious tickling sensation. 'Have you been a bad girl this week, Miss Finnegan?' the therapist whispered.

'Yes,' Keeley moaned. 'Very bad.'

Astrid smiled. 'Then I must administer a punishment.' After wiping her greasy hands on a towel, she opened a drawer in the stainless-steel wall cabinet and removed a birchwood paddle. 'Five strokes today, I think,' she said, running a palm across the instrument's polished surface. 'Are you ready, Miss Finnegan?'

Keeley gripped the sides of the massage table. 'Yes,' she said.

Astrid raised her hand and brought the paddle down lightly on Keeley's right butt cheek. Keeley squirmed, grinding her pelvis into the table. 'Harder,' she instructed. The second stroke landed smartly on Keeley's left cheek and left a bright red imprint.

'Hard enough for you, Miss Finnegan?' Astrid enquired.

'Mmmm . . . mmmm,' Keeley panted. The third stroke sent her lower body into a convulsion. The fourth made her scream out in pleasure; by the fifth, she was in ecstasy, her body flooded with endorphins.

'The punishment is complete,' Astrid declared as she stepped back to admire her handiwork. 'A little soothing cream is required, I think,' she said, surveying her client's scarlet bottom. She opened a small fridge and removed a glass jar. Unscrewing the lid, she scooped a generous dollop of unguent on to each of Keeley's buttocks. Keeley mumured her approval as the chilled lotion hit her inflamed skin. Gently, Astrid used her fingertips to smooth the lotion across Keeley's buttocks in a light circular motion. 'There,' she said as she took a clean towel and spread it across her client's back. 'That completes your treatment for today.'

'Thank you, Astrid, that was wonderful, as always.' Gingerly, Keeley eased herself off the massage table and drew the towel round her, wincing as the material grazed her sore rump. She went to her bathrobe, which was draped over a chair, and reached into the pocket. 'Here you are,' she said, pressing two ten pound notes into the therapist's hands. 'A little something extra for you.'

Astrid smiled. 'The pleasure was all mine.'

Keeley's mood always improved after a session with Astrid, and she was beaming as she made her way back to the female changing area. Once inside, she shrugged off her bathrobe and took a quick shower to slough off the massage oil, wincing as the hot water cascaded across her buttocks. Newly cleansed, she tucked a fluffy complimentary towel round her midriff and emerged into the sumptuous locker room with its marble floor and Tuscan trompe l'œil. The room was split into three distinct sections, each one screened from its neighbour by a bank of coloured lockers. The first section had been taken over by a gaggle of shrill-voiced twenty-somethings. At the heart of the group, a willowy brunette was proudly showing off her recently augumented breasts, while her friends prodded them admiringly. Knowing they would be gossiping for ages, Keeley retrieved her belongings from her locker and walked through to the second section. There she found three women in varying states of undress. One was slathering herself in body lotion, like a swimmer preparing for the Channel; the second was performing stretches in the nude, revealing rather more of her nether regions than was strictly polite; the third was yakking loudly into her mobile phone, gesticulating ostentatiously with her spare hand as she talked. They too gave no sign of an imminent departure. Sighing, Keeley went to the room's third and final section – where, to her relief, she found herself quite alone. Knowing that her privacy could be interrupted at any moment, she tossed her Gucci shoulderbag on a wooden bench and set about scanning the rows of coat hooks that lined the wall. Most of the spa's patrons stowed their belongings in a locker . . . most, but not all. Some, Keeley had discovered, were too trusting by half and, sure enough, several hooks had garments hanging from them. Quick as a flash, she pulled off her towel and hauled on her Juicy tracksuit. She went to the nearest item of clothing – a beaded tunic top – and turned back the collar. Her lip curled in disgust when she saw the label bore the name of a well-known chain store. She went to the next hook and performed the same routine with an appliqué skirt and lace-trimmed vest top. They were both designer brands – but, at a size sixteen and size eighteen respectively, Keeley knew they would be difficult to shift. She crossed the room to inspect a heap of clothes piled messily on a bench. On top of the pile was a striped Miu Miu cardigan. It was pretty enough, but there was a button missing and it was badly worn at the elbows. The white jersey sundress underneath was much more promising, and Keeley's heart leaped when she saw the label: Marni, size 12. Underneath the dress lay a pair of scrunched-up French knickers, and underneath the knickers the pot of gold at the end of the rainbow: a pair of size seven Chloé taupe leather moccasins with cream stitch detailing and a cute gold buckle. They looked almost new, and past experience told Keeley she'd get at least £70 for them on eBay. After checking that she was still unobserved, she picked up the sundress and shoes and shoved them into her already overflowing shoulderbag. Then she pushed her feet into her pink Birkenstocks and quickly exited the changing room.

With head bowed so as not to draw attention to herself, Keeley hurried along the corridor. She was so intent on making her escape that she failed to see the fluorescent signs warning that an emergency cleaning operation was in progress – and, as she rounded the corner at a brisk pace, she tripped over a metal mop bucket that was being pushed by a member of the spa's cleaning staff. As she fell to her knees with a scream, her bag slipped from her shoulder, spilling its contents across the polished floor.

Instantly, the cleaner dropped his mop and squatted down beside her. 'Hey, are you all right, miss?'

'Of course I'm not all right,' Keeley retorted, as she rubbed her bruised shins. 'Why don't you look where you're going?'

The cleaner frowned. 'With all due respect, miss, you came round that corner at a fair old lick. There was nothing I could do.'

Keeley staggered to her feet. 'You're lucky I'm not modelling any more, otherwise I'd be suing St Benedict's for loss of earnings.' Suddenly, she let out a wail. The cleaner's eyes followed the direction of her pointing finger. A piece of white fabric was trailing over the edge of his bucket. He reached down and fished it out of the slimy water with his rubber-gloved hand.

'I don't fucking believe it!' Keeley cried as she wrenched the now-grey Marni dress from the startled cleaner's hands. 'This cost an absolute fortune, and now look at it!'

'I'm terribly sorry, miss. I'm sure the club will pay for it to be dry-cleaned.'

'No amount of cleaning will fix this – it's ruined . . . ruined!' Realizing that she was starting to attract attention to herself, Keeley sighed. 'It doesn't matter; just forget it.'

The cleaner pointed to Keeley's mobile phone, which was lying at the base of a terracotta pot housing a mature yukka. 'At least let me help you pick up your other things.'

'I'm fine,' snapped Keeley. 'You can get back to your floor-wiping.'

'Well, if you're quite sure, miss . . .' When no reply was forthcoming, the man picked up his mop and continued pushing the bucket down the corridor.

Keeley wrung the dress out on to the floor, wrinkling her nose as a vomity stench rose up to greet her, before stuffing it into her bag. Then she set about retrieving her other belongings, which were scattered across the corridor – mobile, house keys, individually wrapped pantyliner – before stomping towards the exit. Suddenly, an unfamiliar voice stopped her in her tracks.

'Hey, Cinderella. Have you lost something?'

Keeley spun round. Standing no more than fifteen feet away was a tall, dark-haired man. His biceps bulged impressively from the sleeves of his well-pressed polo shirt, and in his hand was a taupe leather moccasin. He waved it from side to side. 'I found this under a fire extinguisher. I don't suppose it's yours, is it?'

Keeley smiled. 'Why yes, it is. I took a little tumble back there; it must've fallen out of my bag.' She walked over to the man and held out her hand. 'Thanks.'

The man didn't give her the shoe immediately. Instead, he looked down at Keeley's dainty size-fours in the pink Birkenstocks, then back at the moccasin. 'Aren't these a bit big for you?' he said pleasantly. 'I reckon you could fit two of your feet into one of these.'

Keeley's smile became a scowl. 'I don't see that it's any of your business, to be honest. And now, if you don't mind, I'd like my shoe back. I'm already late for my lunch date.'

'Oh, I'm sorry – here you go.' The man held out the moccasin, his hand brushing against Keeley's as she took it. 'I wouldn't want to keep the lucky guy waiting.'

Keeley stuffed the shoe into her bag. 'Who said I was meeting a man?'

'Well, I just assumed . . . a beautiful girl like you. I'm sure there are guys queuing up to take you out for lunch.'

Keeley regarded the stranger with amusement. She was used to men flirting with her, but they were usually a good deal more subtle. Her eyes flitted to his wrist. A man's watch was always a good indicator of his wealth, and his was large and expensive-looking. Suddenly conscious of her casual appearance, Keeley pushed her wet hair back behind her ears. 'I'm meeting my girlfriends actually,' she said in a friendlier tone.

'Well, have a nice lunch,' the man replied. 'And maybe we'll run into each other again.'

Keeley pursed her rosebud lips coyly and turned on her heel. 'Maybe,' she said over her shoulder.

Harry Hunter watched the woman until she disappeared from view. In her low-slung tracksuit bottoms, she looked every bit as good from the back as she did from the front. He sighed, wondering if he would ever see her again. He glanced at his watch and saw it was time he was heading back to the golf shop. No doubt Lanchester would be most impressed to know he was spending his lunch hour investigating the locker-room thefts — not that he had succeeded in finding anything out, despite loitering for nearly an hour outside the ladies' changing room. The problem was, there were so many beautiful women at St Benedict's, it was hard to keep his mind on the job. As if to prove his point, a statuesque brunette suddenly came tearing down the corridor wearing nothing but a towel. She ran past him and collapsed in a flood of tears at the reception desk.

'Oh my goodness, whatever's the matter?' Harry heard the concerned receptionist say.

'My clothes have been stolen,' the woman in the towel hiccupped. 'I left them in the changing room, and when I came back after my thalassotherapy, they'd disappeared.'

Harry inched closer to the reception desk and bent down, pretending to be tying his shoelace.

The receptionist made a sympathetic face. 'Are you sure you're looking in the right place?'

The woman wiped her eyes with the corner of her towel. 'Quite sure. My cardigan and underwear are still there. It's just my dress and moccasins that are missing.'

'How strange,' the receptionist replied. 'Why don't I come back to the changing room with you and we'll have a good hunt around for them, just in case someone's moved them by mistake?'

'Okay,' the woman sniffed. 'I'll be very upset if we can't find them. My Marni dress was a present from my husband.'

Harry watched them as they disappeared down the corridor towards the ladies' changing room. 'Well, well, well,' he muttered under his breath.

Cindy drummed her fingers on the table impatiently. She'd arranged to meet Laura, Marianne and Keeley for afternoon tea in the high-camp opulence of St Benedict's Ladies' Lounge. It was now ten minutes past the appointed hour and she was beginning to think she'd been stood up, which – after everything she'd done to cultivate these women's friendship – would be a large and rather embarrassing slap in the face. She needn't have worried. Two minutes later, a flushed-looking Keeley rolled up. 'Hi, Cindy, sorry I'm late,' she said breezily, as they exchanged air kisses. 'I've been in the spa all afternoon and I completely lost track of the time.'

'That's okay, hon,' said Cindy. 'There's no sign of the others yet. I hope they haven't gotten the date muddled up.'

'Don't worry, those two are always fashionably late,' said Keeley, wincing as she took a seat, her buttocks still tingling from the treatment Astrid had meted out. 'Let's go ahead and order, shall we? I haven't eaten since brunch, and I seem to have worked up quite an appetite.'

By the time the three-tiered silver stand of dainty sandwiches and pastries had arrived, the foursome was assembled. 'How are you settling in to your new house, Cindy?' Marianne enquired, as she sipped her tea. 'Queen's Crescent is one of the best streets in Kirkhulme, and those houses don't often come up for sale. You're a very lucky girl.'

Cindy beamed, ridiculously grateful that her living arrangements had met with the older woman's approval. 'It sure is a beautiful neighbourhood – and the house is certainly spacious.' She paused to dab her mouth with a linen napkin. 'But, between you and me, the decor and furnishings just scream "bachelor pad". I haven't told Kieran yet, but I'm planning a complete redesign.'

'Oh well, I suppose that's as good a way to spend his money as any,' said Keeley, helping herself to an apricot Danish.

Laura shot her friend a reproachful look. 'Given that Cindy's one of California's top interior designers, I'm quite sure she doesn't need to rely on her husband for financial support.'

'Okay, okay, it was just a throwaway comment,' mumbled Keeley through a mouthful of Danish.

Cindy patted Keeley's arm. 'It's fine, honey, no offence taken.'

'Are you planning to set up your design business here in the UK?' asked Laura.

'You bet,' Cindy exclaimed. 'I couldn't sit at home and do nothing all day.'

Marianne raised an eyebrow. 'Why ever not? We all manage perfectly well.'

'Well, it's just that I wouldn't feel fulfilled – creatively speaking,' said Cindy, choosing her words carefully. 'In any case –'

'I wouldn't exactly say I did *nothing*, Marianne,' Laura interrupted, her voice tinged with irritation. 'I have got two children under the age of three, you know.'

Ignoring her, Marianne turned to Cindy. 'I keep telling her to hire a live-in nanny, but she won't listen.'

'It's just that I can't see the point of having children if you're only going to hand them over to somebody else to bring up,' Laura explained. 'Sam and I manage perfectly well with a part-time au pair.'

Keeley smiled slyly, sensing an opportunity to get her own back for Laura's earlier reprimand. 'D'you know, Cindy, both of Laura's pregnancies were induced – just to fit in with Sam's tour schedule. What a devoted wife, eh?'

Cindy raised an eyebrow. 'Really? Wow, that's, that's . . . amazing.'

'Oh yes,' chipped in Marianne. 'Laura's the most loved-up wife you could ever wish to meet. If Sam asked her to remove her spleen with a hot shoehorn, she'd lift up her shirt and let him get on with it.'

Laura began fussing with the tea strainer, her discomfort obvious. 'I love my husband and I'm prepared to make sacrifices for him. What's wrong with that?'

'Nothing, darling, nothing at all,' said Marianne. 'Except when it puts your health at risk.' She leaned towards Cindy. 'The poor darling suffered complications after the last birth was induced and ended up having a Caesarean. We were all terribly worried about her.'

Laura sighed. 'Can we change the subject? I'm sure Cindy isn't the least bit interested in my gynaecological history; she must think us terribly dull compared to her Californian friends.'

'Of course,' said Marianne, as she checked her reflection in one of the vast ormolu mirrors that lined every wall of the Ladies' Lounge. 'But you do know we've only got your best interests at heart, don't you?' Without waiting for a reply, she turned to Cindy. 'So, tell me, have you seen anything of your famous neighbour – the racing driver fellow? I hear he's practically a recluse.'

Cindy perked up – at last, a subject she was interested in. 'Jackson West? Funny you should mention it. We met for the first time a couple of days ago. I saw him from my balcony; he was wandering through his rose garden at dusk.'

'Did you speak to him?'

'We exchanged a few pleasantries.' Cindy made a little moue. 'But, I must say, he seemed in rather a hurry to get away. I got the impression he felt quite uncomfortable talking to me.'

'If I had a face like that, I daresay I'd be uncomfortable too,' said Marianne. 'The man makes Freddy Krueger look like George Clooney.'

'Marianne!' Laura gasped. 'That's a terrible thing to say.'

'Oh yes, I was forgetting you two were love's young dream, once upon a time.'

Cindy stared at Laura in amazement. '*You* used to date Jackson West?'

Laura looked embarrassed. 'It was a long time ago –

before his accident – and we only went out for a few months. It was no big deal.'

'She's being far too modest,' said Keeley. 'For a while, our friend Laura was quite a celebrity.'

Laura squirmed in her chair. 'We were photographed a few times at parties and award ceremonies, that's all.'

Cindy leaned forward attentively. 'How did you two meet?'

'I used to be a publicist at Anderson Talent in London – that's the sports agency who represented Jackson. We worked together on a couple of projects and just clicked, I suppose.'

Keeley sighed. 'I wouldn't have minded putting in a bit of overtime with him. Jackson West was gorgeous when he was younger.'

'Yes, he was,' said Laura, smiling.

'So what happened? Why did you split up?' asked Cindy eagerly.

'He crashed into a wall, that's what happened.' Laura stroked the rim of her teacup thoughtfully. 'And, when he recovered, all he wanted to do was hide himself away from everyone – including me.'

'God, he must've looked a right mess when they dragged him out of that burning car,' said Keeley with a shudder. 'I bet his own mother wouldn't have recognized him.'

'I wouldn't know,' replied Laura, her voice edged with sadness. 'I never saw him after the accident. I went to the hospital every day for two weeks but he refused to see me.'

Cindy's eyes widened. 'I don't understand. Was he, like, brain damaged or something?'

Laura shrugged. 'I really don't know. After he was

discharged from hospital, I left him dozens of phone messages. I sent letters too, but he didn't return a single one. And it wasn't just me he ignored – it was all his old friends and racing colleagues. It was as if he wanted to cut himself off from everything and everyone he'd ever held dear. Eventually, he left the UK and went to live in some great big château in the Loire, where he could haul up the drawbridge and shut out the world. We all thought he'd turned his back on England for good. And then, six months ago, quite without warning, he came back – to Kirkhulme of all places. I couldn't believe my ears when I heard he'd bought Coldcliffe Hall.'

'It's a stunning house, architecturally speaking,' said Cindy as she indicated the empty milk jug to a passing waiter. 'What I wouldn't give for a peek inside.'

Keeley wrinkled her snub nose. 'Jackson's place gives me the creeps. Have you seen the size of those gargoyles?'

'No, but you know what they say about a man with big gargoyles,' said Marianne.

Laura sighed. 'Just ignore her, Cindy; she's got a one-track mind.'

'Gargoyles notwithstanding, Keeley does have a point,' said Cindy. 'Much as I love it, Coldcliffe Hall *is* faintly sinister; it certainly wouldn't be to everyone's taste. I wonder what was so special about Kirkhulme. Does Jackson have any family connections here?'

Laura shook her head. 'Not that I know of. I'm guessing he just wanted a bit of peace and quiet, like the rest of us.'

'Weren't you tempted to get back in touch – just out of curiosity?'

Laura shrugged nonchalantly. 'Not really. Given that he's gone to such great lengths to avoid human contact, I don't think he would appreciate a reminder from his past. Anyway, it's all water under the bridge now.' Laura folded her napkin neatly into four and laid it on the table, as if to indicate that the subject of Jackson West was now firmly closed. 'Those pastries are delicious, but you mustn't let me eat another one,' she said, pushing her plate away. 'I've been trying to lose weight, but it's proving to be quite a challenge.'

Marianne looked at her in disbelief. 'What are you talking about, darling? There isn't an ounce of fat on you.'

'You haven't seen me with my clothes off. Everything moves south when you have babies,' said Laura, running a hand over her stomach. 'Sam says I should take up tennis.'

'Never mind what Sam says,' snapped Marianne. As if aware that she'd spoken too sharply, her face softened. 'You need *two* people for tennis and, besides, it's very hard on the joints. Why don't you go swimming instead? It's wonderfully relaxing and burns off calories like you wouldn't believe.'

'Hmmm, maybe,' said Laura carelessly. Cindy wondered if there was an atmosphere brewing. She hated atmospheres. She acted quickly to move the conversation to safer ground. 'Have you and Sam been married for long?'

'Nearly five years. We met at a dinner party in London. It was love at first sight – for both of us.'

'You certainly hit the jackpot that night,' said Keeley. 'Rich *and* good-looking.'

Laura smiled indulgently. 'He certainly wasn't rich back then. He'd only just turned pro.'

'When did you move to Cheshire?' asked Cindy.

'Two summers ago. I was perfectly happy in London, but Sam was keen to move back to the north-west – it's where he was born. Naturally, he had to be within spitting distance of a championship golf course, and Kirkhulme seemed like the obvious choice.'

'And Keeley and I took her under our wing straight away, didn't we, darling?' said Marianne.

'You certainly did.' Laura reached across and clasped Marianne's hand. 'And, for that, I shall always be grateful. And now,' she said, her eyes meeting Cindy's, '*I'm* taking *you* under my wing. We golf widows have to look after our own.'

Cindy felt a warm glow spread from the tip of her toes to the top of her head. 'Thanks, Laura, I really appreciate it. Making new friends has been harder than I thought. I was getting kinda worried until you guys came along.'

'Then worry no more. You're one of us now – isn't she, girls?' Both Keeley and Marianne nodded enthusiastically.

A sudden thought crossed Cindy's mind. 'Hey, is Sam competing in the German Masters next month?'

Laura nodded. 'Wild horses wouldn't stop him.'

'Kieran is too. Why don't we arrange to stay in the same hotel? That way, you and I can do a little sightseeing in Cologne while the guys are practising.'

'Oh, *I* shan't be going,' said Laura. 'Someone's got to stay at home and look after the children.'

'Can't you bring them with you?' asked Cindy. 'You

wouldn't be alone; plenty of golfers' wives bring their kids on tour. Hell, why not bring the au pair too?'

Laura looked down at her lap. 'I'd love to; it's ages since Sam and I went away together.' She hesitated. 'But you know what these golfers are like, Cindy. They're very sensitive; they have their little routines. Sam says he finds it too much of a distraction if we're there.'

'I don't know how you put up with all those absences,' said Keeley. 'If I loved Fab as much as you obviously love Sam, I wouldn't want to let him out of my sight.'

'Oh, I always miss him when he goes away, of course I do. But golf's the most important thing in his life – it always has been and it always will be. I'm sure Cindy knows how it is.'

'I guess,' said Cindy. 'But, when Kieran and I have kids, he'd damn well better shoulder his share of responsibility.'

'Don't get me wrong – Sam's wonderful with the children,' Laura said quickly. 'He's teaching Carnie to play golf already – she's not even three yet, but she's already got her own set of mini clubs. I think Sam's secretly hoping she'll grow up to become the next Michelle Wie.'

Cindy smiled, though privately the notion filled her with horror. 'Carnie – that's a cute name.'

'It's short for Carnoustie. She's named after the golf course where Sam won the Scottish Stroke Play Championship.'

'Gee, I guess Sam really does eat, drink and breathe golf. What's your other one called?'

Laura cleared her throat. 'Birdie.'

'Wow, that's so sweet,' said Cindy, putting her hand

over her mouth to hide the smirk that was threatening to break out across her lips.

'Believe me, she got off lightly,' said Marianne. 'If it was a boy, Sam was going to call him Albatross.' She shook her head despairingly. 'Imagine that.'

Six

Sam Bentley was close to climax. Squeezing his eyes tight shut, he forced himself to recall the first round of the British Open at Muirfield, two years earlier. At the third hole, he'd suffered a two-stroke penalty for having an extra driver in his bag — a mistake that had not only made him look like a prize idiot, but potentially cost him £150,000 in winnings. It was, without a doubt, the worst moment of his entire career.

Afterwards, he had given the caddie who'd failed to count his clubs before tee-off the biggest bollocking of his life, before summarily sacking him. Never mind that this was the first mistake the veteran caddie had made in nearly seven years of faithful service: with Sam, there was no such thing as a second chance. Over the next eighteen months, the exacting (some would say downright difficult) golfer hired and fired no fewer than six caddies — all of them men — before he finally found his perfect match.

Abi Gainsbourg was widely regarded as one of the most instinctive caddies operating at St Benedict's. She had picked up her first club at the age of eight, was competing in junior tournaments at twelve, and playing off a handicap of five by her sixteenth birthday. After failing to make the grade as a pro, she'd opted to take up caddying as a career, and had fought to make a name for herself in what was still largely a male-dominated arena.

A tall, athletic twenty-six-year-old with a tousled mane of honey-coloured hair, Abi eschewed the tailored slacks, polo shirts and fleece jackets worn by other caddies in favour of low-slung combats and figure-hugging rollnecks – or, if the weather was warm, a crew-necked T-shirt and a pair of high-cut shorts that showed off her shapely legs to perfection.

People who didn't know any better often viewed caddies as little more than glorified bag carriers, but at the top level the reality was far different. Individuals like Abi were expected to be porter, valet, ordnance survey expert and psychologist all rolled into one and, as such, were highly prized commodities. Sam had poached Abi from one of his biggest rivals at St Benedict's – a Spanish ex-pat, who'd made a name for himself with a third-place finish in the Portuguese Open and fancied himself as the next Seve Ballesteros. Sam's offer to Abi had been an attractive one: a good basic wage, plus fifteen per cent of his prize money. Even so, she had hesitated – and with good reason. Despite his charming public face, Sam had a reputation as a ruthless perfectionist and a hard taskmaster. But, on the golf course at least, Abi was every bit as tough as Sam and, unable to resist a challenge, she'd decided to accept his offer. Her decision to jump ship, delivered during a practice game, prompted the hot-blooded Spanish ex-pat to call her every name under the sun, before hurling his golf bag into the water feature at the fifteenth hole. But Abi – who had now been Sam's caddie for six months, and his lover for four – had no regrets.

Sam's orgasm-delaying technique was working a treat.

As he mentally relived the moment he'd told the aberrant caddie he'd never work in professional golf again, he felt the scrape of Abi's fingernails across his back. Immediately, he quickened his pace, cupping her buttocks in his powerful hands and drawing her pelvis towards him so he could thrust deeper into her. With a loud moan, she pulled him violently down to meet her mouth. Their lips twisted as their tongues explored each other's mouths wildly. Moments later, Abi's head fell to one side and she began a convulsive thrusting against him. Sam smiled, feeling a powerful sense of achievement in a job well done. He liked to excel at everything he did – be it golf, public speaking, or down 'n' dirty fucking. It wasn't that he was an unselfish man – far from it. For Sam, it was simply a matter of pride that the woman always came first.

With Abi taken care of, Sam went for broke. Gripping his lover's hips he began thrusting harder, his muscular thighs contracting with every stroke. The caddie smiled serenely up at him, eyes half closed, arms bent back behind her head. Sam found her slavelike limpness incredibly arousing. He put his lips to her ear. 'Say it, baby,' he whispered.

Abi began licking her lover's neck. She knew precisely what Sam wanted her to say – it was the same thing he wanted her to say every time he was about to come. In fact, the more she said it, the more ridiculous it sounded. Still, if it made him happy . . .

'Say it,' Sam commanded again – more urgently this time.

Abi's full lips parted. 'Hole-in-one,' she said in a low, sexy voice.

Sam moaned in pleasure. 'Again,' he urged.

'Hole. In. One.' Somehow, she managed to make each word sound utterly, unashamedly filthy. Sam's breath was now coming in ragged gasps, his face contorted with pleasure. Abi took a deep breath. 'Hole-in-one, hole-in-one, holeinone, holeinone, holeinone!' she cried. As she reached a crescendo, Sam finally came with a series of noisy grunts, before collapsing on top of her.

They lay joined for a minute or two. Abi stroked the damp tendrils at the nape of Sam's neck, enjoying the fleeting moment of intimacy, even though her spine was pressing painfully into the hard, polished walnut of the St Benedict's trophy-room table. When Sam's pulse was back to its resting rate, he raised himself up off Abi and glanced behind him, reassuring himself that the back of the Queen Anne carver was still wedged securely under the door handle.

'I can't wait for the German Masters,' Abi sighed as she peeled herself off the tabletop. 'At least we'll have the luxury of a hotel room.'

Sam grinned wolfishly. 'I dunno; I quite like all this cloak and dagger stuff. It's like being a teenager again. It gives the whole thing an extra frisson, don't you think . . . the idea that we might get caught in the act.'

Abi walked to the wall and stood on her tiptoes to retrieve her T-shirt, which was draped over a gilt-framed portrait of St Benedict's first president, the Honorable Henry Wykeham, QC. 'Maybe that wouldn't be such a bad thing,' she said softly.

Sam's grin vanished. 'What are you talking about? It would be a fucking disaster – for both of us.'

Abi began combing her hair with her fingers. 'We've been having an affair for the past four months, Sam. And you know what? All this sneaking around is starting to do my head in. I mean, where's this thing going? We've never really talked about it and . . .' She paused, hating to sound whiny. 'It's just I've never done anything like this before and it feels uncomfortable.'

'Done anything like what?'

'Cheated on someone.'

'Oh, and I'm an old hand, am I?'

Abi shrugged. 'Put it this way: it's not the first time you've been unfaithful to Laura, is it?'

Sam began looping his belt through his chinos, buying himself a few precious seconds of thinking time. He was going to have to tread carefully. He didn't want to lose Abi's services as a lover – or as a caddie. 'No,' he said, giving her one of the brooding looks he'd perfected in the bathroom mirror. 'But this is the first time it's meant anything.'

Abi's heartbeat quickened. She was a woman who prided herself on being the consummate professional. Despite her head-turning looks, she was a practical, no-nonsense sort of woman who was used to operating in a man's world and had developed a whole repertoire of curt put-downs to deal with even the friskiest golf pro. She had fought hard – though not, it must be said, very long – to fend off Sam's relentless advances. But, in the end, she'd fallen for him, as most women did – and she'd fallen hard. 'Do you mean that?' she asked.

Sam went over to her and stroked the side of her face, tilting her chin up, so her eyes met his. 'Babe, I've been happier over these past four months than I've been at any time in the whole of my marriage.' Seeing Abi's face soften with emotion, Sam pressed home his advantage. 'Laura's not like you; she doesn't understand what it's like being one of the country's top golfers. She resents the amount of time I have to spend practising, she accuses me of spending too much money on golf equipment and she refuses to come and support me at the overseas tournaments because she doesn't like disrupting the children's routine. I can't win.' He planted a small kiss on his lover's lips. 'Still, at least that means you and I can spend some quality time together at the Masters. I've booked adjoining rooms, so there'll be plenty of opportunity for some after-hours stroke play,' he said, smiling at his own joke.

'You know, Xavier's threatening to come out at the end of the tournament, so we can have a *romantic*' – Abi drew a pair of quote marks in the air – 'weekend break in Cologne but, to be honest, it's the last thing I feel like doing.' She twisted a strand of hair coyly. 'The thing is, Sam, the whole time I'm with him, all I seem to think about is you.'

'It's the same for me, babe,' Sam insisted. 'I can't get you out of my head. But I think you should let Xavier come to Cologne, otherwise he might start getting suspicious.'

'I guess so, but –'

Sam had drawn his finger to his lips, silencing Abi. He could hear the sound of voices in the corridor outside. Recognizing the gruff tones of Alf Joiner, the clubhouse's aged head caretaker, he signalled to Abi to gather up their remaining clothes, while he tiptoed to the door and put his ear to the jamb. After listening to the voices for several seconds he mouthed the word 'fuck'. Gingerly, he moved the chair away from the doorhandle, repositioning it at the head of the table, before grabbing Abi's hand and taking her to the window. 'They're coming to take away the pro-celebrity golf trophy for engraving – with my name. What a fucking irony, eh?' He unbolted the window and drew up the sash, wincing as it rattled in its frame. 'We're going to have to leave by the rear exit.'

Abi's eyes widened in alarm. 'But we're on the first floor.'

'There's a section of flat roof below. Jump on to that and then we can step down on to those wheelie bins below.'

Abi shook her head. 'The things I do for you,' she whispered through gritted teeth.

Mere seconds after Sam and Abi had made their escape, the door to the trophy room swung open. 'So if you could have it back to us by next Tuesday,' Alf was saying to the engraver. 'There's an important directors' meeting on the Wednesday and I don't want any empty cabinets; it makes the room look untidy.' He selected a key from the big bunch attached to a chain round his waist and unlocked a large wall cabinet. 'It's the same name as last year – Sam Bentley,' said Alf, carefully removing the vast Waterford crystal rose bowl from its red velvet mount. 'That bastard wins everything around here.' While the engraver was busy packing the bowl in layers of soft cloth, Alf wandered around the room, checking the tops of the cabinets for dust. As he reached the far wall, he noticed that the bolt on one of the sash windows was undone. 'Bloody cleaners,' he muttered. 'This place would run to rack and ruin if I wasn't here to keep on top of everything.' He screwed the bolt up tightly and as he turned back something soft brushed against his foot. 'What have we got here then?' he mumbled to himself. Alf liked to give a running commentary on whatever he was doing; it helped to reassure him of his usefulness. Frowning, he reached down and picked up a balled scrap of fabric. With a flush of embarrassment, he realized what he was holding in his gnarled hand was a lady's undergarment – and a very scanty undergarment at that. 'All done now, Alf,' said the engraver from the other end of the room. 'Oh, right, yes, just coming,' said the caretaker, hastily stuffing the knickers into the pocket of his overall. The members' antics never ceased to amaze him. They may have fancy airs and graces and money to burn, but most of them were little better than animals.

Out in the sunken garden, in the full glare of the afternoon sun, Marianne was reading a copy of *Vogue*. Except she wasn't really reading. She was far too busy admiring the view. A few feet away, a firm-bodied under-gardener weeded a bed of aspidistras. As he worked, Marianne surveyed him surreptitiously through her sunglasses. He looked to be in his early thirties, strawberry-blond with freckled arms, and wrists strung with plaited-leather bracelets. Not good-looking exactly, but interesting. Very interesting.

As the gardener reached for his spade, Marianne saw that there were two crescent moons of sweat under his arms. Sensing an opportunity, she reached into her bag and pulled out an unopened bottle of Evian. 'Hey,' she called out. 'You look like you could use a drink.'

He looked up and smiled, revealing a row of straight white teeth, dazzling against his sandy complexion. 'Thanks,' he said, wiping his forehead with the heel of his hand. 'But I'm fine, honestly.'

'Don't be silly. It's ninety degrees in the shade. You'll die of dehydration out here.'

Without waiting for an answer, Marianne threw the bottle towards him. He caught it cleanly in one hand. 'Well, if you're sure you don't need it yourself.'

Marianne pushed her sunglasses up into her hair. 'I'm sufficiently lubricated already, thanks.'

The man unscrewed the lid of the bottle and chugged down its contents in one go. 'Cheers,' he said, drawing his thumb and forefinger across the corners of his mouth. 'I needed that.'

'Any time,' said Marianne languidly. She tossed her *Vogue* down on the love seat and stood up. 'I'm Marianne, by the way.'

'Pleased to meet you. I'm James.'

Marianne smoothed a hand over her hair, which was, as always, immaculate. 'Have you been working at St Benedict's long, James?'

'Only a couple of months. I've just relocated from the north-east.'

'I thought that was a Geordie accent I detected.' Marianne gazed around at the four neat tiers of planting, which rose steeply from a central rock garden. 'I must say, you look after this place beautifully,' she said. 'I love

93

it here; it's so peaceful.' She pointed to a privet hedge clipped in the shape of a squirrel. 'Did you do that?'

The gardener grinned. 'I certainly did. Do you like it?'

'It's very impressive.' Marianne took a step closer to the gardener. '*My* bush is very well tended.' She cocked her head on one side. 'Would you like to see it?'

The gardener laughed nervously.

Marianne reached out a hand and stroked the outcrop of tawny hair sprouting from the V of his burgundy polo shirt. 'Forgive me for being so forward, but a woman like me . . .' She licked her lips. 'Let's just say I have a healthy appetite.'

James's eyebrows shot up. 'Are you suggesting what I think you're suggesting?'

'That depends on whether or not you think I'm suggesting a delicious hard fuck somewhere quiet.' At this, the gardener blushed a fetching shade of pomegranate. 'Which I am,' Marianne added matter-of-factly.

James wiped his sweaty palms on his combat trousers. 'I appreciate the offer. I mean, you're a very attractive lady and all. But . . . but . . .' He looked at her helplessly.

Marianne sighed. 'You're married.'

'It's not that.' James's eyes flickered anxiously from side to side. 'I'm worried my boss might come looking for me.'

Marianne arched a brow. 'Bob Daley? I doubt it. I saw him on his lawn tractor not ten minutes ago. He'll be tied up for another half hour at least.' James bit his lip. Marianne saw that he was weakening. 'Oh go on, live dangerously.'

James looked longingly at Marianne's breasts. 'What about my tools?'

'Leave them here. You'll only need one tool where we're going.' And then, before he could raise any further objections, she linked her arm through his and started leading him up the rough stone steps which gave on to the main lawn.

'Where are we going?'

Marianne smiled. 'The shell grotto. Nobody ever goes there.'

This building was one of the few remaining remnants of the grand Victorian estate that had once occupied the St Benedict's site. Built of limestone with a slate roof, the interior walls of the small, circular structure were decorated with an elaborate shell mosaic – not just common or garden mussels, cockles and periwinkles, but more exotic pearl oysters and conches too, gathered on the estate owner's travels to the Caribbean. Located in a far-flung corner of the estate, the grotto had originally served as a whimsical retreat, a place for solitary contemplation, but Marianne had something rather less subtle in mind.

Inside the windowless grotto, the air was cool and slightly musty. It came as a welcome relief from the sun's searing heat. The minute they entered, Marianne grabbed James's hand. 'My, what big, strong hands you have,' she said, stroking the ridge of calluses on his palm. 'I bet they know how to please a woman. Let's see, shall we?' She brought the hand down to the hem of her Pucci tunic dress. James grinned. She wasn't wearing any underwear. Earlier, he had felt apprehensive, not sure how – or indeed, if – he was going to handle this beautiful older woman. But now, sensing Marianne's mounting excitement, he started to feel more confident. With one hand buried between her legs, he used the other to cup the back of her head and draw her face roughly towards his, before pushing his tongue into her mouth. She responded eagerly, wrapping her arms round his waist and crushing her breasts against his chest. After a long, passionate kiss, James turned his attentions to Marianne's neck, nuzzling and sucking the soft, perfumed skin. She gasped out loud as he nipped her with his teeth.

'Don't you like that?' he breathed into her ear.

'I love it,' she whispered. 'Don't stop.'

'Like a bit o' rough, do you?' he said, lifting the hem of her dress and squeezing her bare buttock hard.

'I should say so,' Marianne murmured. Her hand moved to his bulging crotch. 'Now fuck me, darling. Hard as you like.'

Seven

Cindy's heart was pounding. After passing through a reinforced-steel security gate, which slid smoothly open at her approach, she walked towards the imposing stone steps that led to the front door of Coldcliffe Hall. At the top of the steps, she took a moment to smooth her pencil skirt and check her pantyhose for runs. First impressions were vitally important and she couldn't afford to fuck up. Taking a deep breath, she pulled the tassel on the antediluvian doorbell. A sonorous chiming struck up, followed a few seconds later by the scraping of a key in a lock. Cindy summoned up her brightest smile as the door swung open to reveal a plump middle-aged woman in a blue-checked tabard.

'Afternoon,' the woman said curtly. 'Come in.' Cindy stepped through a small vestibule and into a high-ceilinged entrance hall. As she waited for the housekeeper to lock the door behind her – rather unnecessarily, it seemed – she found herself admiring an elegant staircase with an intricate carved newel post and slender mahogany spindles. But before she could subject it to further inspection, her guide had whisked past and was setting off down a gloomy passageway. As Cindy trotted after her, she tried to absorb as much decorative detail as possible, her brain registering an attractive tile floor with encaustic panel insets and a set of line-and-wash architectural drawings displayed at oddly jaunty angles – whether by accident or design, it was impossible to tell. Two-thirds of the way along the passage, the housekeeper stopped and pushed open a door. 'Wait in there,' she said brusquely. 'I'll tell Mr West you're here.' She gave her guest a slightly disparaging up-and-down look, before lumbering flat-footedly down the hall.

Cindy stepped into the room and drank in her sur-roundings. The decor was dramatic, to say the least. Dark red walls battled against plum-painted woodwork and, in the large arched window, floor-length curtains of rust-coloured velvet were swagged artistically. At the opposite end of the room, a tarnished chandelier drooped over an antique sideboard, where a row of stuffed animals formed a baleful welcome committee. The moth-eaten fox watched her warily as she laid her portfolio on a chaise longue that spewed stuffing from a tear in its brocade covering. Cindy shivered. The room wasn't cold, but a vapour of neglect cloaked every corner. As she ran a hand across the oversized granite fireplace, her eye was drawn to the prettiest object in the room – a gilt birdcage, suspended from a tall stand. Inside the cage, a canary sat frozen on a branch of silk leaves. Impulsively, she pushed her finger through the bars, intending to stroke the yellow feathers.

'I found her in an antique shop in Limousin.' The voice came from nowhere. Cindy jumped, almost wrenching her index finger out of its socket. Jackson West was standing three feet away. He was dressed casually in a black tracksuit and thick hiking socks. No wonder she hadn't heard him approach. She smiled, trying not to stare at the livid web of scars that burst across his face and caused the corner of his right eye to droop. 'It's lovely to meet you again, Mr West,' she said, waggling her injured digit. 'I'd shake your hand, but I think I may have dislocated my finger.'

Jackson winced in sympathy. 'I'm sorry, I didn't mean to make you jump.'

Cindy waved his concerns away. 'It's my own fault. I'm too darn nosy for my own good.' She clasped her hands together enthusiastically. 'I must say, you have some beautiful *objets*, Mr West, and the house itself is simply stunning; I've been admiring it from afar for a long while. I was absolutely thrilled when I received your invitation.' This was something of an understatement, for when Jackson's thick cream envelope had dropped on to Cindy's doormat two days earlier, she had practically fainted with ecstasy. 'Oh my God, Kieran!' she'd screamed. 'Jackson West has invited me to Coldcliffe Hall on Saturday afternoon. He wants to talk to me about a design project.' And when Kieran had pointed out that it was very short notice and, in any case, they already had plans for Saturday afternoon – a garden party at the home of his golf coach – she'd begged him to make her apologies. 'Please don't ask to me reschedule Jackson, honey – it'll make him think I'm indifferent, when nothing could be further from the truth.' Kieran, who found it hard to refuse Cindy anything, had readily acquiesced.

Jackson's right eye had started to water. He rubbed it impatiently. Cindy found herself thinking that a Californian plastic surgeon would have made a much better job of his face. 'I'm glad you could come today,' he said, surreptitiously wiping his damp fingers on his tracksuit bottoms. 'I was keen to meet you. I've heard some very good things about your work.'

Cindy raised an eyebrow. 'Really? But how did you know I was an interior designer? I've only been in England a few weeks; the business isn't officially up and running.'

'The St Benedict's grapevine,' said Jackson enigmatically.

'Oh?' said Cindy. 'Are you a member?'

Jackson's eyes dropped to the floor. 'Yes, but I don't get down there very often. I'm a bit of a loner, as you may have gathered from the village gossips.'

'I have to admit I don't know much about you at all, Mr West,' said Cindy. 'I'm afraid I don't take much of an interest in motor racing – or village gossip for that matter.'

The corners of Jackson's mouth curled slowly upwards, offering Cindy a glimpse of the handsome man he must once have been. 'Then you and I are going to get along just famously.' He shifted awkwardly from foot to foot. 'But before we get down to business, I feel I owe you an apology.'

Cindy frowned. 'Whatever for?'

'The other evening, on the balcony. I behaved rather rudely – running away like that.'

'Not at all,' Cindy lied. 'You were obviously lost in thought. I must have startled you, calling out like that. It's me who should be apologizing for making you feel uncomfortable.'

Jackson's eyes dropped to the floor. 'Even so, I could have been a little more friendly. The thing is, when you look like this . . .' He sighed and gestured to his face.

'Let's just say I haven't felt very sociable for quite some time.' To cover his embarrassment, he turned and picked up Cindy's portfolio from the chaise longue. 'May I?' he asked.

'Be my guest.' She cleared her throat discreetly and embarked on a well-rehearsed spiel. 'Since setting up my own business five years ago, I've worked on a huge variety of commissions, everything from beachfront condos to smart city apartments to intimate country retreats. One of my most well-publicized projects was the entire redesign of a three-thousand-square-foot holiday home for a member of the Californian state senate –'

She stopped mid-sentence. Jackson's right hand was raised, revealing scarred fingers – three of which were badly clawed, their tips almost brushing the palm. 'Don't take this the wrong way, Cindy. May I call you Cindy?'

She nodded. 'Of course.'

'I don't need the hard sell; I've done my homework. I received a phone call from Senator Haynes yesterday, as a matter of fact.'

Cindy's face registered surprise. 'You did?' She knew from personal experience that Senator Haynes was an extremely busy man. During the two-month-long refurbishment they'd only met once – the rest of the time she'd dealt with his assistant. He must think Jackson West very important indeed to call him in person.

'The senator didn't hesitate to recommend you; in fact, he was quite effusive in his praise.'

Cindy's lips snapped shut. In that case, she would let her work speak for itself.

For the next few minutes, Jackson perched on the

end of the chaise, examining the portfolio thoughtfully, stopping every now and then to study a particular photograph more closely. 'I like your style,' he murmured. 'It's very dramatic, very self-assured – just the sort of bold hand Coldcliffe needs.'

Cindy beamed. The meeting was already going so much better than she'd hoped. She usually spent at least twenty minutes on her pitch, but now she was feeling confident enough to fast-forward to the next stage. She waited until Jackson had turned the final page of her portfolio and then said lightly, 'Perhaps you could tell me a little more about the project you had in mind?'

Jackson was instantly on his feet. 'I tell you what, why don't I show you?' he said eagerly, setting the portfolio carefully – reverentially, almost – back on the chaise. As he walked towards the door, he touched Cindy lightly on the elbow, indicating that she should exit first. Beneath her chiffon Chloé blouse, the hairs on her arm twitched. There was something infinitely thrilling about being in the presence of a celebrity, albeit a reclusive one.

After making their way back down the passageway, designer and client began to ascend the wide staircase side by side. 'Have you done much work to the house since you moved in?' Cindy asked, her hand embracing the solid mahogany handrail like an old friend.

'Not a thing; everything you see is the previous owner's handiwork and it's all beginning to look rather tired. Ideally, I'd like to update the whole house, but I can't bear the thought of the disruption. I think I'd find it too overwhelming, all those workmen swarming over the place.' He glanced at her through his eyelashes, which were surprisingly long and dark. 'I suppose that sounds a bit silly, coming from a grown man like me.'

Cindy shook her head firmly. 'It's perfectly understandable; you've obviously had a lot to contend with in recent times. And I want you to know that I only hire thoroughly vetted contractors and would be personally supervizing the entire project from beginning to end.' She bit her lip. 'I'm sorry, I'm doing it again, aren't I – being a pushy Californian?' They looked at each other and both burst out laughing; the brittle ice between them was broken.

At the top of the stairs, Jackson led Cindy halfway along the landing to a heavy oak door studded with ornamental ironwork. 'Okay, this is it: the master bedroom suite. Take a look around.' He flung open the door and, with a small bow and a flourish of his hand, stepped aside to let Cindy enter.

The room was palatial – fifty feet long at least – and sparsely furnished with a half tester bed, a sturdy wardrobe and mismatched chest of drawers. Cindy pulled a notebook from her shoulder bag and began jotting down a list of the original features, of which there were many. A fireplace, smaller than the one downstairs, was made of the same dour granite as the three mullion windows, which offered sweeping views over the garden. The floor was handsome sixteen-inch herringbone parquet, which age had burnished to a rich golden hue. The walls were rather less attractive, covered as they were with an ancient lincrusta, which was watermarked and peeling at the edges. Above it lay ornate moulding – bunches of grapes, interspersed with vine leaves, their delicate edges blurred by layer upon layer of clumsily applied emulsion. But by far the room's most stunning feature was the octagonal glass dome that burst from the centre of the ceiling and arched gracefully skywards. Roughly five feet in diameter, it was made of delicate panes of greenish glass, which were fogged unappetizingly with years of grime. After taking down some measurements, Cindy went to explore the en suite, which lay behind a panelled door in the corner of the room. Here, Cindy realized instantly, she would be starting from scratch – for while the sunken bath, gold-plated taps and embossed tiles might have been the height of 1980s chic, they had no place in a building as beautiful as Coldcliffe Hall.

When she returned to the bedroom, Jackson was sitting on the window seat, gazing out across the lawn. When he turned to her, his eyes were bright and shining. 'What do you reckon? Do you think you can work with this space?'

Cindy laid a hand on her breastbone. '*Excuse* me?' Jackson's face fell. 'No, no. I'm being ironic,' she said hastily. 'It's ... it's ...' she struggled to find a fitting adjective '... magnificent!'

Jackson's smile returned. 'Oh good, for one awful moment I thought you were going to say you didn't want to take it on.'

Cindy could hardly believe what she was hearing. The room was a beautiful blank canvas that any designer would give their eye teeth for. 'I've got so many ideas buzzing around in my head, I can't wait to get them down on paper,' she said. 'Can you give me an idea of your budget – just a rough idea, to give me something to work around.'

Jackson made an expansive gesture with his arms. 'Whatever it takes; the sky's the limit.'

Cindy hadn't thought this commission could get any better – but it just had. 'That's great news,' she gushed. 'Okay, Mr West, I'm going to get a costing and some sketches to you as soon as possible – by the end of the week, in fact. I expect you'll want to meet with some other designers, but I can assure you . . .' Cindy's jaw hung open. Jackson was shaking his head.

'That won't be necessary,' he said with more confidence than he had exhibited at any other time during her visit. 'I've already made up my mind. I want *you* to create my new bedroom, Cindy, and I'd like you to start as soon as possible.'

Chef's assistant Richie Grubb had been working at St Benedict's for less than a week. A cocky little shit who thought he knew it all, Richie had already got into trouble for over-seasoning the chicken soup, prompting all twenty litres' worth to be poured down the sink. Having already blotted his copybook, leching after the boss's wife was not, by anyone's standards, a great career move.

That day, Richie was assisting the pantry chef in the preparation of salads, dressings, pâtés and cold hors d'oeuvres. He had just finished decorating a vegetable terrine with juniper berries and was enjoying a cheeky cigarette outside by the bins, when a stunning blonde in combats and a tight T-shirt came sauntering up to him. 'Hey, Richie,' she said, leaning towards him to read the name stitched on his white jacket.

'Hello, gorgeous,' he replied, imagination not being one of his strong suits.

'I don't suppose you could do me a little favour, could you?' asked Abi.

'For you, I'd climb Everest.'

Abi snorted. 'I bet you say that to all the girls.'

'Only the ones with beautiful blue eyes – even if they have got a smear of mud on their cheek.'

Abi's hand flew to her face.

'No, not that cheek, the other one.' Smiling broadly, Richie licked his thumb and reached across to wipe away the offending mark, which had adhered to Abi's dimpled cheek when she'd cleaned Sam's golf clubs with a bucket of soapy water and an old toothbrush. At that precise moment, Xavier happened to be walking past the back door, en route to berate the kitchen porter for allowing the temperature of the fridge to dip half a degree below 32°F, causing frost particles to form on the surface of a freshly prepared syllabub. While he watched his protégé engage in some heavy-duty flirting with his wife, Xavier's jaw tightened. Picking up the nearest weapon to hand – which, unfortunately for Richie, just happened to be a large carving knife still covered in the juices of a well-hung calf – he went to confront him.

'Shit,' said Richie as he saw Xavier striding towards him. 'Coming, Chef,' he said, grinding out his cigarette underfoot. Seconds later, the chef was grabbing him by the collar and flinging him against the bins. 'I was just grabbing a breath of air, Chef,' he bleated as Xavier held the knife to his jugular.

'Keep your hands off my wife, you cretinous, come-gargling motherfucker,' Xavier hissed. He might have quit Paris just three years earlier, but his colloquial English was excellent.

Richie's Adam's apple bobbed up and down as he felt the cold steel pressing uncomfortably against his neck. His eyes flickered towards Abi. 'Your wife, Chef? I swear to God I had no idea; we haven't been formally introduced.'

With his spare hand, Xavier grabbed the collar of Richie's jacket and twisted it, forming a garrotte round his terrified colleague's neck. 'You ignorant English pig. You don't even know my wife's name and already you're running your filthy fingers all over her.'

Despite the restricted blood flow to his throat, Richie managed a small nervous laugh. 'I didn't mean any harm. I was just wiping away a bit of mud.'

'I was just wiping away a bit of mud, *Chef*!' Xavier barked.

'Chef,' Richie squeaked.

Throughout the exchange, Abi had been looking on with a mixture of boredom and amusement. Knowing how her husband resented any interference in the running of his kitchen, she'd held her tongue but now the situation was in danger of spiralling out of control. 'Okay, Xav, the joke's gone far enough,' she sighed. 'Stop being an idiot and let the poor guy go.'

'Joke? Joke? This is no joke!' Xavier cried indignantly. 'You're my wife; I am defending your honour.'

'You're making a complete tit of yourself, more like,' said Abi, gesturing at the window, where a row of white-coated figures was watching the proceedings with obvious amusement. As Xavier turned to look, she stepped forward and yanked his knife-wielding hand away from Richie's face. The chef's assistant stumbled backwards against the bins, coughing and clutching his neck. 'Don't worry, Richie,' said Abi. 'It's all show with him. He wouldn't hurt a fly.'

Xavier frowned crossly. 'What are you doing here anyway?' he asked Abi.

'Looking for you, of course. I wanted to let you know I'm going out tonight. I'm not sure how late I'm going to be so don't bother waiting up.'

'You're hardly ever at home these days,' said Xavier sulkily.

'You can talk,' Abi retorted. 'I can't remember the last time you got home before midnight.'

'I am a chef!' cried Xavier, beating his chest for emphasis. 'This is a vocation, not a job.'

'Yeah, yeah, yeah,' Abi muttered. 'Whatever.'

Xavier's nostrils flared. 'Where are you going anyway?'

'For a drink with Helen.'

'Your friend from school? But you only saw her a couple of nights ago.'

'She's going through a major crisis at the moment. Her boyfriend's dumped her. I need to be there for her.'

'Where are you going?'

Abi pursed her lips. 'What is this, *Twenty Questions*? You're not the boss of me, Xav.'

A wounded look crossed the Frenchman's chiselled features. 'I was just going to say that if you're meeting Helen at the club, I can drive you home when I've finished my shift.'

'Yeah, well, you don't have to worry. We're meeting in town.'

'In that case, you must call me when you're ready to come home and I will pick you up.'

Abi's guts churned in despair. She was weary of excuses to cover up her affair with Sam. 'No, no, it's fine,' she said, her tone gentler now. 'You'll be shattered by the time you've finished your shift. I'll get a cab.'

'As you wish.' Xavier's tone was icy. Seeing Richie still skulking by the bins, he waved the carving knife threateningly. 'What are you staring at, arsehole? Get back to your station; evening service begins in less than an hour.'

'Yes, Chef.'

'And if I ever catch you touching my wife again . . .'

'You won't, Chef. I can assure you of that,' said Richie as he scuttled back to the kitchen.

Setting the cleaver down on top of an upturned bucket, Xavier walked over to his wife and pulled her towards him. 'I'm sorry if I overreacted, *ma chérie*,' he whispered in her ear. 'But I can't help feeling jealous when I see other men flirting with you. I love you so much; I don't know what I would do if you ever left me.'

'Don't be silly,' said Abi. She was glad her face was buried in Xavier's neck, so he couldn't see the guilt in her eyes.

Eight

Ace let out a long low whistle as Keeley emerged from the changing cubicle. 'Wow,' he said, looking her up and down. 'You have *got* to buy those shorts.'

Keeley checked her rear view in the mirror. 'Hmmm . . .' she said, frowning. 'I'm not sure. Don't you think they're a bit . . . well, short?'

'No way,' said Ace. 'Personally, I love seeing a bit of bum cheek poking out, especially when the bum's as sexy as yours.' He turned to his colleague, who was staring fixedly at Keeley's bottom. 'What d'you reckon, Dylan?'

'Fucking gorgeous. Absolutely fucking gorgeous. I'd eat my dinner off that arse.'

Breaking into a smile, Keeley turned towards her admirers. 'You know, I love coming into this shop. You guys always pay me such nice compliments.'

'And you deserve every single one of them,' said Ace. 'Hey, Dylan, you know what would look really good with those? One of those cute cap-sleeve Ts that came in yesterday.' He snapped his fingers. 'Get me an eight in the grey marl, will you?'

Keeley giggled. 'I haven't been a size eight since my modelling days.'

Ace gave her a disbelieving look. 'Really? But you're so slender.' He turned back to Dylan. 'Make that a ten.'

'You'd better get me a twelve as well,' said Keeley as

she stepped back into the changing room and drew the curtain across. 'Some of these designer labels come up very small, don't they?'

'They certainly do,' said Ace, who was well versed in the art of telling his female customers exactly what they wanted to hear.

A few moments later, Dylan returned with the two T-shirts. As he passed them through the curtain, he caught a glimpse of Keeley's naked breasts. It was on days like this that Dylan truly believed he had the best job in the world.

'Hey, guys,' Keeley called out as she pulled the first T-shirt over her head. 'Can you sort me out with some stuff for the weekend?'

Ace made a shushing noise. 'Keep it down, Kee. We've got a new temp working out back.'

'Oops, sorry.' Keeley pushed back the curtain. 'That must be making things tricky for you.'

'You can say that again,' said Ace. 'He's a nosy little so and so too — always asking questions.' His eyes moved down to her braless chest and the two perky nipples poking through the soft jersey fabric. 'That top looks great on you.'

Keeley looked in the mirror and put her hands on her hips. 'Yeah, it's not bad, is it?' She turned round and looked at her bottom one last time. 'Are you sure these shorts don't make me look slutty?'

'You look amazing, trust me.'

Keeley nodded at her reflection. 'Okay then, you've convinced me. Seeing as my boyfriend's treating me, I'll take them both.'

'That footballer's a very lucky bloke,' said Ace, putting his hand over his heart. 'And if you ever dump him, I want to be the first to know.'

'Don't let Astrid hear you say that,' Keeley giggled. 'How are things going with you two?'

'Not bad, thanks, although I don't get to see her half as much as I'd like. They work her like a dog in that spa. You wouldn't believe how much overtime she puts in.'

'Ah well,' said Keeley, biting her lip as she recalled her recent session with the Swedish girl, 'Astrid's massages are legendary. No wonder she's in such hot demand.' She lowered her voice. 'So, anyway, can I get two grams? I've got a busy weekend planned.'

'No problem.' Ace nodded towards the till where Dylan was busy serving another customer. 'You can pay for everything together. I'll give you the usual discount.'

Keeley smiled gratefully. 'Thanks, babe.'

While Keeley was changing, Ace headed for the golf pro's office, which lay next to the stockroom. After closing the door behind him, he went to the safe and punched in the combination, known to only two other people besides him: Jeff and Dylan. He pushed aside a heap of coin bags and reached for the booty beyond. His fingers had just closed round two pre-weighed packages of high-grade Colombian cocaine when he heard the office door creak open. As Ace hastily withdrew his hand from the safe, one of the packages tumbled to the floor. When he turned round, Harry was standing in the doorway.

'Jesus, you nearly gave me a heart attack. I wish you wouldn't creep around like that.' Without taking his eyes off Harry, Ace moved his foot so it was covering the wrap of coke.

Harry smiled apologetically. 'Sorry, mate.' His eyes flitted to the safe and then back to Ace.

'We're running low on change,' said Ace quickly.

'Oh. Right.'

There was a long silence. Harry seemed reluctant to leave.

'Was there something you wanted?' Ace asked.

'Er, yeah.' Another hesitation. 'I'm making some tea. Do you want one?'

'Great. Two sugars, thanks.'

'Coming up.' Harry turned to go.

'Oh, and Harry.'

'Yes?'

'Remember to knock next time.'

A few moments later, Ace was standing at the counter, wrapping Keeley's purchases in tissue paper. After sliding the parcels into one of the shop's smart maroon carriers, he delved briefly in the pocket of his track top, before thrusting his balled fist into the bag.

'There you go,' he said as he handed the bag to Keeley. 'It's all in there, including your little something for the weekend.'

'Cheers, Ace,' said Keeley, as she slid a wedge of cash across the counter. The transaction complete, she said her goodbyes and left the shop. As the door clanged shut behind her, Harry emerged from the back bearing a tray of tea. He did a double take when he caught sight of Keeley's departing figure through the window.

'That girl who just left,' he said as he set the tray down on the counter. 'Who is she?'

Ace sniggered. 'Forget it, mate. She's way out of your league.'

Harry nodded towards the tray. 'Help yourselves, boys. I won't be a minute.' Then, without a word of explanation, he walked out of the shop.

He caught up with Keeley in the leafy arbour that divided St Benedict's well-stocked herb garden from the driving range beyond. When he was almost within touching distance, he called out to her. 'Hey, Cinderella. Remember me?'

Keeley turned round and was surprised to see the dark-haired stranger who'd come to her rescue in the spa a few days earlier. 'Ah, Prince Charming. How could I forget?' she said, pleased that this time at least she was looking her usual well-groomed self. 'Where did you spring from?'

'The golf shop.'

Keeley frowned. 'That's funny, I didn't see you in there.'

'No, you wouldn't have done. I was in the kitchen, making tea.'

Keeley's fingers tightened round her carrier bag. 'Oh, you must be the new temp Ace was talking about.'

'That's right. I'm Harry.'

Keeley took the hand he was offering. 'Keeley. Pleased to meet you.'

'I, uh, don't suppose you've got time for a chat, have you, Keeley?'

Keeley shook her head. She might have known the guy

was going to hit on her. 'I'm afraid not. I've got a yoga class in ten minutes.'

'Later then? I knock off at six, we could meet for a drink in the Chukka Bar.'

Keeley smiled. The man's persistence was flattering, but she'd sooner gargle with nettles than date a shop assistant. 'Somehow, I don't think my boyfriend would be too happy about that,' she said. 'Anyway, look, I've really got to get to my class.'

She started to walk away, but Harry grabbed her upper arm.

'Hey, what do you think you're doing?' Keeley reacted crossly. 'I'm not interested – okay? Read my lips: *en oh* spells no.'

Harry let go of her arm. 'Are you sure you won't reconsider?'

Keeley's patience was wearing thin. 'Look, you freakin' pervert,' she hissed. 'Fuck off or I'll report you to the general manager for sexual harassment.'

Harry tutted. 'You don't want to do that.'

Keeley glared at him. 'Give me one good reason why not.'

Harry held her gaze. 'Let me ask you a question, Keeley. When you leave the changing room after your yoga class, are you going to have a pair of someone else's shoes stashed in your bag?'

Keeley's stomach lurched. 'I don't know what you're talking about.'

'I think you do,' Harry replied calmly. 'A few moments after you left the spa the other day, a very distressed lady came out of the changing room and reported a theft.' He raised an eyebrow. 'No wonder those moccasins weren't in your size.'

Keeley pressed her lips tight together, knowing that silence was her best – indeed, her only – defence.

Harry cocked his head to one side. 'So, how about it then?'

'How about what?' Keeley snapped.

'The Chukka Bar. At six.'

Keeley's nostrils flared. 'It doesn't look like I've got much choice, does it?' Then, with an imperious toss of her head, she flounced off across the lawn.

Two hours later she was sitting in a discreet corner of the Chukka Bar, anxiously sipping a double vodka cranberry. She felt sick to her stomach as she contemplated the consequences of being exposed as a thief. There was no question that she would receive a lifetime ban from St Benedict's, which would be nothing short of disastrous. And when Fabrizio found out, he would be sure to dump her rather than risk sullying his own reputation. Still, that would be the least of her worries if the club's management decided to call in the police.

When Harry arrived, nearly fifteen minutes late, he greeted her warmly and offered to buy her a drink, just as if they were on a regular date. Keeley watched him as he stood at the bar, silently willing him to spontaneously combust. When he returned with their drinks, he enquired politely about her yoga class. Keeley fixed him with a chilly stare. 'I'm supposed to be meeting my boyfriend later, so let's cut the small talk and get to the point, shall we?'

'Fair enough.' Harry pushed his wine glass to one side

and began rolling up his shirt sleeves, exposing an expanse of tanned, muscular forearm.

'I just want to start by saying that whatever you saw – or *thought* you saw – the other day in the spa, you can't prove a thing. You're just a shop boy. Nobody's going to believe your word over mine.' Keeley sat back in her chair and folded her arms across her chest.

'So you admit you stole the moccasins?'

Keeley shrugged. 'Yeah, I stole a pair of second-hand shoes. Big fucking deal.'

'So I guess you stole the Marni dress too.'

Keeley narrowed her eyes.

'And the Gucci blouse,' Harry continued. 'And the Ralph Lauren jeans.'

Keeley's jaw dropped. 'How the fuck do you know about those?'

Harry smiled. 'I may be just a shop boy, but I also happen to be the general manager's godson.'

Keeley gasped. 'You're Lanchester's godson?' She took a fortifying slug of vodka. 'How do I know you're telling the truth?'

'How else would I know about the thefts?' Harry sighed. 'I don't mind telling you that my godfather's very concerned about all this. He's had to deal with some very upset ladies.'

'Upset?' Keeley sneered. 'What have they got to be upset about? They're all fucking minted. They can easily afford to buy replacements.'

Harry looked her in the eye. 'So tell me something, Keeley. Why d'you steal? For the thrill of it?'

Keeley shrugged. 'A girl's got to earn a living somehow.'

'What – you mean you *sell* the clothes?' Harry stared at Keeley in disbelief, taking in the cashmere cardigan and the diamonds glittering in her ear lobes. 'Surely you're not that hard up.'

'What do you care what I do with them?' Keeley retorted, furious that the conversation wasn't panning out the way she'd planned. She gave her inquisitor an arch look. 'So why did you ask me to meet you? Why didn't you just go ahead and grass me up to Lanchester?'

Harry hesitated. He couldn't tell Keeley the real reason – that he'd wanted to be one hundred per cent certain she *was* the thief before he went to Lanchester. He didn't want to end up with egg on his face, not when his slow progress on the drugs investigation had already failed to impress. 'I wanted to give you a chance to explain yourself,' he said. 'To see if there were any' – Harry paused again, conscious that he mustn't sound like an ex-copper – 'what do you call those thingummyjigs ... mitigating circumstances.'

'Oh pur-lease,' said Keeley disgustedly. 'You don't expect me to believe that, do you?' She tossed her hair back. 'It's perfectly clear that there was only one thing on your mind when you suggested this cosy little drink.'

'Oh? And what's that?'

'Sex.'

Harry was taken aback. 'I'm sorry?'

Keeley gave him a withering look. 'Don't pretend you don't know what I'm talking about. Admit it: you asked me here this evening so you could blackmail me into sleeping with you.'

'I absolutely did not!' Harry said indignantly.

Keeley picked up her glass and drained the remainder of her second vodka cranberry. Then she leaned towards him. 'But hey, you're a good-looking guy, so on this occasion I'm prepared to negotiate.' She crossed one leg over the other, so her geometric-print skirt rode up, exposing her firm, St Tropez-ed thighs.

Harry held up a warning hand. 'Keeley, listen. You've got completely the wrong idea about me.'

Keeley placed her hand on Harry's knee. 'Nobody gives blowjobs like me,' she whispered. 'Trust me, I'm the best.'

Harry pushed back his chair. It was an undeniably tempting proposition, but he had to remain professional. 'I can't be bought,' he said firmly. 'I have to follow my conscience.' He stood up. 'I think it's time I went.'

'*Pleeease*, Harry, there *are* other options.'

'Sorry, I'm not interested.' He felt a stab of pity as he looked at Keeley's pretty face with its huge pleading eyes. 'Goodbye, Keeley.'

He started walking towards the exit. Keeley followed. Out in the entrance hall, she moved in front of him and pushed his chest, sending him stumbling back into the wood panelling. In an instant, her body was against his, effectively pinning him to the wall. 'What's the matter?' she said flirtatiously. 'Don't you find me attractive?'

Harry sighed. 'I find you very attractive, Keeley, but that's completely irrelevant.'

'Is it?' Keeley slipped a hand between them and lightly caressed his crotch, eliciting an almost immediate physiological reaction. 'A certain part of your anatomy seems to think otherwise.'

A man in a business suit walked past them and did a double take. Harry blushed and pushed her hand away. 'Please, Keeley; you have to stop this. People are looking.'

Keeley seemed unperturbed. 'We can go somewhere more private if you like.' She took him by the wrist and started leading him down the hallway.

'Keeley, no. This is utterly pointless. Nothing you can say or do is going to make me change my mind.'

'Shut up and get in here.'

Harry looked around at the smooth mahogany-lined walls. 'Get in where?'

Keeley reached out a hand and pushed a seemingly random section of wood panelling at about chest height. Instantly, it sprung open to reveal a concealed cupboard, which was lined with shelves laden with cleaning materials.

'Wow, this is pretty impressive. You wouldn't even know it was here from the outside.' As Harry stood there, admiring the cupboard's construction, Keeley reached into her handbag, pulled out a tube of extra-strong mints, popped one into her mouth and began sucking it as hard as she could. Then she gave Harry a shove, pitching him headfirst into the cupboard. 'Hey, what are you doing?' he said as she closed the door behind them, plunging them into darkness. 'Open that door; I can't see a bloody thing.'

'Good. That way all your other senses will be heightened.'

Harry sighed. 'Okay then, *I'll* open the door.' He took a step forward, but Keeley was blocking his way. He tried to sidestep her, and stubbed his toe on a vacuum cleaner. 'Fuck,' he said through gritted teeth.

In the darkness, Keeley giggled.

'Right, that's it,' said Harry, his tone firmer now. 'This has gone far enough. I'm going to count to ten and if you haven't opened that door by then, I'll . . . I'll . . .'

'You'll what?'

'I'll be forced to take drastic action.' He cleared his throat. 'One. Two. Three.'

Keeley's hand reached for his groin.

'Four, five,' Harry continued.

Keeley crunched on the remnants of her mint as she fumbled with his zipper. Harry knew he should push her hand away, but his arms felt leaden. 'Six.'

Her hand plunged into his underwear. Still he did nothing. 'Seven.'

Suddenly and quite unexpectedly, Harry's cock was engulfed in Keeley's mouth. His voice quavered. 'Eiiiight.'

Keeley began flicking her tongue back and forth across his frenulum in a most distracting fashion.

'Niii—' The private investigator's lips clamped shut as he surrendered to the delicious tingling sensation that was spreading through his cock. It was quite unlike any feeling he'd had before during oral sex – thanks to the extra-strong mint, Keeley's mouth felt hot and cold on him all at the same time.

Three minutes and forty-five seconds later, Harry collapsed sideways onto a shelf unit, sending two bottles of Jeyes Fluid crashing to the floor. His thigh muscles had turned to jelly. Keeley hadn't been lying: it was, by some considerable way, the best blowjob of his life. 'That was awesome,' he gasped as he struggled to an upright position.

Keeley smiled, but before she could graciously accept the compliment, there was a sound in the corridor outside. A moment later, the cupboard was flooded with light.

Caretaker Alf Joiner had seen some strange sights during his thirty-year tenure at St Benedict's, but the one that greeted him now left him slack-jawed with shock. Inside the broom cupboard – *his* broom cupboard – was a partially dressed man. His face was in shadow, but Alf could see that his hands were cupping his naked genitals, while his trousers and underwear were bunched round his knees. In front of him, a young woman was kneeling on the tiled floor. She gave Alf a defiant stare, and then slowly wiped the back of her hand across her mouth.

A surge of anger rose up from Alf's guts. His territory had been violated, there were no two ways about it. 'You filthy perverts,' he whispered, mindful of the other customers who were milling about the entrance hall, just a few feet away. 'Make yourselves decent and get out of my cupboard.'

Quick as a flash, the man had hauled up his trousers and bolted. 'There's plenty more where that came from,' the woman called after him as she rose to her feet.

Alf shook his head despairingly.

'Thanks for the use of the cupboard, grandad,' she said as she brushed past him and sauntered towards the entrance hall, swinging her handbag as if she didn't have a care in the world.

*

Alf was still seething thirty-six hours later when he arrived for his appointment with St Benedict's general manager. His anger resulted not just from the desecration of his precious broom cupboard, but also from the fact that he'd been forced to make an appointment in the first place. Anthony Lanchester's predecessor had been happy to meet with senior members of staff – and the head caretaker was, by virtue of his age and length of service, the most senior of them all – at a moment's notice. And that, Alf firmly believed, was the way it *should* be.

For ten long minutes – time which could have been more usefully spent polishing the ballroom's parquet floor in readiness for a delegation of Japanese businessmen – Alf perched on a leather pouffe a few feet away from Lanchester's secretary, anxiously passing his cloth cap from hand to hand. At long last, a buzzer sounded on the secretary's desk.

'You can go in now,' the secretary said, without lifting her eyes from the computer screen.

'About time too,' Alf muttered as he hauled his arthritic hip from the pouffe.

He found Lanchester sitting behind his desk, performing bicep curls with a large quartz paperweight. 'Ah, Mr Joiner, good morning to you,' the manager said as he replaced the paperweight.

'Is it?'

Ignoring the caretaker's gruff response, Lanchester nodded towards the high-backed chair opposite his desk, which was purposely uncomfortable to discourage visitors from lingering. 'Do take a seat, won't you?'

'I'll stand if it's all the same to you.'

'As you wish.' Lanchester leaned forward across the desk. 'So, I understand you're experiencing some problems. Staff troubles, eh?'

Alf snorted. 'It's not the staff, it's the flamin' punters.'

'Oh? Perhaps you'd care to elucidate.'

'Eeelucy-what?'

Lanchester smiled patronizingly. 'Explain.'

'Oh yes, I'll explain all right.' Alf folded his arms across his chest. 'At it like rabbits they are. All over the club. Everywhere you look. It's a bleedin' disgrace.'

Lanchester's smile faltered. 'I'm sorry, I'm not sure I understand.'

'Rutting. Bonking. Shagging. I'm not sure what the likes of you call it.'

Lanchester held up a hand. 'Let me get this right. You're saying that certain members of St Benedict's are fornicating in public areas.'

Alf nodded vigorously. 'That's *exactly* what I'm saying.'

'And you've seen this with your own eyes?'

'As good as.'

'I see.' Lanchester cleared his throat. 'I'm afraid I'm going to need specifics, old chap – if that's not too embarrassing for you.'

'I'm not the one who should be embarrassed. It's *those* dirty buggers.' Alf felt a twinge in his hip and winced. 'I think I will take the weight off my feet,' he said as he lowered himself on to the chair.

For the next fifteen minutes, Lanchester listened patiently as Alf related, in full and frank detail, the incident in the broom cupboard. When he'd finished, he stared hard at Lanchester. 'So, wotcha gonna do about it?'

Lanchester regarded him thoughtfully. 'So, if I understand you correctly, they weren't engaged in full sex.'

'No,' Alf grudgingly conceded. 'But who's to say they wouldn't have been if I hadn't walked in on them when I did?'

'And do you think you would recognize the participants again?'

'I didn't get a good look at the fella's face, but I've seen *her* around the club loads of times. I could point her out to you, no problem.' He shook his head despairingly. 'On her knees she was, bold as brass. The little madam even had the barefaced cheek to thank me for the use of my facilities.'

'Oh well, that's something I suppose,' Lanchester smirked.

'This ain't a laughing matter,' said Alf sharply. He resented this little upstart making light of his troubles. The old manager would have been a good deal more sympathetic. 'So, I'll ask you again: wotcha gonna do about it?'

Lanchester stared back at Alf, annoyed by his elderly caretaker's attempts to intimidate him. 'I do understand your concerns, Mr Joiner. However, the couple in question did at least conduct their business in an area that afforded them some privacy – and we have to allow our members a certain measure of freedom. It's part of the ethos of St Benedict's.'

'Ethos my arse,' Alf growled, slapping his cloth cap on his thigh for emphasis. 'What about me? What about *my* feelings? That's my bloody cupboard and those filthy perverts were trespassing. If I was general manager, I'd withdraw their memberships. Either that, or we call the rozzers in and do 'em for indecent exposure.'

Lanchester glanced at the wall clock. He'd already spent more time on this matter than it quite clearly merited. 'I have no doubt that it was a deeply distressing experience for you, Mr Joiner,' he said in what he hoped was a calming tone. 'However, with all due respect, it's not, technically speaking, *your* cupboard.' Before Alf had the chance to raise an objection, Lanchester continued swiftly, 'Really, I think the most sensible course of action would be to put the incident behind us and try to forget about it. I daresay it was a one-off.'

'Aah, but that's where you're wrong,' said Alf triumphantly. Leaning to one side, he removed Abi's G-string from the pocket of his overall, where it had been residing for days, like a lucky charm, and tossed the scrap of pink fabric on to Lanchester's desk.

Frowning, Lanchester picked up his Mont Blanc and hooked it through a leg hole. 'What have we here?' he said, holding the pen aloft.

'A pair of ladies' knickers, that's what. I found 'em in the trophy room a few days ago. *And* the window was open.'

Lanchester let the G-string slip off the end of his pen. 'And what, precisely, does that prove?'

'That a couple of your precious bloody members were in there humping,' said Alf. 'They must've heard me coming and made their escape through the window – only they were in such a rush, Little Miss Muffet forgot to put her drawers back on.'

Lanchester had heard enough. As he surveyed his head caretaker's battered face it occurred to him that if wrinkles were like the rings of a tree and could be used to measure age, a rough calculation would leave Alf Joiner little short of a hundred and four. 'Look, old chap,' he said, 'if you're finding the job a bit much to cope with, perhaps it's time to start thinking about retirement.'

Alf struggled to his feet. He'd worked at St Benedict's man and boy. He might moan about the job from time to time, but he had no intention of leaving; they'd have to carry him out in a coffin. 'I'll have you know that I'm a good two years off my pension,' he cried, waving his fist at Lanchester. 'You can't get rid of me, not before I'm good and ready. I know my rights.'

Lanchester sighed. 'Mr Joiner, I can assure you that I have no intention of getting rid of you. I simply suggested –'

'Yeah, well in future you can keep your bloody suggestions to yourself.' Alf tapped his forehead. 'I may be getting on a bit, but the old brain's as sharp as ever and I know when I'm being got at.' He turned and started shuffling towards the door. 'I'll keep out of your way in future, Mr Lanchester, and if you know what's good for you, you'll keep out of mine.'

As the door slammed shut, Lanchester rose from his desk and walked to the window. He'd been thrilled – no, ecstatic – when he'd bagged the general manager's job at St Benedict's and now, gazing out across the manicured grounds, he felt a surge of pride – pride that was tinged with a faint degree of nausea at the thought that he might, just possibly, have bitten off more than he could chew.

As he tracked the progress of an attractive redhead making her way across the lawn in a tiny tennis skirt, impractically teamed with strappy red sandals, Lanchester suddenly became aware of raised voices coming from the adjoining room, which was occupied by his secretary, Janice. For a moment he thought Alf Joiner had returned to make a nuisance of himself, but then he realized that the man remonstrating with Janice had a heavy French accent. Lanchester was just deliberating whether to see what all the fuss was about or remain in the sanctum of his office when the door burst open. Executive chef Xavier Gainsbourg stood on the threshold, glowering razors. Judging by his sweaty brow and gravy-stained uniform, he'd come straight from the kitchen. Behind him, Lanchester's secretary was twittering like a budgie on helium.

'You can't just go barging into Mr Lanchester's office,' she was saying. 'Not without an appointment. He's a very busy man.'

'I don't give a shit about your petty bureaucracy,' Xavier snarled over his shoulder. 'I too am a very busy man. I have a kitchen to run, an army of staff to inspire, a restaurant full of diners salivating at the prospect of my gastronomic creations. Do you think I would waste my precious time coming to see Mr Lanchester if it wasn't a matter of the utmost importance?' He flicked his hand at her. 'Now, why don't you get back to your desk and finish typing up your shopping list.'

'Don't you patronize me, you arrogant swine,' shrieked the secretary as she drew herself up to her full height of five foot two inches and thrust out her shelf-like bosom.

'If your name's not in the appointment book, you're not going in.'

'It's all right, Janice,' Lanchester called out wearily. 'I'm sure I can spare Mr Gainsbourg five minutes.'

The secretary shot Xavier a look of pure hatred before turning on her heel and stomping back to her desk.

'Please, come in, and shut the door behind you,' Lanchester told the chef. 'But you'll have to be quick. I was due in the spa ten minutes ago.'

Xavier walked into the room and collapsed into the chair which had recently been vacated by the head caretaker. He was red-faced and trembling with emotion.

'You look as if you could use a drink,' said Lanchester. He slid open the bottom drawer of his desk. 'I keep a little something in here. Purely for medicinal purposes, you understand.' He removed a bottle of single malt and a cut-glass tumbler. 'One finger or two?'

'Two,' said Xavier, as he undid the top buttons of his chef's jacket.

Lanchester reached back into the drawer for a second tumbler. 'You know what, I think I'll join you. It's been a very trying morning.' He filled both glasses with a generous measure of whisky and pushed one across the desk towards Xavier. The Frenchman downed it in a single gulp and brought the empty tumbler crashing down on the manager's desk.

'Now,' said Lanchester as he sipped cautiously at his own drink. 'Why don't you take a deep breath and tell me what's troubling you.'

Xavier ran a hand through his unkempt quiff. 'Somebody is stealing from the kitchen,' he said slowly.

Lanchester's heart sank. As if he didn't have enough on his plate already. 'And what evidence do you have?' he enquired.

Xavier jabbed at his face. 'The evidence of my own eyes. I've just discovered four lobsters missing from this morning's fish delivery.'

'Cooked?'

'Live.'

The corners of Lanchester's mouth twitched. 'Are you sure they didn't just make a bid for freedom?'

The chef gave him a withering look. 'Please,' he said. 'This is not a joke.'

'No, no, of course not, but I don't think a few un-accounted-for crustaceans are anything to get too upset about.'

Xavier pursed his lips as he fought to control his irritation. 'It's not just the lobsters. Two days ago it was half a pound of pâté de foie gras. And, last week, a bottle of salad dressing and some black cherry compote.'

'Do you have any idea who's responsible?'

Xavier made a slicing motion across his neck. 'If I knew that, the man in question would be dead.'

Lanchester laughed nervously. 'I'll take that as a no.' He set down his tumbler and steepled his fingers under his chin. He could feel his concentration slipping as the whisky started to warm his insides. What's more, he was keen to get to the spa, where he planned to perform an impromptu uniform inspection. He chewed the inside of his cheek as he imagined the line-up of mainly female staff, most of whom were wearing uniforms smaller than one of his freshly pressed pocket handkerchiefs. Perhaps, if he asked nicely, one of the massage therapists would even administer some soothing treatment to the aching tendon in his neck.

'So, what do you intend to do about it?' said Xavier fiercely. 'I cannot tolerate a Judas in my kitchen. We must root him out.'

'Perhaps you could start by keeping a note of the precise dates and times when the foodstuffs are going missing. That way, at least we can see whose shifts the thefts coincide with.'

Xavier flung both hands in the air. 'Is that it? Is that all you are going to do?'

Lanchester sighed. 'I'm afraid it's all I *can* do – at least until we have more evidence. And now, if you'll excuse me, I have some urgent business to attend to in the spa.'

He stood up and walked across the room, intending to open the door, but found the chef blocking his way. 'What could be more important than the kitchen and the happiness of its executive chef?' Xavier cried, thumping his chest with a fist. 'The kitchen is the heart of St Benedict's. Without it there is nothing!'

Lanchester took a step back. 'Please don't shout at me, Mr Gainsbourg. I'm doing my level best to help you, but these are very serious allegations and we must proceed with caution.'

For a long moment, the two men stared at each other. Then Xavier spoke. 'I have a plan.'

Lanchester surveyed the chef doubtfully. 'I'm listening.'

'I shall lay a trap.'

'What sort of trap?'

'Some poison bait: a creamy vichyssoise, laced with rat

poison. And then the culprit will be sick to his thieving stomach.'

Lanchester looked at him aghast. 'Now look here, Mr Gainsbourg, you can't just go taking the law into your own hands.'

Xavier turned his head sulkily towards the window. 'When at my place of work, I answer only to the name "Chef".'

Lanchester sighed. He was fed up of his staff telling him what he should and shouldn't do. 'Well, listen to me, *Chef*,' he said. As he spat the word, a fine spray of spittle shot out from the gap between his front teeth and struck Xavier on the cheek. The chef wiped away the droplets with the back of his hand, making no attempt to hide his disgust. 'I'm in charge here and we're going to play things by my rules or not at all. Understood?'

It was on the tip of Xavier's tongue to tell Lanchester to take his job and shove it up his rectum, but instead he balled his fists and slowly counted to ten. The Frenchman was a maverick, a rule-bender, a free spirit. Much as he loved cooking for the appreciative diners of St Benedict's, he hated being part of the establishment and forced to take orders from the likes of Lanchester. Still, he told himself as he stood there silently fuming, this time next year he'd have his own restaurant in Delchester and would be answerable to no one. Commercial property in the city didn't come cheap, and making his dream a reality was going to cost a vast amount of cash. But Xavier was a resourceful man, and he was already well on his way to raising the money, thanks to a secret business venture, which no one – not even his wife – knew about. The business in question was a risky one and Xavier knew Abi would disapprove, if and when she did find out. But once the restaurant was up and running, and Xavier was the toast of the city, she wouldn't be complaining. 'Understood,' he said, though the word felt like a lump of gristle wedged in his oesophagus.

Nine

Destiny Morris didn't *do* queues. After stepping out of the stretch Hummer, she marched straight up to the shaven-headed doorman, drawing gasps of recognition from the lesser mortals who waited patiently behind the velvet rope. Keeley followed a few respectful paces behind, teetering in her five-inch silver stilettos and feeling supremely confident after the line of coke they'd shared in the back of the limo.

'Evening, ladies,' said the doorman. 'On the guest list, are we? If I could just have your names.'

'Oh for fuck's sake,' said a skinny girl wielding a clipboard. Shoving aside the doorman, she reached down and unclipped the rope. 'Hiya, Destiny, we're so glad you could make it,' she trilled, her voice dripping with sycophancy. 'Coat check's on the left as you go in. VIP room's upstairs.'

'Cheers, babe,' drawled Destiny as she swept into the club, borne on a cloud of fake fur and Eternity by Calvin Klein.

It was the hotly anticipated launch night of Go-Go, Delchester's newest members club, and the place was heaving with beautiful and/or famous young things.

Grabbing Keeley's hand so they wouldn't lose each other in the seething mass of bodies, Destiny led the way up to the mezzanine level, where a menacing quartet of black-suited bouncers guarded the VIP area. Having already received word from the door bitch that Destiny was en route, the bouncers parted to let the girls through, then quickly closed ranks to prevent an inebriated kids' TV presenter in a vomit-stained T-shirt gaining admittance.

After snatching complimentary cocktails from a passing waiter's tray, Destiny and Keeley settled on a faux-zebra-skin sofa, artfully arranging themselves so their best assets – cleavage and legs respectively – were displayed to maximum effect. It being the VIP room, their fellow clubbers studiously avoided gawping, but there were plenty of sidelong glances.

Keeley had known Destiny Morris for less than a year. They'd been introduced by their then boyfriends – a photographer and a very-married advertising executive respectively – who were business associates. The boyfriends had fallen by the wayside, but the girls remained friends and Keeley always looked forward to their rare nights out. As they necked their cocktails – and then helped themselves to another – the talk turned to men, as it usually did.

'How are things going with Fabrizio?' enquired Destiny, who had been single for three weeks after splitting with her latest boyfriend, a BAFTA-award-winning comedian who had turned out to be tragically unfunny in real life.

Keeley shrugged. 'Oh, you know. So-so.'

'Did you manage to get shot of that hideous necklace he gave you?'

'Yeah, I got sixty quid for it on eBay.'

'Hasn't he asked why you're not wearing it?'

'I told him the chain broke while I was out shopping and it slipped off my neck and straight down a drain.'

Destiny chuckled. 'You are awful, Kee – and he *actually* believed you?'

'Fab's such a sucker. He'd believe anything I told him; he's crazy about me.' Keeley curled her lip disdainfully and crossed her legs. As she did so, the pointed tip of her shoe prodded a teenage girl sitting at the next table. Instantly the girl spun round and glared at her. 'Yeah?' said Keeley threateningly.

The girl scowled. 'You just stabbed me with your fucking shoe.' She jabbed an angry finger at her shin. 'Look, you've made a hole in my tights. I ought to make you pay for a new pair.'

Keeley leaned closer to the girl. 'I'd like to see you try,' she hissed.

The girl opened her mouth to fire off a retort, but then she caught sight of Keeley's companion. Instantly, her demeanour changed. 'Oh my God, Destiny!' she squealed, her hands flying to her cheeks. 'I can't believe it's really you. You are, like, *sooo* fucking cool. I loved that shoot you did for *Busted* magazine – you know, the one where you were wearing the PVC catsuit and squirting cream over that other model's boobs.' She paused to catch her breath. 'I'm working as a secretary at the moment; I shouldn't really be in the VIP but my friend knows one of the doormen and he said he'd let us in if we gave him a blowjob later. *Any*way, what I really want to be is a model. I'm saving up for breast implants and then this photographer I know is going to take some pictures so I can send them to all the lads' mags.' She gazed at her heroine worshipfully. 'I think it's wonderful what you've achieved, really I do. You're such an inspiration.'

Destiny forced a smile, revealing the porcelain veneers she'd recently had fitted for a live TV makeover show. She had never set out to be a role model and, frankly, she found the whole business rather tiresome. Still, she told herself, it was girls like this who bought the gossip magazines, which breathlessly reported her every move. In any case, it cost nothing to be civil. 'Thanks, that's nice of you to say so,' she said pleasantly.

The girl held out a damp paper napkin. 'Will you sign this? Or my friends will never believe I've met you.'

'Sure,' said Destiny. 'Do you have a pen?'

'Erm, hang on a minute.' As the girl rummaged in her handbag, Destiny and Keeley exchanged bored looks. 'Here you go,' she said, handing Destiny a blunt eyeliner pencil. The model scrawled her name across the napkin, the edges of the words bleeding into the damp spots. 'Good luck with the implants,' she said as she handed back the napkin. Then, before the girl could engage her in further conversation, she drained her glass and stood up. 'Come on, Kee, let's go and powder our noses.' As they sashayed to the ladies' room, hips swaying beneath their micro skirts, the girl watched them, mesmerized.

'What an arse-licker,' Keeley declared as they pushed open the door of a cubicle, having deposited a crisp tenner in the toilet attendant's saucer to ensure her discretion. 'I don't know how you manage to be so polite. I just wanted to slap her smug little face.'

Destiny shrugged. 'You just get used to it after a while.'

She locked the cubicle door, flipped down the toilet seat and rubbed her hands together greedily. 'Come on then.'

Keeley hitched up her skirt and stuck a hand down the front of her knickers. A moment later, she removed a clear plastic packet filled with cocaine. After tipping roughly a quarter of it onto the toilet lid, she took the credit card Destiny was offering and chopped it into two neat rows. The girls took turns kneeling on the cold tiled floor to hoover up a line through a tightly rolled twenty-pound note. When they were done, Keeley flipped the lock on the cubicle door and led the way to the mirrors, where the girls checked their nostrils for telltale smudges of white.

'Right,' said Destiny, rearranging her breasts in her corset top so they projected over the top like two bowling balls. 'Let's have a little walkabout, shall we . . . see if there's anyone here worth pulling.'

Back in the VIP area, the two girls – arms linked ostentatiously – began a slow circuit of the room. By some unspoken agreement, clusters of clubbers parted to let them through. A couple of acquaintances greeted Destiny by name; she smiled and nodded in a queenly fashion, but didn't engage in conversation. Suddenly, she stopped stone dead, causing Keeley to stumble on her stilettos. 'Well, well, well,' she said, thrusting out a hip. 'I thought this place was supposed to be ultra-exclusive. Clearly I was wrong – it seems that any old slapper can sweet-talk their way in.'

Keeley's heart sank. All at once, she could feel the fun girlie evening she had been so looking forward to slipping away. As she followed the direction of her friend's icy stare, her worst fears were confirmed. On the other side of the room, Destiny's arch-rival Shannon was chatting animatedly to Mick Terry, the dwarfish showbiz editor of the *Delchester Chronicle*. Keeley placed a warning hand on Destiny's shoulder. 'Come on, Des, you don't want to get into another ruck with Shannon, especially not with newspaper reporters around. Why don't we go downstairs for a dance?'

Destiny sniffed. 'Downstairs? With the Muggles? You have *got* to be joking.' Her eyes narrowed. 'Trust me, if I never speak to Shannon Stewart again it would be too soon – but there *was* something I wanted to discuss with Mick.'

'Can't you save it for another time? Judging by the way his nose is practically wedged in Shannon's cleavage, he's pissed as a fart. When he wakes up tomorrow, chances are he won't remember a thing you've said. Why don't you give him a call at the paper tomorrow?'

Destiny tossed her head imperiously. She could be very stubborn when she wanted to. 'But I've got an exclusive for him,' she said in a wheedling tone. 'It can't possibly wait until tomorrow. I'll just have to make sure he writes it all down in his little notebook.'

'What exclusive?' asked Keeley. But her objections were in vain, for her friend was already halfway across the room. Sighing in irritation, Keeley trotted after her.

'Mick! How lovely to see you,' Destiny simpered when she reached the diminutive journalist.

Instantly, Mick's eyes lit up. 'Destiny, sweetheart, you're looking stunning tonight, if I may say so.' He seized the hand Destiny was offering and pressed it greedily to his thin lips. 'This must be my lucky night. I've only got the two best-looking women in the club fighting over me.' He winked seedily and snaked an arm round Destiny's tiny waist.

'Two?' said Destiny disingenuously. She looked showily from left to right. 'Oh, you mean Shannon. Sorry, dear, I didn't see you there.' The other model flashed an insincere smile, before mouthing the word 'bitch' over the top of Mick's balding head. Then, for appearances' sake, the two models exchanged breast-to-breast air kisses. As Mick watched them, he felt something twitch in his bottle-green Y-fronts.

'Shannon here was just telling me all about her new fitness video,' Mick offered.

Destiny's smile hardened. 'You don't say.'

'I'm shooting it next week,' said Shannon airily. '*Shape-up and Salsacise with Shannon*. It's being released in time for the Christmas market. It'll be the perfect stocking filler, eh, Mick?'

The editor grinned lasciviously. 'You can fill my stocking any time, lovie.'

'*Salsacise?*' Destiny sneered. 'I don't know ... these fitness fads are getting more ridiculous by the moment.'

'It's not a fad; it's a highly motivational dance programme that can help you trim inches off your waist, hips and thighs and burn up to five hundred calories an hour,' said Shannon as if reading from an invisible autocue. She looked her nemesis up and down. 'You should try it, Destiny; you could do with toning up those glutes. I tell you what, I'll send you a review copy.'

'Oh there's no need to go to all that trouble,' cooed Destiny. 'I daresay I'll be able to pick it up for next to nothing once it hits the remainder bins, come the New Year.' She reached down to fiddle with the zipper of her spike-heeled boot (the real purpose of this manoeuvre being to give Mick a good eyeful of her cleavage). 'Actually, I've got some *rather* exciting news of my own.'

Shannon arched an over-plucked eyebrow. 'Have you now?' she said disbelievingly.

Destiny turned to Mick, whose eyes were beginning to glaze over after two glasses of wine and three cocktails on an empty stomach. 'It's supposed to be top secret, but you can run it in your column if you like – just so long as you don't credit me as the source.'

Mick patted Destiny's rump. 'Yes, lovie, I'm all ears.'

Destiny cleared her throat. 'So . . . if I said the words, "Celebrity Lust Island", would you know what I was talking about?'

'I wouldn't be worthy of the title Showbiz Editor if I hadn't,' chuckled Mick. 'It's only going to be the most controversial reality show ever seen on British television.' He frowned as he struggled to recollect the details from the TV company's effusive press release. 'Let's see now . . . five newlywed males, selected from the general public, will be despatched to a luxury beach resort in the Caribbean. Over the next three weeks, ten sexy celebrity women will do their very best to seduce them – by fair means or foul – and the contestant who sleeps with the most men pockets the fifty thousand pounds prize money. I spoke to one of the producers a few days ago; they're confirming the celebrity line-up next week.'

'Wow!' exclaimed Keeley. 'That sounds amazing. People are going to be tuning in in their millions.'

'You bet they are,' said Destiny. 'And guess what?'

'What?' said Keeley obligingly.

'Yours truly was invited to audition for the show.'

'When was this?' said Keeley, sticking out her lower lip sulkily. She didn't think she and Destiny *had* secrets. 'How come you didn't mention it before?'

'They made me promise not to tell *anyone*. I shouldn't really be talking about it now. Except . . .' Destiny started jumping up and down and clapping her hands. 'One of the producers phoned me this morning to let me know I've got through! I'm flying to Antigua in six weeks' time.'

Shannon gave a small hard laugh, like a cat coughing up a furball. '*You've* got a place on *Celebrity Lust Island*?'

'Yes, isn't it exciting?'

'It certainly is,' said Mick. 'I'll get that in Thursday's column. It might even be the lead. Hey, d'you think the TV company will let you do an interview with the paper once they've made the official announcement? We can do a nice bikini shoot. You'd be up for that, wouldn't you, Destiny?'

Before she could answer, Shannon started tutting and shaking her head. 'Blimey, they must be desperate.'

'I beg your pardon?' snapped Destiny.

Shannon gave a mocking laugh. 'Never mind scraping the bottom of the barrel – it looks as though those producers have started tunnelling through the earth's crust.'

Destiny's nostrils flared. 'What are you talking about, you silly bitch? The competition in those auditions was fierce; it was dog eat dog, I'm telling you. I'm a star, goddammit; the producers were lucky to get me.'

'In that case, why don't we just remind ourselves exactly what it is you're famous *for*?' said Shannon coolly. 'Let's see, now . . . getting your tits out and falling out of nightclubs drunk. Hardly rocket science, is it?'

Breaking away from Mick, Destiny stepped up to Shannon so their faces were inches apart. 'You're a fine one to talk, Shannon Stewart. What's your biggest achievement? I haven't seen *you* on *University Challenge* recently.'

Shannon put her hands on her hips and leaned forward so her nose was virtually touching Destiny's. 'No, but I *was* in *The Weakest Link* celebrity special last year.'

'Yeah – and what happened? You got voted off in the first round. You are the weakest link, Shannon. Now fuck off.'

Hearing the sound of raised voices, other clubbers had started to sidle up to the group. The rivalry between Destiny and Shannon had been slavishly documented in the tabloids and nobody wanted to miss the latest violent instalment. Tired of pussyfooting around, Shannon decided to move in for the kill. 'In case you'd forgotten, sweetheart, *I* am a professional model. *You*, on the other hand, are a jumped-up slag with delusions of grandeur,' she spat. 'You're so trashy you're practically landfill, Destiny. God knows, you'd suck off your own granddad if you thought there was a bit of publicity in it.'

Almost before she knew what she was doing, Destiny's palm had made contact with Shannon's cheek. A loud crack rang out. Somebody in the crowd applauded. Keeley put her head in her hands. Her big night out was well and truly ruined.

For a moment, Shannon seemed to be in shock. She

clutched her cheek, tears welling up in her huge charcoal-rimmed eyes. 'You fucking cow,' she wailed. 'I'm going to report you for assault – and this time I've got a whole room full of witnesses.'

Not wanting to look like a wuss, Mick attempted – somewhat belatedly, it must be said – to calm the situation down. 'Ladies, ladies,' he said, stepping between the two models. 'Let's not get our G-strings in a twist, eh? Isn't it about time you laid this silly rivalry to rest? You don't need to keep sniping at each other; this town's big enough for both of you.' His voice grew soft and mellifluous. 'How's about we three go somewhere quiet and you girls can talk things through like rational human beings.'

'Oh yeah, bloody brilliant idea, Mick – and what are the odds you'll be secretly taping the whole thing?' Shannon barked. 'Now get out of my way, you fucking midget.' Shoulder-charging the journalist aside, she lunged at Destiny's cleavage. The model yelped and stumbled backwards into Keeley's arms. At the same time, Shannon yanked the top of Destiny's corset with both hands, her teeth gritted with effort. There was the sound of fabric tearing, and then a loud cheer went up from the group of onlookers. As Destiny struggled to an upright position, she glanced down and saw her torn corset hanging round her waist. Her famous breasts were now totally exposed. Clamping her arms across her chest to preserve what little modesty she had, she glared at Shannon, who was bent double with laughter. Across the room, a flashbulb went off. Somebody was taking pictures – and his four-shots-per-second Nikon marked him out as a pro. A bouncer appeared out of nowhere and started grappling with the paparazzo.

Meanwhile, a second bouncer came towards Destiny, his suit jacket held out in front of him like a matador. 'We need to get you out of here before the situation escalates out of control,' he said as he wrapped the jacket round Destiny's bare torso.

'What about that crazy bitch?' said Keeley, jabbing a finger in Shannon's direction. 'She just attacked my friend, without any . . .' Her voice tailed off. 'Well, with *hardly any* provocation.'

'My colleague will take care of her,' said the bouncer calmly. 'Now, please follow me.' He ushered Destiny and Keeley through a side door and down a brightly lit corridor. 'Sorry about this, ladies,' he apologized, as he led them down a draughty flight of stone steps. 'I'm going to have to take you out through the fire escape – only there's half a dozen snappers waiting out front.'

Destiny groaned. 'Jesus, *now* he tells me.' She turned round. 'Come on, Kee. This is going to make a great picture – me and my boobs hanging out of our friend Andy McNab's jacket.' She pulled her lips back like a baboon. 'How do I look? Have I got any lippy on my teeth?'

The bouncer bounded back up the steps, barring Destiny's way. 'I'm sorry, miss. I can't allow you to go back into the club. It's a security risk.'

The model glowered at him. 'Go ahead and ruin my career, why don't you?'

Keeley laid a hand on her arm. 'It's probably for the

best. You don't want the *Celebrity Lust Island* producers thinking you're a cheap tart now, do you?'

'Hmm, I guess not,' said Destiny, conveniently ignoring the fact that this was precisely why the programme-makers had selected her in the first place.

The fire escape led to a litter-strewn side street, where an Audi with blacked-out windows was waiting with its engine running. 'Here we are,' said the bouncer, opening the back door. 'The driver will see you both home safely.'

Keeley gestured to the jacket. 'What about this?'

'Keep it, with the compliments of the management.'

Destiny gave him a haughty look. 'Thanks for nothing.'

As the car made its way through the dark city streets, the girls reflected on the night's drama. 'Well, I think that was quite a successful evening,' said Destiny, sinking back on the leather seats. 'I got to rub Shannon's nose in my reality-TV gig and it looks like I'll get some decent coverage in the *Chronicle*. I just hope that photographer in the club managed to get some decent pictures of my tits.'

Keeley rolled her eyes despairingly. She didn't understand how her friend could be so unashamedly low-rent – when, with a bit of effort, she could easily graduate to the dizzy heights of gameshow hostess or travel presenter.

'It's just a shame I didn't pull,' Destiny continued as she traced the shape of an erect penis in the mist on the car window. 'Three weeks without a shag. I'm absolutely gagging for it.'

'Poor love,' said Keeley, spying a way she could make herself indispensable to Destiny. 'Tell you what, I'll speak to Fabrizio. I'm sure he'll be able to fix you up with one of his mates.'

Destiny outlined a pair of fat testicles with two bold strokes. 'Nah, you're all right. I don't want to be set up with some nice footballer bloke who's going to worship the ground I walk on. I want a hard and fast, no-strings-attached, down 'n' dirty fuck with a stranger – preferably one who's not going to go shooting his mouth off to the bloody papers before I've even got my knickers back on.' She raised her eyes to the heavens. 'I should be so lucky.'

Back in Kirkhulme, Cindy was hard at work, scouring the internet in search of antique brass doorhandles. Two weeks had passed since her first visit to Coldcliffe Hall, and her plans for the bedroom suite were starting to take shape. Since signing the confidentiality contract drawn up by Jackson's lawyer, she had been working on the project virtually non-stop, interviewing contractors and combing the north-west of England for materials, fittings, furniture and accessories that met with her exacting standards. In between these sorties, she had made several trips to Coldcliffe, armed with samples for Jackson's approval. The two had struck up a good rapport, and whenever they disagreed on a design matter, which wasn't very often, Jackson usually ended up bowing to her superior judgement.

Cindy found the reclusive former racing driver intriguing, and her interest had increased ten-fold since she'd learned of his erstwhile romance with her fellow golfer's wife. Despite Cindy's gentle probing, Laura had not said anything more on the subject of Jackson West and the circumstances that led to their break-up – which was why, as Cindy sat in Kieran's well-appointed home office, she found herself idly Googling: *Jackson West AND Belgian Grand Prix AND crash*. In less than a second, she was rewarded with nearly a quarter of a million results. As she scrolled down the first page, her eye was caught by a headline from the BBC's website: *Jackson West 'critical' after high-speed crash*. The accompanying news report was brief:

Jackson West remains seriously ill in hospital after crashing his McLaren yesterday during the Belgian Grand Prix. Following the accident, the British Formula One star was taken to the Sart-Tilman hospital, where doctors described his condition as critical, but stable.

West – widely regarded as one of Europe's brightest racing talents – lost control of his car as he entered the track's infamous Eau Rouge corner at an estimated speed of 150mph. After crashing into the tyre barrier, his car exploded in a fireball. Marshals were on the scene in seconds and quickly put out the blaze – but not before West had suffered third-degree burns to his face and hands. It later emerged that, in his confusion, the badly concussed driver had pulled off his protective gloves and helmet.

A hospital spokesman said his parents were at his bedside and, at the request of his family, no further information would be released. McLaren has now launched a full investigation into the crash.

Cindy clicked the Back button on her browser and continued down the page of results. Another headline jumped out at her, this one from the *Evening Standard*. *Jackson West returns home after near-fatal crash*. Cindy clicked on the link, her eyes widening in shock as a colour photo of Jackson appeared, his features almost unrecognizable, buried as they were beneath a layer of charred, leathery skin. He looked scared and he was holding up a hand as if to ward off the cameraman.

Jackson West had to fight his way through a horde of waiting photographers when he returned to his Chelsea home for the first time since the accident that nearly claimed his life. More than two months after the crash at the Belgian Grand Prix, the extent of West's horrific injuries was still plain to see. Doctors are optimistic that the scars to his face and hands will improve with time – although the mental scars may take longer to heal.

Earlier this week, West issued a brief statement through his lawyer announcing his retirement from Formula One and asking to be left in peace. Meanwhile, a source close to the racing driver revealed that he had refused to see anyone outside his immediate family as he recovered in hospital – not even his girlfriend of three months, PR executive Laura Horrocks.

'All Jackson's friends are desperately worried about him,' the source said. 'Ever since the accident, all their letters, emails and phone calls have gone unanswered. It's as if he wants nothing more to do with them. Understandably, Laura's pretty devastated, but she's trying to put a brave face on it.'

'Poor Laura,' muttered Cindy as she returned to the search page and entered a new set of criteria: *Jackson West AND Kirkhulme*. It led her to a story from 'Jemima's Diary', the *Kirkhulme Gazette*'s twee weekly gossip column:

Get ready with the Moët, folks – it looks as if we'll soon have yet another celebrity in our midst. My spies tell me that the proud new owner of Coldcliffe Hall, that spooky gothic pile on Queen's Crescent, is none other than Jackson West. The Formula One star, who was horribly disfigured in a racing accident, has been living in France for the past three years – but now it seems he's hankering after life in the slow lane. By a strange quirk of fate, Kirkhulme is already home to one of Jackson's old flames, Laura Bentley, who's now been snapped up by swoonsome golf ace Sam.

Woodward & Stockley, the estate agents handling the sale of Coldcliffe – formerly owned by three generations of the Milton family – refused to confirm the rumour. 'I've been sworn to secrecy,' sales manager Roger Beverly-Smith whispered in my shell-like. 'Suffice to say, the new owner is looking forward to some much-needed peace and quiet.' So, Jackson, if you're reading this, I'll be dropping by with a welcome basket of home-baked goodies in the not-too-distant future!

Deep in thought, Cindy rose and went to the window. As she gazed at Coldcliffe's bell tower, she couldn't help thinking it was a strange quirk of fate indeed that had brought Jackson West to Laura's doorstep.

Ten

It wasn't even ten o'clock, but the eight golf pros sitting round the dinner table in one of St Benedict's lavish private rooms were already half-cut. They were a close-knit group, and one of them was about to tie the knot – hence the final-night-of-freedom festivities, organized by best man, Jeff Goodbody. Given that it was marriage number three for the forty-six-year-old groom, it was a relatively civilized affair. A pair of pretty waitresses had served a roast venison supper and a selection of fine wines, and now the men were enjoying cigars and digestifs before settling down to a game of poker. Sam Bentley, however, was in the mood for something a little stronger than brandy. It was a long time since he'd had a night out with the boys and he was keen to make the most of it.

'I'm going to pay a visit to the gents,' he said as he reached into the pocket of his Jil Sander blazer, which was hanging on the back of his chair, and removed a large amount of cocaine in a clear plastic bag.

The groom, a former runner-up at the British Open, did a double take. 'Jesus, Sam, how much coke have you got there?'

'I dunno, five grams or so.'

'You must spend a fortune on that stuff.'

Sam stood up. 'Yeah, well, I get a good discount for

buying in bulk.' He looked around the table. 'Anyone care to join me?'

Jeff gestured to his cigar. 'I'll be there in a minute, mate. Just let me finish this Montecristo.'

Sam nodded and started walking towards the door. Halfway there, he collided with a plaster bust of Debussy, almost knocking it off its plinth. 'You know what, I think I might be pissed,' he said, putting a hand on the wall to steady himself.

'What a lightweight,' the groom jeered. 'We're only just getting started here.'

'Yeah, yeah,' Sam retorted. 'You won't be laughing when I whup your asses at poker.'

At this, a shower of good-natured catcalls and balled-up napkins rained down on him. 'See you in a minute, fellas,' Sam said as he staggered from the room. Outside, he passed the waitress station, where the two girls, clad in figure-hugging black-and-white uniforms, were chatting until the stags summoned them by old-fashioned hand bell.

'Hey, ladies,' he said, raising a hand in greeting. 'I hope we're not working you too hard.'

'Of course not,' said the prettier of the two. 'We're really enjoying ourselves.'

'Pleased to hear it,' Sam replied. 'And don't worry, we'll be sure to leave you a good tip.'

The two waitresses watched the golfer's unsteady progress down the corridor. As he rounded the corner, the waitress who'd spoken to him gave her colleague a sly look. Then she went running after him.

Sam was pushing open the door of the gents when he heard her voice. 'Mr Bentley, may I have a word?'

He turned round and smiled when he saw the girl standing there. She was very young, twenty-two at most, with smooth cappuccino-coloured skin and long hair, tied back in a high ponytail. She smoothed her hands over her hips, as if to draw his attention to her impressive curves. 'I was wondering if I could ask you a favour,' she said.

Sam's hand fell from the doorhandle. 'Of course, sweetheart. What can I do for you?'

'My little brother's a huge fan of yours,' the waitress said. 'He'll be so excited when I tell him I've met you in person. I don't suppose I could get an autograph for him, could I?'

Sam flashed one of the famous grins he reserved for fans and TV cameras. 'No problem. Have you got a pen and some paper?'

The girl reached into the pocket of her apron and pulled out a biro and a waitress pad. 'Here,' she said, holding them out towards him.

Even later, Sam wasn't sure who made the first move. One minute he was signing his name, the next they were pressed up against an antique console table, kissing frenziedly. Much to Sam's annoyance, their impromptu snog was cut short after just a few moments when he felt a hand tugging at his arm. He removed his tongue from the waitress's mouth, and glanced irritably over his shoulder.

It was Jeff Goodbody. 'Steady on, mate,' Jeff said in a low voice. 'If you want to do that sort of thing, best go somewhere private, eh?' He pulled a key chain from his pocket and removed one of the dozen or so keys. As head golf pro, he pretty much had free run of St Benedict's. 'This is for the video conferencing suite,' he said. 'It'll be empty at this time of night. Turn left at the end of the corridor and it's the third door on the right.'

Before Sam had a chance to reply, Elissa was snatching the key from Jeff's hand and leading him down the corridor. He turned back over his shoulder and shrugged at Jeff, as if to say, *Sorry, mate, I can't help it if women find me irresistible.* Jeff gave him the thumbs-up. He'd known Sam for years, and this wasn't the first time he'd seen him in a clinch with a woman who wasn't his wife. Nor, he was quite certain, would it be the last.

The minute they were in the video conferencing suite, the girl thrust up against Sam with such enthusiasm she managed to send a flipchart easel and a collection of fat-nibbed felt-tips flying. Sam was used to girls throwing themselves at him, but this one was something else. 'Whoa there,' he said as he gently unwrapped her arms from his neck. 'Let's not rush this, okay?'

A petulant frown crossed the girl's face. 'I can't be gone for too long. My friend says she'll cover me for half an hour or so, but any more than that and she'll think I'm taking the piss.'

'Ah, so you planned this, did you?'

'So what if I did?'

Sam smiled. 'It doesn't bother me, sweetheart.'

The girl reached out to stroke his hair. 'I couldn't believe it when I heard you were part of tonight's stag party,' she said. 'I've fancied you for ages.'

Sam narrowed his eyes as he struggled to focus on her breasts. 'You're pretty tasty yourself.'

'I look better with my clothes off. But you don't have to take my word for that.' The girl walked over to an overhead projector, mounted on a dais, and switched it on, illuminating the large screen mounted on the room's rear wall. Then she stood directly in front of the screen and began to perform a slow strip, each movement casting a giant, provocative shadow. First, she untied her apron and tossed it to the floor. Next, she reached a hand to the nape of her neck and, after a fair degree of contortion, pulled down the zip of her dress. As the black, knee-length sheath fell to the floor, Sam found himself staring at a spectacular body, covered only by a balconette bra and the tiniest of black lace G-strings.

'Mmmm,' Sam murmured appreciatively. 'You look good enough to eat.'

'So eat me,' she said, stepping out of the dress and kicking off her patent leather Mary Janes. She walked over to Sam and pressed her body against his. As they kissed hungrily, the girl's hands began unbuckling Sam's belt. He pulled away from her. 'I can see you're in a hurry, sweetheart, but do you mind if I do a line first?'

The girl shrugged. 'Whatever.'

Sam pulled out his packet of coke and looked around the room for a suitable surface to chop it out, his eyes finally alighting on the gilt Regency mirror above the fireplace. It was heavier than it looked and he staggered under its weight as he carried it back to the conference table. After depositing a small mound of coke on the glass from his stash, Sam expertly chopped it into a fat line with his credit card, before snorting it through a rolled-up fifty-pound note.

'Do you want some?' he asked, pinching his nostrils.

The girl shook her head. 'No, you're all right.'

'Oh go on, just a tiny bit. I hate doing drugs on my own.' Sam licked his index finger and pressed it to the mirror, scooping up the leftover grains of white powder. 'Here,' he said, pushing his finger inside her mouth and rubbing it against her gums. She didn't resist.

'Do you do this often?' he asked her.

She frowned. 'Do what?'

'Seduce your customers?'

She flicked her ponytail over her shoulder. 'Does it matter?'

'Not really.'

The girl reached behind her back to unhook her bra. 'Look, I've really got to get back soon. Is it okay if we just get on with it?'

'Sure,' said Sam as he began to remove his trousers and underpants. The girl watched him with a coldness he found unnerving, but now he'd got this far he couldn't very well lose face by backing out. Before he tossed his trousers on the floor, he removed his wallet from the pocket.

The girl frowned. 'What are you doing?'

Sam held up a condom in a wrapper. 'Just getting one of these.'

'It's okay, I'm on the Pill.'

Sam tore off the top of the wrapper. 'No offence, but there's no harm in being extra careful, is there?'

The waitress rolled her eyes. Sam thought she seemed annoyed. Despite the coke, he could feel his desire ebbing by the minute. He looked down at his limp cock. 'How about you give me a hand here?'

The waitress sank to her knees and obligingly took his manhood in her mouth. Sam closed his eyes and tried to imagine himself on the gently sloping green at Carnoustie, scene of his greatest professional triumph. As he visualized himself taking the shot that would make him the Scottish Stroke Play Champion, he felt his cock stiffening. Keen for this encounter to be brought to a rapid conclusion, he pushed the girl's shoulders away, and reached for the condom. It was only as he thrust into the waitress's pliant young body – which was positioned, at his request, on all fours on the soft wool carpet – that Sam realized he didn't even know her name.

Less than fifteen minutes later, the girl rejoined her colleague at the waitress station.

'How was it?' her friend asked eagerly.

The girl sighed. 'Pretty crappy. But I got this.' Delving into her apron pocket, she produced her waitress pad with Sam's signature scrawled across the top page.

Her colleague grinned. 'What are you going to do with it?'

The girl tore off the page, crushed it into a ball and tossed it into the old ice bucket where they tipped out the used ashtrays. 'That's what I'm going to do with it, Becky.'

Her friend winked. 'Sooo . . . did he give you anything else?'

'You bet he did.' The girl reached back into her pocket and removed a used condom, knotted at the top and bulging with semen. 'Look at this, Bex. Worth its weight in gold, this is.'

*

Not far away, in another of St Benedict's private rooms, the monthly meeting of Kirkhulme Rotary Club's board of directors was drawing to a close. It had been a long and unusually heated affair and most of the participants were keen to make a quick exit. Neville Fairbanks, barrister-at-law, had told his wife he would be home by ten but the meeting had overrun and it was already half past. No doubt the little woman would be getting anxious. He could picture her now: scrawny shoulders tensed in anticipation, ears pricked for the sound of his Jaguar crunching on the gravel. In the kitchen, a Marks and Spencer pre-prepared meal would be sitting in the microwave, plastic lid pricked and ready; an individual syrup sponge with custard waiting in the wings – and, if he was *really* lucky, a single glass of Shiraz. The inevitability of it all made Neville's heart sink. Well, he told himself as he turned right outside the clubhouse and made his way down the stone pathway that led to St Benedict's luxurious spa complex, the silly neurotic creature could damn well worry a bit longer.

Just as he had hoped, the sauna – a cedar cabin nestling in a pretty clearing some thirty feet away from the main building – was deserted. After pouring a scoop of anise-scented water on to the hot coals, Neville breathed a contented sigh as he settled down on a bench to sweat out a day's worth of stress. Less than a minute later, his good mood was shattered when the cabin door swung open. Neville watched with barely concealed irritation as a woman appeared through the threads of steam. She was deeply tanned and her hair was arranged in a deliberately dishevelled up-do with stray tendrils framing the face and neck. He glared disapprovingly at the towel that was wrapped round her midriff. As a barrister, Neville had a highly developed sense of right and wrong – and the intruder was in flagrant breach of the sign on the door which stated that: 'Bathing costumes must be worn.'

The woman took a seat on the opposite bench. 'Good evening,' she said in a husky tone.

'Evening,' Neville replied briskly. He didn't much care for small talk, especially when he was trying to relax. He closed his eyes, hoping to dissuade the newcomer from further conversation, giving Marianne the perfect opportunity to inspect her prey unobserved. She hadn't got a very good look at him when she spotted him exiting the men's changing room a short time earlier. Now she saw that his face was quite attractive – he had well-shaped lips, a square jaw and what appeared to be a full head of hair. That was the good news. The bad news was he was at least two stone overweight. As she surveyed his torso critically, Marianne winced at the sight of his ample man boobs, which were mottled from the steam and laced with rivulets of sweat. Still, desperate times called for desperate measures – and, that particular evening, Marianne was nothing if not desperate.

'I must say, I didn't expect to see anyone else here,' she remarked casually. 'I usually have the place to myself at this time of night.'

Neville's eyes snapped open. 'Yes, I was enjoying the peace and quiet,' he said pointedly. He reached across and ladled another scoop of water on to the coals. Marianne noticed how the action caused his love handles to quiver unpleasantly.

'It's terribly hot in here,' she said, fanning herself with a hand.

'Well, it is a sauna after all.'

Marianne tittered, although there had been nothing light-hearted about Neville's observation. 'It's just a pity we have to cover ourselves up,' she continued. 'The Scandinavians think nothing of going naked into a public sauna.'

Neville curled his lip. 'How dreadfully unhygienic.'

'Not if you take a shower first.' Marianne crossed one freshly waxed leg over the other. 'I sometimes think we Brits are too straight-laced; we could learn a lot from the Swedes.'

'Such as.' Neville's voice was flat and lifeless, the words presented as a statement rather than a question.

'Their liberal attitude towards sex, for example.'

Neville smirked. He'd got a right one here. He'd give it another two minutes, for politeness' sake, and then head for the plunge pool.

Uncrossing her legs, Marianne let her head fall back. With a stagy sigh, she began to massage an imaginary ache in her shoulder. At the same time, her knees accidentally-on-purpose fell apart.

Neville gulped. Beneath her towel, Marianne was naked and the pose afforded him a clear view of her genitalia. The barrister wiped his forehead with the back of his hand and looked away. A moment later, he risked another peek. Marianne's eyes were now closed and her legs spread even wider. Neville was mesmerized. In twenty-five years of marriage, his wife had never allowed him to scrutinize her 'toilet parts', as she off-puttingly described them. He tried to tear his eyes away from the dark cleft between Marianne's legs and found he couldn't. As he gawped, he became aware of a swelling in his swim shorts. Without taking his eyes off Marianne, he reached along the bench beside him, feeling for his towel, and then remembered he'd left it in the changing room. He placed both hands in his lap in a vain attempt to mask his arousal.

Marianne opened one eye. Neville was so busy staring between her legs, he didn't notice at first. Suddenly, she drew her knees together, causing the barrister to jump guiltily. Marianne wagged a finger. 'Naughty boy,' she reprimanded him teasingly. 'Caught you looking, didn't I?'

Neville's face, already pink from the steam, turned scarlet. 'I-I-I don't know what you're talking about,' he stammered.

Marianne stood up. 'I think you do,' she said as she locked the cabin door with the simple depression of a round button on the handle. She turned back to Neville and stared at his crotch. 'My, oh my. What have we here?' she said. 'I wouldn't mind a closer look.' She walked across and laid a hand on Neville's thigh. 'May I?' The barrister nodded mutely. His brilliant mind had turned to jelly. The only sensations he was aware of were the heat of the sauna and the throbbing in his groin.

Marianne sank to her knees. Frankly, it pained her to service such an unappealing specimen, but she'd gone without sex for six days now, and needs must. Widening her eyes like a child under the Christmas tree, she slipped a hand inside Neville's shorts. 'Oh my goodness,' she exclaimed, giving the hot and hairy handful a few expert pulls to make sure he was hard enough. 'What a big boy you are.' If anything, Neville's offering was of slightly below average length and girth, but Marianne knew a man's ego required as much stroking as his cock. With her other hand she released her towel. It fell away, exposing an expanse of toned flesh. A bubble of drool appeared at the corner of Neville's mouth. This was the sort of thing that only happened in the pages of the magazines he liked to peruse in his study when his wife had gone to bed. Warily, he placed his hands on Marianne's breasts, as if waiting for further instructions to be communicated. Marianne removed his right hand from her breast and guided it between her legs. 'Right you are, missy,' he murmured, exploring her with his sausagey fingers. Marianne's body was quick to respond, and the moment Neville judged her ready for him he hooked a thumb either side of his waist and levered his shorts down over his pot belly. A quick shimmy and they were at his knees. One further shake and they fell to his ankles – which seemed as far as he was prepared to dismiss them. Marianne required no further encouragement. Pushing Neville back on to the bench, she mounted him in one swift movement.

'Atta girl,' Neville panted, as he saw to the task of fucking a middle-aged woman in a sauna, while his wife waited patiently at home. Now *this* would be something to tell the boys at the Rotary Club.

Three-quarters of a mile away, Keeley was hosting a midweek dinner party – not in her own flat, where there wasn't room to swing a cat, but at Fabrizio's stunning chapel conversion, which occupied a prime location overlooking Kirkhulme's village green. While the footballer was leading their guests up to the mezzanine dining area, Keeley was ensconced in the Smallbone kitchen, plating up a gourmet meal. Not that she had actually cooked any of it (in Keeley's opinion, life was far too short to grate a root vegetable). Instead, she'd ordered everything in from a local catering firm (and paid for it with Fabrizio's credit card, naturally). The menu consisted of individual asparagus and Gruyére tartes, followed by slow-roasted lamb shank with fondant potatoes, and butterscotch crème brûlée to finish. All it needed was a few simple touches – a scattering of rocket, a sprinkle of rosemary, a quick blast of a blowtorch, and Keeley would be able to pass it off as homemade. It was most unusual to find Keeley playing hostess – as a general rule of thumb, she found dinner parties energy sapping and stressful. However, this particular soirée was born out of necessity, rather than choice.

Until Cindy's arrival, Laura had been the closest thing Keeley had to a best friend in Kirkhulme. They shopped together regularly, lunched at St Benedict's at least twice a week and spoke on the phone most days. Keeley had always assumed, perhaps naively, that their friendship was strong enough to withstand any threat, but in recent weeks she'd noticed a subtle shift in the dynamic of their little group. It had come to her attention that Laura and Cindy were developing quite a bond; in fact, these days she rarely saw one without the other. When Keeley thought about it, it wasn't that surprising. The pair had a lot in common: not only were they the same age, but their husbands were both top-flight golfers – and, as

Laura was fond of saying, no woman could appreciate what it was like being married to a pro sportsman until she'd experienced it first-hand. But just because Keeley recognized their compatibility, it didn't mean she was happy about the burgeoning friendship. She was worried; there were no two ways about it. Keeley wasn't like the other women at St Benedict's. She didn't have a glamorous career, or a big inheritance, or a famous husband, and consequently she'd had to work twice as hard to get where she was. But now she could feel her hard-earned status slipping away. Unless she acted immediately to reassert herself, she ran the risk of becoming an also-ran – a substitute on the benches, called into action only when the first-choice player was unavailable. Reckoning that the best course of action was to ingratiate herself with the enemy, Keeley had decided to invite Cindy and her husband Kieran to dinner. She hadn't bothered explaining her sudden desire to play domestic goddess to Fabrizio, fearing it would take far too long and push her reserves of patience to the limit. However, this really was quite unfair of her, since Fabrizio's English was coming on in leaps and bounds, to the extent that he was now almost fluent.

Having distressed the edges of her tartes with a rolling pin in an attempt to make them look less professional, Keeley arranged the four starter plates on a tray. As she ascended the spiral staircase to the mezzanine, she could hear Cindy gushing over Fabrizio's interior design. 'I love what you've done with this space,' she was saying as she stroked the wallpaper with its delicate pattern of songbirds and citrus trees. 'Is this hand-painted Chinese silk?'

'It's no good asking *him*,' Keeley said, setting the tray down on the antique dining table. 'What Fabrizio knows about decorating you could fit on the back of a matchbox.'

Cindy, who found Keeley rather dismissive at times, ignored her. Smiling at the footballer, she said in a kind voice, 'Well, one thing's for sure: you've got very good taste in houses.'

Fabrizio gave a bashful grin. 'Thank you, but I'm afraid it's only rented. I wanted to get a feel for village life before I made any big investments.'

'Very sensible too,' said Kieran as he took a seat at the table. 'Although you'll never lose money on property in Kirkhulme. How long have you been in England now, Fabrizio?'

'Nearly four months.'

'Have you settled in okay?'

'Yes, thank you. I have made lots of friends at the football club.' He smiled goofily at Keeley. 'And I've met a wonderful woman, so I think I will be very happy here.'

'That's good,' said Cindy. 'It can be very difficult finding your feet in a strange country.'

'Of course!' Fabrizio exclaimed. 'You too are a fo-fo-fo—'

'Foreigner,' said Keeley, raising her eyes to the heavens.

'Fore-ig-norrrr,' said Fabrizo, labouring over the word. 'You too are a foreigner, Cindy, although it sounds as if you've made yourself at home. Keeley tells me you're working for Jackson West.'

'That's right,' said Cindy. 'I'm really enjoying it. I shall be sorry when the project's finished.'

Fabrizio picked up a bottle of Burgundy and began

filling glasses. 'I'm a big fan of Formula One,' he said. 'The racing world lost a great driver when Mr West announced his retirement. Do you think he'll ever be tempted back to the sport?'

'I can't see it somehow,' Cindy replied. 'I should think he'd find walking into a room full of people a frightening prospect, never mind getting back behind the wheel of a racing car.'

'What a freak,' Keeley muttered.

Fabrizio frowned. 'You seem to be forgetting that the man nearly lost his life.'

'That crash was years ago,' Keeley said airily. 'Why can't he just get over himself?'

'Jackson's a very sensitive man,' said Cindy, rather more sharply than she intended. 'Don't be too judgemental.'

Keeley took a sip of wine, trying to mask her annoyance at the American woman's criticism. 'Hey, guess what, Fab,' she said, turning to her boyfriend. 'You know my friend Laura? She used to go out with Jackson – years ago, when they both lived in London.'

'Really – and now they live in the same village? How strange.'

'Well, they do say Kirkhulme's one of the most desirable places to live in Britain,' said Kieran. 'The electoral roll already reads like a *Who's Who*, so it's hardly surprising that another millionaire sportsman decided to make it his home.'

Keeley looked at Cindy. 'Do you think Jackson even knows that one of his ex-girlfriends is living less than half a mile away?'

'I've no idea,' Cindy replied. 'Jackson and I don't really

talk about personal stuff. Most of our conversations are about colour combining and thread count; that's about as exciting as it gets.'

Keeley pushed her half-eaten starter to one side. 'Laura doesn't like talking about Jackson – have you noticed? Whenever I ask her about him, she always tries to change the subject.'

'She's a happily married woman,' Kieran interjected. 'It's hardly surprising that she doesn't want to dwell on the past.'

Keeley leaned across the table. 'Tell me something, Kieran. What do you make of Sam Bentley?'

Kieran looked surprised. 'Sam? He's an awesome golfer; I mean the guy is seriously talented.'

'I'm sure he is,' said Keeley. 'But what I meant was, what do you think of him *personally*.'

'Oh, right. Well, to be fair, I hardly know him. You have to remember that I haven't played in Europe for a couple of years. Obviously, Cindy has become quite friendly with Laura' – he flashed a look at his wife – 'but Sam and I haven't got beyond the stage of exchanging pleasantries on the golf course. He seems nice enough though.'

'But you spend so much time at St Benedict's, I bet you hear tons of gossip,' Keeley said eagerly.

Kieran looked at her blankly. 'No, not really,' he said. 'I'm too busy concentrating on my game to pay much attention to tittle-tattle.'

Keeley seemed disappointed. She thought for a moment, and then said mysteriously: 'According to Laura, Sam's a *very* difficult man.'

Kieran coughed. 'Is he?' he ventured. Cindy, meanwhile,

pretended to be busy chasing a mound of rocket round her plate.

'Yes, I think Laura's been having quite a hard time of it lately,' Keeley continued, unabashed. 'But she keeps her feelings very well hidden, so you'd never know it – not unless you'd known her for a long time, like I have.' She gave Cindy a knowing look, keen to distinguish her relationship with Laura as one of greater depth and emotional intimacy.

'Poor Laura,' Kieran remarked. 'I've only met her a couple of times but she seems like such a nice woman.'

'Oh, but she is,' Keeley gushed. 'She's the best friend anyone could have. She was *sooo* supportive when I split up with Chip.' She looked at Cindy hopefully. 'Chip Weinberger. He's American too . . . I expect you've heard of him.' Cindy shook her head and chewed silently on a mouthful of rocket. 'No? Oh well, he's a pretty big cheese around these parts. He owns Cheshire's largest theme park; he's absolutely loaded.'

There was an uneasy silence. Keeley cleared her throat ostentatiously. 'Anyway, what was I saying? Ah yes, Sam.' She glanced around the table, making sure she had everyone's attention. 'This mustn't go any further, but I have it on very good authority that Sam's been playing away from home.' She looked at the others expectantly, as if waiting for a round of applause.

Fabrizio looked horrified. 'Keeley!' he exclaimed. 'I can't believe you just said that.' He looked at the McAllisters. 'I'm so sorry,' he said. 'Please, just ignore her.'

Keeley shot her boyfriend a poisonous look. 'Cindy's a good friend of Laura's, so I'm sure she'd want to hear about anything that affects her well-being,' she said defiantly. 'Isn't that right, Cindy?'

Cindy set her knife and fork in the six o'clock position. She was shocked at Keeley's indiscretion – but somehow not by the discovery that Sam Bentley might be having an affair. She remembered how he'd looked her up and down appreciatively the first time they'd met, even though his wife had been standing less than two feet away. 'It's really none of my business what Sam Bentley gets up to in private,' she said evenly.

'But don't you see? That's the awful thing,' said Keeley excitedly. 'Sam *isn't* doing it in private; he's positively flaunting his bit on the side.' Her eyes narrowed. 'I wouldn't be surprised if half of St Benedict's didn't already know about him and Abi.'

Cindy's blood ran cold. Laura had mentioned her husband's caddie several times in conversation and she knew her friend liked – and, more importantly, trusted – the younger woman. 'I assume you're talking about Abi Gainsbourg,' she said tightly.

'Yeah, the little slut – and her a married woman as well.'

Cindy frowned. 'Are you sure this isn't just idle gossip, Keeley? Because, if it is, I'm not sure you should be spreading it.'

'No, it bloody well isn't,' came Keeley's indignant reply. 'Fabrizio saw them last week with his own eyes. They were in one of the gazebos behind the clubhouse and Sam was all over her.' The footballer stared into his wine glass, clearly embarrassed. Keeley banged her hand down on the table in front of him. 'Tell them, Fab,' she commanded.

169

'Perhaps they were talking tactics,' he suggested. 'She is his caddie after all.'

'Oh *pur-lease*! You said he had his arm round her. In any case, why would they bother sneaking into the gazebo unless they were up to no good – answer me that, huh?' Her nostrils flared angrily. 'No, they're definitely having an affair. I bet they're at it every opportunity they get. It's a miracle Laura hasn't found out already.'

Cindy frowned. 'You're not going to say anything to her, are you?'

'*I'd* want to know if *my* husband was shagging someone else, wouldn't you?'

Cindy glanced at Kieran. 'Well yes, of course I would. But this is all just speculation. Putting your arm round someone hardly constitutes an affair. Perhaps Abi was upset about something; Sam might have been comforting her.'

'Oh yeah, take *his* side, why don't you?'

Cindy sighed. 'Listen, honey, I care about Laura as much as you do. I'm not taking sides. All I'm saying is, don't go shooting your mouth off until you've got proof of your allegation. After all, there's no point worrying Laura unneccessarily.'

Keeley snorted. '*Proof?* What I am supposed to do – hang around the golf course in the hope of catching Sam giving Abi a quick one at the eighteenth hole?'

'Come on, ladies, let's not fall out over this,' said Kieran, who could see from the delicate blue vein jumping in Cindy's temple that she was struggling to remain calm. 'Have you shared your suspicions with anyone else, Keeley?'

'Nope.'

'Good, because I think we should keep this to ourselves for the time being. When – and *if* – one of us notices anything untoward in Sam's behaviour towards Abi, we can reassess the situation.'

'Excellent idea,' said Fabrizio. 'Keeley shouldn't have said anything in the first place and I apologize if she's put you in a difficult position.'

Keeley scowled, but kept her mouth shut.

'Good, so we're all agreed – not a word to Laura,' said Cindy. 'Keeley?'

'Okay, okay, I won't say anything. But I'll be watching that bastard like a hawk from now on.' Keeley got up from the table and reached for the tray, which was propped up against the wall behind her. 'Now, if everybody's *quite* finished, I'll go and get the main course,' she said brusquely.

She carried the dirty dishes back to the kitchen, grateful for a few moments alone. Snatching up the oven gloves, she yanked open the oven door and was rewarded with a blast of hot, garlicky air. Turning her face to one side, she hauled out the earthenware dish of lamb and slammed it down on the granite worktop. Tossing aside the oven gloves, she opened a cabinet door and pulled out a bottle of cooking sherry. She unscrewed the lid and took a slug straight from the bottle. Keeley was beginning to wish she had never organized this dinner party. Getting drunk was definitely her best option.

Eleven

Dusk was falling over Bunker Hill, a local beauty spot just off the Kirkhulme bypass. The dog walkers and picnickers had long since departed and the public car park was empty, save for a middle-aged couple in a red Fiat Punto. A little while later, they were joined by a second vehicle – a smart black Range Rover with personalized number plates. It performed a slow sweep of the car park, before finally coming to a halt some twenty feet from the Fiat. The driver killed his engine and waited, mouth dry with anticipation. Seconds later, the Fiat's interior light flashed on and off twice. Sam Bentley, sitting behind the wheel of the Range Rover, smiled to himself: his luck was in. He checked his appearance in the rear-view mirror and made a small adjustment to his blond Rod Stewart wig, which was looking a little shabby, having made its debut at a New Year's Eve party some six years earlier. Satisfied with his disguise, he reached into the glove box and pulled out a torch and a pair of latex surgeon's gloves. He didn't know if he'd require the latter, but there was no harm in being prepared. Climbing out of the car, he activated the central locking and walked over to the Fiat, his soft Gucci loafers barely making a sound on the tarmac. As he approached the car, the passenger window slid down to reveal a not-unattractive brunette in a low-cut top.

'Are you playing tonight?' Sam asked.

The man in the driver's seat leaned over. 'We certainly are,' he replied.

Sam held up the torch. 'It's getting dark. Do you mind if I use this for a better view?'

'Be my guest, mate.'

The woman flashed Sam a come-hither smile. 'Enjoy the show,' she said, before peeling off her T-shirt to reveal a pair of large and unfettered breasts. Sam licked his lips and flicked on the torch. The brunette had just started to recline her seat when a sudden movement in the undergrowth made Sam start. He swung his torch towards a bushy hawthorn. 'Who's there?' he demanded. A stocky figure in jeans and a waterproof jacket lurched out of the shadows. He nodded a greeting at Sam. 'Room for another one?' he asked casually. Sam shrugged – the more the merrier as far as he was concerned. He turned to the couple in the Fiat. The woman looked the newcomer briefly up and down before nodding her approval.

The two men stood shoulder to shoulder at the passenger window as the couple assumed their starting positions. Having reclined her seat as far back as it would go, the woman hitched up her skirt round her waist, revealing black suspenders straining over dimpled thighs, and no knickers. The man, who had been masturbating furiously since Sam's appearance, yanked his already unzipped trousers and boxer shorts down to his knees and climbed on top of her. His partner raised her legs, bracing her feet on the dashboard, and then, without any hint of self-consciousness, the pair began fucking with gusto.

Sam had been an active participant in the Cheshire

dogging scene for several months. He'd stumbled across the largely nocturnal activity by accident while driving home after a golf match. Desperate for a piss, he'd pulled off the bypass into the Bunker Hill car park, fully expecting it to be deserted. Instead, he'd found half a dozen or so men clustered around a campervan, which was rocking furiously from side to side. He decided to get out of his car for a closer look. What he saw had left him shocked. Shocked and hugely aroused. A cursory search of the internet later that evening revealed that there were dozens of 'play and display' car parks all over Cheshire – as well as hundreds of willing couples and singles, who were up for one-on-one, group sex, wife-swapping, in the car, on the car, up against a tree, on a picnic bench . . . the possibilities were endless. Sam, who indulged in his hobby once or twice a week, was what is known in dogging circles as a 'piker': a lone male who likes to watch others having sex. Watch – and, if invited, participate in foreplay. Hence the gloves (Sam was a stickler for personal hygiene). Some evenings he simply bowled up to a tried-and-tested venue on spec; other times he met contacts at a pre-scheduled time and place, the arrangements having been made via anonymous online message boards. Needless to say, neither Sam's wife nor his lover knew anything about his proclivities. There was no doubt in his mind that Laura would be absolutely horrified. Abi, on the other hand, was more broad-minded. In fact, he'd been thinking about letting her in on his little secret in the hope of persuading her to join in the fun and games.

The performance in the Fiat had drawn to a noisy

climax. As the couple broke apart, Sam's companion sloped silently back into the shadows. Sam switched off his torch. 'Thanks, that was a great show,' he called out, ever conscious of etiquette. He turned to go, but the woman called him back. 'Hey, handsome, fancy a hand job?' she said, leering through the open window.

It was a tempting offer; Sam was fit to burst. He glanced at his watch. 'Sorry,' he said with a rueful smile. 'I've got to get going. Another time maybe.'

The woman flipped down her sun visor and removed a business card from the pocket. 'Here's our mobile number,' she said. 'Get in touch whenever.' The golfer took the card, flashed one of his killer smiles, and hurried back to his car. A few moments later, he was back on the bypass and speeding towards a National Trust car park, some four miles south of Delchester. Despite the unfamiliar venue, Sam was hugely excited about his next assignation, which had been arranged via email with a husband-and-wife combo who were new to the game. The husband had contacted him after reading the personal ad Sam had posted on a dogging website, and explained that he and his wife were looking for a 'discreet and gentle introduction' to the sport. Never one to look a gift horse in the mouth, Sam was looking forward to showing them the ropes.

The following Sunday morning, Laura woke with a start. For a moment she lay motionless, heart pounding, unsure of who or what had jerked her rudely into consciousness. Then it came again – the familiar high-pitched squawking of a teething infant. Groaning, she checked the alarm clock: 7.02 a.m. Bugger. So much for the lie-in she so desperately needed. Since Birdie's arrival, Laura had averaged no more than six hours' sleep a night. What's more, her daughter's sleeping pattern seemed to be getting worse, not better. She rolled over and surveyed her husband, who lay comatose beside her, one arm flung above his head, exhaling giant guttural sighs. She tried to work out the odds of persuading him to see to Birdie and – given that he was sure to be incubating a hangover – judged them to be precisely nil.

Sam had left the house the previous morning for a practice session with his golf coach, swearing he'd be back mid-afternoon when he was scheduled to accompany Carnie to a fairies and wizards birthday party (it being an event for three-year-olds, at least one responsible adult per child was expected to be in attendance). But, just as Laura was attaching Carnie's pink Tinkerbell wings, Sam had phoned to say he'd been held up at the club and didn't know when he was going to be able to get away.

'Oh, *Saaam*,' she said, hating the whining tone in her voice. 'You *promised* to take Carnie to that party.'

'Can't the au pair take her?' He sounded tense, distracted.

'That's not the point – you know how much she was looking forward to showing off her famous daddy to all her little friends.'

'I know, I'm sorry,' he muttered.

'It's not me you should be apologizing to.'

'Yeah, yeah; don't give me a hard time. You know I'll make it up to Carnie.'

Resisting the temptation to ask: *How — by giving her another expensive toy she doesn't need?* Laura said sulkily: 'So what's important enough to drag you away from your family anyway?'

At the other end of the phone, Sam exhaled irritably. 'Listen, Laura. It's a bit awkward right now. We'll talk when I get back.' And then, in a warmer tone: 'Tell you what, why don't I pick up a nice bottle of wine on the way home?' At this, Laura felt a ridiculous frisson of excitement. It seemed like ages since she and Sam had spent an entire evening together, just the two of them. In recent weeks they'd become ships in the night, their conversation consisting of hurried exchanges about over-due library books and whose turn it was to fill the car with petrol. It wasn't an entirely unprecedented turn of events. Sam was always more distant in the run-up to a big tournament — not just physically, but emotionally too — and it was something Laura had grown used to over the years. All the same, she'd never known him to put in quite so much practice as he had done for the German Masters, which was now less than a month away.

'Anyway, I've really got to go now,' he continued. 'I'll see you and the girls later.'

'Love you,' she said. But all she got in return was the dial tone.

It had gone midnight by the time Sam finally rolled home, drunk and stinking of cigarette smoke. He'd woken Laura up as he turned on the halogen spots in the en suite, before pissing noisily all over the toilet seat. 'Where the hell have you been? I thought we were going to talk,' she said as he collapsed into bed beside her. 'I was worried about you. I kept phoning and phoning, but your mobile's been switched off all evening.'

Sam's voice was slurry. 'Gotta get shome schleep, 's gonna be a big day tomorrow.'

'Big day? What are you talking about?' she said crossly. 'All we've got planned is a trip to the garden centre.' Sam's reply came in the form of a loud snore.

As Birdie's experimental *are-you-there-Mummy?* yelps gave way to a full-throated Kiri Te Kanawa aria, Laura shucked off the duvet and pushed her feet into the soft sheepskin mules that she always felt signified her descent into middle age. Still half asleep, she lumbered to the nursery, where she found Birdie peering anxiously through the bars of her cot, tears rolling down her fat cheeks.

'Hello, you. What time do you call this?' said Laura as she scooped her daughter out of the cot and hoisted her on to a hip. 'Come on then, madam. Let's see if you've succeeded in waking up your sister.'

Through the half-open door of Carnie's pink-and-white princess bedroom, Laura could see her firstborn sitting cross-legged in her miniature four-poster. Nestling beside her was the disgusting stuffed koala that she adored. Laura was mystified by the attraction: her daughter had a cupboard full of the finest toys a wealthy parent could buy and what did she choose to lavish her affection on? A boss-eyed bear from a charity shop. 'You've been very, very naughty,' Carnie was saying to Mr Koala. 'You didn't come to Annabel's party like you said you would – and you know what that means.' The koala stared mutely ahead. 'You have to buy me a new toy: a Surfer Girl Barbie.' She paused. '*And* an Angelina Ballerina tutu.'

Laura sighed. Only three years old, and already her daughter knew everything there was to know about the fine art of buying forgiveness. She nudged the door open with her elbow and walked into the room. 'Morning, sweetheart, ready for some breakfast?'

Carnie stuck her thumb in her mouth. 'I wan' Dadda to make my breakfast.'

'Daddy's asleep, darling.'

Carnie's face lit up. 'Let's get into bed with Dadda!'

There was nothing Laura would have liked more – all four of them cuddled up in bed on a Sunday morning, just like a regular family. But there was no point entertaining the idea – not when Sam was bound to wake up with a sore head and a temper to match. 'Daddy got in very late last night, so why don't we give him another half hour?' Laura said in her best Mary Poppins voice. 'And when he's awake, we can make him breakfast in bed. How about that?'

The look on Carnie's face suggested she didn't think very much of the idea, but she clambered out of bed, pulled on her pink quilted dressing gown and took the hand her mother was offering.

Laura had been five months' pregnant with Carnoustie when she married Sam – although she liked to think he would have asked her to marry him anyway. Her due date coincided with the British Open and the birth was induced so as not to disrupt Sam's playing schedule. It had been a similar story with Birdie, who was due slap bang in the middle of the European Masters. In her heart, Laura would have loved to have had natural births, but at the time it was a sacrifice she was willing to make. After all, they were both working towards the same goal: Sam's success as a golfer. Still, she sometimes wondered what it would take for him to pull out of a tournament for someone else's sake.

Downstairs in the kitchen, Laura stared wistfully at the round table by the French windows, where she'd laid out crockery and cereal boxes the night before. Sunday mornings were the one time Sam was guaranteed to be at home and she'd been looking forward to a relaxed family breakfast. Oh well, she comforted herself, at least this way she'd be able to tuck into a couple of calorie-packed croissants without having to endure Sam's reproachful stare. She'd put on three and a half stone when she was pregnant with Birdie and was still struggling to shed the final ten pounds – as Sam was fond of reminding her. After settling Birdie into her high chair, Laura flicked on the kettle and went to collect the Sunday papers from the doormat. She only ever read the broadsheets herself, but Sam liked a tabloid for the football. Back in the kitchen she tossed both newspapers on to the table and set about preparing the girls' breakfast.

'What do you want to eat?' she asked Carnie as she fished Birdie's bottle out of the sterilizer. 'Toast or Weetabix?'

'Pop Tarts!' cried the three-year-old.

'They're full of sugar, darling. They'll make you hyper.'

'Marta lets me have Pop Tarts,' said Carnie, eyeing her mother slyly.

Laura raised an eyebrow. 'Does she now?' She made a mental note to speak to the au pair, who had strict instructions to limit the children's intake of sugar and additives. 'Well, Marta's not here, which means they're off the menu, I'm afraid.'

Carnie threw her head back. 'I . . . wan' . . . Pop . . . Tarts,' she wailed, gulping for air in between each word as if she were about to burst into tears.

Laura sighed. She really couldn't cope with a tantrum at this time of the morning. 'How about a crumpet?' she said. 'Mmm, a delicious hot crumpet with honey.'

Carnie frowned. 'Chocolate spread.' She was a tough negotiator.

'Okay, it's a deal.'

Laura opened a cupboard to hunt for the chocolate spread. The minute her back was turned, Birdie made a play for the sugar bowl, upending it on to the table. 'Oh, Birdie, now look what you've done.' As Laura swabbed the drifts of sugar with a dishcloth, she glanced idly at the tabloid on the other side of the table. *Golf star's shameful sex secret*, screamed the front-page headline. Normally, Laura would have ignored such a lurid story, but the golfing connection had piqued her interest. With her free hand, she turned to the next page, which carried a blurry snapshot, apparently taken with a hidden camera, and began to read.

This photo reveals the perverted pastime of 'dogging' fan Sam Bentley. The golfing ace, pictured in a secluded car park as he cruised for casual sex with strangers, was talking to two *Sunday Herald* reporters posing as man and wife.

Laura let out a ragged cry as she fell on to the nearest dining chair.

'That's a funny noise,' said Carnie as she came tottering over from the fridge with a bottle of banana milk.

'Mummy's just had some bad news,' said Laura in a voice that was little more than a whisper. Swallowing hard, she read on.

The car park is just three miles from the £1.5 million home in the Cheshire village of Kirkhulme which Bentley (currently ranked 15th in Europe), shares with wife Laura and their two young daughters. The 36-year-old, who was wearing a bizarre Rod Stewart-style wig, advertises his services openly on a XXX-rated website, using the alias 'Colonel Bogey' ('bogey' being a well-known golfing term for one stroke over par). During a half-hour chat with our reporters, Bentley provided them with a comprehensive insight into dogging, and:

BRAGGED about his detailed knowledge of the sordid practice.

DESCRIBED in explicit detail dogging 'etiquette', revealing how some like to romp while being watched and others prefer to spectate.

OFFERED to take our undercover team on a tour of his favourite haunts.

BEGGED for our reporters' mobile phone number after they made their excuses and left – and texted them the next day to say: 'If u fancy sum fun, I'll be at the cr prk 2nite at 9.'

Yesterday morning, we confronted Bentley as he arrived at the exclusive St Benedict's country club in Kirkhulme – a village which famously boasts more millionaires per square mile than anywhere else in the country. When we told him we were planning to expose his kinky hobby, he refused to comment and drove away at speed. The golfer now faces a showdown with his wife – and something tells us he's heading straight for the doghouse. Turn to pages 5 and 6 for the full story.

Laura's breath was coming in short shallow gasps. No wonder she felt light-headed. She pulled the newspaper closer and scrutinized the photo. Despite its lack of definition, the figure in the blond wig was unmistakeably Sam. A sick feeling rose in her stomach. She raised a fist to her mouth; her arm seemed to ache with the effort. Carnie was chattering away nineteen to the dozen, but the only sound Laura could hear was the blood rushing in her ears. As she stared at the picture, a fresh wave of nausea swept over her. Clutching a tea towel to her mouth, she made a dash for the downstairs cloakroom.

After purging her stomach of its contents, Laura returned to the kitchen to finish making the children's breakfast. She moved like an automaton – pouring juice, buttering crumpets and spooning organic baby rice into Birdie's eager mouth. Inside her head her brain was doing backflips, as she struggled to process the information from the newspaper. As she filed the dirty crockery in the dishwasher, she thought about shaking Sam awake and screaming at him. Screaming until her tonsils bled. But then she had a much better idea. She went to the living room and looked out of the window; Sam's Range Rover was parked outside. She curled her lip in disgust – so her husband wasn't just a pervert, he was a drunk driver too. He would've been well over the limit as he drove home through the country lanes. The reporters who confronted him at the club would certainly have told him the story was running in today's paper. No wonder he'd been so reluctant to come home, preferring to go on the lash and then slink home in the dead of night like the lying, cheating scumbag he was. She noticed Sam's sports jacket, slung across the back of an armchair. Feeling in the pockets she found his car keys, nestling beside a business card, the cheap kind you get from a machine at the shopping centre. It bore the names *Martin & Shelley*, a mobile phone number and an email address: *martshell@ doggersdelight.co.uk*. Laura swallowed hard. She could well imagine what line of business *they* were in. Crushing the card in the palm of her hand, she returned to the kitchen. 'Mummy's got to go for a little drive,' she said in a brittle voice. 'You girls are going to have to go in the buggy for five minutes where I know you'll be safe.'

'But, Mummy, you're wearing your nightie,' Carnie piped up. Laura didn't reply. Picking up a child in each arm, she carried them to the large entrance hall, where the tandem buggy was leaning against the wall. Setting Carnie down, she unfolded the buggy and strapped Birdie into the rear seat. All the baby blankets were upstairs, so she yanked a fleece jacket from the coatstand and tucked it around her younger daughter, who was gurgling contentedly. Laura turned to Carnie. 'It's chilly outside, you'd better put this on over your dressing gown,' she said, holding out a miniature duffel coat.

Carnie obligingly stuffed her arms into the sleeves. 'What about you, Mummy? Won't you be cold?'

'I'll live,' muttered Laura. 'Come on, sweetheart, get in the buggy.'

'I don't wan' to go in da buggy.'

Laura sighed. 'You have to, I don't want you running out in front of the car.'

'Can't I come in the car wid' you?' Carnie wheedled.

'No, you can't.' Carnie began to wail. 'I tell you what: if you're a good girl and you do what Mummy says, you can have a packet of choccy buttons when we get back.'

Carnie cocked her head on one side, apparently weighing up the deal. 'Okaaaay!' she said in a sing-song voice as she clambered into the front seat of the buggy. As soon as she was safely strapped in, Laura flung open the front door and manoeuvred the buggy over the step. 'Mummy's left something back in the house,' she told Carnie as she flicked the brake on. 'Bet I'm back before you can count to twenty.'

'One . . . two . . . three . . .' Carnie began. Laura turned on her heel and marched to the ground-floor games room, where Sam kept the tools of his trade. He was obsessive about his golf gear. Every piece of equipment had to be thoroughly cleaned and stacked in its rightful place at the end of each game and practice session – a task which more often than not fell to Abi Gainsbourg. Laura thought of Abi, shaking her head sadly as she imagined the caddie's horror when she learned of her boss's disgrace. She might even hand in her notice, and then where would Sam be?

Laura walked briskly along the line of golf bags, each and every set of clubs custom-made to suit Sam's size, strength, swing speed and shot characteristics. To the untrained eye, one set looked much the same as another, but Laura knew exactly what she was looking for: the Adams matchplay clubs. They were Sam's lucky clubs, the ones he used in every championship match – and, as he was fond of telling people, 'virtually priceless'. Quickly identifying the clubs by their blue leather carry case, Laura hiked the bag on to her shoulder and made her way back to the entrance hall, stopping en route to pick up Sam's car keys. At the foot of the stairs, she stopped and listened, but there was no sound of movement from above.

'You were aaages,' Carnie said disapprovingly as her mother reappeared. 'Bad Mummy.' Her eyes widened when she spied the golf bag. 'Are you going to play golf? Can I play too? Can I, can I?'

'No, sweetheart. You stay there and look after Birdie. Mummy's got to do a little job and then she'll be right back.' Ignoring her daughter's wail of protest, Laura set off down the red brick driveway. Her heart felt hard and sharp in her chest, like a lump of quartz. Every few steps, she pulled a club out of the golf bag and dropped it on the drive lengthways, until all fifteen clubs were laid out like the steps of a ladder. Without bothering to survey her handiwork, she carelessly tossed the empty bag into a flowerbed and made her way towards the quadruple garage, which lay some twenty feet from the house. Sam's car was parked outside. She climbed into the driver's seat and turned on the ignition. 'Right then, you dirty bastard,' she said through clenched teeth. 'Let's see how you like this.' She wound down the electric window, then hit the car horn with the palm of her hand, holding it there for several seconds. She craned her neck out of the window and looked up at the elegant Georgian windows of the master bedroom. There was no sign of life. Thinking she was witnessing some sort of game, Carnie clapped her hands together delightedly. 'Beep the horn again, Mummy,' she shrieked. Laura obliged, this time holding the horn down for longer. She looked up at the window again – still no response. It wasn't until she'd performed the same routine another half dozen times that Sam's bewildered face finally appeared at the bedroom window. Pressing both palms against the glass, he looked first at the car and then back at the girls sitting in the buggy. Laura pushed the horn again. The sash flew open and Sam leaned out. 'What the fuck's going on, Laura?' he shouted, raising a hand to shield his eyes against the morning sunshine.

'Just doing some spring cleaning,' Laura called back gaily. 'You've got all those sets of golf clubs sitting in the games room gathering dust. I thought it was about time we got rid of some of them.'

Sam scratched his head. 'Uh?' he said.

'The Adams matchplay clubs, for example. You won't miss them – will you?'

Sam was instantly alert. 'What are you talking about? You know they're my lucky clubs. They're virtually –'

'Priceless?' Laura shouted grimly.

'Yeah, priceless.' Sam squinted down into the garden. 'Hang on a minute . . . why is my golf bag lying in the middle of those rose bushes?' His gaze drifted past the bag. 'And why are my clubs scattered all over the freaking drive?' His look of confusion turned to one of consternation. 'Laura, what the hell are you playing at?' His hands flew to his head as the penny dropped. 'Now, darling, you're not going to do anything silly, are you?'

Laura drummed her fingers on the steering wheel. 'What? You mean like get my sleazy car-park antics splashed across a Sunday tabloid?' she screamed, suddenly losing control. 'Perish the thought.' She began to rev the engine threateningly.

Sam gulped. 'Laura, wait. I can explain.'

'Too late!' she trilled, pushing the gear stick into first. Sam watched, frozen in horror, as his wife released the handbrake and set off down the driveway. He let out an anguished cry as the Range Rover bounced over his nine iron, reducing the finely tuned shaft to a twisted lump of metal. 'You bitch,' he sobbed, banging his fist on the window frame. 'You fucking bitch.' His Redline RPM driver was next to be sacrificed, as the vehicle's fat tyres made light work of its superbly crafted titanium head. Sam's hands flew to his face. He could hardly bear to watch – but watch he did as the Range Rover continued its rampage. As Laura approached the final club, she seemed to hesitate. Sam clasped his hands together in prayer. 'Not the broomhandle, please God, not the broomhandle . . .' But his wife had saved the best till last. Remembering how Sam had kissed his precious broomhandle putter after storming to victory at Carnoustie, she was going to make sure it received the swan song it deserved. Revving the car, she positively flew over the putter, almost snapping its distinctive long shaft in two. Then, as if to make sure she'd done the job properly, she put the car into reverse and drove back over the entire set of clubs. When she was done, she climbed out of the car and threw a triumphant look at Sam. Tears were rolling down his cheeks and his lips were twisted in a bitter grimace. 'I may as well come down there and let you drive over *me* now,' he sobbed. 'Is that what you want, Laura?'

His wife gave him a withering look. 'Oh for goodness' sake, stop being such a drama queen. Get your pathetic arse downstairs now. You've got some almighty explaining to do.'

'I mean, really . . . whatever was the man thinking?' said Marianne as she distributed fragrant lapsang souchong in china cups. 'Prowling around public car parks after dark while his loyal wife and darling daughters are waiting for him at home. It simply beggars belief.' She patted Laura's hand. 'My heart goes out to you, it really does. You must be absolutely furious. Frankly, I'm amazed you haven't thrown him out of the house – it's only what he deserves.'

'Don't worry, Sam's not having an easy time of it,' said Laura. 'I've told him I don't want him anywhere near me, so he's been sleeping in the attic for the past few nights. I did think about making him move into a hotel but that would only be more fodder for the tabloids.' She gave a little sigh. 'In any case, it would be very disruptive for the girls, and my biggest concern is that *they* shouldn't suffer. Thank goodness they're too young to understand what's going on.'

Cindy smiled sympathetically. 'And what about you, honey?' she asked. 'How are *you* feeling?'

Laura shrugged. 'Oh you know . . . as well as can be expected. Sam and I have talked and talked – or at least, *he*'s talked, I've mainly shouted and cried – but I still don't feel I'm any closer to understanding what possessed him to get caught up in such a revolting pastime. He claims it was a momentary act of madness, a way of relieving a build-up of stress.'

'Hmmm, well he was certainly relieving a build-up of *something*,' Keeley muttered.

Laura's cheeks turned pink. 'In his defence, Sam *has* been under a lot of pressure lately, what with the German Masters just round the corner.' She looked down at her teacup. Even to her own ears, the words didn't sound convincing.

'He's taking you for a fool,' Marianne said sharply. '"Momentary act of madness" indeed. According to the newspaper, he's been at it for months. And, by all accounts, he put quite a bit of effort into it – trawling websites, making contacts, setting up secret meetings. It's a wonder he had time to fit any golf practice in.'

Keeley nodded her agreement. 'The shocking thing is, I've always considered myself to be fairly broad-minded. But I didn't even know people *did* things like that in car parks.' She passed her teacup to Marianne for refilling. 'I wonder why they call it "dogging".'

Laura winced. 'I do hate that word. It sounds so, so . . .'

'Bestial?' offered Marianne as she passed round a plate of shortbread fingers.

'Exactly.'

'All men are dogs, darling. I discovered that a long time ago. You just have to decide how far you're prepared to let them stray.'

'What a depressing notion,' said Laura, shaking her head at the offer of a biscuit and then changing her mind and taking two. 'Still, I suppose the one saving grace in all of this is that, technically, Sam hasn't actually been unfaithful.'

Keeley raised an eyebrow. '*Hasn't* he? He might have stopped short of penetration, but he did tell those under-cover reporters he'd had oral sex on several occasions. I remember the quote quite clearly, it was at the bottom of page five – and I don't know about anyone else, but I'd say that having your dick sucked through a car window comes pretty close to infidelity.'

Cindy glared at the younger woman. '*Thank* you, Keeley. In case you'd forgotten, we're supposed to be making Laura feel better about this whole sorry mess, not rubbing her nose in the lurid details.'

'Oh yeah, sorry,' Keeley grimaced. 'I wasn't thinking.'

Laura managed a weak smile. 'It's okay, you've all been very supportive. I don't know what I would've done without your phone calls and texts over the past few days.'

It had been five days since the tabloid exposé and the friends were gathered at Marianne's house for a sympathy session. This was the first time any of them had seen Laura and they were desperate for the juicy details, though none – with the possible exception of Keeley – would have cared to admit it.

'I'm just so angry,' Laura continued. 'I can't believe

Sam would jeopardize our relationship – not to mention his precious career – for fifteen minutes of fun with a complete stranger. And of course it's dreadfully humiliating too. I've hardly left the house since the story broke. I can't bear the thought of people looking at me and pointing the finger: there's the wife who couldn't keep her husband happy in bed.' She paused to lick a shortbread crumb from the corner of her mouth. 'I'll admit that our sex life hasn't exactly been red-hot of late but, when you've got two young kids, passion has to take a back seat.'

'Of course it does,' said Marianne. 'And you mustn't make excuses for him. Sam's got to take responsibility for his own actions.'

'Has he always been a bit, you know, kinky?' Keeley asked.

Laura shrugged. 'No more than the next bloke. He likes me to wear suspenders and, when we're having sex, he . . .' She hesitated. 'No, I really shouldn't say. It's not fair on Sam.'

'Oh come on, darling,' said Marianne. 'We're all friends here.'

Laura smiled impishly. 'Oh, all right then, but it mustn't go any further.' The three women leaned forward eagerly. 'When we're having sex, Sam always makes me shout out "hole-in-one" over and over again, just as he's about to come. He gets very cross if I don't play along with it.'

Keeley burst into shrieks of laughter. 'That's the funniest thing I've heard in ages. That man really does have golf on the brain, twenty-four/seven.'

'Yeah, he does,' said Laura, suddenly serious. 'And

that's why all those evenings he wasn't at home with me and the girls, I assumed he was at the club, practising. Now I know the truth.' She blinked hard, fighting back tears. 'But I don't know why I'm so surprised. This is typical of Sam – always putting his own selfish needs first, never giving a thought for anyone else.'

'Still, it sounds as if you hit him where it hurt,' said Cindy, trying to lift the mood. 'Driving over those golf clubs was a stroke of genius.'

Laura took a paper hanky from the gold-plated dispenser on Marianne's occasional table and blew her nose noisily. 'Honestly, you should have seen his face when he came out on to the driveway and saw the extent of the damage. He picked up that broomhandle putter and cradled it in his arms as if it were a dying child.'

Marianne tutted. 'It's about time Sam got his priorities straight. He's got to realize that you and the girls are more important than his stupid golf clubs.'

'Try telling him that,' said Laura. 'I knew what he was like when I married him. The trouble is, I'm not sure if it's what I want any more. I don't care about the house or the cars or the five-star holidays. I just want someone who's always there; someone who'll ask me if I've had a good day and put their arms round me when I've had a bad one.'

Keeley's eyes widened. 'Are you saying you might leave him?'

'I don't know that I'm brave enough.'

'Of course you are,' exclaimed Keeley. 'You'd manage perfectly well on your own, and don't forget that Sam would have to fork out a fair wedge in alimony.'

Laura stared out of Marianne's living-room window, into the manicured garden beyond. 'It's not that simple, Keeley. I don't want to be a single mum.'

'But will you ever be able to trust him again?' said Marianne. 'I know I wouldn't, if I were in your shoes.'

'And then there's the stuff we *don't* know about,' Keeley remarked casually.

Laura frowned. 'What do you mean?'

'Well . . .' Keeley began. She caught Cindy's eye and thought she detected something threatening in the other woman's expression. She pressed on regardless. 'Has it crossed your mind that as well as all this dogging stuff, Sam might be, you know, having a full-blown affair?'

'Keeley!' exclaimed Marianne. 'I hardly think that's appropriate. Hasn't Laura got enough to contend with without –'

'The answer's *yes*,' said Laura, cutting across Marianne. 'Not that Sam's given me any reason to think it might be true.'

Cindy glowered at Keeley, daring her to say something about Abi. To her relief, the other woman remained quiet. There was a long silence, broken only by the chinking of teacups on saucers, and then Laura said, 'Listen, girls, would you mind awfully if we changed the subject? Otherwise, I think I may be about to burst into tears.'

Twelve

Xavier Gainsbourg muttered an expletive in French and stuffed his hands under his armpits. It was an hour and ten minutes since he'd been shut inside the walk-in cold store and his fingers were starting to turn blue. The walk-in had a safety mechanism, which allowed it to be opened from the inside. In other words, his incarceration was entirely self-inflicted. At the end of lunchtime service, the chef had waited for the final porter to depart, before slipping unseen into the cold store's icy, pitch-dark interior. It being a Sunday, none of the staff had any reason to return to the kitchen until it reopened on Monday morning – unless, that is, they were up to no good.

Ever since his meeting with Lanchester a week earlier, Xavier had been performing a discreet, twice-daily stock-take, which revealed that small quantities of food – all of it luxury items or dishes made to Xavier's own personal recipe – were regularly going missing. Many of the thefts apparently occurred during service, when Xavier was far too busy to monitor the movements of each and every one of his colleagues. However, the thief had also struck twice on a Sunday, when the kitchen was closed – and, if he tried his luck a third time, Xavier wanted to be there to greet him. It filled him with rage to think that one of his staff, whom he had painstakingly nurtured, albeit in the brutish fashion peculiar to chefs, should betray him in such a way. He might have been chilled to the bone, huddled there in his winter coat and woollen beret, but the chef was prepared to lie in wait all night if need be.

Nearly three hours had passed when Xavier heard the sound of footsteps. His heartbeat quickened as he moved back into the furthest recesses of the cold store and crouched down behind some sacks of swedes. A moment later, the overhead light came on, temporarily blinding him. When his vision returned, he found himself squinting through the gap between the sacks at Seamus O'Gorman. The young sous was casually dressed in jeans and a demin jacket and there was a leather satchel slung over his shoulder. Xavier's fingers inched across the floor towards his weapon: a cordless industrial blender, whose razor-sharp cutting blades were capable of pureeing 110 lb of potatoes in less than three minutes. Seamus took his time perusing the shelves before finally selecting two containers of caviar and a bottle of truffle oil. Xavier's nostrils flared in anger as Seamus slipped the items into his satchel and then turned back for a slab of well-matured Roquefort. He waited until the sous's hand was on the doorhandle, and then said in a loud, clear voice. 'Not so fast, Monsieur O'Gorman.'

As Seamus spun round, the satchel fell from his shoulder. The bottle of truffle oil shattered instantly, spilling its viscous contents across the tiled floor. He looked around wildly. 'Who's there?' he said in a frightened voice.

Xavier emerged from behind the sacks, blender in hand.

'Chef,' Seamus gasped. 'What are you doing here?'

'I could ask the same question of you,' said Xavier coldly. 'But of course I already know the answer.' He stared down at the satchel, its contents now scattered across the floor.

Seamus held up his hands. 'It's not how it looks, Chef, honest.'

'Don't take me for an ignoramus,' Xavier bellowed. 'I know exactly what you've been up to.'

Seamus started backing towards the door. As he did so, he slipped on a pool of truffle oil, cracking his head on the edge of a shelf unit as he fell to the floor. Xavier was on him in an instant. He straddled the dazed chef, flicked the switch on the industrial blender and raised it in the air like a dagger. With his other hand, he gripped Seamus by the throat. 'You shit-eating cocksucker,' he spat. 'What have you done with all the food you stole? Sold it to your fuckwit friends in the pub? Stuffed your fat face with it? Eh? Eh?'

Unable to speak due to the pressure on his windpipe, Seamus made a choking sound. Xavier brought the whirring blades of the blender closer to his face. 'If you don't tell me, I swear I'm going to make mincemeat of your eyeballs,' he cried.

Seamus's arms and legs began flailing wildly. He kicked over a tower of wooden crates, sending a week's worth of avocados flying. One struck Xavier's elbow, causing him to loosen his grip on the sous chef's throat. In that moment, Seamus twisted his body and pitched Xavier sideways, sending the blender skittering under a shelf unit. The chef let out an almighty bellow and brought his knee up between Seamus's legs. As the sous clutched his testicles in agony, Xavier lunged for the nearest weapon – a catering-sized tub of crème fraiche. Tearing off the lid, he flung the tub's contents in his apprentice's face, temporarily blinding him.

'Your own mother won't recognize you by the time I've finished,' he said as he bent down and slapped Seamus hard across the face.

'Please, Chef, I can explain,' Seamus wailed. He curled up in a ball and put his hands over his head.

'It's too late for explanations, you whining little bed-wetter. Now stand up and face me like a man.'

As Seamus struggled to his feet, Xavier put his fists up and began dancing around him like a boxer.

Suddenly a voice spoke. 'What the heckedy-heck's going on here then?'

Xavier looked over his shoulder. Head caretaker Alf Joiner was standing at the entrance to the cold store.

'This is a private matter,' snapped Xavier. 'Please remove yourself from my kitchen.'

Alf pointed to Seamus. 'Why is he covered in cream?'

Xavier sighed and dropped his fists. 'It would take too long to explain.'

Alf frowned. 'Hey, this isn't some kind of kinky sex game, is it? I've heard about you artistic types.'

'How dare you suggest a thing,' said Xavier, puffing out his chest as if to emphasize his masculinity. 'I'll have you know that I caught this lowlife stealing from the kitchen. I was just issuing his punishment.'

Alf pushed his flat cap to one side and scratched his head. 'Whatever you say, guv'nor.'

Suddenly Seamus made a dash for the door, shoving Alf aside in his haste to escape.

Xavier let out an anguished cry, but made no attempt to pursue the thief. All of a sudden, the fight had gone out of him. 'You're fired, Seamus,' he shouted. 'And God help you if you ever show your face in my kitchen again.'

Alf surveyed the floor, which was now covered in a glutinous mixture of trampled avocados, oil and cream. 'I hope you're not expecting the cleaners to clear up this mess, Mr Gainsbourg.'

'It's "Chef",' Xavier snapped.

'I beg your pardon?'

' "Chef": that is my title; that is how you must address me.'

Alf chuckled. 'I'm not one of your kitchen flunkies. I was working at St Benedict's when you were just a twinkle in your pa's eye.' He kicked an avocado with his foot. 'Now wait here while I get you a mop and bucket.'

Xavier was disconsolate standing in the ruins of the cold store. He hated it when things didn't go his way. He bent down to pick up the waxed-paper package of Roquefort, which miraculously had escaped the melee unscathed. As he did so, he noticed a folded scrap of paper that was laying half in and half out of Seamus's abandoned satchel. Opening it, he saw that it contained a handwritten recipe. He recognized it straight away. It was his own legendary beetroot terrine with horseradish and dill cream, a dish that had taken him nearly three years to perfect. Xavier never wrote anything down; all his recipes were committed to memory – but it wouldn't be too difficult for an eagle-eyed sous to pick up the recipe. 'You fucking swine, Seamus,' he hissed. 'If I ever see you again, I'm going to cut off your balls, make them into pâté and serve it to your sister on a silver salver.'

Out on the driving range, Marianne was struggling to master the rudiments of golf – or rather *pretending* to struggle. The fifty-one-year-old was, as ever, immaculately turned out in white capri pants, white cap-sleeve T-shirt and baby-pink towelling visor, to match the pink Ralph Lauren sweater that was looped casually round her shoulders. Scrutinizing her performance was Scott Mason, St Benedict's newest golf coach.

'I don't know what's wrong with me; I just can't seem to get it right,' sighed Marianne, after missing the ball for the third swing in a row. 'My hand-eye coordination really is abysmal. No wonder I never made the school hockey team.' In truth, Marianne's hand-eye coordination was excellent as Scott's recently retired predecessor – with whom Marianne had enjoyed weekly golf lessons for nearly a year – had been fond of remarking. She shot Scott a flirtatious sideways glance. 'What on earth are you going to do with me?'

The twenty-eight-year-old coach smiled patiently. 'Don't panic, Mrs Kennedy. It's only your first lesson and nobody gets it right straight away. Your swing's not bad actually, but your grip's all wrong. Here, let me show you again.'

A delicious shudder rippled through Marianne's lower regions as Scott's arms encircled her for the second time that morning. As he positioned his hands over hers on the club, she pushed out her bottom – pert and toned as a woman's half her age, thanks to regular gym workouts – so that it nestled snugly against her tutor's crotch.

'Goodness, what big muscles you have,' she murmured, gazing at his brawny forearms.

'Thanks,' said Scott, his warm, chewing-gum-scented breath teasing the back of her neck. He adjusted her hands so that the index finger of her left hand interlocked with her right-hand pinky. 'Okay, Mrs Kennedy. You need to grip the shaft with enough force to feel the club head as it moves – but not so tightly that your wrists are tensed.'

'Grip the *shaft*,' Marianne repeated, enjoying the taste of the word in her mouth. 'I should be able to manage that.'

Scott gently pushed Marianne's elbows closer to her body. 'Okay, we're nearly there, Mrs Kennedy, but you're still squeezing too hard. You have to be gentle. Hold the club as if you're holding a baby bird.'

Marianne gave a tinkling laugh, turning her head so she could inhale another whiff of Scott's lemony after-shave. 'A baby bird? What a wonderful analogy. Believe me, I can be *verrry* gentle when the situation demands it.'

Suppressing a smirk, Scott released his pupil and took a step back. 'There now, that's just about perfect,' he said, stroking his square jaw approvingly. 'Your husband's going to be very impressed when he sees what you've learned.'

Marianne fixed him with a stare. 'I don't have a husband,' she said. 'He died.'

'Oh. I'm sorry to hear that, Mrs Kennedy.'

'Don't be,' said Marianne firmly. 'It was the best thing that ever happened to me.'

Scott laughed nervously, not sure if his client were joking. She wasn't. 'Okay, Mrs Kennedy, let's work on your posture now, shall we?'

'You're the boss, darling,' purred Marianne, as the golf pro placed a new golf ball on the plastic tee.

'Concentrate now. Head straight, please, eyes looking directly ahead. Drop your right shoulder slightly. Feet shoulder width apart ... good. Now flex your knees slightly and – swing!'

There was a loud crack as ball, tee and a clod of earth went flying through the air together. Marianne shrugged. 'Oh well, at least I managed to hit the ball this time.'

Scott patted her on the shoulder. 'You've done very well, Mrs Kennedy. We're going to have you out on that fairway in no time.' He glanced at his watch. 'We'll work on your ball control next time, but that's it for today, I'm afraid.'

Marianne mimicked an expression of dismay. 'No! Already? Goodness, doesn't time fly when you're having fun?' She glanced around the driving range, which – it being a Saturday – was full to capacity. 'You know, Scott, practising in front of all these people makes me dreadfully self-conscious.' She moistened her lips with her tongue. 'I know you haven't been at St Benedict's for very long, but a very good friend of mine told me, in the strictest confidence, that you sometimes give private lessons – for *special* clients – in the comfort of their own homes.'

Scott grinned sheepishly and ran a hand through his floppy fringe. 'You've heard about those, have you?'

'I daresay the club doesn't like you doing private work, but I won't breathe a word to anyone, I promise.'

Scott looked Marianne up and down, deliberating. 'To be honest,' he said finally, 'I think you could really benefit from a private session.'

Marianne smiled. 'Wonderful – and how much do you usually charge for a one-to-one?'

'Two hundred an hour. Cash or personal cheque only, I'm afraid.'

Marianne raised an eyebrow. 'Two hundred? In that case, you *must* be good.'

'Oh I am, Mrs Kennedy, the very best,' said Scott, running a hand over his six-pack. 'Trust me, we'll have you gripping that shaft like a pro in no time.'

Despite the onset of middle age, Marianne was still a handsome woman. Her deportment was gracious, her voice well modulated, her tailoring flawless. Every inch of her screamed old money. But the reality was very different. No one, not even her closest friends, knew she'd once made her living as an Avon lady. For years, Marianne had trudged the east Lancashire streets that comprised her patch, a fake smile plastered across her over-made-up face, as she hawked pansticks and polka-dot tote bags to sour-faced young mums and glamorous grannies. Meanwhile, her late husband, Clive, had pursued a similarly unexceptional career as a carpet fitter. They didn't have much money, but they were happy enough – or at least as happy as any couple who'd been married for twenty-two childless years *could* be. They lived in an unassuming suburban terrace, took an annual holiday on the Costa Brava, enjoyed a bottle of Blue Nun at the weekend – nothing remarkable. And then, one Saturday night, their lives were turned upside down. By six numbers. *And* the bonus ball. Five lucky ticket holders shared the jackpot of £14.2 million – and Clive was one of them.

Marianne, who'd always been the sensible sort, urged her husband to take financial advice, to seek out a high-interest savings account, to top up his pension and invest in stocks and shares. But Clive thought he knew better. It was his money, he said, and he'd spend it any which way he liked. After handing in his notice at work, he went on a massive week-long spending spree. He blew a hundred grand at a classic-car dealership in a single afternoon. He bought a state-of-the art stereo system, a rubber dinghy, a multi-gym, six pairs of handmade Italian leather shoes, a tank of tropical fish and a pair of bad-tempered chinchillas. Marianne tried her best to rein him in, but Clive was unstoppable. He splashed out on a 48-inch Dolby surround-sound television, a solid-gold sovereign ring, an antique umbrella stand and a wardrobe full of Tacchini separates. And when a jealous neighbour scraped a key along the side of Clive's vintage E-type, he traded in their terrace for a mock-Tudor mansion with an indoor swimming pool and CCTV.

Over a period of months, Clive changed from the quiet, easygoing man Marianne had fallen in love with at the age of nineteen, to a boorish, cocky jack-the-lad. He abandoned all his old friends and took to drinking alone in smart city-centre bars, before coming home in the small hours, stinking of cigars and other women's perfume. Clive had never responded well to nagging, and Marianne thought that if she simply bided her time, he would eventually get tired of carousing, and realize that what he was looking for was already waiting for him at home. But then he took up with a blonde barmaid called Jodie who was young enough to be his daughter, and when Marianne found her Ann Summers bra and a used condom wrapped in tissue in the back of the E-type, she couldn't hold her tongue any longer. So she confronted Clive and threatened to leave him if he didn't give up his little tart. He laughed in her face. 'What? Leave all this?' he sneered, gesturing around their vast, triple-aspect living room with its cream leather sofas and onyx coffee table. 'Go on then, I dare you. And let's see how far you get.' Marianne hung her head, lips pressed tight together. She could never go back to their old life; in any case, she had nowhere else to go – and Clive knew it. So she killed him – or as good as.

Clive had suffered from asthma his whole life. As a boy, he'd been hospitalized twice for the condition, but over the years he'd learned to control his symptoms by avoiding known triggers – notably pollen and animal hair – and carrying his inhaler with him at all times. Two days after dropping his bombshell on Marianne, he came home, smashed as usual, and promptly fell asleep in the living room, not noticing that Marianne had left one of the Velux windows open. It was early summer and Clive's new garden was well stocked with mature plants and exotic grasses, whose deadly spores drifted, unseen, on the balmy night air.

Some time later, Clive woke with a dry throat and a tightness in his chest. He staggered to the kitchen and gulped down a glass of water, but within minutes he was bent double, coughing and gasping for breath. He went back into the living room and groped on the floor for the jacket he'd been wearing earlier – but, when he reached into the pocket, his inhaler wasn't there. Unbeknown to him, it was lying on Jodie's bedroom floor, where he'd spent the earlier part of the evening. Knowing there was a spare in the bathroom cabinet, Clive started to climb the staircase on his hands and knees. His pulse was racing and he could feel the rush of blood in his ears and a dull pounding in his chest. Ahead of him, the stairs stretched endlessly. 'Marianne,' he called out in a ragged voice.

Marianne's eyes flickered open. She was a famously light sleeper. Clive used to joke that he couldn't fart without waking her. She heard him call her name again; his voice was weaker now. 'Marianne. I . . . need . . . my . . . inhaler.' She flung back the bedclothes and went to the top of the stairs. Her husband lay in a crumpled heap on the half-landing. Even in the dim light, Marianne could see that his skin had turned a peculiar ashy shade. 'Bathroom . . . cabinet,' he wheezed. 'Left . . . hand . . . side.'

Marianne frowned. 'I'm sorry, darling, I can't hear you. You'll have to speak up.'

Clive raised his head and extended an arm towards her. His eyes were bulging and his lips had started to turn blue. 'Help . . . me,' he said.

Now, Marianne wasn't an innately cruel person, but that night something inside her snapped. 'Help your fucking self,' she said. And, with that, she turned on her heel and went back to bed.

She didn't call an ambulance till morning, by which time Clive's body was quite cold. The coroner recorded a verdict of death by natural causes, having concluded that a severe asthma attack had sent the victim into respiratory arrest. Marianne – clad in black Armani, bought with one of the bundles of fifty-pound notes she'd found stuffed at the back of Clive's underwear drawer – wept at the inquest. People thought she was grieving for her dead husband – but, really, they were tears of relief. Clive had never bothered to make a will and, after a certain amount of legal wrangling thanks to a troublesome distant cousin, Marianne was named his sole beneficiary.

She then set about spending what was left of Clive's winnings wisely. She hired a top-flight financial advisor, who helped her make a series of canny investments in property and shares – enough to provide a comfortable annual income. She took elocution lessons and quickly lost her soft Lancashire burr, and hired an image consultant to teach her about style and colour combining. Marianne had always been an attractive woman, but now she could afford to be stunning. A breast enlargement, liposuction and Botox, plus £4,000 worth of cosmetic dentistry made her feel like a whole new woman. Then she sold the ugly mock-Tudor mansion and moved fifty miles away, to a chocolate-box cottage in Kirkhulme. Having reverted to her maiden name, so no one would be able to identify her as the 'lottery millionaire's wife', she launched herself on the Cheshire scene with gusto. Thanks to her newfound wealth and social graces, Marianne found it easy to make friends at St Benedict's.

Most people took her at face value, but if anyone delved deeper, she said her late husband had made his money in top-end car dealing.

Until his death, Clive was the only man Marianne had ever slept with. But she'd always had a high sex drive and, now that she was a free agent, she set about unashamedly satisfying her sexual needs. She picked up men wherever she could – at the club, in the supermarket, waiting in line at the post office. She seduced the mechanic who serviced her Audi, and the engineer who came to fix her boiler and the lad who came to mow the lawn. She quickly discovered she preferred younger men, who had hard bodies and good stamina. Marianne didn't want a relationship, just high-quality uncomplicated sex. She was happy to go for dinner first, if it helped get them in the mood; to indulge their Mrs Robinson fantasies; to experiment with role play, sex toys, a little light bondage, but, at the end of the day, they played it by her rules – or they didn't play at all. Her next lover was going to be young Scott Mason. Of that, she was certain.

Thirteen

For the first time in goodness knows how long, Keeley Finnigan had been dumped – and she was fuming. Not because she was particularly fond of Fabrizio: as all her friends knew, she found the footballer and his halting English more irritating than a yeast infection. What's more, she hated the way he fawned over her, treating her as if she were a precious piece of Clarice Cliff that might fall and break at any moment. No, Keeley's displeasure was simply down to the fact that she preferred to finish relationships on her own terms, usually after the extraction of some final parting gift or, at the very least, an introduction to an eligible single friend of theirs. By contrast, the split with Fabrizio had been sudden and messy, and now Keeley found herself in the embarrassing position of being 'in between' boyfriends. It wouldn't take her long to find a replacement – three weeks, tops – but in the meantime there would be no expensive additions to her wardrobe, no Michelin-starred meals out, no cobalt-blue Porsche to gun down the Kirkhulme bypass. And it was all the fault of that stupid interfering Ryan Stoker.

It had been clear to Keeley from the start that Fabrizio's goalkeeping buddy didn't much care for her. She assumed he found her shallow and grasping. After all, plenty of men did (although that didn't stop most of them wanting to fuck her). Whenever they went out as a threesome, Ryan was always making sarcastic asides – most of which, thankfully, went over the top of Fabrizio's head – and sometimes he looked at Keeley with such loathing, his eyes seemed to burn a hole right through her. She'd been relieved when Fabrizio's English improved enough so that they no longer required the services of an interpreter. But now it appeared that Ryan had been biding his time ever since, just waiting for a chance to drive a wedge between them – and, careless girl that she was, Keeley presented him with just such an opportunity the night she agreed to have a drink with Joe Carter.

Keeley had been sleeping with Joe for the best part of three years. He was average in almost every respect – average-looking, average income, average intelligence, average in bed – and, normally, Keeley wouldn't have given him the time of day. But, in his capacity as senior membership advisor at St Benedict's, Joe was in a position to give Keeley something no one else could: namely, a small gold card with the words 'VIP Member' embossed in sexy black letters. Best of all, it cost her absolutely nothing . . . nothing, that is, except a monthly sex session, which was no great hardship for Keeley and a massive thrill for Joe, whose long-term girlfriend had a furry top lip and the thighs of a female wrestler. Given that theirs was a purely sexual relationship, Keeley and Joe rarely went out in public together. But, on the day in question, Joe had called his lover a couple of hours before they were due to meet at his Delchester maisonette for an hour-long session between his not-very-clean sheets to suggest a quick drink in town, before they got down to it. Keeley almost demurred – Joe was pleasant enough, but hardly scintillating company. Then she decided that, actually, she wouldn't mind a nice glass of something, especially since Joe was paying. She'd just endured a very stressful shopping expedition, during which a jumped-up Karen Millen sales girl had declined to let her return a spangled halter-top, refusing to believe her claim that it was the wrong size, and triumphantly pointing out the large wine stain on the front. And so, against her better judgement, Keeley agreed to meet Joe at a venue of his choice. They should've gone somewhere quiet – a backstreet pub where nobody Keeley knew would be seen dead. But instead Joe, wanting to show her off, had named a smart city-centre vodka bar. Exhausted from her confrontation with the shop assistant, Keeley hadn't put up much of a fight.

The pair spent a perfectly pleasant hour or so drinking martinis, and were just preparing to leave when Ryan Stoker walked in with a girl he'd met at a nightclub two nights previously. Keeley, who had her back to the door and was a little giddy from the martinis, didn't notice him at first. But the goalie noticed Keeley, and he watched from a dimly lit corner with interest as Joe ran his hand up her bare leg and under her rose-print sundress, before leaning in close to whisper something in her ear. A few moments later, Keeley threw back her head and laughed, presenting Joe with an expanse of smooth neck and collar-bone, which he then proceeded to shower with kisses.

As Keeley and Joe made their way towards the door, Ryan appeared from the shadows and caught Keeley's arm. 'Evening, Kee,' he said. 'Fancy seeing you here.'

Keeley's heart sank. 'Hi, Ryan,' she muttered, wondering how much the footballer had seen. 'Sorry I can't stop to chat. We were just leaving.'

A mischievous smile played about Ryan's lips. 'What a shame,' he said. He turned to Joe. 'Aren't you going to introduce me to your —' he cleared his throat pointedly — '*friend*?'

'No, I'm bloody not,' Keeley started to say, but Joe — who wasn't going to pass up an introduction to one of his sporting heroes — was already gripping Ryan's hand.

'Joe Carter. Nice to meet you, Mr Stoker. I've seen you at St Benedict's; I work in memberships.'

Ryan narrowed his eyes. 'Oh yeah, I thought you looked familiar. Well, enjoy the rest of the evening, whatever it is you're doing.' He looked at Keeley. 'I'll tell Fab you were asking after him, shall I?' he said, his voice dripping with sarcasm.

'What-*evah*,' Keeley replied as she grabbed Joe's elbow and marched him out of the door.

It was too much to hope that Ryan would keep his mouth shut. Later, when Fabrizio confronted her, Keeley denied everything. She insisted that Ryan must have imagined Joe's hand snaking up her leg and the way he'd traced her vertebrae one by one as he helped her on with her cardigan. 'He's an old school friend,' she insisted. 'He just happens to be a very touchy-feely person.'

Fabrizio may have been a fool for falling in love with Keeley in the first place, but he wasn't stupid. 'Ryan's right,' he said. 'You don't love me and you never will.'

Keeley had cried, cajoled, promised to give Fabrizio one of her famous blowjobs — but, to his credit, he refused to weaken. 'You've taken me for a ride,' he said, showing off his new linguistic skills. 'I never want to see you again.'

Keeley was horrified. She nearly always managed to remain on good terms with her exes – one never knew when they might come in handy – and a Premiership footballer was a particularly useful contact to have. 'Not even as friends?' she'd said, lower lip trembling.

'Not even as friends,' he'd confirmed. He held out his hand. 'And now I would be grateful for the return of my keys.'

Sighing, Keeley had rummaged in her handbag for the set of house keys, tied with a red silk bow, which Fabrizio had presented to her on their sixth date. 'Here,' she said, slapping them into his hand. 'Take the flaming things.' She made a great show of fumbling with the fastening of her Cartier watch. 'I suppose you want this back too.'

A look of disgust crossed the footballer's face. 'What do you take me for?' he said. 'The watch . . . *all* my gifts to you . . . were given in love. I am a gentleman; I would never dream of asking for their return.'

Keeley breathed a sigh of relief. 'Oh, okay. I thought I'd better check.'

So now, here she was, single and skint, with no new prospects in sight. But at least she still had her VIP membership at St Benedict's – and, as Fabrizio turned his back on her and walked away, Keeley's first thought was to seek solace in the club's luxurious spa.

Keeley was one of a select group of club members who knew there was more on offer at the spa's women-only

relaxation suite than massages and complimentary thera-
pies. At certain times and in certain locations, the suite
became a discreet hive of lesbian activity – some of it
administered by the club's highly qualified therapy team;
other acts occurring spontaneously between consenting
members of the clientele.

Keeley had always regarded herself as bi-curious, rather
than bisexual – although the truth was, her curiosity had
been satisfied a long time ago. She'd never had a full-
blown relationship with a woman, nor could she imagine
doing so, and her Sapphic experiences had only ever
been about satisfying an immediate sexual need. Her
experimentation had begun at the age of eighteen when
she found herself sharing a Parisian hotel room with a
French model called Beatrice during a three-day fashion
shoot for an in-flight magazine. On the final evening, all
the models had gone clubbing together and Keeley had
got hopelessly drunk on pastis. She'd woken in the middle
of the night with a parched throat and a naked Beatrice
standing beside her bed. Before a sleep-befuddled Keeley
had had a chance to object, Beatrice was slipping into
bed beside her and pushing down the spaghetti straps of
her nightdress. Beatrice didn't speak much English, but
no words were needed – not when her mouth and hands
were well versed in the language of pleasure. By the time
the sun came up, both girls were covered in a sheen of
sweat, and Keeley's eyes had been opened to a whole new
world of possibilities. She never saw Beatrice again, but
in the months and years that followed, she enjoyed a
string of enjoyable, but essentially meaningless, lesbian
liaisons. Indeed, some of her best sexual experiences to

date had been with women. She didn't have a particular type as far as looks were concerned – blondes, brunettes, redheads, she was open to any offer. That said, she did have a soft spot for large breasts, given that she herself was flat as the Fens.

As Keeley flashed her membership card at the spa's white-coated receptionist, she thought longingly of her favourite therapist, Astrid. Unfortunately, the Swedish girl didn't come cheap – and, without Fabrizio to subsidize her, Keeley couldn't afford to indulge. Today, she would have to make do with a dip in one of the relaxation suite's aromatherapy hot tubs, which were free to VIP members. With any luck, she's find some like-minded female with whom she'd be able to retire to one of the roomy changing cubicles for a little stress relief.

After changing into a fake Versace bikini, Keeley spritzed some perfume behind her ears and headed for the hot tubs. Big enough for two at a pinch, each sunken tub was surrounded on three sides by a Chinese-style lacquered screen, which afforded bathers a modicum of privacy. But with the temperature outside in the eighties, most of the spa's regular patrons had decamped to the outdoor swimming pond and all the baths were empty – save for one, which was occupied by a taut-faced forty-something with a trout pout and a Gloria Swanson-style turban. The woman smiled pleasantly as Keeley walked past. Keeley nodded a greeting and hurried towards the bath at the furthest end of the room. Kicking off her flip-flops, she took a complimentary towel from the freshly laundered stack beside the tub, folded it into a triangle and draped it over the top of the screen, thereby signalling her availability for sexual activity. She climbed into the tub, sighing as the warm, fragrant water enveloped her body. Closing her eyes, she began mentally replaying her conversation with Fabrizio – only this time she was the one doing the dumping. Suddenly, a familiar voice interrupted her reverie.

'Hiya, babe, how ya doing?'

Keeley's eyes snapped open. Standing beside the tub was a curvaceous blonde in a skimpy white bikini, her enormous breasts casting a generous shadow on the limestone floor.

Keeley broke into a smile. 'Destiny!' she exclaimed. 'It's been absolutely ages. Where've you been hiding? I've left tons of messages on your voicemail but you never call me back.'

Destiny spat a wad of well-masticated chewing gum into her hand and glued it to the lacquered screen. 'Yeah, sorry 'bout that. Things have been really hectic lately. I've had to do heaps of publicity for *Celebrity Lust Island*; the media interest has been unbelievable. I fly out in five days and I absolutely cannot wait – especially now I've seen photos of the blokes on offer. They are *lush*.' She fanned herself with a hand, pretending to be having a hot flush. 'Seriously, babe, they'd better have a big supply of condoms on that island, cos I'm gonna be shagging for Britain.'

'It sounds great; you must be really excited,' said Keeley forlornly. At first, she'd been pleased about Destiny's big TV break, but the more she thought about it, the more she wished her friend weren't heading for Antigua. As it was, she didn't see as much of the model as she'd like –

and, once the show aired, Destiny was going to be a big star and wouldn't have time for the likes of Keeley.

'And, don't forget, one sleb gets voted off each week, so you gotta keep voting for me,' said Destiny.

'Of course I will,' Keeley lied. 'My finger's going to be on that redial button morning, noon and night.'

Her sarcasm was lost on Destiny. 'Thanks,' she said, smiling gratefully. 'Actually, there's another reason I'm glad I ran into you.'

'Oh yes?' said Keeley, perking up.

Destiny's voice dropped to a whisper. 'I want to buy some coke. Will you come to the golf shop with me? Only I'm not sure who I should speak to.'

'Sure,' said Keeley, stupidly glad to be of service. 'I know all the guys in the shop.'

'Cool.' Destiny tapped the face of the large dive watch that hung loosely from her twig-like wrist. 'Is it okay if we go now, only I've got a big party this evening and I need to get home and choose my outfit.'

'A party?' said Keeley, her face lighting up. 'Hey, would it be okay if I tagged along? It's ages since I had a good night out.'

'Sorry, babe,' said Destiny. 'No can do. It's strictly invite only.'

'Oh. Okay. Never mind then.' Keeley assumed a woeful expression. 'It's just that Fab dumped me this morning, so I could do with cheering up.' She paused, waiting for Destiny to offer her condolences. None were forthcoming. 'Another time maybe?' she said hesitantly.

'Uh-huh,' said Destiny. She clapped her hands together impatiently. 'So, shall we get going then?'

Keeley didn't answer immediately. Instead, she lifted an arm out of the water and stroked it languidly. If Destiny couldn't even be bothered to wangle her an invitation to the party, she could damn well wait for her coke. 'I'll take you to the shop in a little while,' she said archly. 'But first I need to have ten minutes in the tub. I'm so stressed out right now. Splitting up with Fab has really knocked me for six.' She gestured to the circular bath. 'Care to join me?'

Destiny shrugged as if she didn't much care either way. 'Okay then, ten minutes.' She pulled a scrunchie off her wrist and used it to secure her mane of hair in a high ponytail. 'Mmm, this smells nice,' she said as she stepped into the scented water and sank down beside Keeley.

'It's a blend of geranium and ginger,' said Keeley. 'To improve circulation and balance the emotions.'

'Really?' said Destiny disinterestedly. She sighed and closed her eyes. Keeley used the opportunity to subject her famous friend to a critical appraisal. Destiny's face was no prettier than her own, she decided, and those hair extensions really were rank. But the body . . . the body was spectacular. More important than that, Destiny had the sort of go-getting, self-promoting, exhibitionist personality needed in order to get one's face plastered across the tabloids.

Destiny's eyelids fluttered open. 'Hey, you'll never guess what I heard the other day.'

Keeley pointed at Destiny's left breast, which had escaped from its mooring, and was now bobbing freely on the surface of the water like a huge inflatable.

Destiny tutted. 'These damn things are always escaping,' she said proudly.

Keeley rolled her eyes. 'Well, if you will buy clothes three sizes too small for you.'

Destiny giggled as she shoehorned the offending mammary back into her bikini top. 'Anyway, as I was saying, I heard some juicy gossip the other day, from a very reliable source.'

'Go on,' said Keeley eagerly.

'Well, apparently there's all sorts of stuff goes on in here. Stuff like you *would* not believe.'

Keeley's lips curled upwards. 'You don't say.'

'Yeah, I was shocked when I found out about it. Absolutely gobsmacked.' Destiny dropped her voice to a whisper. 'It involves girl-on-girl action.' She shook her head censoriously. 'Honestly, the nerve of some people.'

Keeley's smile widened. 'Girl-on-girl action,' she repeated. 'Here, in the relaxation suite?'

'Yeah, Monday nights and Thursday afternoons is when it all kicks off,' Destiny said breathlessly. 'Apparently, there's this secret signal which shows if someone's game-on. And then, if another girl likes the look of them, they'll tip them the wink and then they both sneak off to one of the changing cubicles and do whatever it is lezzers do. Incredible, huh? You'd think a place like St Benedict's would have rules about that sort of thing.'

'Secret signal,' said Keeley thoughtfully. 'What sort of secret signal?'

'Well,' said Destiny. 'According to my friend in-the-know, you fold your towel in a certain way and display it in a prominent place.'

In a slow, deliberate gesture, Keeley looked up at her towel, which was still hanging over the lacquered screen. 'Like that, you mean?'

Destiny followed her gaze. For a few moments she stared at the towel as the cogs in her brain clunked into gear. Then her mouth dropped open. 'Oh my God, Keeley! Are you a lesbo?'

'Certainly not,' Keeley sniffed. 'You know me – I like a big hard cock as much as the next girl. It's just that sometimes, when I'm in a certain mood, I like to have sex with women.'

Destiny's hands flew to her face. 'Keeley! I can't believe you just said that.'

Keeley shrugged. 'It's no big deal. It's just a different kind of sex. Women are the experts. They know exactly how other women's bodies work; there's none of that awful fumbling around.' She looked Destiny in the eye. 'Their lips are softer too.' For a long moment, the two women stared at each other. And then Keeley leaned forward, cupped Destiny's jaw in her hand and kissed her full on the lips. The model's lips were warm and cushiony and tasted faintly of spearmint. When Destiny didn't resist, she pushed her tongue gently into the model's mouth. For a second, Destiny's body seemed to freeze and then she reciprocated, sliding her own tongue into Keeley's eager mouth. When Destiny finally came up for air, several minutes later, she was gasping like a trout on a riverbank. 'Wow,' she said, pushing damp tendrils of hair out of her face. 'I see what you mean.'

Keeley smiled lazily. Underneath the lightly foaming

water, she slipped a hand onto Destiny's inner thigh. 'You know how fond of you I am, don't you, Des?'

A nervous look crossed Destiny's features. 'Erm, yeah.'

Keeley licked her lips. 'So how about it then?'

'How about what?'

Keeley jerked her head in the direction of the changing rooms. 'Me and you in one of the cubicles. I promise you won't regret it. I can do things no man has even dreamed of.'

'Ewww!' squealed Destiny as she pushed Keeley's hand away roughly. 'You have *got* to be kidding. She folded her arms protectively across her chest. 'Okay, so I've had a few threesomes in my time, but that was different. I'm not a lesbian – do you understand?'

'All right, all right,' said Keeley. 'No need to get your knickers in a twist. It was only a suggestion.'

Destiny stood up, sending a wave of geranium-flavoured water into Keeley's mouth. 'Yeah, well, you can keep your perverted suggestions to yourself.' She stepped out of the tub and snatched a complimentary towel from the pile, wrapping it round her shoulders like a cloak. 'I'm off. I'm not staying around here to be taken advantage of.'

Keeley reached a hand out towards her friend. 'Oh c'mon, Des, don't be like that. What about the coke?'

'Forget it. I'll sort myself out.' She gave Keeley a hard look. 'You're not going to tell anyone about this, are you?'

Keeley sighed. 'Of course not.'

'I don't know any more,' Destiny spat. 'You're not the

person I thought you were.' And, with that, she turned on her heel and marched off in the direction of the exit.

Keeley walked back to the changing area with a heavy heart. The day was going from bad to worse. As she stood beneath the shower, rinsing off the pungent aromatherapy oils, her mood sank even further as she contempleted the prospect of a lonely night in. Depressingly, the fridge in her pokey kitchen was empty, save for an overripe Camembert and half a bottle of Cabernet Sauvignon. It was weeks since she'd done a food shop; she either cooked at Fab's or they ate out. What's more, she had no cash in her purse and an overdraft that already ran into four figures. There was only one thing for it: she was going to have to find another rich boyfriend – and fast.

When she emerged from the shower, Keeley found herself utterly alone in the changing room. As she towelled herself dry, her eye was drawn to one of the stainless steel lockers on the opposite wall. Although its key had been removed, the locker door was partially open and beyond it she could see the glint of something shiny. She glanced around the room; it was deserted. Wrapping the towel round her midriff, she walked over to the locker, pushing the door back on its hinges. Inside was a large make-up bag and a pile of neatly folded clothes. Nestling on top of the clothes and catching the light was a pretty silver watch. Keeley leaned forward for a closer look, her pulse quickening as she made out the words *Baume & Mercier*. Then she noticed the rounded tips of two shoes poking out from underneath the heap of clothes. Carefully, she eased them out. 'Nice,' she murmured when she realized she was looking at a pair of size four black-and-white Marc Jacobs pumps. Each shoe had been customized with a tiny pair of initials, *A F*, picked out in gold thread on the inside edge. They looked almost new and past experience told her that – initials notwithstanding – they would fetch at least seventy pounds on eBay – and as for the watch . . .

Keeley flashed another glance around the locker room to check she was still alone. Then she picked up the watch and the Marc Jacobs pumps, carried them back across the room and stuffed them into her sports bag. Presumably, the items belonged to the relaxation suite's only patron – the bitch in the turban – and, judging by the amount she'd spent on plastic surgery, she could easily afford to buy replacements. Keen to make a quick getaway, Keeley hauled her tracksuit on over her damp bikini, pushed her feet into her leather flip-flops and hurried out of the changing room.

Harry Hunter was heading towards the clubhouse, en route to a meeting with Lanchester, when he spotted Keeley walking briskly in the opposite direction. Smiling, he raised a hand and waved at her. Following their unscripted encounter in the broom cupboard two weeks previously, the pair had struck a mutually beneficial agreement. Sometimes, the exchange took place in a quiet corner of St Benedict's, but usually Harry went to Keeley's flat, a cramped top-floor studio, which seemed to be bursting at the seams with girly paraphernalia. There were shoes spilling out of wardrobes, make-up scattered across the dining table, and bottles of nail polish and expensive perfume jostling for position on every window sill. Harry had learned from Ace that Keeley was dating Delchester United's star striker and sometimes, as he stood in her living room with his trousers round his ankles, he wondered if she had any morals at all. Mind you, he was a fine one to talk. Lanchester would doubtless be horrified to discover that he had abandoned his investigations into the changing-room thefts in exchange for a bi-weekly blowjob from the best in the business.

As they drew level with one another, Keeley hugged the sports bag she was carrying closer to her body. The gesture didn't go unnoticed by Harry, who couldn't help wondering what contraband the bag contained. But, given his promise never to raise the subject of Keeley's kleptomania again, he kept his thoughts to himself.

'Hey,' he said. 'How's it going?'

Keeley sighed wearily. 'I've had better days.'

'Oh? What's happened?'

'My boyfriend's dumped me.'

Without thinking, Harry broke into a grin. Covering his mouth with his hand, he hastily rearranged his features into a more sympathetic expression. 'I'm sorry to hear that. Is there no chance you might get back together?'

Keeley shook her head. 'There's more chance of me modelling for Stella McCartney.' She gave a loud sniff and rubbed her nose with the back of her hand. 'And, as if that wasn't depressing enough, I've just fallen out with one of my best friends.'

Harry placed a comforting hand on her shoulder. 'It's okay, Keeley, don't go upsetting yourself.'

She looked up at him. Her eyes were dry and hard as

zircons. 'I'm not upset,' she said coolly. 'I've just got a touch of hayfever.' She stared at the hand on her shoulder until Harry took the hint and let it fall away.

'So,' he said, shoving his hands in his pockets to affect casualness. 'I guess that means you'll be free on Saturday night then.'

Keeley scowled. 'Rub it in, why don't you?'

'Sorry. It's just that I was thinking of going into town to see the new Bond movie on Saturday. You're welcome to join me if you've got nothing better to do.'

Keeley folded her arms across her chest. 'Are you asking me out on a date?'

'You know what, I think I just might be.'

Keeley stuck her chin in the air disdainfully. 'Let's get one thing straight, Harry Hunter. I wouldn't go out with you if you were the only man at St Benedict's. Two blowjobs a week, nothing more. That was our deal.'

Harry shrugged. 'Fair enough. But what if I was a millionaire? Would you go out with me then?'

'Probably.'

'I'd better find myself a new job then, hadn't I?' Harry rubbed his hands together greedily. 'So, I'll see you at your place next Tuesday. What time do you want me?'

'Four p.m. And you'll have to be quick about it. I've got an appointment for a cut and blow-dry at four thirty.' With that, Keeley tossed her hair over her shoulders and began walking away. Harry watched her until she had disappeared from sight.

It hadn't taken Harry long to realize he had a problem on his hands, although it wasn't the kind of problem he could ever have anticipated. The young PI may have been inexperienced but he wasn't stupid, and it was clear, right from the beginning, that drugs were being dealt from the club shop in generous quantities. Despite his colleagues' attempts at discretion, he'd quickly sussed that the office safe housed more than cash. And only a fool could have failed to notice the steady stream of customers who shunned his offers of assistance, preferring instead to whisper a quiet word in Ace's ear, before heading for the till to collect a carrier bag which appeared to be – but almost certainly wasn't – empty. The one thing Harry didn't know was the identity of the supplier, the Mr Big who was raking in thousands of pounds a week from the seemingly insatiable members of St Benedict's. He had his suspicions all right – but, under the circumstances, he wasn't sure he wanted to air them.

Much to his amazement, Harry discovered that he loved working in the club shop. He enjoyed everything about it – the easy banter on the shop floor, the flirting with female customers, even the methodical nature of the weekly stocktake. It was the first job he'd had where he actually looked forward to getting up in the morning. Except, of course, it wasn't a real job – and therein lay the problem. The more time Harry spent at the club, the more he felt at home in its louche atmosphere, and he knew it would be a wrench when the time came for him to leave. St Benedict's had that effect on people. It drew them into its enchanted web, and made their lives before seem dull and ordinary. To complicate matters further, he'd developed a fun camaraderie with Jeff, Ace and Dylan who, despite their initial wariness, now frequently included him in their after-hours drinking sessions, where they'd regale him with club gossip and outrageous tales of their sexual conquests. Harry didn't see that their drug dealing was hurting anyone – indeed, some might say they were performing a valuable community service – and to spill the beans on their activities, illegal or not, would seem to him like a dreadful betrayal.

Every four or five days, Harry was summoned to the general manager's office to report on his latest findings. So far, he'd done a good job of fobbing Lanchester off, hinting at tantalizing new leads and promising breakthroughs that never quite materialized. But now his employer was starting to get impatient, which was why he had issued an unexpected summons, via a curt message in Harry's staff pigeonhole. As the private investigator assumed his usual position on the high-backed chair opposite the manager's desk, he felt a sickening sense of dread.

'You've been working undercover for six weeks, Mr Hunter, and I must admit, I *am* a little frustrated with the way things are going,' Lanchester began. 'I was rather hoping we'd have this unsavoury business sewn up by now. You haven't even been able to confirm what I already know – that your colleagues in the shop are dealing drugs – never mind identify their supplier.'

Harry smiled pleasantly. 'I'm sorry you feel that way, Mr Lanchester. But, as I explained right at the beginning, these things take time.'

'Yes, but time costs money,' Lanchester snapped. 'I mean, what do you do in that shop all day?'

Harry shrugged. 'Stock shelves, make tea, assist customers.'

The manager glared at him. 'Perhaps that's where you're going wrong.'

'I'm sorry?'

'You're supposed to be my eyes and ears in that shop. You need to be more proactive – ask a few questions, snoop around in the office . . . you know, do all that stuff private investigators are supposed to do.'

'With all due respect, Mr Lanchester, you seem to be forgetting that when it comes to surveillance work, *I'm* the expert here,' said Harry, lowering his voice an octave in an attempt to appear more authoritative.

Lanchester sighed. 'Yes, I realize that, and I'm not casting aspersions on your competence. But I've only got a limited resource, and I need to see some results.'

Harry looked at his lap and nodded. 'I understand and, rest assured, I am going to be pulling out all the stops from now on.'

Lanchester folded his arms across his chest. 'What about the thefts from the ladies' changing room? I've just had a call from one of the receptionists at the spa. There's been another incident. A very expensive watch and a pair of designer shoes have gone missing and the owner is most upset. She was threatening to go to the local paper until I offered her free golf lessons and a year's worth of colonic irrigation.'

Harry cleared his throat. Keeley had apparently stepped up a gear – now, she had graduated to jewellery. 'Oh dear,' he said lamely. 'I've been to the spa a couple of times for some covert observation, but sadly I've drawn a blank. To be honest, I think it's better if I focus all my energies on the shop for the time being.'

Lanchester sighed again. 'Look here, old chap, I'm beginning to wonder if we shouldn't just call it quits.'

Harry felt a churning sensation somewhere between his bowels and his small intestine. 'Please, just give me a couple more weeks,' he said. 'I'm getting close to a breakthrough – I can feel it in my bones.'

Lanchester shook his head despairingly. 'Ten days, Harry; just until the gala dinner. And then, I'm afraid, I really am going to have to let you go.'

'Fine,' said Harry. 'I won't let you down, Mr Lanchester, I promise.'

Fourteen

Scott Mason was in his second season as a professional gigolo. He had stumbled on this lucrative part-time career while working as an assistant golf pro at a country club in the West Midlands. A good-looking man, he was used to clients coming on to him, but he'd never dreamed of taking it any further. And then one day, without any sort of preamble, a hard-nosed corporate lawyer he'd given a couple of golf lessons to, but had never so much as flirted with, offered him £200 to sleep with her. Shocked – and more than a little insulted – Scott demurred. But the lawyer was used to tough negotiation. The next time he gave her a lesson she offered him £300. And the lesson after that, £400. It was then that Scott thought, 'Why not?' The lawyer was pushing forty and twenty-five pounds overweight, but she was still attractive. In any case, Scott's car needed a new set of tyres and his credit cards were already maxed out. It was all relatively painless. The lawyer hired a hotel room. Scott serviced her – twice – and left before dawn. Job done. Afterwards, the lawyer recommended him to a friend of hers. And *she* recommended him to a couple of others. And so it went on. He didn't advertise; he met all his clients on the driving range – or else they came to him by word of mouth. Soon, he was making more from sex than he was from teaching golf. But he was never tempted to quit the day job. He didn't want to be *just* a gigolo – and, besides, golf lessons made great foreplay. Scott had always been upwardly mobile and after a little while he decided to quit his Midlands club in search of richer pickings. So far, St Benedict's, playground for the wealthy and bored, had more than lived up to his expectations.

Scott took his work very seriously. His chest was waxed, his hands were manicured, his aftershave was subtle. He spoke in a clear, confident tone and never used coarse language – except in bed (and then only by prior agreement). He was always prompt when arriving at the arranged venue – but once the performance had begun, he was *never* in a hurry. In fact, making a client beg for it was one of his specialities. He listened carefully to his client's needs and preferences before initiating any form of sexual activity. He knew that insecurity is the enemy of the female libido – which was why he liked to lavish his clients with compliments, to make them feel desired, and desirable. During the act itself, he practised breath control and helped direct the woman's sexual energy with the aid of massage and G-spot manipulation. His client's pleasure was paramount; indeed more than one had credited him with generating their first orgasm. Generally speaking, Scott's appointments lasted no more than a couple of hours. But he was also available for dinner dates, evenings at the theatre, weddings, funerals, bar mitzvahs, business functions and weekend getaways. The majority of his customers were single women who didn't have the time – or the energy – for a relationship, but still needed sex. Others were married to stressed-out executives who couldn't satisfy them and visited him, with or without the agreement of their husbands. Most simply wanted a good fucking, but occasionally they veered off the straight and narrow. Among his more challenging clients were a pair of lesbians who required him to do the vacuuming – naked – while they performed cunnilingus on the sofa, a woman who offered him £5,000 to have sex on her husband's grave, and a mother who beat his bare buttocks with a plastic fish slice as he pleasured her daughter in the marital bed.

Scott always took a good deal of pride in his work, but he went the extra mile for new clients in the hope they'd become regulars. For his appointment with Marianne, he had selected a freshly pressed Prada sports T-shirt, tennis shorts and white Reeboks. It was a cute, sporty look his older clients loved. Pulling up outside her pretty cottage two minutes ahead of schedule, he parked his Golf outside the triple garage, as instructed. There was just time to check his hair in the rear-view mirror and take a hit of breath freshener before making his entrance.

When Marianne came to the door, she was barefoot and casually dressed in a baby-pink tracksuit, her shoulder-length hair tied back in a loose ponytail. 'Scott,' she murmured, her eyes roaming his body approvingly. Taking his hand, she pulled him into the house. 'Would you like something to drink?' she said as she showed him into one of her three reception rooms. 'To wet your whistle before we get started.' She bit her bottom lip provocatively.

Scott smiled. This one was hot to trot all right. 'Only if you're having one,' he said lightly.

'There's a bottle of Sancerre in the fridge,' she said. 'I'll be two ticks. Why don't you make yourself comfortable?'

Scott remained standing after Marianne had left the room. He never sat down before the client. As he waited, with a delicious sense of anticipation and just a soupçon of nervousness, he drank in his luxurious surroundings: the grand piano, the Charles Eames chairs, the two Burmese cats sprawled on the sofa – the trappings of the super-rich that confirmed he'd moved into a different league. A few moments later, Marianne returned carrying two glasses of wine. After handing one to him, she settled into the sofa beside the cats, drawing her feet up on to the cushions. There was no more room on the sofa, so Scott took a seat on a wing-backed armchair and assumed an unapologetically macho pose with his legs wide apart.

For five minutes or so, they sipped their wine and made polite conversation about Marianne's cats and the wonderful weather they were having. Scott was used to this; first-timers usually required a bit of small talk to help them relax. Then Marianne pulled down the zipper of her top by a couple of inches, revealing the top of a cream lace bra. 'I've never paid for sex before,' she said, stroking her collarbone with slow, deliberate strokes. 'I'm interested to see if it's going to be any different from the free sort.'

'Well, you can rest assured that your pleasure is my priority,' said Scott smoothly. 'So I do hope you won't be disappointed.' He stared deep into his client's eyes. 'You have a beautiful mouth. It's very sensual.'

Marianne raised an eyebrow. 'Really,' she said flatly.

'Yes, and that shade of pink brings out the blue in your eyes.'

Marianne released a small derisive snort. 'Save it for

your other clients, Scott. I don't need warming up, believe me.'

Scott nodded submissively. 'Whatever you say, Mrs Kennedy. You're the boss.' It was rapidly becoming clear that Marianne was going to be an exceptionally demanding client. But that was fine – Scott liked a challenge. 'Did you have anything in particular in mind for this afternoon?' he enquired. 'I'm able to accommodate almost any request.'

Marianne smiled serenely. 'Yes, as a matter of fact I did.' She gestured with her head towards the door. 'Shall we?'

'Absolutely,' said Scott, putting down his wine glass on a side table, careful to set it on a coaster so it wouldn't mark the glass top. He followed Marianne to an opulent Louis Quartorze-themed boudoir, whose kingsize bed already had the covers folded back, hotel-style. On the table next to it, a packet of ribbed condoms lay unopened. Without saying a word, Marianne disappeared into a walk-in wardrobe, and when she emerged she was carrying a white cotton coat of the sort worn by a doctor or a lab technician. 'I'd like you to put this on over your clothes,' she instructed him. When he took the coat, he saw that underneath it Marianne had a stethoscope draped over her arm.

Scott couldn't help smiling as he took the items. He was used to anticipating his client's needs, and he wouldn't have pegged Marianne as the role-playing type.

'Is something funny?' asked Marianne icily.

'Absolutely not,' replied Scott, conjuring up a more serious expression. He found Marianne intriguing. On the driving range she had been flirtatious – suggestive even – but now she was utterly aloof. For a man who was used to women falling at his feet, it was a big turn-on.

'Okay, I'm leaving the room now and, when I come back in, I want you to act like a doctor, okay?'

'Sure,' said Scott as he hooked the stethoscope round his muscular neck.

'And I'm your patient.'

'Got it.'

She looked at his legs, bare beneath the coat, and frowned. 'Hang on a minute.' She disappeared back into the wardrobe. 'Here,' she said, tossing him a pair of men's suit trousers. 'Put these on.'

Marianne left the room and closed the door behind her. A minute or two later, Scott heard a brisk knocking. 'Come in,' he said in a stern voice. The door opened and Marianne stood on the threshold, her tracksuit now covered by a beige trenchcoat.

'Ah, Mrs Kennedy. Please come in. Here, let me help you with that coat.' Marianne stood passively as Scott slipped the coat off her shoulders, his hand deliberately grazing her left breast as he did so. He hooked the coat over the door and patted the bed. 'Why don't you pop yourself up here on the examination couch?'

Marianne did as she was told and sat on the bed. Scott moved beside her and stood cupping his chin in his hand in what he hoped was a suitably medical manner. 'Now, Mrs Kennedy, what seems to be the problem?'

Marianne assumed a pained expression and put her hand on her chest. 'It's my lungs, Doctor. I'm having difficulty breathing.'

Scott frowned. 'Oh? I'd better have a closer look. Could you lie back on the couch, please?'

Marianne did as she was told. 'May I?' said Scott, taking Marianne's zipper between forefinger and thumb.

'Yes, Doctor,' she said weakly.

Slowly, Scott pulled down the zipper until the tracksuit top fell apart, exposing Marianne's stomach (flat as a schoolgirl's after the previous day's high colonic) and the cantilevered breasts, encased in an intricate network of Rigby & Peller lace. Marianne sighed and let her head flop to one side.

'I'm just going to have a little listen and see if I can detect any irregularities.' Scott removed the stethoscope from round his neck and placed the tips in his ears. He set the chest piece between Marianne's breasts. 'Could you cough, please.' Marianne obliged.

Scott tutted. 'I'm going to have to remove your brassiere,' he said apologetically. 'The underwire seems to be interfering with my reading.' The corners of Marianne's lips twitched in amusement. 'Yes, Doctor,' she murmured. She lifted herself up, so that Scott could unhook her bra.

'Ah yes, that's much better,' said Scott as he slid the bra off and tossed it on the floor. He found himself admiring Marianne's breasts. For a woman of her age, they were remarkably firm. He cupped her right breast in his hand and gently teased the nipple with his thumb. Marianne's eyes fluttered. 'How does this affect your breathing?' he asked.

'It makes it easier,' Marianne gasped.

'Are you sure, Mrs Kennedy? Only you seem a little short of breath.'

In lieu of a reply, Marianne's hand reached under Scott's white coat until it found the stiff bulge between his legs. 'Fuck me, Doctor,' she whimpered.

Scott wagged a forefinger. 'Absolutely not, Mrs Kennedy. I'd be struck off if the authorities got wind of it.'

Marianne undid Scott's flies and worked her hand through the opening. 'But I won't tell anyone – it'll be our little secret.'

'Really, Mrs Kennedy, this is highly irregular.' Scott shuddered as Marianne reached inside his tennis shorts and freed his nesting cock from captivity.

'Fuck me,' she commanded. 'Please.' And with that, the good doctor felt duty-bound to oblige.

Eighteen minutes and forty-two seconds later, Scott fell back on the pillows, having just experienced one of the best orgasms of his entire life. 'Wow,' he said, placing a hand on his chest and feeling the thump of his racing heart. 'That was amazing.'

Marianne stretched languidly, like one of her Burmese cats. 'I've told you before, you're wasting your breath. I don't need your fake flattery.'

'No, really, I mean it,' said Scott, raising himself up on one elbow to look at her. 'Your pelvic floor muscles have incredible strength. How do you make them pulse like that?'

'Years of practice,' said Marianne smugly, drawing the linen sheet over her breasts.

There was a brief silence.

'So, how was it for you?' asked Scott.

'Very nice, thank you.' Marianne's tone was indifferent, bored even. Scott was nonplussed. His clients usually lavished him with praise, post-performance. To hide his disappointment, he busied himself with removing the condom from his rapidly softening penis. Marianne pulled a tissue from the box on the bedside table and held it out to him.

'Thanks,' he said, wrapping the knotted condom in the tissue. Marianne gave a loud yawn. Scott was quick to react. 'Would you like me to go now?'

'Why? Have you got another appointment this afternoon?'

'No.'

'Golf lessons?'

'It's my afternoon off.'

Marianne's eyes flickered over Scott's toned pecs and impressive six-pack. 'Why don't you keep me company for a while? Let's take a shower and then perhaps you could help me work on my putting technique in the garden. Who knows, I might even have worked up an appetite by dinner time.'

It was a quarter past midnight when Scott finally left Marianne's home. The young golf pro had been well paid for his services – but, as he reversed out of the drive, he realized that, actually, it hadn't felt like work at all.

Three streets away, Kieran McAllister was sleeping like a baby. He'd had an exceptionally good day on the golf course and was lost in his favourite dream – the one that saw him holding the Ryder Cup aloft after leading the European team to victory. Beside him, his wife Cindy lay wide awake, staring at the chichi reproduction ceiling rose and wondering where she was going to find the pair of squat Victorian candelabra she had in mind for the mantelpiece in Jackson's bedroom. The room felt unbearably stuffy and, as Cindy flipped her pillow in search of a cool spot, she found herself thinking longingly of the air con that came as standard in practically every Santa Barbara residence.

Finally, after half an hour of tossing and turning, she climbed out of bed and padded over to the French windows. Carefully, so as not to wake Kieran, she opened them and stepped on to the balcony barefoot, sighing as a gentle breeze ruffled her cotton nightdress. As usual, her gaze was drawn to Coldcliffe Hall and the twin turrets rising majestically into the star-filled sky. It seemed she wasn't the only one who couldn't sleep, for chinks of light shone through some of Jackson's downstairs curtains, fighting against the inky darkness outside. Suddenly, quite without warning, the sunken lights round the swimming pool came on, flooding the surrounding area with a soft yellow glow. Moments later, a pair of figures – one male, one female – emerged from the hundred-year-old conservatory at the rear of the house and began walking across the lawn. They were some distance away, and it took Cindy a moment or two to realize that both were stark naked. She could just make out the dark tufts of pubic hair and the pale shape of the man's penis. Smiling in amusement, she leaned over the wrought-iron balustrade for a better view. Although she couldn't see the couple's facial features, she recognized Jackson by his distinctive loping gait. As the pair made their way towards the swimming pool, the woman broke into a run. She shouted something over her shoulder, but the words were unintelligible. A moment later, Jackson started running after her. He caught up with his prey in half a dozen strides and scooped her up in his arms, carrying her the final few feet to the pool's tiled edge, where he held her over the water and made as if to drop her in while she thrashed her legs in mock alarm. As Cindy watched them, she couldn't help feeling like a voyeur – but, try as she might, she couldn't tear her eyes away from the intimate courtship ritual being played out in front of her.

After a little coaxing, Jackson submitted to the woman's pleas for mercy and set her back down on her feet. Then he walked round to the deep end and entered the water in an effortless swallow dive. His companion applauded him as he surfaced, then she sat down at the pool's edge and gingerly lowered herself in. As they frolicked in the water, hugging and kissing, their laughter rose up to Cindy in her eyrie. She wondered who the woman could be. Certainly, Jackson had never mentioned a girlfriend to her – but, then again, for all their cosy chats over cups of coffee in his kitchen, the ex-racing driver remained intensely guarded about his private life. Cindy leaned further over the balcony, frowning in frustration . . . what she wouldn't give to be a fly on a rose bush in Jackson's garden. And then a tantalizing thought struck her: there *was* a way of getting a closer look at the action, but only if she were prepared to cast her morals aside. She didn't agonize for too long. A few moments later, she was tiptoeing aross the bedroom to the office where Kieran – a keen race goer – kept a pair of powerful binoculars. By the time Cindy had returned to the balcony, Jackson had clambered out of the pool, and was standing beside a patio table, filling two glasses from a bottle. Lifting the binoculars to her eyes, Cindy trained them on the bottle, adjusting the focus until a distinctive gold Krug label swam into view. Behind it, Jackson's penis bobbed distractingly. Cindy adjusted the focus again and saw that, for a slender man, he was surprisingly well endowed. She tracked him as he carried the glasses of champagne to the swimming pool. As he bent down and passed one to his companion, Cindy focused the binoculars on the woman's face. What she saw was so shocking it made her cry out loud. She dropped the binoculars from her eyes and turned back to the bedroom. Kieran grunted, but didn't wake up. Cindy squinted hard at the swimming pool, unable to believe what she'd just seen. Then she brought the binoculars back to her face. The facts were inescapable: the woman in Jackson's swimming pool was Laura Bentley.

Fifteen

It was a late summer's day – the kind of stultifying, windless, pollen-rich day that makes you want to take all your clothes off and jump in the nearest fountain. The cloudless sky was an intense luminous blue and beneath it stretched a vast, shimmering lake, surrounded by sturdy Scots pines. In the car park overlooking the lake, Sam sat in his Range Rover with the windows closed and the air con blasting. Beside him, Abi sat stone-faced, staring out across the lake. In an attempt to appear suitably anguished, Sam ran his hands through his thick hair. 'Look, Abi, I made a mistake and I'm so, so sorry,' he said, blinking hard in the hope of squeezing out a tear or two. 'Please, just give me one more chance.'

It was the second time in three weeks that he'd been forced to issue a grovelling apology for his actions. When the dogging story broke, Abi was visiting relatives in France with her husband, and Sam had been bracing himself for his lover's return. There was no way he could stop Abi finding out about his unusual hobby – not when everyone at St Benedict's was agog with the news. Personally, Sam didn't know what all the fuss was about. It wasn't as if he'd slept with a prostitute or an underage girl; in fact he hadn't slept with *anybody*. All he'd done was watch consenting adults exchange bodily fluids. Oh, and he'd accepted a few blowjobs. Big fat fucking deal. And even though there'd been a fair bit of piss-taking from the guys at the club, most of it was good-natured and one or two had even expressed an interest in trying dogging for themselves.

But Abi was a woman – and, in Sam's experience, women viewed such matters differently. To make life even more difficult, they were by nature less forgiving than men, Laura being a case in point. Publicly, at least, his wife was standing by him – but the truth was, they were barely on speaking terms – and Sam's instincts told him Abi was going to be equally pissed off when she discovered what he'd been up to. So when she'd called him, within hours of her plane touching down at Delchester Airport, to suggest a drive in the country, he'd been expecting the worst. It was now forty-five minutes since they'd parked up at the lake; forty-five minutes during which Sam had staged a convincing show of regret. Abi, meanwhile, demonstrated surprising restraint as she listened to what he had to say, only occasionally interrupting to ask a question or mutter a swear word. And now that his performance was over, all Sam could do was await the verdict.

For a moment, Abi was silent, apparently digesting his final impassioned plea, and then she spoke. 'A mistake,' she repeated coldly. 'That's a bit of an understatement, don't you think?'

Sam nodded, trying to mask his irritation. He hated the way women always had to analyse every last detail; he would rather Abi just binned him now, if that were her ultimate intention. 'No, you're absolutely right,' he agreed. 'It's more than a mistake. I fucked up. Big time.'

'It's just so sordid,' Abi went on. 'I mean, what sort of woman has sex in a public place while a bunch of strangers watch?'

'You should try it sometime,' said Sam. 'You never know, you might like it.' Seeing Abi's look of disgust, he added quickly: 'It was a joke, okay?'

'What are you trying to say – that I'm not adventurous, sexually?' Abi asked tightly.

'Yes . . . I mean, no,' said Sam. 'What I mean to say is, dogging's a different sort of thrill entirely.' He couldn't help smiling as he remembered how he'd stood in a pub car park after closing as three men queued up to service a comely redhead sprawled across a car bonnet. 'It's furtive, illicit.'

'And so is shagging me behind Laura's back,' Abi retorted. 'Isn't that furtive enough for you?'

Sam sighed. 'The fact I went dogging is no reflection on you, Abi. You've got to believe me: there is nothing deficient about our sex life.' For once, Sam was telling the truth. Indeed, honesty was such an unusual departure from his standard modus operandi that he sent out a subconscious alert – a 'you've got to believe me' or a 'to be perfectly frank' – whenever he felt a moment of sincerity coming on.

'And what about your sex life with Laura?' Abi enquired sarcastically. 'Is there anything deficient about *that*?'

'I've told you before,' said Sam, easily recognizing Abi's attempt to catch him out. 'Laura and I haven't had sex for months – not since before Birdie was born.' In contrast to Sam's previous statement, this was a blatant lie.

'Hmmm,' said Abi. 'But I bet she still wanted to bash your brains out when she opened that newspaper.'

Sam sighed. 'I daresay she did. Unfortunately, she decided to take out her aggression on my golf clubs instead.'

Abi looked at him quizzically. 'She did what?'

'She took my Adams matchplay clubs and ran over them in the Range Rover.'

Abi's face softened in sympathy. 'Oh, you poor love. Those were your lucky clubs. You must be devastated.'

Sam nodded, pleased that he'd elicited some sympathy at last. 'They're just twisted lumps of metal now, every last one of them,' he said dolefully. 'I've kept them, though – God knows why; they're no use to me now. I just couldn't bear to throw them away.'

Abi reached across and squeezed Sam's thigh, feeling his pain. 'I know it won't be the same, but you can always get a new set made,' she said soothingly. 'I must admit, I wouldn't have thought Laura had it in her. She always seems so . . . I don't know . . . *nice*.'

'Yeah, I must admit I didn't think she'd take it quite so badly,' said Sam. 'She can still barely bring herself to look at me. I've been sleeping in the attic for the past two weeks.'

'Do you think she's going to leave you?'

Sam shook his head. 'I doubt it. I think she's just sulking; she'll snap out of it soon enough.' He reached across the handbrake and took his lover's hand. 'Anyway, that's enough about Laura. What about us? *You're* not going to leave me, are you?' Sam knew full well he wasn't in love with Abi Gainsbourg, but he wasn't ready to lose her – not yet. She was sharp and funny and good in bed. Besides, with the German Masters looming, he couldn't afford to lose the best caddie he'd ever had.

Abi stroked her thumb along the palm of Sam's hand. 'I just want you to tell me one thing.'

'Anything, sweetheart. Fire away.'

'Do you love me – I mean *really* love me?'

Sam tutted. 'I can't believe you need to ask.'

'Say it then.'

He looked deep into her eyes. 'Abi, I love you.'

'In that case, why don't you leave Laura?'

Sam gulped. This was the very scenario he'd been dreading. 'What?'

'I'm tired of all this sneaking around – meeting in hotel rooms, trying to snatch a few precious hours with each other. If you leave Laura, we can be together all the time.'

'Erm, there *is* the small matter of your husband to consider.'

Abi took a deep breath. 'I'd leave him in a minute. If you asked me to.'

Sam looked at Abi the way a lab rat looks at a medical researcher: aware that animal experiments need to be conducted for the sake of human progress, but still somehow pleading for release. 'Oh come on, Abi, don't make me choose. Laura's just had a baby; she's at her most vulnerable. I can't leave her now.'

Abi yanked her hand away from Sam and folded her arms across her chest. 'Birdie's eight months old,' she said sharply. 'If you're *ever* going to leave Laura, I'd say that now's as good a time as any. And if you're not serious about me – about *us* – then I can't see the point in continuing this relationship.' She gave a little sniff. 'In which case, I'd have to resign as your caddie.'

'Don't be like that, baby,' said Sam in a wheedling tone. 'There's nothing I'd like more than to wake up next to your beautiful body every morning. But we mustn't make any rash decisions; we need to take the time to think this through properly.'

'How much time?'

Sam scratched his head as he did some quick mental arithmetic, factoring in the German Masters and the time it would take to find a replacement caddie. 'Oh, I dunno . . . a month?'

'One month,' Abi repeated. 'Okay, I can live with that.'

'So am I forgiven for being a naughty boy?'

Abi smiled. 'Oh go on then, you smooth-talking bastard.'

'You won't regret it,' said Sam as he reached out and caressed Abi's cheek. 'Hey, it's the club's gala dinner a week on Saturday. How do you fancy coming as my official guest?' An annual black-tie event, the gala dinner traditionally marked the end of a hectic summer season at St Benedict's. It was a prestigious affair, consisting of a drinks reception, lavish banquet, awards ceremony and dancing. Numbers were strictly limited and tickets often changed hands for hundreds of pounds above their face value.

Abi frowned. 'But you'll be taking Laura, won't you?'

Sam shook his head. 'Uh-uh. Even if she's talking to me by then, she won't want to come. She hasn't dared show her face at the club since that dogging story was splashed all over the paper. She reckons everyone's talking about her behind her back – which, to be fair, they probably are.'

'I'd love to go, but I don't know that it's such a good idea. Xav's going to be doing the catering, for one thing.'

'So what? He'll be stuck out in the kitchen, won't he?'

'Yeah, I guess so,' said Abi hesitantly. 'But won't the other guests be suspicious when they see us together?'

'Why should they? What could be more natural than the club's top golfer wanting his loyal caddie to be at his side when he steps up to accept the award for Sportsman of the Year?'

Abi smiled. 'You're a cocky little shit and no mistake.'

'So you'll come then?'

'Yeah, I'll come.'

Sam leaned across and planted a kiss on the end of Abi's nose. 'Laura's going out with her silly American friend tonight, and Marta's agreed to babysit – which means I've got the entire evening free. *Sooo* . . . why don't you and I get together for a little fun?'

Abi licked her full lips. 'I suppose I could be tempted. Xav's working tonight.'

'Good girl,' said Sam. 'And guess what? I've got a little treat for us.' He nodded towards the glove box. 'Go on, open it.'

Abi did as she was told. Her face lit up when she saw the small plastic packet filled with white powder. She reached for it greedily. 'Ooh, let's have some now.' Sam placed a warning hand on her arm. 'Not here, sweetie. Let's save it for later, eh? I'm in enough trouble already without being nicked for drugs possession.' He flashed a vulpine smile. 'I missed you so much when you were in

France,' he said, massaging Abi's knee through her taupe linen skirt. 'I can't wait to get you naked.'

'I missed you too,' said Abi. 'More than you can imagine.'

She leaned over to kiss him. As their tongues locked together, Sam's hand moved from Abi's knee to her breast. He pushed his tongue deeper inside her mouth, and began to flick his thumb back and forth across her stiffening nipple. Abi made little gasps of appreciation as she squirmed in her seat, thrusting her body against Sam's. The pair were so engrossed in each other they didn't see the elderly man approaching the car, walking stick held angrily aloft. Seconds later, there was a loud rapping at the window. Sam broke away from Abi and turned to look over his shoulder. The man was peering through the window. His lips were moving but it was impossible to make out what he was saying over the roar of the air conditioning. Sam activated the electric window. 'Can I help you?' he asked politely.

'Yes, you can. You can bloody well clear off,' said the man, his liver-spotted hands gripping the bottom edge of the window.

Sam was put out. Being something of a local celebrity, he'd assumed the man had been about to ask for an autograph. 'I beg your pardon?' he said indignantly.

'This is a public place. There are families with kiddies here,' the man growled. 'We don't want your sort here.'

'And what sort might that be?'

'Deviants.'

Sam opened the car door, almost knocking the man to the ground. 'Hey, who are you calling a deviant?'

Abi grabbed the back of Sam's polo shirt. 'Leave it, Sam. He's not worth it.'

Reluctantly, Sam slammed the car door shut. 'Cheeky fucking bastard,' he snarled as he watched the man hobble off to rejoin a group of anglers. 'Who the hell does he think he is, telling me to clear off? I've as much right to be here as he has.' He turned to look at Abi, who was sniggering behind her hand like a schoolgirl. 'What are you laughing at?' he said crossly.

'Oh c'mon, Sam, you've got to see the funny side. I thought for a minute you were going to punch that guy's lights out. That would've made a good front-page story: "Disgraced golfer attacks defenceless OAP".' She erupted in a fresh fit of the giggles.

In that moment, Sam knew he could never marry a woman like Abi. She was far too disrespectful. Not like Laura; sure, his wife had her moods, but she was loyal to a fault. Or so he thought.

By the time he dropped Abi off in the pub car park round the corner from her flat, Sam was feeling well pleased with himself. His mother had often told him he could charm the birds out of the trees and, yet again, he'd proved her right. Now all he had to do was keep his caddie sweet until after the German Masters, and he'd be home and dry.

As he hit the Kirkhulme bypass and slipped into fifth gear, Sam glanced at the clock on the dash: four fifty-three. If he went straight home, he'd be able to spend some quality time with his youngest daughter before she went to bed. Then again, there were still a good two and half hours of daylight left, and his golf clubs were in the boot of the car. In Sam's mind, there was no competition.

When he got to St Benedict's, he parked up and called home on his mobile. The phone rang for ages before finally the au pair answered.

'Hey, Marta, it's me. Can you get Laura?'

'She's out.'

Sam frowned. Laura had been spending increasing amounts of time away from home lately, and it irked him. 'Do you know where she's gone?'

'No, Mr Bentley.'

'Did she say when she'd be back?'

'No, Mr Bentley.'

'I keep telling you, call me Sam,' he snapped.

There was a stony silence. Sam sighed. In his view, the Spanish girl was a hard piece of work. Fiercely loyal to Laura, so far she was the only woman who had proved immune to his charms.

'Well, when she gets back, tell her I'm putting in a couple of hours' practice at the club,' he said. 'I'll be home by eight.'

'Okay, Mr Bentley.' Marta put the phone down without bothering to say goodbye.

Sam's mood didn't improve when he opened the boot and found it empty. He let out a string of expletives, belatedly remembering that he'd taken his practice clubs out of the car for cleaning the night before. He slammed the lid down, flinching as he felt a twinge in his left shoulder blade – the vestige of an old golfing injury. He'd have to book a session with the sports physio in the morning but, in the meantime, a nice relaxing massage would loosen him up. If Laura was out enjoying herself, why should he rush to get home?

At the spa, an attractive receptionist greeted him warmly. She, like all the staff at St Benedict's, knew Sam Bentley by sight. 'We normally advise members to book at least twenty-four hours in advance, but I'll see what I can do for you,' she said, smiling coquettishly.

Sam folded his arms on the reception desk and leaned forward, so he could get a better view of her cleavage. 'Cheers, sweetheart, I'd really appreciate it.'

The girl tapped some keys on her computer. 'Did you have a particular therapist in mind?'

Sam was about to say no, but then he remembered the stunning Amazon from the golf shop. 'There's a tall blonde girl, with a Scandinavian accent. Sorry, I can't remember her name.'

'Ah, you mean Astrid.'

Sam snapped his fingers. 'Yeah, Astrid, that's her.'

'She's very popular. I should think she'll be fully booked for the rest of the day, but let's see, shall we?' The receptionist punched some more keys. 'Oh, you're in luck. She's had a cancellation for six o'clock. How would that suit?'

Sam beamed. 'Perfect. Just time for a couple of drinks in the clubhouse.'

The receptionist smiled back. 'Great, we'll see you back at six, Mr Bentley.'

Astrid was every bit as gorgeous as Sam remembered. 'I've been meaning to make an appointment with you ever since we met in the golf shop,' he said as he lay face down on the couch, naked, save for a towel draped across his buttocks. 'I don't mind admitting, you made quite an impression on me.'

'Did I?' she said coolly.

'Absolutely. You're a very striking girl, but I'm sure you've been told that lots of times before.'

Astrid made a little noise in the back of her throat, as if to confirm Sam's assumption. For a few minutes she worked in silence, performing gliding strokes with her fingertips down the length of Sam's spine. As the golfer submitted to her firm touch, he closed his eyes and imagined what she would look like naked.

'Can I ask you something?' he said as she began kneading his shoulders.

'Of course.'

'Are you and Ace, you know . . . an item?'

'We're seeing each other, yes.'

'He's a nice lad.'

'I know.'

'Is it serious?'

Astrid began applying circular pressure to Sam's scapula. 'Not yet, but who knows what'll happen in the future.'

Sam was silent for a while as he considered the various options. Usually, he had a good sense of whether or not a woman was game on but, with his face pressed into the couch, it was impossible to read Astrid's body language. Before very long, he came up with a plan. He waited until Astrid had turned her attentions to his lower back, then he gave a cry and jerked his leg at the same time.

Astrid's hands stopped moving. 'Are you okay?'

'I've got a touch of cramp in my calf; do you mind if I get up for a sec?'

'No. Have a little walk around, stretch the muscles out.'

Sam rolled over, holding the towel over his private parts. As he raised himself into a sitting position, he simulated another spasm. Wincing in pretend agony, he clutched his calf and let the towel fall to the floor, exposing his semi-erect penis. 'Jesus, I'm sorry,' he said, without a trace of embarrassment.

Astrid raised a disbelieving eyebrow. 'No problem.' She picked up his towel from the floor. 'Here you go.'

Sam didn't take the towel from her. Instead, he sat on the edge of the couch, legs slightly apart. They made eye contact, then slowly, and very deliberately, Sam looked at his crotch. 'Sorry about the semi,' he said with a smirk. 'Only, like I say, you're a very beautiful woman.'

Astrid looked at him disdainfully, then flung the towel at his lap with enough force to make his testicles contract. 'Cover yourself up, Mr Bentley, and lie back down on the couch before you make a fool of yourself.'

Sam's face fell. No woman had ever rejected him quite so harshly. 'Lie back down,' Astrid repeated. There was a faint air of menace in her tone. Despite his bruised ego, Sam found himself complying. A moment later, he felt the masseuse's hands attacking his back in short, sharp chopping motions.

'You are an extremely rude man, Mr Bentley. I think you need to be taught a lesson.'

Sam lifted his head off the couch. 'Now hang on a minute, all I did was –'

'Silence!' Astrid barked. 'You must not speak to

Mistress Valkyrie unless she addresses you directly.' And then, quite unexpectedly, she snatched the towel from his buttocks. Sam smiled to himself – so the therapist had just been playing hard to get. He heard the sound of a drawer opening and wondered what her next move was going to be. A few moments later, the answer came in the shape of a firm thwack across his buttocks. Sam raised himself up on to his forearms and looked over his shoulder. To his amazement, Astrid was brandishing a riding crop. She smiled cruelly and pushed the end of the crop in the cleft between his buttocks. 'Oh yes, Mr Bentley,' she said, working the crop gently up and down, stimulating his perineum and balls. 'Celebrity or not, I'm going to teach you a lesson you'll never forget.'

Sam smiled as he sank back down on the couch. This was going to be good. This was going to be very good.

For the next twenty minutes, Astrid meted out the most exquisite torture Sam had ever experienced, and by the end of it the ache in his shoulder blade was a distant memory. Afterwards, he slipped on his bathrobe, flinching slightly as the terry towelling brushed against his inflamed skin, and thanked Astrid for her expert attentions. She gave a small nod by way of acknowledgement, and began tidying away the tools of her trade.

'There will be no charge for this taster session, but subsequent visits cost a hundred and eighty pounds per half hour,' she recited in a businesslike tone. 'Mistress Valkyrie will be happy to accommodate specific requests. You can book at reception in the usual way; just ask for Astrid's *tukta* therapy.'

Sam raised an eyebrow. '*Tukta?*'

'It's Swedish,' said Astrid. 'Roughly translated, it means "discipline".'

Sam was wearing a broad grin as he headed for the changing rooms. Although he was a man of varied sexual tastes, S&M was something he had never tried before – but now he was beginning to think he'd been missing out all these years. In the shower, he surveyed his reddened buttocks over one shoulder and wondered if one day in the not too distant future, when Laura was speaking to him, he could cajole her into playing the dominatrix. Little did he know that his wife had something – or rather, some*one* – else on her mind.

On the other side of Kirkhulme, Laura was wandering through Coldcliffe's sprawling gardens, arm in arm with Jackson. They were still in the heady, couldn't-keep-their-hands-off-each-other, early stages of their rekindled relationship, where every minute apart was a minute too long. As they talked and laughed together, they assumed, not unreasonably, that they were safe from prying eyes. Meanwhile, up on the balcony, screened by a trough of leafy bamboo, Cindy was monitoring their every move. Ever since she'd seen the pair cavorting in the swimming pool two days earlier, she'd kept a close eye on activities in her neighbour's garden – and now her patience had been rewarded.

She watched through the binoculars as Jackson bent down to pick up a fallen bloom from a gardenia. He tucked it behind Laura's ear, upon which she caught his hand and brought it to her lips. Cindy couldn't help smiling. It seemed as if the pair were very much in love and, with a husband like Sam, nobody could blame Laura for being tempted. Jackson West may have lost his looks, but he was kind and intelligent – and, in Cindy's book, that counted for a good deal.

Suddenly, a bumblebee rose up from one of the galvanized zinc planters that were dotted about the balcony and flew straight into Cindy's line of vision. With her binoculars still trained on the lovebirds, who now had their tongues down each other's throats, Cindy took a step to the side, whereupon her heel struck the sharp edge of a planter, causing her to lose her balance. As she fell, her arms flailed desperately, but there was nothing to hold on to. With a loud cry, she crashed through the bamboo screen and landed heavily against the iron balustrade.

A few moments later, a voice called out to her. 'Cindy, is that you? Are you all right?'

From her semi-prone position, Cindy turned her head and peered through an ironwork scroll. To her acute embarrassment, Laura and Jackson were standing at the foot of the red brick wall that separated the two gardens.

'Laura, fancy seeing you here!' she exclaimed as she staggered to her feet. 'Don't worry about me, honey, I'm fine. I was watering the wisteria when I tripped on one of these darned pots. Kieran's always telling me I've got too many plants out here.'

Laura gave her friend a gently mocking look. 'Watering the wisteria?' She pointed to Cindy's chest. 'So what's with those?'

Cindy looked down. The binoculars had survived the fall and were still hanging from a leather strap round her neck. 'Oh, these. I, uh, thought I might do a spot of birdwatching. You can see for miles up here.'

Laura threw back her head and laughed. 'It's okay, Cindy, you don't have to lie. I think I know what you were doing.' She turned to Jackson. 'Cindy looks as if she could use a cup of tea. Why don't you go in and put the kettle on, darling?'

Five minutes later, Cindy was sitting on a damask-covered armchair in Coldcliffe's living room, her hands cupping a mug of Earl Grey. On the sofa opposite, Laura and Jackson sat shoulder to shoulder.

'So,' said Laura as she pointedly placed a hand on Jackson's thigh. 'I expect you're wondering how long we've been having an affair.'

'I don't think that's any of my business.' Cindy blushed, knowing that the binoculars belied her words.

'Well, I'm going to tell you: two weeks, five days and nine hours. That's right, isn't it, darling?' Laura gave Jackson a look suffused with such love and tenderness, it left Cindy in no doubt about the strength of her feelings for him.

Jackson nodded. 'Yes, my love, and I haven't stopped pinching myself.'

Cindy took a sip of tea. A thousand questions buzzed in her head, but she didn't want to overstep the mark. 'How did it happen?' she said. 'I thought you two lost contact years ago.'

'We did,' said Laura. 'Sam was the one who brought us back together.'

'I saw the dogging story in the newspaper,' Jackson explained.

'And he sent me the most wonderful bouquet of flowers.'

'With a note, telling her to call me if she needed someone to talk to – which she did.'

Laura rested her head on her lover's shoulder. 'We spoke for nearly an hour. Then Jackson invited me to Coldcliffe, and the minute I set eyes on him all the old feelings came flooding back.'

'And vice versa.'

Cindy looked from one to the other. 'Jeez, you make it sound awful simple.'

Jackson smiled mistily. 'I never thought this day would come. Laura's been in my thoughts and dreams for so long.' He made an apologetic face. 'I hope you won't be offended, Cindy, but that's the real reason I asked you to redesign my bedroom.'

Cindy frowned. 'I'm sorry, I don't understand.'

'I heard on the village grapevine that you were friends with Laura, and when I discovered you were an interior designer . . . well, I suppose I saw it as a way of getting close to her.'

Cindy's lips tightened. 'I see.'

'But that's not to say Jackson doesn't think you're a brilliant designer,' said Laura. 'Isn't that right, darling?'

'Of course,' agreed Jackson. 'You're a genius, Cindy; I love your work.'

Cindy smiled graciously, although she couldn't help feeling a little hurt that talent alone hadn't been enough to win her the commission. 'So why, in all the time I've been working for you, have you never once brought up Laura's name in conversation?'

'I was waiting for the right moment,' Jackson replied. 'In fact, I've been waiting for the right moment to get in touch with Laura ever since I moved to Coldcliffe.'

Cindy looked at him disbelievingly. 'But, if you knew where she lived, why didn't you just drop her a note?'

Jackson sighed. 'I knew Laura was married – happily, or so I thought – with a couple of kids, and I didn't think it was fair for me to come barging back into her life unannounced. Besides, I was frightened she wouldn't want to know. After the way I treated her, I wouldn't have been surprised if she never wanted to see or speak to me again – but I knew I had to at least try, or spend the rest of my life regretting it.' He brought his gaze level with Cindy's. 'You might as well know, it's no coincidence I moved to Kirkhulme. I came here for Laura.'

Laura squeezed his hand encouragingly. 'Go on, tell her the whole story.'

For the next half an hour, Cindy listened raptly as Jackson talked, in terrifying detail, about the fateful racing accident that destroyed his career, and the lengthy recuperation that followed. Her heart went out to him as he described the third-degree burns, which had left his face scarred beyond recognition.

'I'll never forget the first time they gave me a mirror in hospital,' he said as he gazed into his mug and swirled the dregs of tea absent-mindedly. 'The only part of my face I recognized was my eyes. And then I started to wonder how Laura would feel when she saw her once-handsome boyfriend reduced to a well-cooked wreck. How could I kiss her when I had no lips to offer? How could I hold her when my hands were twisted and useless?'

To Cindy's dismay, a tear appeared in the corner of Jackson's drooping right eye and began to descend his scarred cheek.

'It's okay,' she said soothingly. 'You don't have to go on with this if it's too painful.'

Jackson shook his head. 'No, it's fine. It's good for me to talk about what happened, at least that's what my therapist told me.'

A delicious shiver of anticipation ran the full length of Cindy's spine. 'Okay, honey, I'm listening,' she said.

'Laura flew to Belgium after the accident and she showed up at the hospital every day for two weeks. Without a second thought, I told the nurses to send her away. I thought I was protecting her, but really I was protecting myself. I couldn't bear to see the pity in her eyes, or watch her tears fall on to my hospital sheets. I know now that my behaviour was irrational. But I was in shock; I wasn't thinking straight. I was convinced that, ultimately, Laura would abandon me, for what woman in her right mind would want to be with the hideous monster I saw in that mirror? To my mind, the only way to shield myself from the pain of rejection was to reject her first.' Jackson gave a bitter laugh. 'Everyone knows that racing drivers are among the most selfish creatures on earth, and I was no different.

'When I left hospital, I decided that I couldn't stay in England, where there were too many painful reminders of the past. In any case, the press had made my life a misery, with their endless demands for interviews and photo exclusives. And so, a few months after I came out of hospital, I decided to move to France. In time, the scars on my hands and face healed, but I was plagued with nightmares where I relived the terror of being trapped in my burning car. I'd wake up in a cold sweat, my chest covered in red welts where I'd clawed my body, trying to release an imaginary safety belt.' Suddenly, he stopped and stared up at the anaglypta-covered ceiling.

'You're doing very well,' Laura whispered.

Jackson took a few deep breaths, then resumed his story. 'After a couple of years of this, I realized I couldn't overcome my demons alone. I needed help, professional help, so I found an English-speaking psychotherapist, who diagnosed me with a form of post-traumatic shock. Although I'd blanked Laura from my mind with some degree of success, it became clear during the course of my psychotherapy that some remnants of her still lingered. And once I started talking about her I found I couldn't stop. My therapist came to the conclusion that the unresolved nature of our relationship was a serious threat to my recovery. In confirming what I already suspected, he gave me permission to let Laura back into my heart – and, as the memories returned, she began to occupy my thoughts more and more. I became obsessed with finding out what had happened to her in the years since that fateful grand prix and, when my internet searches proved fruitless, I hired a private investigator to track her down. She was easy enough to find. Within a week, the PI had told me everything I needed to know: that Laura had left her job and home in London, and was living in Cheshire with one of England's top golfers. I thought that once I had satisfied my curiosity, that would be an end to it. Laura was taken, end of story.

At last I could lay her ghost to rest. But I was wrong.'

At this juncture, Jackson paused to give Laura a lingering kiss on the mouth. Cindy hardly knew where to look; the air around them was fairly bristling with sexual electricity. His hunger sated, he resumed his monologue.

'My parents had been keen for me to move back to the UK for some time, where I suppose they thought they could keep an eye on me. And so, in the same casual way I elected to move to France, I decided it was time for me to return to England, where I had – and indeed still have – various business interests, including a sizeable commercial-property portfolio. The big question was where? I had no desire to return to London – or any city for that matter. My parents tried to lure me to their home town in Hertfordshire, but I was determined to keep them at arm's length. Other than that, my needs were relatively simple: I wanted to be in a village environment, in a smart area with good transport links. Cheshire seemed to fit the bill perfectly. I told myself it was just coincidence – the fact that Laura was living in that very county. In truth, it was anything but.

'Given my generous budget, the relocator I employed concentrated her search in the affluent east of the county, as I knew she would. As the estate agents' details started to arrive by email, I found myself rejecting properties on entirely unreasonable grounds: the garden was too big, there was no swimming pool, I didn't like the colour of the front door. And then, after several months of disappointment, I received the details for Coldcliffe Hall. My heart missed a beat when I saw the location: Kirkhulme. It seemed like fate. The property wasn't even officially on the market; my relocator had been tipped off by an estate agent that the owners were thinking of selling. Conveniently overlooking the fact that the house and gardens were impractically large, I called her up immediately and told her to do whatever it took to secure the property. The deal was done without me even visiting the place. Ten weeks later, I was moving in.'

'I was so excited when I heard that Jackson had moved to Kirkhulme,' Laura said. 'I mean *really* excited.'

Cindy frowned. 'In that case, why didn't you try to get in touch with him?'

'I wanted to – not because I thought there was any chance of us getting back together, mind you; just to show there were no hard feelings on my part. But, when I mentioned it to Sam, he went through the roof.'

'He was jealous?'

Laura nodded. 'After Jackson's accident, I was so hurt and confused when he refused to see me in hospital. And when I realized he wasn't going to change his mind – that I had, to all intents and purposes, been dumped – I was absolutely devastated. Two months later, Sam came along. He was the one who picked up the pieces and put me back together. He said that getting back in touch with Jackson would only make me upset all over again. I tried to tell him that all I wanted to do was lay a ghost to rest. But he made such a fuss that in the end I found myself agreeing not to contact Jackson. All the same, I couldn't help hoping that one day I'd bump into him in the village or at St Benedict's.' She made a face at Cindy. 'I couldn't believe it when you told me he'd hired you to work on his house. Whenever his name came up in conversation,

I had to fight the urge not to bombard you with questions – although I *was* tempted to ask if you needed an assistant.'

Cindy smiled. 'But then Sam was caught dogging and that gave Jackson the perfect excuse to get in touch.'

Laura nodded. 'For obvious reasons, we've gone to great lengths to keep our relationship a secret, but we didn't figure on you and your super-powered binoculars.'

Cindy bit her lip. 'Listen, guys, I'm really sorry. I shouldn't have spied on you.'

Laura waved her concerns away. 'Don't worry. I'm glad you found us out – I've been dying to tell someone.' Suddenly, she sat bolt upright. 'You haven't told anyone else, have you?'

Cindy shook her head. 'Not a soul.'

'Good, and that's the way we'd like to keep it.' Laura glanced at Jackson. 'After all, it's still early days.'

'Of course, honey; you know you can trust me.' Cindy gave a little sigh as she stroked the armchair's faded damask. 'Only it's going to be hard keeping it from Kieran. We don't have secrets from one another.'

'I realize it's asking a lot of you, but I'm sure he would understand.' Laura reached over and patted her friend's arm. 'You're very lucky to have such a happy marriage and a husband who loves and respects you as much as Kieran does.'

Cindy smiled. 'I know I am. And there isn't a day goes by when I don't count my blessings.'

Sixteen

Scott Mason couldn't help smiling as he drank in the magnificent sight of Marianne's buttocks rising and falling. Any woman who slept with Scott always came back for more, and he now had a twice-weekly arrangement with the wealthy widow. Sometimes, Marianne just wanted sex and she'd be yanking Scott's clothes off almost before he was inside her front door, rubbing her body up against him like a bitch on heat. Other times, she preferred the sex to be preceded by a pseudo date – a trip to the cinema or a meal in a smart restaurant – and it was these rendezvous that Scott enjoyed the most. Although he was getting paid handsomely for his services, the fact was he genuinely enjoyed spending time with Marianne. Despite her frosty exterior, he found her to be a lively, intelligent woman with a waspish sense of humour. But, best of all, he liked her independence and the fact she was beholden to no one, least of all a man. And Scott wasn't the only one who looked forward to their time together. Marianne found the young golf coach a breath of fresh air. There was something appealingly uncomplicated about him. He was charming, but not obsequious, confident but not cocky, street smart but not intellectual – and, more important than all of that, he was a genius in the sack. Usually, Marianne had several lovers on the go at once, but since hiring Scott as her stud she hadn't slept with another man.

Considering the difference in their ages and backgrounds, Scott and Marianne had a remarkable number of things in common – a passion for Beaujolais, film noir and Burt Bacharach being three of them – and when Marianne discovered that Scott shared her love of horse riding, she jumped at the chance to organize a surprise outing. 'Hey, handsome,' she'd said as she opened the door to him, clad in a crisp white shirt and skintight jodhpurs. 'Today, I'm going to take you pony-trekking.' She ran a hand down his body, tracing a line from his muscular pecs to the equally impressive bulge in his crotch. 'It'll help us work up an appetite.'

Half an hour later they had collected their mounts from the local stables, located in the heart of the picturesque Delchester Country Park, and were trotting in single file along a meandering bridle path. With Marianne taking the lead on her favourite piebald mare, Scott found himself mesmerized by his client's spectacular rear aspect – the slender waist, flaring dramatically into a pair of shapely buttocks which bounced up and down as she performed a rising trot. As he mentally undressed Marianne, imagining what she'd look like naked in the saddle, he found himself nursing an erection. 'Damn,' he murmured as he stuffed a hand down his jeans and tried to rearrange his manhood, which was rubbing uncomfortably on the seam of his boxers.

'Is everything okay back there?' said Marianne, glancing over her shoulder.

Scott gave one of the roguish smiles that made Marianne's heart beat just a tiny bit faster. 'Couldn't be better,' he said. 'I was just admiring the view.'

As they followed the bridle path through a pretty copse, Scott's fantasy stepped up a gear. Now he imagined tearing his silver-haired Godiva from the pony, pinning her to an oak tree and pushing his knee between her thighs. Perhaps there'd be an opportunity later that afternoon to act out his fantasy for real — not that he would have dreamed of suggesting such a thing. Marianne was the client; she was in control — although, just recently, Scott had found himself thinking that *he* wouldn't mind taking charge just for once. He didn't know much about Marianne's previous relationships — she rarely talked about her past — but he had a theory that, for all her independence, what Marianne really wanted was a strong man to take her in hand.

Soon, the copse opened out into a stretch of heathland, dotted with heather and coconut-scented gorse. Marianne decided to pick up the pace and squeezed her lower legs against the mare's flanks, urging her into a brisk canter. Scott followed suit but, being a less experienced rider, he opted for a more sedate pace. As the canter became a gallop, Marianne leaned forward in the saddle, laughing as the wind whipped her hair across her face. The heath narrowed, giving way to another wooded area, and Marianne tightened her thighs and gave a short pull on the reins to bring the pony back to a trot. She turned around to see where her companion was. 'Come on, slow coach,' she yelled playfully. 'Last one to the woods is a sissy.' She didn't see the low-hanging branch until it was too late. It struck her square between the eyes, causing her to drop the reins. As Marianne felt herself slip from the saddle, she instinctively brought her arms close to her body and curled into a ball, knowing this was the best way to minimize injury. She hit the ground with a dull thud and flipped on to her back, where she lay, stunned, staring up at the sky. After an indeterminate length of time, she heard the sound of hooves and then Scott was beside her.

'Jesus, Marianne. Are you all right?' he said as he dismounted and looped the reins round a slender sapling. He crouched on the ground beside her, his face contorted with concern. Marianne's eyes were open, but she was clearly dazed and a vivid streak of blood was running down the bridge of her nose.

She smiled woozily. 'I'm fine,' she said as she struggled to raise herself into a sitting position.

'Don't try to move – you're still in shock,' said Scott, gently pushing her shoulders back to the ground. He lifted his hand in front of her eyes. 'How many fingers am I holding up?'

'Two.'

'Good, you're not suffering from blurred vision.' He stared into her eyes. 'And your pupils aren't dilated. Do you feel dizzy or sick?'

Marianne shook her head. 'No, but I've got an almighty headache.'

'I'm not surprised. You took quite a knock.' Scott pulled a clean white handkerchief from his pocket and gently wiped the blood away. 'It looks as if you've had a lucky escape. This wound isn't too deep so it won't need stitches – and you're not exhibiting any signs of concussion. But I still think you should lie there for a few more minutes and catch your breath.'

Marianne was touched by Scott's concern. 'I didn't know you were such a medical expert,' she said as he loosened the chinstrap of her riding hat.

'I've had some pretty intensive first-aid training. It's a requirement of the job.'

'Oh, and which job might that be: the gigoloing or the golf coaching?'

Scott grinned sheepishly. 'The coaching. You'd be amazed at the damage a flying golf ball can do.' He pushed a strand of platinum hair out of Marianne's eyes. 'I'm glad you're okay. I was quite worried about you for a minute.'

As his eyes locked on to hers, Marianne felt something stir deep inside her – and, just for once, the sensation wasn't focused around her nether regions. She looked away, suddenly self-conscious. 'Where are the ponies?' she said to mask her awkwardness.

Scott pointed to where the two animals were grazing side by side on an outcrop of heather. 'They're happy as Larry,' he said. He turned back to Marianne. 'Are you getting cold? Why don't I cover you with my jacket?'

'Stop fussing, Scott,' she said. Then, more tenderly: 'You don't need to worry about me. I'm a tough old boot.'

'And also a very beautiful one,' he said.

'Yeah, right,' said Marianne, rolling her eyes. 'I bet you say that to all your clients.'

Scott sighed. 'Why do you always do that?'

'Do what?'

'Refuse to accept my compliments.'

Marianne stared at Scott. 'I'm not a fool,' she said wearily. 'I'm a fifty-one-year-old woman, who knows when she's being sweet-talked.'

Scott looked pained. 'I've never tried to sweet-talk you, Marianne. In fact, I've never said a single thing to you that I didn't mean.'

Marianne suddenly felt bad. She shouldn't have sniped at Scott. It was just her well-honed defence mechanisms springing into action. She couldn't help feeling vulnerable, lying there on the ground. 'Well, in that case, I'm sorry, Scott,' she said. 'I just presumed –'

'Yeah, well, you presumed wrong,' Scott said quietly. He leaned towards her. 'Put your arms round my neck and I'll lift you into a sitting position.'

Marianne did as she was told. It was a strange, but not unpleasant feeling, being utterly dependent on someone else for a change.

'You know, you're very defensive,' Scott remarked when Marianne was upright and leaning with her back against the very same tree that had felled her. 'And forgive my cod psychology, but that rather makes me think some-body must have hurt you very badly in the past.'

Marianne bit her lip. She never discussed her marriage and she wasn't about to bare her soul now, even if she was feeling a bit light-headed (though whether this was from the blow to her head or a result of being in such close proximity to Scott was hard to say).

'I don't mean to pry – I can see that you're a very private person – but I want you to know that you can talk to me any time you like,' Scott continued, sitting cross-legged beside her. 'I'm a good listener.'

Marianne gave an acid laugh. 'And how much would that cost me?'

Scott looked down at the ground. 'Actually, I've

been meaning to talk to you about that . . . the money, that is.'

'Oh?' said Marianne as she brushed moss from the sleeve of her blouse. 'Don't tell me, you're putting up your prices?'

Scott shook his head. 'No. You see, the thing is, I don't want your money any more.'

Marianne's lips formed a tight line. 'I see,' she said coldly. 'What's the problem? Had enough of fucking a woman old enough to be your mother, have you? Keen to get your hands on some younger, fresher meat?'

Scott looked horrified. He gripped Marianne's shoulders. 'Don't say that,' he said angrily. 'That's not what I meant; you must know that.'

Marianne could feel his hot breath against her face and see the pinpricks of dark stubble dotted across his jaw like iron filings. 'No?' she said calmly. 'So what did you mean?'

Scott didn't answer. Instead he took her face in his hands and kissed her the way he'd never kissed any of his clients before. In spite of her cold, hard mind, Marianne's heart arched like a swallow making a circle of the sky, turning south for the winter.

In the spa at St Benedict's, the two beauty therapists worked with silent efficiency. Their clients, clad in shower caps and paper G-strings, lay side by side on a pair of treatment couches. Having covered the women's bodies in a thick paste of seaweed and mineral salts, the therapists began wrapping them tightly from neck to ankle in warm cotton bandages. Thus cocooned, each woman was covered with a thermal blanket before being left in the semi-darkness to sweat out her impurities.

'Isn't this divine?' sighed Keeley. 'Thanks ever so much for treating me, Marianne.'

Marianne smiled benignly, knowing full well that Keeley could no longer afford to indulge in her usual weekly round of pampering treatments since having been dumped by Fabrizio. 'You're welcome, darling. Frankly, I'm glad of the company. It's so deathly dull lying here on one's own, trussed up like a chicken.' She turned her head – the only part of her body with unrestricted movement – towards the younger woman. 'And, actually, there *was* something I wanted to talk to you about.'

'Oh yes?' said Keeley eagerly. It was ages since she'd had a proper gossip with Marianne – and, with Laura and Cindy thicker than ever, she'd begun to feel a tad neglected.

'It's about Scott,' Marianne continued. 'He's beginning to become a problem.'

'Ah,' said Keeley. 'St Benedict's resident stud. I've heard he's in hot demand, especially now that summer's coming to an end.'

Marianne frowned. 'I wouldn't have thought demand for Scott's services was seasonal.'

'Oh, sure it is. Think about it: you've got all those ladies-who-lunch flocking back to Cheshire from their Caribbean island hideaways. So, imagine you'd spent the entire summer trapped with your dull, overweight, millionaire husband. What's the first thing you'd want to do as soon as you got back to Kirkhulme?'

'Have a good seeing to?'

'Precisely. And nobody's better than Scott Mason. Or at least that's what I've heard – of course I haven't experienced his skills for myself, never having actually been desperate enough to *pay* for sex.' She winced, realizing her blunder. 'Sorry, Marianne. No offence.'

'None taken, darling.' Keeley could be monstrously tactless at times, but Marianne knew her friend's heart was in the right place. 'And you're absolutely right about Scott: he's nothing short of a legend in bed.' Despite the strictures of the bandages, Marianne felt a tingle in her groin as she recalled how the young golf coach had driven her back home after the riding accident, gently bathed her wound and then given her the best goddamned shag of her life.

'So what's the problem?' Keeley asked.

'The problem is, I think I might be falling for him.'

'*Noooo!*' Keeley gasped. 'You're having me on, you must be.'

'Would I joke about something like that?'

'But I didn't think you wanted another relationship. You've always said you'd never love another man after your husband died.'

Marianne sniffed. 'I know I did, but I'm entitled to change my mind. Don't get too excited though – I only said "might" be falling for him.'

'Wow,' said Keeley. 'Well, I can't blame you – Scott's a very sexy guy. But it's going to make things a bit awkward, isn't it?'

'How do you mean?'

'You know . . . seeing him, having sex with him, knowing he doesn't feel the same way about you.'

Marianne's nostrils flared like a stallion's. 'Who says he doesn't?'

'Well, it stands to reason, doesn't it? I mean, don't get me wrong, you're a very attractive woman, Marianne, but you *are* old enough to be his mother.' She paused. 'And *then* some.'

'For your information,' Marianne said superciliously, 'Scott Mason is in love with me. He told me so when we were riding yesterday.' She pursed her lips. '*Horse* riding, that is.'

Keeley's eyes grew wide as dinner plates. 'Seriously?'

'As God is my witness. He doesn't want me to pay him for sex any more; he thinks we should start a proper relationship.' She thrust out her chin. 'I told him I'd think about it and let him know.'

Keeley was silent as she digested this surprising piece of information. It didn't seem fair that Marianne, who functioned perfectly well on her own, should have such a tempting proposition handed to her on a plate, while she, Keeley, who was next-to-useless without a man to take care of her, hadn't had so much as a sniff of interest for an entire week. Still, she comforted herself, Scott Mason was hardly a high-roller and wouldn't be able to keep a woman like her in shoes, never mind diamonds.

'What about the gigoloing?' she asked. 'How could you go out with him, knowing he was shagging half the village?'

'I think that's a bit of an exaggeration – but, in any case, Scott says he'll give it up. That's how serious he is about me.' Her eyes misted over. 'He says he's never felt this way about a woman before.'

Keeley frowned. 'But how do you know he's not just after your money?' she said, convinced she would unearth some negative in Marianne's news, if she looked hard enough.

'I don't,' said Marianne evenly. 'But something tells me I've finally found a man I can trust. Don't ask me why; just call it instinct.'

'It sounds as if you've already made up your mind to go for it.'

Marianne smiled. 'Do you know, Kee, I think I just might. I've been on my own for a long while now – completely out of choice, I might add – but I think it's about time I lowered my guard and let someone else into my life.'

'I'm very pleased for you,' said Keeley, trying to sound like she meant it. 'I think you and Scott make a lovely couple.'

'We do, don't we?' said Marianne smugly. 'And I know the perfect stage for our first public appearance together.' She paused for an imaginary drum roll. 'The gala dinner.'

Keeley groaned. The gala dinner was the Holy Grail for any social climber worth her salt and, until a week ago, *she* had been on the guest list, courtesy of Fabrizio. As a member of St Benedict's glitterati, the footballer had received a pair of complimentary tickets months ago – but now he'd doubtless be taking some other girl. Keeley looked at Marianne accusingly. '*You're* going to the gala dinner? How did you manage to swing that? Tickets are rarer than a blue Hermès Birkin bag.'

'It's all down to Scott,' said Marianne. 'Every golf coach got a pair of tickets as a thank you for generating a record amount of income for the club this season. And he's asked *moi* to go as his official guest.' She smiled, imagining the envious looks she'd get when she walked into St Benedict's grand art deco ballroom on the young golf coach's arm. 'The only trouble is, I haven't got a thing to wear. I fancy a piece of vintage couture; something really elegant and sophisticated. Dior perhaps, or Valentino. You can help me choose it if you like.'

'Great,' Keeley replied dully.

'Oh, I'm sorry, darling,' said Marianne. 'I didn't mean to gloat. Can't your friend – that membership advisor chappie – sneak you in through the back door?'

Keeley shook her head. 'No chance; I've already asked Joe, but he says it's more than his job's worth.' She narrowed her eyes. 'I'd kill to go that dinner. Anyone who's anyone at Benedict's will be there; it'll be the best chance I'll have all year to bag myself a rich boyfriend.' She stuck out her lower lip. 'I bet Laura's going. Sam will have got complimentary tickets for sure. It's so unfair.'

'How *is* Laura? I haven't seen her in ages.'

'Me neither; she's been very elusive recently. I spoke to her on the phone yesterday, but the baby was crying and I could tell she was distracted. I suggested meeting for lunch, but she said she was having childcare problems – but it was obviously an excuse because when I bumped into Cindy in the post office a couple of days earlier, she happened to mention in passing that Marta's gone full-time. That struck me as odd because Laura used to swear she'd never have a full-time nanny. Honestly, Marianne, I don't know what's happened to her lately. She's changed; she seems so . . . I don't know . . . secretive.'

'That's a shame. You two used to be so close.'

Keeley bit her lip. 'I know this is going to sound silly, but it seems that ever since Cindy arrived in Kirkhulme, I've been surplus to requirements. Or at least that's the way it feels.'

'Nonsense,' said Marianne firmly. 'Laura's not like that. I expect she just needs a bit of space till she's worked through things with Sam.' She fluttered her eyelashes reproachfully. 'Frankly, any woman in their right mind would've given him the heave-ho, but you know how Laura believes in all that sanctity-of-the-family shit. She'd rather gouge out her own eyes than deprive those gorgeous little girls of their father. Let's just hope her trust isn't misplaced.'

Keeley nodded, remembering Fabrizio's description of Sam and Abi's embrace in the gazebo. In recent weeks, she'd seen the pair several times at St Benedict's – practising on the golf course, enjoying a lunchtime drink together – but nothing in their behaviour suggested they were anything other than friends. Nevertheless, Keeley was a firm believer in there being no smoke without fire and, when she'd bumped into Abi in the Chukka Bar toilets the day before, she'd given her a filthy look and then deliberately let the exit door swing back in her face.

'Anyway,' Marianne went on. 'You've don't need to wait on Laura; you've got plenty of other friends. Speaking of which, did you see that story about Destiny in today's paper?'

'No. What's she done now?'

'Her house has been broken into. I guess the thieves knew she was away filming in Antigua. The strange thing is, they didn't touch her valuables. According to her agent, the only things missing are various items of an "intensely personal nature" – whatever that means.'

'Poor Destiny,' said Keeley. 'Have you been watching *Celebrity Lust Island*?'

'Of course,' replied Marianne. 'Destiny's doing rather well, isn't she? How many men has she slept with now? Two, isn't it?'

'Three,' corrected Keeley. 'You've got to watch to-night's show; it's going to be an absolute corker. Destiny's going to have a massive catfight with Shannon. It was all over this morning's paper.'

'Shannon Stewart? But that ghastly trollop isn't one of the contestants.'

Keeley grinned. 'She is now. She flew into Antigua yesterday morning. The producers have brought her in as a surprise replacement for that hoity-toity twit girl, Cordelia Nye-Browne.'

'The one who broke her ankle falling out of a hammock?'

'Yeah, stupid cow,' said Keeley. 'I mean, fancy trying to have oral sex in a hammock. It was bound to end in tears. Still, the producers have played a blinder bringing in Shannon. Everyone knows she and Des are sworn enemies.'

'Ooh, this is going to be good,' said Marianne gleefully. 'How did Shannon make her grand entrance?'

'You know that part of the show where all the celebrity babes parade around the swimming pool in their bikinis and then each one of the guys picks his date for the day?'

Marianne nodded. 'And the last girl left standing is on the next plane home.'

'That's it. Now, Des is obviously feeling confident because she's convinced that Jake – the fella she had sex with the night before – is going to pick her. But then the presenter reveals that they've found a last-minute replacement for Cordelia. That's Shannon's cue to emerge from one of the villas in a hot-pink bikini, hips wiggling, boobs jiggling. The camera homes in on Destiny's face and her jaw practically hits the floor. But, somehow, she manages to keep a grip of herself as she watches the first three guys pick their dates. And then it's Jake's turn. He looks at Shannon. Then he looks at Des. Then he looks back at Shannon and says: "I'll take you, darlin'." That's when Destiny completely loses it. She goes running over to Shannon, screaming, "This is *my* show, you effing bitch," slaps her round the face and pushes her into the swimming pool.'

Marianne let out a loud guffaw. 'That's our Destiny,' she said. 'Classy as ever.' Keeley started to giggle too, and before long the pair were laughing so much they had tears rolling down their seaweed-plastered cheeks.

Freshly purged and pleased at having been taken into Marianne's confidence, Keeley was glowing in every sense of the word as she walked the short distance home from St Benedict's. The only blot on the horizon was her lack of funds. She was certain the millionaire of her dreams was just round the corner, but in the meantime she had to find a way to put food on the table. There was nothing for it, she was going to have to do what she always did in times of financial crisis: hit eBay. Remembering the watch and the Marc Jacobs pumps that were still stashed in her sports bag, Keeley felt an unfamiliar stab of remorse. She brushed it away, telling herself firmly, needs must. On a whim, she stopped at the off licence in the high street and spent her last fiver on a bottle of red wine, which would help make the task ahead more palatable.

As she walked through the front door of her studio flat, which opened straight on to the fifteen-foot-square living space, Keeley's heart leaped as she saw the light on her answerphone blinking. She'd got talking to a middle-aged and not unattractive property developer on the croquet lawn at St Benedict's five days earlier and had insisted on giving him her number, even though he was wearing a wedding ring. She'd been waiting for him to call ever since. Pressing *play*, she went to the tiny kitchen-ette to pour herself a glass of wine. A few seconds later, a staccato voice told her she had two new messages. The first was from her bank, informing her that she had exceeded her overdraft limit. 'Yeah, I know. *You* try living on thin air,' she snapped as she wound the corkscrew into the bottle. There was a beep and then the second caller began to speak.

'Hiya, it's Ryan. Listen, Kee, I know you and I haven't exactly got along in the past, but I've got a proposition for you.'

'Bloody cheek,' Keeley muttered as she eased the cork out of the bottle.

'I know this is short notice,' the message continued. 'But I've got two tickets to the gala dinner on Saturday. I was supposed to take this girl I've been seeing, but she's just blown me out. So I was wondering if you fancied coming with me instead. I'll sort out a car to take you home and stuff. Oh, and just in case you were wondering, Fab isn't going. He'll be in Florence at his niece's christening. Anyway, you've got my mobile number. Let me know if you're up for it. See ya.'

Keeley's scowl became a grin. 'Ryan Stoker, you little beauty!' she cried, punching the air with her fist. Then a thought struck her: why would Ryan want to take her to the gala dinner when he didn't even like her? 'Guilty conscience?' she mused out loud. 'Yeah, that'll be it.' She raised her wine glass in a silent toast to the goalie. There was no doubt about it: things were definitely looking up.

Seventeen

Cindy McAllister was busy swagging curtains. Her work at Coldcliffe Hall was coming to an end and she was spending her final day executing the all-important finishing touches. Satisfied that the pleats in the rich aquamarine silk were all of a uniform width, she secured the drape with a hand-beaded double-tassel tieback, before stepping back to survey the effect. Immediately, her critical eye was drawn to several loose threads trailing from the hem. Frowning, she went to get her scissors from the cantilevered wooden toolbox that contained all her design essentials. But even before she'd unclipped the brass catch she remembered that she'd removed the scissors the night before in order to sew a loose button on Kieran's chinos, and had stupidly forgotten to return them to the box. Cindy sighed in annoyance, realizing that she'd have to tramp downstairs to borrow the pair of scissors that resided in the knife block in Jackson's kitchen.

As she descended the sweeping staircase, Cindy congratulated herself for the hundredth time on scoring such a lucky break. Although her contract prevented her from discussing the Coldcliffe project, word of her work there had quickly spread around the village. She'd already received several phone enquiries, as well as a brief flattering mention in 'Jemima's Diary'. Fiercely ambitious, Cindy had given herself just eighteen months to become the design darling of the Cheshire set – and she knew instinctively that she was already well on her way.

When she reached the bottom of the stairs, Cindy doubled back along the hallway, moving soundlessly in the comfortable ballet flats she always wore when she was working. Her hand had just made contact with the heavy oak door that led to the vast kitchen-diner when something stopped her in her tracks. There were two voices coming from the room beyond, which she recognized as belonging to Jackson and his housekeeper. Judging by the former's tone, Mrs Driver was receiving a telling off. Cindy couldn't help smiling. She didn't much care for Jackson's employee. She was too smug, too knowing – and even though Cindy was a top interior designer and Mrs Driver was nothing more than a glorified cleaner, the older woman always behaved as if she were somehow superior to Cindy. Not wanting to barge in on a private conversation, Cindy's hand fell away from the door. She knew she should turn round and go back upstairs, but something held her rooted to the spot.

'You stupid woman,' Jackson was saying. 'How could you be so careless?'

'I thought he knew,' Mrs Driver responded sulkily.

'You could have ruined everything, just by one careless slip of the tongue.'

'But I didn't, did I?'

'You were lucky, that's all. If you make a mistake like this again, you'll be out on your ear. Have I made myself clear?'

'Perfectly clear, Jackson.' Despite the stern tenor of the conversation, there was a note of intimacy about it that struck Cindy as odd. She had never heard Mrs Driver use Jackson's first name before – it was always 'Mr West'.

Suddenly, at the other end of the hall, the doorbell began to chime. Cindy started guiltily.

'That'll be Laura,' she heard Jackson say.

There was a pause and then Mrs Driver asked: 'How did she get through the security gate?'

'I gave her the entry code.'

'Oh,' said Mrs Driver, her disapproval evident.

'Go and answer the door, will you? Tell her I'm in the garden and ask her to wait in the morning room. That'll give me a chance to clean up in here.'

With her heart in her mouth, Cindy turned and scurried back down the hall. Knowing there was no time to ascend the staircase, she pushed open the first door she came to and was surprised to find herself in an unfamiliar room: a grand dining hall with scarlet walls and French windows opening out on to the garden. She stood behind the door, heart pounding, as Mrs Driver plodded down the hall. The housekeeper's footsteps were receding when Cindy subconsciously shifted her weight, causing the floorboard beneath her to emit a loud creak. The footsteps stopped. Cindy bit her lip. The footsteps started up again, but now they were coming back towards her. When Mrs Driver reached the dining room, she paused. On the other side of the door, Cindy could hear her breathing hoarsely.

'Mrs McAllister, is that you?' the housekeeper said querulously.

Cindy groaned inwardly. She had her reputation to think of and it wouldn't do to be caught snooping around

285

a client's house. She would have to brazen it out. Pasting a smile on her face, she stepped out from behind the door. 'Yes, Mrs Driver,' she said pleasantly. 'I was looking for a pair of scissors.'

The housekeeper gave her a strange, hard look. 'In the dining room?'

'Yes, I thought I'd seen a sewing box in here.'

Mrs Driver raised an eyebrow as if further explanation was required.

'Earlier that is, when Jackson gave me a tour of the house,' Cindy hastily ad-libbed. She shrugged. 'But I can't find one, so I must've been mistaken.'

The doorbell pealed again. Mrs Driver pinched her thin lips together. 'I'd better let Mrs Bentley in and then I'll see to you,' she said curtly.

'Thank you,' said Cindy. But Mrs Driver was already halfway to the front door.

A few moments later, Laura stepped across the threshold. Her nose and forehead were rosy from the sun and she was carrying a wicker basket over her arm.

'Hi, Cindy,' she said cheerily when she spotted her friend hovering at the foot of the staircase. 'I wondered if I'd find you here.'

'It's my last day, more's the pity,' said Cindy as she kissed the cheek Laura was offering. 'I've loved working here; I'm really going to miss this old place.' She gestured to the basket. 'Are you taking Jackson out for a picnic?'

'Oh no, it's just some homemade gingerbread, made with my grandmother's secret recipe.' Laura giggled. 'I'm trying to fatten him up.' She peeled back a checked cloth to reveal a waxed package nestling beside a cardboard punnet of strawberries. 'And I've brought him some fruit too. I'm worried he's not getting enough vitamin C; he always looks so pale.'

Cindy smiled. Jackson had certainly brought out Laura's mothering instinct. 'That's because he doesn't get outdoors enough. There's nothing wrong with that guy that a few days in the sun won't cure.'

'Hey, there's a thought,' said Laura as they traipsed down the hall behind Mrs Driver.

'What's that, honey?'

'Jackson and I could take a little holiday together. A long weekend in Rome would be nice – or Florence. I've always wanted to go to Florence.'

Cindy raised an eyebrow. 'Isn't that a little impractical? Who'd take care of Carnie and Birdie?'

'I'm sure I could come to some arrangement with Marta.'

'What about Sam?'

Laura shrugged. 'What *about* him?'

'Well, how would you explain your absence?'

'I daresay I could think of some excuse,' said Laura wearily. 'Although frankly, after what he's put me through, I think I'd be perfectly justified in just taking off.'

'So things are still difficult between you two?'

'We're speaking again – just – and I suppose he's trying to make amends in his own pathetic way. Yesterday, he bought me an orchid.' She gave a hard laugh. 'But it's going to take more than flowers to earn my forgiveness.'

Mrs Driver threw open the door to the morning room and stepped aside to let the two women enter. 'Mr West's in the garden,' she said in a monotone. 'I'll tell him you're here. Shall I take that basket, Mrs Bentley?'

'Yes, please, if you wouldn't mind. A pot of tea would be nice too.'

'Very good,' said Mrs Driver – although her tone suggested that putting the kettle on would be nothing less than a massive inconvenience.

Cindy waited until the housekeeper had closed the door behind her. 'Listen, honey, I don't mean to criticize, but you really ought to be careful what you say in front of the hired help.' She shot a worried look at the door, as if Mrs Driver might be hovering outside it, eye pressed to the keyhole. 'There's something very odd about that woman; I just don't feel comfortable around her. How do you know that the minute she gets out of here, she's not gossiping to everyone in the village?'

'Oh, you don't need to worry about Mrs Driver,' said Laura as she settled on a wingback chair. 'Jackson's known her for years. She used to work for him in France, you know.'

Cindy walked to the window and stared out at the unkempt lawn. 'In that case, he must be very fond of her, because she's certainly not much of a housekeeper.' She ran her fingertip across the windowsill and held it up for inspection. 'This obviously hasn't seen a duster for some time.'

'Oh well, it's a big house; I imagine it's quite hard for one person to keep clean.'

Cindy nodded. She admired the way Laura was always so willing to see the best in people. 'So, anyway, how are things going with you and Jackson?'

Laura beamed. 'Oh, Cindy, you've no idea; it's been absolutely amazing. Jackson's the complete opposite of Sam. He's so thoughtful and caring; he treats me like a princess.' She looked down at her lap coyly. 'I've lost count of the number of times he's told me he loves me.'

'And do you love him?'

Laura laughed. 'Of course I do. It's blatantly obvious, isn't it?'

Laura and Jackson's affair was barely four weeks old, but it seemed to Cindy that the romance was moving at breakneck speed. As she had worked at Coldcliffe, she'd sometimes caught sight of the pair from the bedroom window as they walked hand in hand through the gardens. Jackson's devotion to Laura was plain to see. Already, Cindy had noticed a dramatic change in the former racing driver: his eyes were brighter, he was more animated, his shuffling gait had been replaced by a confident swagger – and it seemed that Laura was equally smitten. Cindy knew she should be happy for her friend, but she couldn't help feeling there was something cloying and artificial about the romance. It was a fantasy affair, the sugar-coated Disney version – all played out amid the gothic surrealism of Coldcliffe Hall. Cindy hated to be unchari-table, but she couldn't help wondering if Jackson was in love with the real Laura – the eminently practical mother-of-two with wet wipes in her handbag and baby sick on her shoulder – or just the bountiful Snow White who arrived at his door smelling of Issy Miyake and fresh-baked gingerbread.

As Cindy weighed up the likelihood that the romance would outlast the summer, the door burst open and

Jackson appeared. A palpable energy radiated from him and seemed to fill the room. Laura jumped out of her chair and went rushing across the room to meet him. Cindy half expected her to leap into his arms and wrap her legs round his waist, the way she'd seen some of the American golfers' wives do when their husbands completed the winning putt in a tournament.

'Laura, darling, how are you?' Jackson said, enveloping her in a bear hug.

'All the better for seeing you,' she replied, burrowing her face into his neck.

Jackson began stroking Laura's hair. 'I'm so sorry I kept you waiting. I was out in the garden, checking the swimming pool. I've got to get it drained soon, before the leaves start falling.'

As Cindy observed the lovers, locked in their suffocating embrace, she thought she saw a faint look of bewilderment creep into Jackson's expression, as though he somehow doubted the quality of his present happiness. A moment later, it was gone. She watched Jackson whisper something in Laura's ear, prompting her to cling to him with a fresh rush of emotion. Lost in their own private world, they seemed to have forgotten Cindy. Indeed, Jackson had yet to even acknowledge her presence. Cindy looked once more at them. Then she slipped out of the room and back up the stairs, leaving them alone together.

There was more than one eavesdropper in Kirkhulme that afternoon. In the woods that lay on the south side of the village, Richie Grubb was foraging for wild mushrooms. Ever since his flirtatious encounter with Abi by the dustbins, the chef's assistant had been in Xavier's bad books. As if being forced to clean the ovens and chop chillies till his fingers burned wasn't humiliation enough, Richie had now been ordered to the woods to gather the meaty chanterelles, which grew in abundance there. Being a sullen little sod, he'd taken his time about the task, pausing to smoke several roll-ups and take a long call on his mobile from his on-off girlfriend, who worked as a barmaid in the village pub.

With all the interruptions, it took Richie the best part of two hours to fill his basket. He was just about to set off back to St Benedict's when he heard the sound of a woman sobbing. Frowning, he looked around. The noise seemed to be coming from a small clearing, screened by a row of silver birches, some fifty yards away. Despite his lackadaisical attitude, Richie wasn't completely heartless and, thinking that the woman might be in some sort of trouble, he abandoned his basket and set off to investigate. The mossy earth was soft and spongy underfoot and his trainers barely made a sound as he walked towards the clearing. What he saw when he peered between the birch trees' slender trunks left him open-mouthed in shock. On the ground lay a blanket, and on the blanket lay Abi Gainsbourg. Her skirt was hiked up round her hips and in between her parted legs lay a man, his bare arse exposed to the elements. His face was buried in Abi's neck, but Richie knew it couldn't be Xavier, for the chef was in the kitchen at St Benedict's, overseeing the production of a French-themed afternoon tea for the well-heeled members of the Kirkhulme Ladies' Guild. Smirking to himself, Richie realized it wasn't sobbing he had heard, but Abi's mews of pleasure.

The couple were far too engrossed in the job at hand to notice they had company, but, just to be on the safe side, Richie crept back a few paces and hunkered down behind a fallen tree. 'You little slapper,' he murmured as he watched Abi gasping and writhing. Having already felt the sharp edge – quite literally – of Xavier's temper, he wouldn't like to be in her lover's shoes, if and when the chef discovered his wife's infidelity.

Richie observed the copulating couple with lurid fascination – until, after five minutes or so, Abi began whinnying and bucking like a prize brood mare. Richie couldn't help giggling to himself. Instantly, he clapped his hand over his mouth – but it was too late. Abi had raised herself up on to her elbows and was staring out beyond the line of silver birches.

'Who's there?' she called out in a nervous voice.

Her lover barely broke rhythm. 'Don't worry, it's just the wind in the trees,' he told her breathlessly as he forced her shoulders back to the ground with the weight of his torso.

Knowing he risked discovery if he stayed any longer, Richie scuttled away. He was whistling as he emerged from the woods, basket in hand, and set off on the short walk back to St Benedict's.

The following morning, Abi was horrified to discover an anonymous missive in her staff pigeonhole, formed, in best pulp-detective-fiction fashion, from letters cut from newspaper.

*i kNOw WHat yOu diD iN THE wOOds. AnD iF yOU
DOn't wAnT yOUR oLD mAN tO fiND oUT
yoU'd BEtteR mEet me iN tHE sTabLe YaRd At 6Pm.*

It was with a keen sense of excitement that Richie
made his way to the appointed location well ahead of
time, just in case his quarry showed up early. Situated in
St Benedict's northerly reaches, the stable block had been
out of commission for years, and was now used for
storage, if and when the need arose. Few staff ever had
occasion to visit it, and Richie knew he would be able to
conduct his business unobserved. After checking he was
alone, he slipped like a shadow into one of the empty
stables, where he kept lookout through a dusty window
pane.

Abi arrived bang on time, looking hot as ever in denim
cut-offs and a strapless shocking-pink top that finished
halfway down her midriff. Richie watched her as she
stood in the middle of the yard and performed a slow
360° turn, waiting until her back was turned before
emerging from his hiding place.

'Hey, Abi,' he said, affecting casualness. 'Glad you
could make it.'

She pivoted round. 'You,' she said disgustedly. 'I might
have known.'

Richie looked her up and down. He was going to enjoy
this. 'So, Mrs Gainsbourg,' he said in a mellifluous voice,
'we're quite the little goer on the sly, aren't we? I couldn't
believe it when I saw you in the woods yesterday, moaning
and groaning like a good un.'

A blush rose to Abi's cheeks. 'Whatever you saw – or

thought you saw – in the woods, you've got the wrong idea.'

Richie tittered. 'I dunno, it looked pretty clear-cut from where I was standing. Your fancy man was giving you a good old rogering and no mistake.'

Abi folded her arms defiantly. 'What is it you want from me, Richie?'

'Ooh, not very much, not when you consider what's at stake. Let's see . . .' Richie paused and cupped his chin in his hand. 'Five thousand pounds should be enough to make me forget what I saw. I'd say that was a bit of a bargain, wouldn't you?'

Abi made a face. 'Five thousand pounds? You must be joking. Where do you think I'm going to get that sort of money from?'

'Your husband's one of Cheshire's finest chefs. I'm sure he won't notice if you make a little withdrawal from the joint bank account.' He reached out a hand and stroked Abi's cheek. 'Of course, if you haven't got the readies, you could always pay me in kind.'

The caddie shook off his pawing hoof. 'Richie Grubb, I wouldn't swap bodily fluids with you if the future of the human race depended on it.'

'No?' Richie said, his nostrils flaring in anger. 'Well, in that case I'm going to have to tell Chef all about the rare species I found on my little mushroom-picking expedition. What's it called now? Ah yes, the lesser-spotted adulteress.'

Abi's jaw tensed. She decided to take a gamble. 'You haven't thought this through very well, have you?' she said, sounding more confident than she felt. 'You don't even know who this so-called "fancy man" is.'

'Yes, I do,' Richie said indignantly.

'Who is he then?'

'I'm not saying.'

'You're not saying because you don't know.'

Richie pressed his lips together, annoyed at having been caught out.

'I knew it.' Abi let out a derisory laugh. 'You can't prove a thing. And if you do say anything to my husband, I shall tell him you've made the story up, as a way of getting back at him for holding that carving knife to your neck after he caught you flirting with me.'

Richie stared at the ground, silently fuming. She was right: he hadn't thought this blackmail plot through at all. His head had been too full of images of Abi's long legs clamped round his waist.

'Seriously, Richie, I'd think long and hard before you open your big mouth. Xav will probably get you sacked if he finds out you've been spreading vile rumours about his wife. That's after he's wrapped a cheese wire round your neck.'

The caddie gave him one last pitying look. Then she turned on her heel and walked away, her flip-flops sending up little clouds of dust in her wake.

Eighteen

'Wow,' said Kieran as he eyed Jackson West's classic Aston Martin DB5 through the bars of the steel security gate. '*That* is one cool motor.'

Cindy smiled as she pressed the buzzer on the intercom. 'Jackson's quite a car enthusiast. That's something else you two have in common.'

'Something else besides what?'

'Why, me of course,' said Cindy, playfully pinching her husband's muscular bicep.

A few moments went by, during which the intercom remained resolutely silent.

'Why is nobody answering this goddamn thing?' said Cindy. 'I'm sure Jackson's home. I saw him from the balcony not fifteen minutes ago.'

Kieran slipped an arm round his wife's waist. 'Never mind. We can always call back another time.'

'But I really wanted you to meet him today,' said Cindy, resting her head on his shoulder. 'If you guys hit it off – which I'm sure you will – I was going to invite him to dinner.'

Kieran's lips tightened. 'With Laura?'

'Why, yes. I think that would be nice, don't you?'

Kieran didn't say anything, but he didn't have to. He had one of those faces that betrayed every little emotion, and it was immediately clear he didn't think that entertaining his wife's best friend and her new lover would be nice in the slightest. It was two days since he'd learned of the affair. Although Cindy had been sworn to secrecy, she'd found herself compromised beyond endurance when Laura had asked another favour. She wanted to know if she could leave her car in the McAllisters' driveway when she visited Jackson, fearful that the neighbourhood gossips would see it parked outside Coldcliffe Hall. Naturally, Kieran would have to be informed of such an arrangement – and so, with Laura's reluctant consent, Cindy had revealed the affair to her post-coital husband as they lay in bed together. Being someone who took his marriage vows literally, Kieran was shocked at first, and then disapproving. But he loved his wife passionately and, knowing how hard she'd worked to build her friendship with Laura, he felt he had no choice but to accommodate the adulteress's parking requirements. Now, Cindy was asking him to get involved even further. For a man like Kieran, it was a tough call.

As Cindy waited impatiently beside the intercom, she reached into her handbag and fingered the crisp white envelope that contained the final invoice for her work at Coldcliffe Hall – a hefty five-figure sum that would get her new business off to a flying start. The invoice was just an excuse, however; the real reason for her unscheduled visit was to resurrect her friendship with Jackson, which seemed to have lost its impetus in recent weeks. Since getting together with Laura, he'd become increasingly distant – not unfriendly exactly, just a little cool. He'd often be closeted in his office or home gym when Cindy arrived, where once he would have been waiting in the kitchen, a steaming cafetière and two oversized mugs ready on the table. Even his enthusiasm for the redesign seemed to have waned. When an excited Cindy had invited him to inspect the finished article, he'd performed a brisk circuit of the bedroom and en suite, before pronouncing himself 'very pleased indeed'. But his eyes were dead as he spoke the words. It was if his mind were somewhere else – which, as Cindy was forced to acknowledge, was hardly surprising. He'd just been reunited with the love of his life and it was reasonable to assume that Laura occupied most of his waking thoughts – and doubtless a fair proportion of his sleeping ones too. Even so, Cindy had assumed that once she'd finished work on the bedroom she and Jackson would continue to socialize together – but, so far, the hoped-for invites had failed to materialize. In an attempt to reinforce the flimsy friendship, Cindy had persuaded Kieran to accompany her to Coldcliffe Hall in the naïve expectation that the two sportsmen would form an instant rapport, thus paving the way for a whole string of future get-togethers.

Sighing, Cindy pushed the buzzer a second time. A few seconds later, she was rewarded with a crackle of static. 'Yes,' said a hollow female voice.

Cindy put her mouth to the intercom. 'Hi, Mrs Driver, it's Cindy.'

'How can I help you?' After a pause she added 'Mrs McAllister' in a dilatory, grudging way.

'I'm sorry for dropping by unannounced, but my husband and I wondered if we might come in for a few minutes. We'd like to speak with Jackson.'

'He's out.'

'Are you sure he isn't just in the garden? I saw him out there a few minutes ago.'

'Quite sure.'

Cindy frowned. While Mrs Driver had never been exactly welcoming, she had at least maintained a modicum of civility. 'Perhaps we could call back this afternoon,' she persisted. 'Do you know what time he's due back?'

Another pointed silence. 'Mr West's out for the whole day.'

Cindy looked at Kieran and shrugged. 'Fine,' she said curtly. She reached into her handbag. 'I've brought my invoice. Can I come up to the house and leave it with you?'

Mrs Driver coughed irritably. 'There's a postbox on the gate. Put it in there and I'll see that he gets it.' With that, there was another crackle of static and she was gone.

'And goodbye to you too, honey,' muttered Cindy.

Kieran took the envelope from her hand and dropped it into the postbox. 'So I won't have the honour of an audience with the great Jackson West today after all.'

'No,' said Cindy dejectedly. 'I guess not.' She took a last, longing look at the house. As her gaze drifted upwards, she thought she caught a movement at one of the second-floor windows. Shielding her eyes against the sunlight, she looked again. The window was empty, but it seemed that the grinning winged gargoyle that crouched above it was mocking her. 'Come on,' she said, taking Kieran's hand. 'Let's go home.'

The club shop at St Benedict's was heaving with customers. A gaggle of American underwear buyers – in town for Delchester's annual international lingerie fair –

was visiting St Benedict's for a day of sports and pampering. They'd descended on the shop en masse, where the selection of golf-themed novelties and cute designer leisurewear had sent them into raptures. Suffice to say, the till hadn't stopped ringing all morning.

With Ace taking the cash and Dylan endlessly gift wrapping solid silver golf-ball key rings bearing the St Benedict's monogram, and boxes of 'Handmade Kirkhulme Luxury Shortbread, produced by the ton in a factory just outside Dundee, it fell to Harry to man the changing rooms. He was currently lavishing his attentions on a broad-beamed dame with a drawling southern accent, who had her heart set on a 1920s-inspired golfing ensemble. Having been ensconced in the changing room for an extravagant amount of time, during which Harry had overheard much huffing and puffing and several 'hot dangs!', the woman finally emerged into the shop, her arse broad as a bus in a pair of green twill plus fours.

'What do you think?' she said, performing a surprisingly dainty twirl.

'Oh, madam, you look ravishing,' Harry gushed, clapping his hands together in ersatz delight.

The woman glowed. 'The girls at the golf club back home are going to be green with envy when they see me dressed like this.'

Harry fluttered his eyelids camply. 'Ooh yes, they'll be scratching your eyes out.' He took a step back, stared at the mid-priced, wool-mix V-neck the woman had picked from the sale rail and gave a slightly disapproving frown, the way he'd seen Ace do a hundred times before.

'What's the matter?' the woman said.

Harry hesitated for a second, as if reluctant to speak his mind. 'It's just – and I do hope you won't take offence – I don't think that sweater does you any favours.'

The woman glanced down at her torso.

'I mean, it's not bad,' Harry said quickly. 'But it looks a little ... well, *cheap*.' He walked over to a wooden shelving unit where a rainbow of soft, and very expensive, angora sweaters lay neatly folded. 'Let's see. Not the pink ... far too girlie for a woman as sophisticated as you. How about the lemon ...' He threw a glance at his customer's florid complexion. 'Hmmm ... maybe not. I don't think it'll work with your delicate colouring.' He turned back to the shelves. 'Ah yes, the teal, this is more like it.' He rummaged through the pile for a size sixteen and presented it to the woman. She caught the dangling price tag between forefinger and thumb and surveyed it doubtfully.

'Oh dear, this was quite a bit more than I was hoping to spend.'

'Yes, but feel the quality. The angora comes from locally bred Kirkhulme rabbits. Fed on a strict diet of spring greens and sow's milk.' Harry lowered his voice as if he were about to reveal the secret of eternal youth. 'It makes the wool that little bit softer.' He reached out and rubbed the sweater gently against her cheek. 'See.'

The woman blushed. It was a long time since she'd received such personal service from a shop assistant – especially one young enough to be her son. 'Mmmm,' she said, closing her eyes. 'I see what you mean.'

Harry pushed the sweater into her hands. 'Go on, it won't hurt to try it on.'

The woman burst into a smile. 'Oh, all right then. You've twisted my arm.'

Fifteen minutes later, Harry was walking to the counter with an armful of clothes, while the woman finished getting dressed. Besides the angora sweater and plus fours, Harry had managed to foist on her a poplin club shirt with mother of pearl buttons, two pairs of argyle socks and a plaid tam o'shanter.

'Nice work, fella,' said Ace as he began ringing up the purchases. 'I can't believe you managed to flog her one of those hideous teal numbers; I thought we'd have a job to *give* those away. You're a natural-born salesman and no mistake.'

Harry smiled, basking in Ace's praise. The truth was, he'd never been cut out to be a policeman – or, for that matter, a private investigator – and it was a relief to finally find something he was good at. His colleagues had been generous in teaching him the tricks of the trade. They had, understandably, been rather less forthcoming on the subject of the lucrative sideline that, by Harry's reckoning, accounted for more than half the shop's business.

Right on cue, the door swung open and Sam Bentley appeared. Harry watched as he swaggered up to the counter acting, as usual, as if he owned the place. For all the golfer's good looks and easy charm, there was something vaguely sinister about him; something that made Harry think he wouldn't trust the man as far as he could throw him. He hadn't been in the least bit surprised when he'd read about Sam's dogging exploits in the paper. According to Jeff, Sam's wife was still barely speaking to him – and Harry didn't blame her one little bit.

'Hey guys,' said Sam as he dropped his bulging rucksack on the counter, carelessly knocking over a dispenser of golf lesson flyers. 'Is Jeff about?'

Ace shook his head. 'Sorry, mate, he's teaching this morning.' Without further preamble, he jerked his head towards the rear of the shop. 'We got some new Fairway & Greene zip vests in yesterday,' he said in a loud voice, which Harry couldn't help feeling was for his benefit. 'Do you want to come out back and take a look?'

'Great,' said Sam, hauling the rucksack over his shoulder. 'Lead the way.'

As they walked to the back of the shop, Harry sidled up to Dylan. 'How come that guy always gets special treatment, even on a day like today when we're rushed off our feet?'

Dylan gave him a loaded look. 'Let's just say you don't want to mess with a man like Sam Bentley. He's very influential at St Benedict's – in more ways than you can possibly imagine.'

Harry resisted the urge to probe Dylan further. The less he knew, the less information he would be tempted to impart. 'Nuff said, ' he muttered.

The next couple of hours flew by and by lunchtime Harry was exhausted – exhausted but at the same time exhilarated. In sales terms, it had been his best morning's work in the shop to date and he knew Jeff would be pleased when he checked the morning's receipts. The final excitable underwear buyer having departed, Harry was about to take a well-earned break when Lanchester materialized unexpectedly. 'Good afternoon, gentlemen,' he said, tweaking his suit cuffs officiously. 'How's business today?'

'Fan-bloody-tastic,' said Ace, reaching out to ruffle Harry's hair. 'Your godson here has singlehandedly shifted nearly two grand's worth of clothing this morning. You should be very proud of him.'

'Oh, I am,' said Lanchester, baring his gappy teeth in something that passed for a smile. 'Harry always puts his heart and soul into everything he does, don't you, son?'

'I dunno about that,' said Harry, squirming at Lanchester's claims of kinship. He slipped his arms into his lightweight summer jacket. 'Anyway, listen, I was just popping out for my lunch break, so I'll catch up with you later, okay?'

Lanchester stepped into his path. 'Actually, Harry, it was you I came to see. I was wondering if I might have a word. In private.'

Harry's heart sank. He had a feeling he knew what this was going to be about. 'Of course. Why don't we take a walk around the grounds?'

'Excellent idea,' said Lanchester, putting a paternal arm round his shoulders and guiding him through the door.

'So,' Lanchester began as they set off at a brisk pace across the front lawn. 'It sounds as if you've made quite an impression on your colleagues.'

Harry thought he detected a faintly mocking tone in the general manager's voice. 'I'm just trying to fit in, that's all.'

'Well, you seem to have done a very good job. At this rate, you'll be running for Salesman of the Year.' Lanchester turned his head to glare at a courting couple who were engaged in some heavy-duty frottage, just yards from the croquet lawn. 'Filthmongers,' he said under his breath as he removed a two-way radio from the holster round his waist. After putting out a call for the nearest member of staff to tactfully prise the pair apart, he turned back to Harry. 'Now, where was I? Ah yes . . . fitting in. Now, as I'm sure you're aware, your ten-day grace period comes to an end tomorrow Harry.' He slid the radio back into its holster. 'So, old chap, what have you got to show for it?'

Harry bit his lip. He thought of his new friends, Ace and Dylan, who would certainly lose their jobs if he grassed them up. Then his thoughts turned to Sam Bentley and his mysterious trips to the back room. Harry had no allegiance to the golfer but, if he shared his suspicions about him with Lanchester, the whole operation would doubtless come crashing down, taking Ace and Dylan with it.

'Well?' the general manager said impatiently.

Harry shook his head. 'I'm sorry, Mr Lanchester. I'm afraid I've hit a brick wall. There's no evidence whatsoever to support your notion that drugs are being dealt from the shop.'

Lanchester tutted. 'I'm very, very disappointed in you, Harry,' he said in the sort of tone teachers use to pupils caught smoking behind the bike sheds. 'I've spent thousands on this investigation, and now I discover it's all been a complete waste of time.'

'I tell you what,' said Harry. 'I'll do you a deal. Forget my private investigator's fee. Just pay me the same wage as Ace and Dylan, and we'll call it quits.'

Lanchester looked at him in surprise. 'That's very reasonable of you, old chap.'

'However, there is one condition.'

'Go on.'

'You let me carry on working part-time in the shop until the end of the year.'

Lanchester stopped walking and turned to face Harry. 'Why on earth would you want to do that?'

Harry looked him in the eye. 'Because I enjoy it and I'm good at it.' He raised a warning finger. 'I'm not going to do any spying for you, mind. I just want to be a regular employee.'

Lanchester thought for a moment, then he offered Harry his hand. 'Okay, it's a deal.'

'You won't regret this,' Harry said as he grasped the manager's hand. 'I'm going to be the best salesman you ever had.'

'I don't doubt it.' Lanchester gave a great sigh. 'But this still leaves me with a major headache. I *know* drugs are being dealt from that shop, but I daren't risk the club's reputation by calling in the police. What am I supposed to do now?'

Harry smiled. 'You know what my advice would be?'

The general manager raised a querying eyebrow.

'Ignore it.'

'But . . . but . . . but . . . that's a preposterous suggestion,' Lanchester erupted, a sibilant shower of spittle issuing from the gap between his front teeth. 'I can't just sit back and do nothing.'

Harry shrugged. 'Why not?'

'Because my conscience won't let me.'

Harry wrapped his arm round the manager's shoulders. 'Look here, *old chap*. I haven't been at St Benedict's very long, but it's pretty obvious that this place doesn't operate by the normal laws of society. The club members . . . well, let's just say they have their own moral code. In my opinion, you're fighting a losing battle by trying to change things, so, if I were you, I'd just let them get on with it. Either that or dig yourself into an early grave with the stress of it all.' He let his arm fall away. 'And now, if you'll excuse me, I'm going to salvage what's left of my lunch break and then I've got to get back to my customers.'

As Lanchester watched Harry go, it suddenly dawned on him that the younger man might just have a point.

Nineteen

For the first time in ages Sam had the house to himself. Marta was enjoying a day off and Laura had taken the girls to the Delchester Country Park for a teddy bears' picnic. Sam wouldn't have minded accompanying them, but he hadn't been invited – and he didn't want to push his luck by asking. Laura was being horribly stubborn. It had been four weeks since she'd run over his golf clubs and Sam was still exiled to the attic. He didn't know what more he could do. He'd apologized till he was blue in the face; he'd bought her flowers, chocolates, tickets to the theatre; even offered to take her and the girls on an exotic holiday once the German Masters was out of the way – but still she looked at him with loathing, addressing him in a hurt, accusing way as if he'd inadvertently brought dog shit into the house on the sole of his shoe. And when he'd dared enquire when he might rejoin her in the marital bed, she'd simply shrugged and said: 'If and when I can find it in my heart to forgive you.' He wouldn't have minded so much if she'd looked half as unhappy as he felt. But *she* wasn't the one mooching around, grey-faced and bleary-eyed from lack of sleep; quite the opposite. His wife seemed perversely perky: her skin glowed, her eyes were bright, her dark curls seemed even bouncier than usual. Sam assumed she'd been seeking solace in the beauty salon. He never, not for one moment, entertained the thought that his wife might be having an affair. Laura was too sweet, too straightforward. Unlike him, she lacked the guile to carry off such duplicity – the kind of cold-blooded cunning that enabled him to say 'I love you' to another person and know the words were a lie. But now, as he stared at the unfamiliar rose-print tulle thong in Laura's underwear drawer, he was beginning to revise his opinion.

To the best of his knowledge, Laura hadn't worn a thong since Birdie was born. He wished she would. He loved his wife's arse – it was full and round and eminently spankable – but these days it always seemed to be encased in sensible support pants that disguised her post-baby bulge. Sighing, Sam dropped the thong back in Laura's drawer and continued to forage. A few moments later, he unearthed the matching bra – and not just any bra, but a cheeky peek-a-boo number. Like the thong, its price tag was still attached, hinting at a recent purchase. He fingered its lacy cups, wondering when – and, more importantly, *for whom* – Laura planned to wear it. The notion that Laura might be having sex with another man made him want to drive his fist through the nearest wall. He loved his wife and he would fight to the death to protect her. She was everything to him: lover, best friend, social secretary and, most crucially of all, the mother of his children. What's more, although he undoubtedly took her for granted sometimes, Sam had never underestimated Laura's vital contribution to the success of his golfing career. He knew that without her his well-ordered life would quite simply fall apart. Sure he'd had his fair share of affairs in the past, but none of them meant anything.

Even Abi was just a bit of fun, a way of breaking up the monotony of domestic life – although just lately, she had become an albatross round his neck. The previous evening, she'd called him on his mobile in a bit of a state. Apparently, one of the young lads who worked with Xavier had seen them shagging in the woods a couple of days earlier and had subsequently made a clumsy attempt to blackmail her. 'I think I managed to shut him up,' she'd said. 'He hasn't got any proof – he didn't even see your face.'

At this, Sam breathed a sigh of relief. 'So what's the problem?'

She'd made a huffing noise then, as if she were losing patience with him. 'I know I agreed that we'd carry on as we were for the time being, but this has changed things. Surely you can see that?'

'Not really.'

'Of course it has,' she'd twittered. 'If Richie's seen us together, the chances are other people have too. And even if he doesn't say anything to Xav – which I'm pretty sure he won't – he's bound to let something slip to one of his mates. Then people will start gossiping and –'

'Look, Abi,' said Sam, breaking across her. 'Do you mind just getting to the point? Laura's upstairs putting Carnie to bed, and I promised I'd read her a bedtime story.'

'Oh,' said Abi. 'Quite the devoted father all of a sudden, aren't we?'

'Don't be like that, babe.'

There was a long, sulky silence. 'I just think we should come clean now,' Abi said finally. 'Because, believe me, it's only a matter of time before Xav or Laura finds out about us from someone else.'

'Yeah, yeah, I hear what you're saying,' said Sam, wondering if Abi had made the whole tale up as a way of forcing his hand. 'But it's not the right time. Laura's very fragile right now. You know what she did to my golf clubs. I'm worried that next time she might hurt herself – or even, God forbid, the kids.' It was a cheap shot, but it had done the trick.

'Fine,' said Abi tightly. 'We'll play it your way.'

As Sam closed his wife's underwear drawer, he tried to imagine how he'd feel if it turned out Laura *was* having an affair. He gave a great sigh, deciding that it was simply too horrible to contemplate. He was surrounded by negative energy, and his head ached with the strain of trying to keep all the balls in the air. He sat on the edge of the bed and began to count his out-breaths, a meditation technique his sports psychologist had taught him. He needed to focus, to remember what was important. His biggest priority right now was the German Masters; everything else would have to wait.

In the kitchen at St Benedict's, Xavier had just finished a gruelling eleven-hour shift. The Frenchman had spent much of the day perfecting his dishes for the gala dinner, which was now just forty-eight hours away. His innovative tasting menu was destined to be one of the evening's highlights and boasted such daring creations as red cabbage gazpacho, salmon poached with liquorice, and warm chocolate fondant with peanut butter ice cream and artichoke caramel. After barking out some final instructions to his maître d', Xavier unbuttoned his white coat and flung it in the laundry bin.

One of the sous chefs looked up from the sauce he was whisking. 'Leaving on time, Chef? That's not like you.'

'It's my anniversary,' Xavier replied. 'I can't be late because I have a very romantic surprise planned for my beautiful wife.'

'Hear that?' the sous remarked to the commis. 'These French guys really know how to lay on the charm with a trowel. No wonder Chef's got half the restaurant's female patrons gagging to see the size of his boning knife.'

'Cheeky fucker,' Xavier said, cuffing his colleague's head good-naturedly. 'Now keep your mind on that hollandaise or it'll curdle, just like your brains.' He raised a hand in farewell. 'I'll see you all in the morning.' Across the kitchen, a chorus of goodbyes rang out. Despite his fiery temperament, Xavier was admired and respected by his colleagues. There wasn't a man among them who didn't fully appreciate the immense skill and dedication it took to earn a Michelin star.

As Xavier walked towards the swing doors, he noticed Richie Grubb labouring over the icing on a choux pastry and vanilla cream horseshoe. Instantly, his good humour evaporated.

'Can't you do anything right, shit-for-brains?' the chef yelled as he surveyed Richie's efforts. 'This is a fucking disaster. There's far too much icing here; it's going to completely overpower the vanilla cream. Throw it away and start again.'

'Yes, Chef,' Richie muttered.

Xavier glared at his assistant. 'I must have been mad to take you on. Do you know what you are?'

'No, Chef.'

'A fucking liability.' And then, with one final disgusted toss of his head, Xavier disappeared through the swing doors.

Richie laughed softly to himself as he tipped the ruined dessert into the bin. 'A fucking liability, am I? You're not wrong there, Chef.'

Xavier was excited as he made his way to the staffroom, imagining Abi's delight when she discovered what he had in store for their anniversary. Soon, he'd be bringing her back to St Benedict's for a lavish dinner *à deux*. But they wouldn't be eating in the club's restaurant, where Abi had dined many times before. No, Xavier had something much more unique in mind for his precious love.

In a remote corner of the club's sprawling grounds stood a ruined nineteenth-century folly. Built of brick and flint, it resembled a miniature castle, complete with turrets and castellations, and would have had pride of place in the gardens of the grand Victorian mansion that had once occupied the site. It was here, amid the ruins, that Xavier planned to celebrate his anniversary. The soirée had required a fair degree of planning and a good deal of help from his friends at St Benedict's. Earlier that day, a couple of kitchen porters had set up a table and chairs inside the folly, and decorated the crumbling walls with outdoor candles and huge terracotta pots of richly-scented jasmine and lavender, generously loaned by head grounds-man, Bob Daley. When Xavier and Abi arrived, a waiter would greet them with champagne cocktails, while a lone violinist played Stravinsky. Later, as the sun slipped behind the treetops, a five-course banquet would be served, ferried by golf buggy from the restaurant kitchen. And then, at the end of the evening, the chef would present his wife with a platinum eternity ring, which he'd had engraved with their intertwined initials. The love token had cost him a hefty sum, but now that his secret business venture was beginning to reap dividends, he could afford to splash out. He'd known there was big money to be made in the world of horse racing, though his success to date had far exceeded his wildest expectations.

Xavier had always been a gambling man, and when one of his regular restaurant patrons – a woman who just happened to be one of Cheshire's top female racehorse trainers – offered him a twenty-five per cent stake in a chestnut filly, he'd jumped at the chance. He'd kept the deal a secret from Abi, who disapproved of his gambling and would have baulked at the hefty monthly training fees. That way, if Flight of Fancy failed to perform, Xavier could quietly give up his stake and his wife would be none the wiser. But if the filly came good – as she was beginning to, scoring two wins in the past three months alone – he would make a clean breast of it. One more win, he told himself, then he would 'fess up to Abi, and together they would enjoy the fruits of his success.

In the staffroom, Xavier collected his crash helmet from his locker, before checking his pigeonhole for messages. There was a handwritten note from Lanchester's secretary, requesting his presence in the general manager's office at ten a.m. for a final gala dinner briefing. Underneath it lay a single sheet of A4, folded into thirds. He opened it out. It contained a bald message, formed from cut-up newspaper.

YOUr WiFe's FUCkINg aNOtHer BlokE. I KnOw, cOs I'vE SeeN thE dIRtY BItCH At iT. HAppY anNIVeRSArY, cHEF.

A wave of revulsion washed over Xavier. For several minutes, he stared at the poison words in a state of shock. He wondered fleetingly if it were some kind of joke – but none of his friends at St Benedict's would do such a thing, especially not on his anniversary of all days. As various horrifying possibilities crowded his brain, the door to the staffroom swung open and Bob Daley appeared.

'Hi, Xavier, all set for tonight, are you?' the head gardener enquired as he made his way towards the bank of pigeonholes.

Xavier dragged his eyes away from the page and looked blankly at his friend. 'Tonight?'

'Your anniversary.' Bob chuckled. 'Don't tell me you've forgotten, not after I've nearly done my back in dragging all those terracotta pots up to the folly.'

Xavier forced a smile, though it seemed as if his jaw would crack with the effort. 'No, of course not.' He dropped the paper into his upturned crash helmet. 'I'd better get home. Abi will be waiting.' Then he strode from the room quickly, so Bob wouldn't see the tears forming in his eyes. Five minutes later, he was bombing down the bypass on his Vespa, weaving in and out of the rush-hour traffic like a madman, not sure of what he would do when he arrived home. Just knowing that he wanted to hurt someone. Badly.

Pushing open the door to his third-floor apartment, Xavier was greeted by the sound of running water. It seemed his wife was taking a shower in readiness for the big night ahead. On another occasion he might have stripped off to join her – or, at the very least, shouted a loving greeting through the door – but today he marched straight past the bathroom like a man possessed. He went to the living room and stood by the window, torturing himself with thoughts of Abi in another man's arms. She was his soulmate, his muse, his sweet English rose. He couldn't bear to think of life without her. As he stood there, slowly clenching and unclenching his fists, he heard the muffled sound of a bossa nova ring tone, which signalled the arrival of a text message on his wife's mobile. Normally, Xavier would have ignored it, but now he stalked around the room until he tracked the sound to Abi's backpack, which lay beside the sofa. His hand hesitated on the zipper as he strained to see if he could still hear the shower. He could. With his wife thus occupied, he unzipped the bag and pulled out her phone. Its illuminated screen listed the caller ID as 'unknown'. Without hesitation, he opened the message.

hey sxy. roses r red gerkins r green.
i luv ur legs and wots in btwn!
miss ya babe. see u at the wkend.

Xavier bit down hard on his lip until he tasted blood. The timing of the message was cruelly perfect. Now he knew, beyond a shadow of a doubt, that the anonymous letter was correct: his wife *was* having an affair – but with whom? A single tear worked its way through his lids and descended down his cheek. Brushing it away angrily, he read the message a second time, the hateful words branding themselves on his heart. Not wanting Abi to know he'd intercepted the message, he hastily deleted it. Then he checked her inbox in search of other incriminating texts: it was empty. His wife had covered her tracks well. He shoved the phone into the backpack and zipped it up.

'Xav!' The chef spun round at the sound of his name. Abi was standing naked in the doorway, her wet hair sending rivulets of water down her shoulders and breasts. 'I didn't hear you come in,' she said.

'I've just walked through the door.' He stared into her eyes, trying to hold it together, though his throat was tight and dry.

Abi walked up to him and kissed him on the mouth. 'So when am I going to find out about this anniversary surprise of yours?'

'At sunset.' Xavier swallowed hard. '*Ma chérie.*' He glanced at his watch. 'Which is due to occur in precisely one hour and fourteen minutes.'

'I'd better get a move on then.' She ran a hand across his forehead, smoothing back his hair. 'Are you okay?' she asked. 'You look a bit pale.'

'I'm tired,' Xavier replied curtly. 'I've been working since six a.m.'

Abi made a sympathetic face. 'Poor baby. We won't

stay out too late, okay?' She stood on tiptoes to kiss the end of his nose. 'It won't take me long to get ready. Just give me another fifteen minutes.'

As he watched Abi walk away, her slender body swaying erotically, Xavier felt as if his heart were breaking. He was sorely tempted to drive to St Benedict's and take a pickaxe to the folly. He would smash the terracotta pots to smithereens, turn the wooden table and chairs into kindling and trample the rose petals that had been scattered across the ruin's mossy carpet to a fragrant pulp. But that wasn't going to happen. Instead, he would lead his wife to the ruins, sit there in the soft candlelight and feed her morsels of food from the end of his fork, as if he hadn't a care in the world. He wasn't going to confront her with the evidence. Not tonight. Not until he'd discovered the identity of her secret lover. And, when he did, he was going to make him wish he'd never been born.

Twenty

Elissa Jones smoothed a hand over the white frilled apron tied round her waist and felt a warm glow at the thought of the seven-week-old foetus nestling in her womb. A third-year sociology student at Delchester University, she supplemented her grant by working as a silver-service waitress for corporate events and various private functions at St Benedict's. But, if things went according to plan, she and her baby would soon be living a life of luxury.

Stepping up to the mirror, she pulled back her long black hair into a tight ponytail, a style which only served to accentuate her spectacular cheekbones, before attaching her waitress hat with a couple of hairgrips. She smiled at her reflection. Pregnant or not, she still felt sexy in her cute black-and-white uniform. Two coats of mascara and a slick of clear lipgloss and she was ready for action. She was just stowing her belongings in a locker when Becky, her friend and fellow waitress, came tearing into the staff changing room.

'Blimey, Bex, you're cutting it fine, aren't you?' said Elissa, glancing at the wall clock.

'Tell me about it,' Becky replied breathlessly. 'There was a car smash on the bypass and the bloody bus got held up for ages.' She flung down her tote bag and went to the clothes rail where her freshly laundered uniform was hanging in a clear plastic sheath. 'Tonight's going to be such a laugh,' she said, peeling off her T-shirt. 'I've heard the guest list includes at least half a dozen footballers, and I reckon if we wiggle our booties as we're clearing away those plates, we should be able to persuade a couple of them to take us drinking in town afterwards.'

Elissa patted her stomach. 'I'm afraid my drinking days are over, at least for a while.'

Becky grimaced. 'Shit, yeah. I was forgetting about that.' She yanked her black dress off its hanger and pulled it over her head. 'So, tonight's the big night, eh?'

Elissa nodded. 'I can't wait to see the look on his face when he finds out.'

'Don't you think you'd be better off breaking the news in private?'

'No way. I need to make the whole thing as public as possible. That way, he's less likely to try and duck out of his responsibilities.'

Becky gave her friend a concerned look. 'Are you sure you want to go through with this pregnancy, Liss? He'd probably give you a good pay-off if you had an abortion.'

Elissa nodded. 'Quite sure. This isn't just a money-making scam; it's a lifestyle choice. This way, I get the best of both worlds: a baby, and a regular income – at least until the kid's eighteen.'

Suddenly, the door to the changing room swung open and in walked the girls' boss, Alison – a mono-browed matron whose bark was widely acknowledged to be worse than her bite.

'Come on, girls, chop chop,' she said, clapping her hands together. 'There's no time for gossiping. The first guests will be arriving in less than an hour.' She pointed at Elissa. 'You, get to the atrium with the others. And you' – she pointed to Becky – 'have got five minutes to finish getting ready. After that, I'm going to start docking your wages.'

Out in the atrium, there was a palpable air of excitement. Over the years, the gala dinner had assumed an almost legendary status. Jobs among the waiting staff were as highly prized as a place on the guest list itself, and only the youngest, most attractive individuals had been selected to serve the assorted celebs, aristocrats and dignataries, who would shortly be descending on St Benedict's lavishly decorated ballroom. As soon as her staff was assembled, Alison called for silence before embarking on her usual pep talk.

'Okay, people, as you know, this is a very important night for St Benedict's, so I need you all to be on top of your game. And, remember, you're not just here to serve the food; you're here to provide a bit of eye candy. So, if somebody grabs your arse, don't make a song and dance about it. Just smile and pretend you're enjoying it.' She folded her arms across her generous bosom, surveying her eager-faced acolytes. 'Boys, I hope you've kept the aftershave subtle; girls, don't forget to freshen up your make-up at regular intervals.' She caught the eye of a tall girl with wet-look fuchsia lips. 'Tania dear, you're going to have to tone down that lippy, or the guests are going to think we've got a hooker on the payroll.' The girl blushed and looked down at her feet. 'Now, don't forget the golden rules: no drinking, no smoking, no drug-taking. But what you get up to once the lights have gone up and you've taken off your uniform is your own business. Oh, and if I catch 'anyone accepting a tip, they'll be sent home immediately.' She beamed, displaying a row of small pointed teeth. 'Righty-ho, let's go next door and familiarize ourselves with the layout of the dining tables, shall we?'

Each gala dinner had a theme and this year it was Renaissance Venice. For the past three days, an army of set designers had worked round the clock to create a grand Venetian piazza, complete with domed basilica, fountains, a trio of elegant arched bridges and even an indoor canal, where a fleet of gold-painted gondolas waited to ferry the guests to their tables. For several minutes, the awestruck waiters and waitresses wandered around the vast room, marvelling at the transformation.

'Isn't this amazing?' said Becky, running her hand over a plaster replica of Michaelangelo's *David*. 'Imagine how much all this must have cost.'

'I know,' said Elissa. 'And the sad thing is, most of the guests will be too drunk to appreciate it.'

Becky raised an eyebrow. 'Drunk – or coked up to the eyeballs.'

Elissa bent down and trailed her fingers in the shallow water of the canal, which curved in a graceful S through the centre of the room. 'What do you reckon the odds are of somebody ending up in here before the night's out?'

Becky sniggered. 'Surely it's a foregone conclusion. I'll say this for the good folk of St Benedict's: they know how to have a good time.' She squatted down beside her friend. 'This place is so cool. I wish *I* could afford a membership.'

'Then you're going to have to find yourself a rich man,' said Elissa. She stroked her belly thoughtfully. 'Just like I have.'

Half a mile away, Keeley was getting ready in the cramped confines of her studio flat. Unable to afford a new outfit, she'd plumped for a vintage number that Fabrizio had treated her to – a 1940s crêpe de Chine goddess gown, teamed with a jet choker (another gift from an erstwhile boyfriend) and the Marc Jacobs pumps she'd filched from the changing room at St Benedict's. Like the Baume & Mercier watch, the shoes had reached their reserve price on eBay two days earlier, but Keeley reckoned they deserved one final outing before being despatched to their new owner – and, luckily, they fitted her perfectly. Having spent the best part of half an hour fixing her hair into an elegant Geisha girl *shimada*, she turned her attention to her face. In an ideal world, she would have had her make-up applied at a salon, but tonight she was relying on the tester-sized freebies she'd begged off the Bobbi Brown counter at Harvey Nics. As she brushed silver-grey shadow across her eyelids, Keeley couldn't help hoping that tonight was going to be her lucky night. If she didn't find a boyfriend soon, she was going to have to think seriously about getting a job. The mere thought of it made her feel quite queasy. She picked up a cotton bud and ran it over the corners of her eyes, smudging the shadow to create a smouldering effect, and then reached for her mascara, widening her eyes as she stroked the wand across her long lashes. 'You've got to sort your life out, girl,' she said aloud to her reflection. 'Maybe it's time you thought about settling down, instead of always flitting from one man to the next.' She gave a little shudder. She was still only twenty-seven, but already she had an uncomfortable sense that life was passing her by.

Suddenly, the buzzer on the intercom sounded, causing Keeley to jab her eye with the mascara wand. 'Bugger,' she said, holding her finger under her eye as it started to water. She went to the open window and leaned out. Ryan Stoker was standing on the garden path. He was wearing an expensive-looking lounge suit and Aviator sunglasses. At the kerb, a Bentley Continental sat with its engine idling and a uniformed driver at the wheel. Keeley was impressed.

'Oi, Ryan,' she called down to him. 'You're early.'

The goalkeeper looked up, a rueful smile on his face. 'And a very good evening to you too, Ms Finnegan.'

Keeley smiled apologetically, remembering belatedly that Ryan was doing *her* a favour, and not the other way round. 'Sorry,' she said. 'It's just that I haven't finished getting ready yet. Can you give me another ten minutes?'

'No problem,' said Ryan. 'Take all the time you need. I'll wait in the car, shall I? Unless you want to invite me up, that is.'

'No, you're all right, I won't be long,' said Keeley hastily, not wanting Ryan to see her humble living conditions. 'Hey, you haven't forgotten my mask, have you?' In keeping with the Venetian theme, all guests were expected to wear masks – and when Keeley had phoned Ryan to accept his invitation, the footballer had thoughtfully offered to purchase this vital accessory.

'No, Keeley, I haven't forgotten,' Ryan replied with

exaggerated weariness. Then he turned round and walked back to the car.

As she finished applying her make-up, Keeley found herself wondering what Ryan's game plan was. She certainly didn't want to be stuck with him all evening, and presumed that he felt the same way. Naturally they'd sit together for the dinner itself, where they'd arranged to share a table with Marianne, Scott, Cindy and Kieran – but later, when it came to the dancing, they'd both be free to mingle. A final spritz of DKNY and Keeley was ready. 'Hmmm, not bad,' she said as she checked her appearance in the full-length mirror that was screwed to the back of the front door to save space. After collecting her silk clutch bag and a chiffon wrap, she ran down the three flights of stairs to the Bentley, where the driver was waiting with the door open.

'Wow,' said Ryan, taking off his sunglasses as Keeley slid in beside him. 'You look amazing.'

Keeley was taken aback by the compliment. The whole time she'd been seeing his teammate, Ryan had never made any comment on her appearance – positive or otherwise. 'Why, thank you, Ryan. You're not looking bad yourself.' She reached out to stroke the lapel of his jacket. 'I've never seen you in a suit before. What is it?'

'Hugo Boss.'

'*Verrry* nice.' As the Bentley pulled smoothly away, Keeley noticed a plastic bag on the parcel shelf. 'Is my mask in there? May I see it?'

Ryan reached for the bag. 'This is mine,' he said, producing a relatively sober green-and-gold Columbino half-mask. 'And this one is for you.' He handed her an elaborate gilded mask, trimmed with black and gold ostrich feathers and decorated round the eyeholes with tiny sparkling gemstones.

'Oh, Ryan, it's beautiful,' Keeley exclaimed, holding the mask up to her face. 'And see, it matches my outfit perfectly.' Without thinking, she reached across and kissed him on the cheek. He smelled pleasingly of soap and Brylcreem.

Ryan seemed embarrassed. 'Easy,' he said. 'It's only a mask.'

For a long moment, neither of them spoke. The footballer stared straight ahead, his expression inscrutable.

'Does Fabrizio know we're going to the dinner together?' Keeley said at length, more for something to fill the silence than a desperate interest in the answer.

Ryan's expression didn't change. 'Nope.'

'Aren't you worried what he'll say when he finds out?'

'Why, are you?'

Keeley shook her head. 'He might think it's a bit odd though – you know, his best friend taking out his ex-girlfriend.' She coughed self-consciously. 'I mean I know it's not a date or anything, but even so . . .'

'To be honest, I shouldn't think he'd be that bothered. In any case, he won't be around for much longer. He's going back to Italy in a couple of months' time.'

Keeley's eyes widened. 'He is?'

'Yeah, don't you read the sports pages?'

'Why on earth should I?'

'Because then you'd know that Fab's just signed a massive deal with Lazio, which means the lucky bugger's going to be one of the best-paid players in *Série A*.'

'How nice for him,' Keeley said in a brittle voice.

'Don't tell me you're going to miss him.'

'Of course I am,' she said indignantly. 'Fabrizio and I were very close.'

Ryan raised a dubious brow. 'But he used to irritate the hell out of you; you know he did.'

'And what the hell would *you* know about my feelings?' Keeley snapped. 'You're the reason we broke up. Remember?'

Ryan's face clouded over. 'No, Keeley, the reason Fab dumped you is because you were knocking off some other bloke. *Remember?*'

Keeley bit her lip and turned to stare out of the window. A few moments later, she felt Ryan's hand on her knee. 'Hey, let's not fall out,' he said. 'I want us to have a nice time tonight, okay?'

'I'll do my best,' replied Keeley tightly. She crossed her legs and Ryan's hand fell away.

At the entrance to St Benedict's, half a dozen paparazzi were lying in wait. They leaped into action when they saw the Bentley approach, surrounding it and thrusting their cameras at the windows, even before they knew who was inside. 'I don't know how you footballers cope with all this attention,' said Keeley as the car swept through the security gates and up the long driveway to the clubhouse. 'It would drive me mad, never having any privacy.'

Ryan looked at her disbelievingly. 'But you used to be a model. I would've thought you'd love all the attention.'

'Yeah, but modelling's different. You turn up, you pose for the camera, you go home. Job done. Whereas you lot

. . . you're never off limits.' She winked. 'See, Mr Smarty Pants. You don't know as much about me as you think you do.'

The pre-dinner cocktail reception was in full swing by the time they entered the atrium – and judging by the rows of Bentleys, Astons, Porsches and Mercs lined up outside, the entire Cheshire set was in attendance. Keeley felt a delicious sense of anticipation as they descended the marble steps and were absorbed into the throng. She gazed around in delight, soaking up the atmosphere and admiring the bling that was dripping from ears, rattling on wrists and bouncing on creamy décolletages. The air was thick with the pungent aroma of money and privilege – and naturally there wasn't a woman present who didn't look as if she were hosting a tapeworm. Ryan offered to get some drinks, leaving Keeley to go in search of her friends. As she wove her way among the excited guests, she caught sight of Astrid, standing alone beside one of the atrium's graceful arched windows. Her mask was dangling from her wrist and she was smoking what appeared to be a large spliff in a tortoiseshell cigarette holder.

'Hi, Astrid,' said Keeley, peeking out from behind her own mask. 'I didn't know you were coming tonight.'

'Keeley! How lovely to see you,' exclaimed Astrid. She pursed her lips and blew a quivering smoke ring into the air. 'You haven't been to see me in ages. I'm feeling *verrry* neglected.'

'I've missed our sessions too,' said Keeley. 'More than you can imagine. It's just that I'm a bit strapped for cash right now.'

Astrid frowned in sympathy. 'You should have said something sooner. I'm sure Mistress Valkyrie can arrange a special discount for one of her favourite clients.'

Keeley smiled. 'Really? That would be great.'

Astrid reached out a hand and stroked the other woman's cheek with her fingertips. 'Why don't you make an appointment for Monday evening?' she said softly. 'I've got a new calfskin strop I'm just *aching* to try out.' She paused and ran her tongue round her scarlet-painted lips. All at once, Keeley felt a delicious tingling sensation in her buttocks.

Suddenly, a horned devil appeared at Astrid's side. 'I'm not interrupting anything, am I?' he said as he handed one of the highball glasses he was carrying to the masseuse.

Keeley narrowed her eyes suspiciously, prompting Satan to lift his mask.

'Ace,' Keeley said, clapping her hands together delightedly. 'How the devil are you?'

Ace shook his head. 'Very funny.' He draped an arm round Astrid's shoulders. 'I couldn't be better, thanks. After all, I am going out with the best-looking bird at St Benedict's.' He gave Keeley a wink. 'Present company excepted, of course.'

'God, Ace, you're smoother than a freshly Botoxed forehead,' said Keeley, laughing. 'How did you guys manage to get tickets anyway? I heard the staff allocation was practically non-existent this year.'

Astrid gave Ace an admiring look. 'You know my boyfriend. He can lay his hands on just about anything.'

Ace grinned. 'One of my customers owed me a favour after I got him a load of pills at short notice. I'm not

329

naming any names, but he's a business heavyweight with a lot of clout at St Benedict's. So, I called in the favour and asked him to get me four tickets for tonight.'

'*Four* tickets?' said Keeley in surprise. 'He *must* be influential. What did you do with the others? Sell them on for double their face value, I bet.'

'Nah, I couldn't very well go and not take these two reprobates, could I?' Ace made a beckoning motion. 'Come on, fellas. No need to hover on the sidelines.'

Keeley turned round to see Dylan standing there, maskless and gurning. 'Hi, Keeley,' he said, blinking furiously. 'You look amazing.'

'She does, doesn't she?' came a voice behind him.

Dylan stepped to one side to reveal a tall figure, the upper part of his face covered by a Phantom of the Opera mask. Despite the man's disguise, Keeley had no trouble recognizing him. 'Well, well, well. Harry Hunter. Fancy seeing you here.' She looked her sometime lover up and down, checking out his fashionably retro velvet lounge suit.

Harry offered Keeley the glass of champagne he was carrying. 'Here, why don't you have this?' he said. 'I can easily get another.'

'Thanks, but you're okay. My friend's just gone to get some drinks, as a matter of fact.'

Harry raised his eyebrows. 'Oh? And what friend might that be?'

'Ryan Stoker.' Keeley smiled archly. 'I expect you've heard of him.'

'Blimey,' said Ace. 'Don't tell me you've managed to pull another premiership footballer already, Kee?'

'Oh no, I'm not shagging him,' said Keeley hastily. 'We're mates, that's all.' She cast her eyes around the room. 'We supposed to be meeting some friends of mine. I suppose I ought to see if I can find them.' Her eyes wandered back to Harry. 'Perhaps I'll catch up with you later.'

'Yes,' he said. 'I hope so.'

It didn't take Keeley long to locate Marianne and Co. They were standing in an alcove, watching the band, who were performing rousing excerpts from *La Bohème*.

'Hi, guys,' Keeley trilled.

'Darling!' Marianne exclaimed as she enveloped her friend in a hug. 'I'm so glad you're here.'

'That's a real cute dress, Keeley; the forties is definitely your era,' said Cindy, who looked stunning in a low-cut Roberto Cavalli gown, which showed off her impressive bosom to maximum effect.

'And what a fabulous mask,' said Marianne, squinting through her own disguise, which was shaped like a crescent moon and trimmed with a foot-high plume of marabou.

Keeley smiled. 'Ryan bought it for me.'

'How thoughtful of him.' Marianne looked over her friend's shoulder. 'Where's he hiding?'

'He'll be here in a minute; he's just gone to get some drinks.'

Cindy looked surprised. 'You've come with Ryan? But wasn't he behind your break-up with Fabrizio?'

'Well, yes, in a manner of speaking,' Keeley admitted. 'But it's all water under the bridge now. In fact, thinking about it, Ryan probably did me a favour. Fab wasn't right for me: *I* knew it, *you* knew it, everyone knew it – everyone, that is, except Fab.'

'Well, I'm just glad Ryan decided to make amends by giving you his spare ticket,' said Marianne. She beamed at her companions. 'Isn't it nice that we're all here together with our gorgeous escorts?' She shot a lustful glance at Scott, who was engrossed in a conversation about computer golf simulators with Kieran. 'It's just a shame Laura couldn't make it. I called her this morning and begged her to change her mind about coming, but she's still feeling sensitive about that nasty dogging business. I told her it's old gossip – that the only thing people want to talk about now is Bibi Montague's botched facelift. But she said she's just not ready to face people.' Marianne shrugged. 'What can you do?'

Keeley turned to Cindy. 'Have *you* seen Laura recently?' she said, unable to keep the accusing tone out of her voice. 'She's been lying low for weeks. Marianne and I are starting to get quite worried about her.'

Cindy shook her head. 'Not for a little while, but I'm sure she's fine.' She took a sip of mojito to hide her awkwardness. The truth was, she'd seen Laura just the day before as she parked her car in the McAllisters' driveway, en route to her latest tryst with Jackson. Not that the two women had actually spoken; Laura had simply waved at Cindy through the glass as she hurried past the living-room window.

'I can't imagine how she fills her days without St Benedict's,' Marianne wondered out loud. 'It can't be good for her, being cooped up in that house all day.'

'I expect she's just taking some time out to work through things with Sam.' Cindy shifted from foot to foot. She was a terrible liar. To make matters worse, Scott had just excused himself to go to the bathroom and Kieran was now standing silently at her side, solid and handsome in his dinner suit and bow tie. She could feel the disapproval coming off him in waves. In the wake of their fruitless visit to Coldcliffe Hall, they'd ended up having – if not a row, then certainly a heated debate, over Cindy's involvement in Laura's 'web of deceit', as Kieran put it. 'She's cheating on her husband and I don't see why you should carry on covering for her,' he'd said. 'It'll all end in tears. Mark my words.' And now, as Cindy stood there, desperately trying to think of a way to shift the topic of conversation on to safer ground, she was suddenly overwhelmed by a curious and inexplicable sense of impending doom. Thankfully, Kieran came to her rescue by distracting the others' attention. 'Laura might not have been able to make it, but Sam's here,' he said, pointing to one of the stone caryatids that appeared to support the atrium's magnificent coffered ceiling. 'See, there he is.'

Keeley turned to look. Sam was leaning against the pillar, disguised as a leering harlequin. Next to him, and standing so close their shoulders were almost touching, was Abi, her delicate features concealed by a sequinned half-mask. Opposite them was another couple Keeley didn't recognize. 'Did Sam come with Abi Gainsbourg?' she enquired.

'Yes, I saw them arrive together,' Marianne replied. 'They were just in front of Scott and me in the queue for the cloakroom.'

Keeley pursed her lips. 'So *he's* out enjoying himself, while Laura's stuck at home with the kids.'

'You can hardly blame Sam for wanting to be here,' said Scott, who had now rejoined the group. 'Not when he's up for Sportsman of the Year.'

Marianne put her arm round her lover's waist, smiling as their hips connected. 'And with Xavier tied up in the kitchen I guess it made sense for Sam to treat Abi to a night out.'

'Hmmm, just so long as that's all he's treating her to,' Keeley remarked under her breath.

Marianne frowned. 'Sorry, darling, I didn't catch that. The band's awfully loud.'

'Nothing,' Keeley muttered. 'So who's that couple Sam and Abi are talking to? These damn masks are a pain in the arse. It's impossible to work out who anyone is.'

'That's Jeff Goodbody and his wife, Jo,' said Scott. 'Sam and Jeff go way back. They used to play against each other as amateurs.'

At that moment, Keeley felt a gentle nudge in the small of her back. Realizing that it was Ryan with the drinks, she took his elbow and drew him into the group.

'Everyone, I'd like you to meet Ryan Stoker,' she said, relieving her escort of one of the bellinis he was carrying.

'Hi, guys,' said the footballer, pushing back his mask so that it sat on top of his head, giving him a strange four-dimensional look. 'I feel like such a twat in this thing.'

'I know the feeling,' said Scott, reaching out to shake his hand. 'How are you, Ryan, mate? Nice to see you again.'

Keeley and Marianne exchanged surprised looks. 'Do you two know each other?' they said in unison.

'I've had a couple of golf lessons from Scott,' said Ryan. 'Not that you'd notice. My game's still rubbish.'

Scott clapped Ryan on the back. 'You're used to a bigger ball, that's your problem, mate.'

'Yeah, I'd stick to what you're good at if I were you, and leave the golf to the professionals,' joked Kieran. 'And, Ryan, I have to say you played a blinder against City last Saturday. That penalty save was nothing short of heroic.'

Keeley breathed a sigh of relief. She wouldn't have to worry about nursemaiding Ryan. He'd be in good hands with Scott and Kieran. As the conversation turned to Delchester United's encouraging start to the new season, Keeley found her gaze drifting back to Sam and Abi. She had to admit that Abi looked stunning in a Grecian-style off-the-shoulder dress and strappy sandals, her long hair twisted into a loose chignon. As someone who'd had a fair few flings with married men herself, Keeley had no doubt the pair were more than just good friends. There was something in the way Abi looked at Sam – head tilted coyly to one side, forefinger twirling a loose tendril of hair – which suggested an intimacy that went far beyond the golf course.

As Keeley turned back to her friends, she caught sight of a familiar face – or, rather, a familiar body – weaving her way through the crowd. Despite her dramatic Persian cat eye mask, Destiny's famous curves, encased in a skin-tight silver lamé sheath, were unmistakeable. She sashayed towards the band while dozens of pairs of eyes – male *and* female – tracked her progress. Fresh from her sojourn on *Celebrity Lust Island,* Destiny was now more famous than ever. Not only had she won the competition, bagging the £50,000 prize money, but her sexploits had earned her acres of tabloid coverage, as well as a lucrative advertising deal for a range of feminine wipes.

Despite their falling-out, Keeley was keen to show off her association with the glamour model for the benefit of any would-be suitors. 'Hey, Destiny!' she called out, standing on her tiptoes and waving her hand above her head ostentatiously. Failing to get a response, she flipped her mask up over her head. 'It's me, Keeley,' she said as Destiny drew level. The model paused and looked her right in the eye. Then she gave a superior little toss of her head and marched straight past without saying a word. Keeley's face dropped. To cover her embarrassment, she pulled her mask back over her face and looked around anxiously, hoping not too many people had noticed the snub.

Marianne flashed the younger woman a sympathetic look. 'You girls still not talking, eh?'

'Apparently not,' said Keeley flatly. 'But who needs friends like Destiny anyway? She always was too big for her boots, and now she's won that stupid TV show her ego must be the size of Saturn and all its bloody rings. I don't think I could bear to be around her, to be perfectly honest.'

'Wasn't the show finale fantastic?' said Marianne, clapping her hands together. 'It went right to the wire, didn't it? I thought Shannon was going to pass out when the presenter revealed that Destiny had beaten her by one solitary shag.'

'Is Shannon here tonight?' Keeley asked. But before Marianne could reply, a loud gong sounded, signalling that the ballroom was now ready to receive the dinner guests. As she and the others finished their drinks and prepared to join the queue for gondolas, Keeley looked around for Sam and Abi but they were nowhere to be seen.

Outside, golfer and caddie were making their own entertainment in one of the wooden gazebos that studded St Benedict's lush grounds. 'That's better,' said Sam as he collected the last few grains of white powder on his fingertip and rubbed them across his gums. 'Now we can really enjoy ourselves.'

'Do you think anyone saw us leave?' said Abi, looking anxiously towards the clubhouse.

'Who cares?' Sam smiled lazily as he felt the effects of the drug kick in.

Abi wagged her finger. 'Seriously, Sam, we've got to be really careful tonight. Xavier's in the kitchen, remember. He knows I've come here with you, but it would only take one of the waiting staff to see you with your hand on my knee under the dinner table and –'

'Yeah, yeah, I get the picture,' said Sam, cutting her off. Abi used to be such a laugh, but now all she ever did was nag him – and he already had a wife for that. 'So how was your surprise anniversary dinner?' he asked. 'All hearts, flowers and escargots, washed down with a bottle of vintage *je ne sais quoi*, was it?'

Abi grinned. 'Something like that. I was quite touched, actually; Xav had gone to so much trouble.' Her smile faded. 'I felt really guilty, sitting there, holding his hand and telling him I loved him when all I could think about was you.'

'Are you having second thoughts about leaving him?' Sam asked hopefully.

Abi looked at him aghast. 'God no, of course not.' She reached out a hand and tenderly cupped the side of Sam's face. 'As far as I'm concerned, the sooner you and I can be together, the better. I know our other halves are going to be dreadfully hurt, but I can't see any way round it. You can't fight a love like ours – and, God knows, we've tried.' She looked back towards the clubhouse. Faint strains of the overture from *Madame Butterfly* drifted across the lawn. 'Shall we go back in? It must be nearly time for the dinner.'

'What's the rush?' said Sam. 'Nobody's going to miss us for a little while.' He reached out and grabbed Abi's arse, feeling the familiar stirring in his loins when he discovered she wasn't wearing any underwear. 'You're so damn hot,' he said, taking her earlobe in his mouth and sucking it hard.

Abi moved her hand; her cigarette was dangerously close to Sam's suit sleeve. 'Yeah, and so will you be if you don't watch yourself with this fag.'

Sam grabbed the cigarette and flung it to the floor of the gazebo, grinding it into the dirt with his heel. Seizing Abi's head between his hands, he thrust his tongue into her mouth. The young caddie responded with enthusiasm, grabbing a hunk of Sam's hair with one hand, while the other sought out his stiffening cock.

'Oh, baby,' Sam moaned as he fumbled with his

cummerbund. 'I think I'm going to explode.' His flies successfully unbuttoned, he pushed Abi up against the wall of the gazebo and worked a hand under her dress. She gasped as his hand made contact with the soft skin of her inner thighs.

'We shouldn't be doing this,' Abi whispered. 'Not here. What if someone sees us?'

By way of response, Sam parted Abi's legs with his knee and reached into his trousers. As usual, the caddie was powerless to resist.

Not far away, Anthony Lanchester was striding purposefully up the long driveway that led to the clubhouse. He was returning from the main entrance gate, where a scuffle had broken out between a guest and one of the more persistent paparazzi. By the time Lanchester arrived, security guards had managed to sweet-talk the guest back into his limo. Meanwhile, the disgruntled paparazzo sat on the grass verge nursing a bloody nose and a broken Hasselblad. Keen to avoid any police involvement, Lanchester handed the assault victim an absorbent dressing from the medical kit he was carrying and assured him the management would cover the cost of any repairs to his camera. After some brief negotiation, during which the snapper successfully added a six-month club membership to his compensation package, the two shook hands. The crisis averted, Lanchester was making his way back to the clubhouse, chest puffed out in pride at a job well done, when the unmistakeable sound of a couple having sexual relations drifted towards him. Gasping in irritation, he stopped and stared about him. The noises seemed to be coming from a wooden gazebo nestled at the foot of the gently sloping front lawn. There were moans and yelps and guttural expletives that made Lanchester frown in the manner of a churchgoing teetotaller. Suddenly, a woman's voice called out. She spoke quickly, running her words together. 'Hole-in-one,' she seemed to be saying. 'Holeinoneholeinoneholeinone.' Lanchester glanced anxiously towards the ballroom's vast terrace where a cluster of dinner guests was enjoying a spectacular sunset, drinks in hand. Sounds carried easily in the still night air and, with the orchestra apparently taking a break, it was surely only a matter of time before the copulators' bestial cacophony wafted up to them.

Inside the gazebo, Sam and Abi were seconds away from a simultaneous orgasm when all at once, the caddie heard the crackle of radio static.

'Shit,' she said as she pushed Sam off her and began scrabbling on the floor for her mask.

'Hey, what are you doing?' said a bewildered Sam. 'I haven't finished yet.'

'Oh, but I think you have, sir.'

Sam spun round. The general manager of St Benedict's was standing in the doorway. In one hand, he held a radio; in the other, a small red box emblazoned with a white cross. The golfer looked at Abi, who was frozen against the wall of the gazebo, mask pressed to her face with both hands. Sam shuffled forward from the shadows, his movements hindered somewhat by the trousers and underwear bunched round his ankles. Lanchester coughed in embarrassment as his eyes took in the wilting erection bobbing between the man's legs, before his gaze travelled slowly upwards. As soon as he realized who he was dealing with, the general manager's expression changed from disgust to alarm.

'Oh, Mr Bentley, it's you. I'm terribly sorry, sir. I was walking through the grounds when I heard some strange noises. I thought I'd better investigate.'

Sam gestured to Abi. 'My wife and I were just enjoying an intimate moment,' he said cockily. 'Do you have a problem with that?'

Lanchester began backing away. 'No, no, of course not, Mr Bentley, sir. Please accept my sincerest apologies for the interruption. I shall leave you and your, er, wife in peace.' He licked his lips nervously. 'However, perhaps I could ask you to keep the noise levels down. For the sake of our other dinner guests, you understand.'

'No problem,' said Sam. He turned to Abi. 'Did you hear that, sweetheart? I know I drive you wild, but you're going to have to put a sock in it.'

The woman made no reply and Lanchester sensed her mortification was even greater than his, if such a thing were possible. He also registered that she had blonde hair. Laura Bentley was a brunette. 'Enjoy the rest of your evening,' he said stiffly. Then he turned and walked away.

As he retraced his steps across the lawn, Lanchester let out a great sigh. Harry Hunter was right: he *was* fighting a losing battle. 'That's it,' he said out loud. 'I've had enough. From now on, if they want to behave like savages, they bloody well can.' And at that moment, it felt as if a great weight had been lifted from his shoulders.

*

Inside the ballroom, Keeley and her party were being delivered to their dining table by a handsome moustachioed gondolier. When Keeley saw Marianne flash her golf coach a loving look as he helped her out of the boat, she couldn't help smiling. Only a few short weeks ago, the older woman would have made a play for the gondolier, no doubt about it, but tonight she only had eyes for Scott. Although she was pleased to see Marianne so loved up, Keeley couldn't help feeling a pang of loss. Her friends were dropping like flies. Destiny was blanking her, Laura had become a virtual hermit and now that Marianne was besotted with a man young enough to be her son, she was certain to have less time for the lunches and shopping expeditions that were Keeley's lifeblood. As she sought out her place card at the dining table, she couldn't help sighing at the unfairness of it all.

'Penny for 'em?' said Ryan, pulling out her chair with a flourish.

Keeley was impressed by her escort's chivalry. The footballer was certainly on his best behaviour. He'd never so much as held a door open for her before. 'Sorry, I was miles away,' she murmured.

Ryan took the seat beside her. 'I hope I'm not boring you,' he said, tossing his mask on the table.

'Of course you're not.' Keeley looked at him. He smiled back at her and she noticed for the first time that he had a cute dimple in his left cheek. 'Can I ask you something, Ryan?' she said.

'Sure.'

'Why did you invite me here tonight? I didn't think you even liked me.'

'That's not true. I just didn't like the way you gave Fab the runaround.'

'But you could've given your spare ticket to anyone. You must know loads of girls.'

Ryan shrugged. 'I wanted to give it to someone who'd really appreciate it, that's all.' He picked up his mask and began fiddling with the elastic.

'Sorry,' said Keeley, sensing his discomfort. 'It's mean of me to put you on the spot like that. The fact is, I already know why you invited me.'

Ryan's eyebrows shot up. 'You do?'

'Yeah, because you feel guilty about grassing me up to Fab.' She raised an eyebrow. 'I'm right, aren't I?'

Ryan licked his lips. 'Well, yes, I guess that's part of the reason.' He was about to say something else, but checked himself, clearing his throat to conceal the manoeuvre.

'Anyway, I'm really glad you did invite me. I'm having a brilliant time,' Keeley chattered. 'Now let's get some drinks in. I'm spitting feathers here.'

While Ryan attempted to collar a passing wine waiter, Keeley's eyes flitted from table to table, checking out the talent. There were plenty of good-looking men in the room, nearly all of them accompanied. But Keeley wasn't the sort of girl to let a detail like that stand in her way. She'd just have to be discreet about it: a covert look here, a whispered word there, a phone number slipped into a suit pocket. She'd done it dozens of times before. As her gaze drifted around the room, she noticed Sam and Abi making a late entrance, heads bowed as if they didn't want to draw attention to themselves. They took their seats at a table near the front of the room, beside the

343

wooden podium that had been set up for the prize-giving ceremony, due to take place after dinner. They were sitting with Jeff Goodbody and his wife and some other people she didn't recognize. It didn't escape Keeley's notice that Abi's chignon, which had been smooth and well secured earlier in the evening, was now looking decidedly unkempt and strands of hair were hanging down over her shoulders. Even more tellingly, the fastening on Sam's cummerbund had mysteriously worked its way round to the front of his torso. Keeley shook her head; those two were at it, she was sure as she could be. She turned to Cindy, intending to draw her attention to the pair's dishevelled appearance – and then, suddenly, her heart was in her mouth.

Sitting at the next table was the middle-aged woman with the trout pout who'd been in the spa the day Keeley had been spurned by Destiny. The woman was almost certainly the owner of the Baume & Mercier watch – currently winging its way by special delivery to a lucky bidder in Virginia Water – and the Marc Jacobs pumps with the embroidered initials that were now adorning Keeley's feet. As Keeley watched in horror, a stocky man with a florid complexion and public-school accent descended on the woman. 'Annabel darling,' he brayed. 'How good to see you. I was saying to Gracie only the other day, "We haven't seen the Frenches for simply ages. We must have them round for dinner".' As the woman twittered a response, Keeley gulped. Annabel French. The initials matched those on the pumps. This was her victim, there was no doubt about it. As the man returned to his own table, Annabel French happened to glance in

Keeley's direction. Their eyes locked together and Annabel frowned as if she recognized her fellow guest but couldn't quite place her. Keeley looked away quickly and pretended to be studying the menu.

'Are you all right, honey?' said Cindy, leaning to one side to allow the waiter to fill her wine glass. 'You look a little flushed.'

'I'm just a bit hot, that's all,' replied Keeley, fanning her face with the menu. 'I'll be fine in a minute.'

Keeley spent the first two courses in a state of nervous anxiety. Xavier's tasting menu was to die for, but the food tasted like cardboard in her mouth. She did her best to act normally as she chatted with the others round the table, but all she could think of was the ugly scene that would ensue if her victim spotted the pumps. The shoes were very distinctive and clearly one of a kind. The minute Annabel French saw them she would know they were hers. Given that the tablecloths only reached halfway to the floor and Annabel was sitting less than three feet away, Keeley knew it was only a matter of time. While the gazpacho bowls were being whisked away, Keeley came to a decision: she would have to take the pumps off. It was either that or spend the rest of the dinner with her stomach in knots. She waited until the waitress was serving the third course – a delicate green tea and tarragon mousse – before easing the pumps off one by one, using the toes of the opposing foot. She was about to reach discreetly under the table, intending to pick up the shoes and lay them on her lap when, out of the corner of her eye, she noticed Annabel French's napkin falling to the floor. As she watched her bend down to retrieve it,

Keeley realized that in approximately two seconds' time Annabel's line of sight would be mere inches away from the pumps. Acting almost by reflex, Keeley's foot swept the pumps to her right-hand side, under Ryan's chair where they would be safely out of view. At the same time, her foot brushed against one of Ryan's soft Italian loafers. Ryan, who was deep in conversation with Scott, continued chatting to the golf coach as if he hadn't noticed.

Pleased that she'd managed to avoid detection, Keeley picked up her fork and started to eat with renewed gusto. 'Isn't this mousse divine?' she remarked to Cindy. 'Xavier's so talented. I wonder if his wife appreciates him.' She glared at Sam and Abi, who were chatting animatedly, staring deep into one another's eyes. 'It certainly doesn't look like it from where I'm sitting.'

Cindy followed the direction of Keeley's gaze. 'You're not still worried about those two, are you?'

'Oh come on, Cindy. Are you blind? Just look at their body language. They're having an affair; I'd stake my Louis Vuitton luggage on it. And somebody really ought to tell Laura.'

Cindy sighed. She'd had enough of the Bentleys' tangled love lives. 'It's your call, Keeley,' she said. 'I don't want to get involved.'

Keeley was about to ask Cindy how *she'd* feel if it were Kieran having the affair and nobody bothered to tell her, when all of a sudden she felt a gentle pressure on the side of her right foot. She looked at Ryan. He was still talking to Scott and his upper body was facing away from her. The next moment, the pressure was replaced by a gentle stroking action. Keeley was so shocked she let out a little gasp. Ryan didn't react, but Marianne broke off her conversation with Kieran and gave her friend a questioning look. Keeley pointed to the mousse. 'I have a sensitive tooth,' she lied. She waited until the others had resumed their conversation and then risked a peek under the table. To her astonishment, she saw that Ryan had eased off one of his loafers and his stockinged foot was now caressing her bare one with surprising delicacy. She bit her lip, suppressing a smile. When she'd brushed against Ryan's foot earlier, he'd obviously thought she was playing footsie with him – and now he was reciprocating. Keeley allowed the footballer to continue his ministrations while she sipped her wine, wondering how best to extract herself from the situation without causing offence. Then a sudden realization dawned on her: perhaps she'd had too much to drink, but the fact was, she was rather enjoying the attention from her old adversary. On impulse, she extended an arm under the tablecloth and placed it on Ryan's thigh. His powerful quadricep quivered beneath her touch. Pausing momentarily in his conversation with Scott, the footballer reached for his glass of wine. As his eyes met Keeley's, he broke into a shy smile.

By the end of the meal everyone in the ballroom was well fed – not to mention well lubricated. A rowdy applause broke out as St Benedict's portly president, Charles Peach, OBE (or 'Fruity', as he was known by almost everyone) ascended the podium, clutching a set of well-thumbed prompt cards and two gold-plated figurines. It was the moment everyone had been waiting for:

the prize-giving ceremony. As Fruity made a great show of positioning the figurines on top of his lectern, Sam rubbed his hands together. 'Here we go,' he whispered to Abi. 'My name had better be on one of those bloody trophies or I'm resigning my membership.'

The caddie – wired from copious quantities of alcohol and cocaine – grinned maniacally as she reached for her cigarette packet. 'Don't worry, babe,' she drawled. 'You're the best. Everyone knows it.'

Once the applause and cat-calling had died down, Fruity embarked on his traditional meandering and self-congratulatory speech about the club's achievements over the past year – the record amounts raised for charity, the opening of the new squash courts and the fitness studio's employment of Madonna's former ashtanga yoga instructor. Half an hour later, he was finally ready to make the only announcement anybody cared about: the Sportsman and Sportswoman of the Year awards. Always hotly contested, the awards celebrated not only an individual's physical and professional achievements, but also their charity fundraising efforts. As widely anticipated, the women's award went to Bunty Cowper. A member of St Benedict's for the past two decades, Bunty had recently been named British crown green bowling ladies' singles champion and was famed for her bulging forearms and risqué above-the-knee pleated skirts. There was stiffer competition for the men's award – due mainly to the influx of pro footballers to the club over the previous year. Sam took a fortifying swig of Remy Martin and leaned forward eagerly as Fruity prepared to make the announcement.

'And the award for Sportsman of the Year goes to . . .' the president paused, eking out the suspense. '. . . Mr Samuel Bent-leeeeeeey!' Sam jumped up and punched the air with his fist as the room erupted into enthusiastic applause. Although his fellow golfers knew him to be an arrogant and utterly self-absorbed individual, Sam remained a popular and charismatic figure among the members of St Benedict's, who were blinded by his handsome face and dazzling smile. 'But before I hand over this splendid trophy,' Fruity continued, 'we have, in the customary manner, a short film to mark Sam's considerable achievements over this past year.' He turned to the huge plasma screen, mounted behind the podium, which had already paid tribute to Bunty Cowper. On cue, Sam appeared, striding manfully across the green at St Benedict's, hair rippling in the wind, buttocks taut in sky-blue Tommy Hilfiger golf trousers, five-iron slung casually over his shoulder – all set against the rousing backdrop of Bonnie Tyler's 'Holding Out for a Hero'.

'Hey, that's the pro-celebrity golf tournament,' said Sam, grinning at his digital doppelganger. 'I look great, don't I?' he murmured to Abi. 'See the way those trousers hug my butt.'

Sam had no sooner finished speaking when the plasma screen suddenly went dark. A ripple of disapproval spread through the audience. Fruity stepped up to the mic, wringing his hands. 'Sorry, folks, we seem to be having some technical difficulties. We'll get it sorted out just as soon as we can.'

Sam banged the table with the palm of his hand, causing the coffee spoons to rattle in their saucers. 'Fucking idiots,' he said aggressively. 'Why do they have to go and ruin my big night?'

Jeff Goodbody put a calming hand on Sam's shoulder. 'Easy, Sam. People are watching you, remember.'

The golfer responded immediately, breaking into a broad smile and giving an exaggerated 'oh well, it can't be helped' shrug for the benefit of the tables nearest to him.

A moment later, the screen came back to life. Fruity clapped his hands together. 'Ah, good. We seem to be back in business.' Then his jaw dropped – for the face on the screen wasn't Sam's, but Jeff Goodbody's.

Sam looked at Jeff. 'What the fuck's going on?'

Jeff shook his head, but his face had turned quite pale. Beside him, his wife set down the petit four that had been halfway to her mouth and watched the screen with interest.

As the camera panned around, it became clear that the footage had been taken inside some sort of outbuilding, which several of the more observant guests recognized as St Benedict's ancient potting shed. The camera operator's hand was wobbling badly and at first it was difficult to see what was going on, but then as the camera zoomed in on Jeff's torso, it became clear that the golf coach was not only naked from the waist down, but also sporting a large erection. There was a collective intake of breath from the dinner guests, followed by an outbreak of tittering. The Jeff sitting at the dinner table let out a groan and buried his head in his hands. His wife, meanwhile, had snatched up her napkin and was pressing it to her lips as if she might be sick.

On the podium, Fruity's face had frozen in a rictus of horror. A few moments later, he came to his senses and began frantically looking around for a member of the club's audio-visual department. There was none in sight. 'Somebody stop that tape!' he cried, shaking his fist at the screen. His request was ignored and the footage rolled on.

'Ooh, Jeff, you're a *very* big boy,' a female voice purred over the speakers. A cheer went up from the audience, who were delighted to discover that the tape had audio.

Jeff winked at his unseen companion. 'We aim to please,' he said, putting his hands on his hips and turning to one side, so the camera could capture his tumescence in profile. He reached out a hand. 'My turn now,' he said. 'I want to film that awesome body of yours for posterity.'

As the camera changed hands, the dinner guests were treated to a close-up of a wooden trug. The next instant, a pair of enormous breasts filled the screen. Their proud owner cupped them in her hands, offering them to the camera.

'You dirty bitch,' said Jeff. His voice had grown quite hoarse. 'I can see I'm going to have to give you a good hard seeing to.'

The woman giggled. 'All good things come to those who wait.' Her voice took on a teasing, mellifluous tone. 'Have you got some candy for me, Uncle Jeff? I've been a very good girl.'

Jeff set the camera down on a workbench. It tracked him as he walked over to a chocolate linen jacket, which was hanging over one of the tall rakes ranged against the wall. Reaching into the jacket pocket, he pulled out a clear plastic wrap, filled with white powder. He handed the wrap over, before returning to the camera. 'That'll get you in the mood,' he said as the lens moved over his companion's flat stomach and up towards her face. A second collective gasp went up, followed by the sound of dozens of chair legs scraping across the floor as the dinner guests turned to look at the woman whose face was now staring out from the plasma screen.

All the time the film had been rolling, Destiny Morris had been sitting silently at her table, surrounded by assorted flunkies and hangers-on, praying that somebody, somewhere, would press stop on the video machine and spare her humiliation. But it was too late.

The model watched horrified through her fingers as the tape showed her chopping up the coke with a credit card on the surface of a make-up mirror before greedily snorting all three lines through the plastic shell of a cheap biro. When she was done, she looked up at the camera pie-eyed, blobs of white powder still hanging from her nostrils. 'Okay. Let's fuck,' she said baldly. Then she lay on the potting-shed floor, which had been covered with a piece of sacking, and spread her legs wide. At that moment, the screen went blank. A chorus of boos went up from the audience. Without saying a word, Jo Good-body picked up a brimming water jug and deposited its contents over her husband's head, before storming out of the room in tears. For a moment, Jeff sat there, water dripping down his collar, a slice of lemon wedged behind his ear, wondering whether or not to brazen it out.

'Bad luck, mate,' Sam muttered under his breath as he held out a napkin. The golf coach took the napkin and wiped it across his face. Then he stood up and shuffled towards the door, knowing that his career at St Benedict's lay in tatters.

A stunned silence filled the room, broken only by a few embarrassed coughs. Even the club president, who usually had ample reserves of bluster, was lost for words. Suddenly, a pert figure dressed in black emerged from the shadows of an alcove and marched up to the podium.

'Now look here, you can't just —' Fruity started to say as the gatecrasher mounted the dais.

'Zip it, you old fart,' she said, elbowing him roughly aside.

Destiny made a huffing noise as she eyed her nemesis. 'Shannon Stewart. I might have known,' she muttered.

Leaning into the mic, Shannon put her hand above her eyes, surveying the dinner guests like a captain looking out to sea. 'Destiny? Where are you, *girlfriend*?' she said with a super-sarcastic emphasis on the final word. She held a video tape aloft. 'I think this belongs to you. Didn't you say there was a reward for its safe return?'

Destiny slammed her hands on the table and rose to her feet. 'You conniving little thief,' she yelled, her voice echoing around the ballroom. 'That tape is *my* private property; it was stolen from my house when I was away in Antigua — and you're the evil bitch who did it.'

'I wouldn't go making wild accusations if I were you. Not in front of all these witnesses,' Shannon said with a superior smile. 'You've no proof I stole the tape. Let's just say it found its way into my hands via a third party — and now I'm returning it to you. I simply thought the ladies and gentlemen of St Benedict's ought to see it first, just so they can see exactly what a dirty, husband-stealing, cokehead slapper you really are.'

At this, Destiny let out a high-pitched banshee screech and went running up to the podium as fast as her five-inch stilettoes could carry her. Fruity made a half-hearted attempt to intercept the enraged model, but she shoved him aside and hurled herself at Shannon. Lectern and mic went flying as both girls crashed to the ground in a tangle of legs and hair. Destiny quickly got the upper hand as she straddled Shannon and pinned her arms to the ground, before working up a good gob of spittle and firing it into her enemy's face. But her victory was destined to be short-lived. Moments later, she was grabbed by a dinner-suited security man, who effortlessly heaved her over his shoulder in a fireman's lift and carried her from the room as she bellowed expletives and pummelled his back with her fists. A sobbing Shannon was escorted away in a similarly undignified fashion, with the president's threat of a lifetime ban ringing in her ears. As the dust settled, Fruity scuttled over to the twenty-four-piece orchestra, who had been watching the proceedings with amusement, and ordered them to start playing. The evening wasn't quite working out as he'd hoped. Little did he know that the worst was yet to come.

Cindy picked up her empty Armagnac glass and waved it at a passing drinks waiter. 'After what I've just seen, I need something to calm my nerves,' she explained to Marianne. 'I know you said I was in for a spectacular evening, but I must admit that wasn't the sort of entertainment I was expecting.'

'Nothing that goes on at St Benedict's surprises me any more,' Marianne declared as she puffed on a slim cigar. 'Although I must admit I didn't think Jeff Goodbody was the type.'

'Me neither,' said Scott. 'Jeff and Destiny: who would've thought it? And as for the drugs . . .' He let out a long, low whistle.

Marianne exhaled a cloud of pungent smoke. 'Keeley's going to be gutted when she finds out what she's missed. We'll have to give her all the gory details when she gets back.'

Cindy turned towards the ballroom's elegant French windows, which opened out on to the terrace. 'She's been gone for ages. Do you think I should see if she's okay?'

Marianne shook her head. 'She'll be fine with Ryan. I'd leave them to it if I were you. I know Keeley said she was feeling faint, but I have a sneaking suspicion she was telling fibs.'

'Why on earth would she do that?'

Marianne winked. 'Use your imagination, darling.'

Outside, in a corner of the terrace that was screened from the ballroom windows by a line of leafy bamboos, Ryan and a barefoot Keeley had been snogging for the best part of ten minutes. 'I can't believe we're doing this,' Keeley whispered in Ryan's ear when finally she came up for breath.

'I can,' said Ryan as he worked his hands up and down her waist and hips. 'As a matter of fact, I've imagined kissing you lots of times before.'

Keeley looked at him in surprise. 'But you were so

mean to me the whole time I was going out with Fab. I was convinced you hated my guts.'

'Yeah, well . . . like I said before, I didn't think you and Fab were right for each other. But me, on the other hand . . .' Ryan's dimple appeared in his cheek. 'Let's just say I think I know how to handle a girl like you.'

'I see,' said Keeley teasingly. 'And what sort of girl might that be?'

'Oh, you know . . . high maintenance, easily bored, likes to get her own way.'

'You cheeky bugger,' said Keeley as she wrapped her arms round the footballer's broad shoulders and offered her mouth up to his.

Less than a mile away, in the master bedroom suite at Coldcliffe Hall, another pair of lovebirds were locked in a post-coital embrace.

'So,' said Jackson as he pulled one of Laura's fat curls and watched it spring satisfyingly back into place. 'Are you sure this is what you want? I don't want you to feel I'm pressuring you.'

Laura looked up at him. Her face was suffused with happiness. 'I've never been more sure of anything in my life.'

'My sweet Laura,' said Jackson, his voice cracking with emotion. 'I never thought this day would come. I was so scared you'd take one look at the monster I've become and run away.'

Laura's fingers flew to his lips. 'Hush,' she said fiercely. 'You're not a monster. I never want to hear you speak that word again.'

Jackson closed his eyes, savouring the sweet taste of success. He'd dreamed of this moment for so long, he could hardly dare believe it was finally happening. 'You've made me so happy,' he whispered into Laura's hair. 'Happier than I imagined it was possible for a man to be.'

Laura sighed with pleasure and drew Jackson closer, raining kisses across his scarred cheek. 'So. Now. All. We. Have. To. Do. Is. Tell. Sam,' she said, punctuating each word with a kiss.

'And when shall we do that, my love?'

Laura smiled coyly. 'There's no time like the present.'

'First thing tomorrow then?'

'I was thinking sooner than that.'

Jackson looked at Laura with a mixture of shock and delight. 'Tonight? You're kidding, aren't you?'

Laura shook her head as she shucked off the thousand-count Egyptian cotton sheet that was now crumpled and damp with perspiration after their prolonged love-making. 'Come on. If we go now, we can catch Sam before he leaves St Benedict's. I'd rather have it out with him there than wait till he gets home and risk waking the girls.'

'What about Marta? She thinks you went to the cinema with a friend. Won't she wonder where on earth you've got to?'

Laura picked her rose-print tulle bra and matching thong off the bedroom floor. She'd bought them specially and Jackson had been more than appreciative. 'Don't worry about Marta. She's staying the night. I told her not to wait up for me.'

For a moment Jackson lay stock still, like a rabbit frozen in the headlights.

'Come on,' Laura urged as she stepped into the thong. 'Before I lose my nerve.'

It took them less than five minutes to reach St Benedict's in Jackson's vintage Aston. As they stepped out of the car, Jackson noticed that Laura was shivering.

'Are you okay?' he asked, his eyes full of concern.

'I'm fine, just a bit chilly. I stupidly forgot to pick up my pashmina before we left.'

Jackson locked the car and moved to Laura's side, wrapping a protective arm round her shoulders. 'It's gone midnight, you know. We don't have to do this now. It can always wait until the morning.'

'No,' said Laura firmly. 'I want to get it out of the way tonight – and then tomorrow, if it's okay with you, the girls and I can move into Coldcliffe.'

'It's more than okay,' said Jackson, kissing the top of her head. 'It's bloody brilliant.'

As they walked the short distance to the clubhouse, Laura felt strangely light-headed. Sam was in for a big shock. It wasn't like her to be so impetuous; she'd always been the sensible one in their partnership. But she'd had enough of being Sam's doormat and now, just for once, she was going to put herself first.

Back in the ballroom, the orchestra was playing the last song of the evening – a cover of Roxy Music's 'Jealous Guy' – and the dancefloor was filled with smooching couples. In a candlelit alcove, Sam and Abi were working their way through a bottle of Jack Daniel's. On the table in front of them sat Sam's Sportsman of the Year trophy, which the club president had unceremoniously thrust into the golfer's hand an hour earlier. Sam was still smarting from the indignity of it. 'I can't believe Fruity let those stupid models ruin the award ceremony,' he griped. 'I spent two hours last night writing my speech.'

'My poor baby,' said Abi, stroking a damp tendril of hair from her lover's forehead.

'Careful,' Sam slurred, brushing her hand away. 'People'll start to talk.'

'You know what, Sam, I'm past caring,' said Abi as she stubbed her cigarette out on the tabletop. 'Come on, let's dance.' Ignoring Sam's protests, she led him on to the dance floor and pressed her body close to his.

Keeley watched them intently as they swayed in time to the music. Suddenly, her head, which had been resting on Ryan's shoulder, snapped up. 'Gotcha!' she hissed.

'What are you on about, Kee?' the footballer mumbled into her hair.

She smiled thinly. 'Sam Bentley's having an affair with his caddie. I've been saying it for weeks and now I've got proof.'

Ryan looked over his shoulder. 'They're just dancing, aren't they? No harm in that.'

'Where's her hand then?'

Ryan blinked hard. He, like most of the dinner guests, was rather the worse for wear. 'Sorry. You've lost me.'

Keeley spun Ryan round so he had a better view of the couple. 'See. Abi's left hand is on Sam's shoulder. Her right hand is stroking Sam's todger.'

Ryan dropped his gaze. His eyes widened. 'Oh my God, so it is.'

'*Un-beee-lievable*. The dogging was bad enough, but fucking his caddie too . . .' Keeley shook her head despairingly. 'First thing tomorrow, I'm calling Laura and telling her what a lying, cheating scumbag she's married to.'

'Does it have to be *first* thing in the morning?' said Ryan with a mischievous glint in his eye. 'Only, I thought we could have a lie in and then I could make you breakfast.'

'Ryan Stoker!' cried Keeley, opening her mouth in mock shock. 'Are you asking me to spend the night with you?' She didn't need to answer yes or no. The smile on her face said it all.

Harry watched from his table as Keeley gave Ryan a lingering kiss. 'That was quick work,' he muttered under his breath. He picked up his bottle of beer and found that it was empty. Sighing, he turned to Dylan, who was lolling against his shoulder, semi-comatose. 'Come on, mate, I think it's time to get you home,' he said. 'There's nothing more for us here.'

The lone doorman could scarcely believe his eyes when he saw Jackson West approaching the clubhouse. He'd heard that the legendary racing driver was living in Kirkhulme, but had never seen him around the village; nor had anyone he knew. Stranger still, Jackson was accompanied by the wife of St Benedict's best-known golf pro. The doorman gave a deferent bow. 'Good evening, sir . . . madam.'

Jackson nodded a greeting. 'Mrs Bentley's come to meet her husband,' he said in a low voice. 'It's cold out here. May we wait inside?'

'But of course, sir,' said the bemused doorman, pushing open the swing door and stepping aside to allow them entry. 'And can I say what a great pleasure it is to see you here at St Benedict's, Mr West. I've always been a great admirer of yours.'

Jackson managed the ghost of a smile as he walked past the doorman and ushered Laura into the warmth of the atrium. Earlier, he'd been excited about the thought of confronting Sam, but now that he was actually here Jackson was starting to feel anxious at the thought of being on public display. His eyes flickered apprehensively over the pair of ornate arched doors that led to the ballroom. 'So what's the plan?' he said, suddenly aware that he and Laura hadn't thought this through at all. 'Do we wait for Sam to come out and then take him some place quiet for a chat?'

'I guess so.' Laura started walking towards the doors. 'Hear that?' she said, cocking her head to one side. '"Jealous Guy". Pretty ironic, huh?'

'Hey, where are you going? I think it's best if we wait here, don't you?'

'I just want to take a quick peek,' said Laura, without breaking stride. 'So I can see what I've missed.' She pulled open one of the heavy doors and peered round the corner. The ballroom resembled a beautiful painting, albeit one by Hieronymus Bosch. The floor was covered in discarded masks, many of them trodden to a pulp, and guests in various states of inebriation lay slumped across dinner chairs and plush banquettes. At one table, a woman sat in a state of semi-undress, kissing a man passionately, while a second man fondled her naked breasts. Meanwhile, underneath a scale replica of the Bridge of Sighs, one of the young men Laura had seen working in the club shop was having full sex with a striking blonde. Beside them, less than six feet away, a teenage heiress shovelled cocaine into her nose on the end of a house key. As Laura's gaze turned to the couples revolving slowly around the dancefloor, she caught sight of Marianne, wrapped around a young man who she recognized as one of the club's golf coaches. And there was Keeley too, her head resting on Ryan Stoker's shoulder. Close by, Cindy and Kieran swayed to the music, gazing lovingly into each other's eyes. Laura smiled and made a mental note that, as soon as this messy business with Sam was sorted out, she was going to treat her friends to a' posh dinner and tell them all about her new lover. She turned away, intending to go back to Jackson, who was hovering uncertainly a few feet away, but, as she did so, she caught sight of her husband. Laura froze. Sam was dancing with Abi Gainsbourg. She knew he was taking the caddie to the event; that wasn't the problem. What had taken her by surprise was their obvious intimacy. Not only were their arms wrapped round each other, but Sam's face was turned towards Abi's neck, his lips grazing her skin. Both of them looked wasted. As Laura watched, Abi whispered something in Sam's ear. The golfer laughed, and pulled the caddie closer, grinding his pelvis against hers. It was too much for Laura. Without a second thought, she stalked over to her husband and tapped him on the shoulder.

When Sam saw her, his arms fell from Abi's waist and he stumbled backwards, clearly shocked. 'Jesus, Laura. What are you doing here?'

Laura looked the pair up and down disdainfully. 'So this is what you two get up to the minute my back's turned,' she said, shouting to be heard over the orchestra.

Sam started backing away from Abi. 'Listen, Laura, it's not how it looks. I've had a few drinks – and you know how tactile I am when I'm pissed.'

'Tactile?' Laura shrieked. 'You were all over her like a flaming octopus.' She glared at Abi. 'And what about you, *madam*? Does Xavier know you're dancing cheek to cheek with another woman's husband?'

The orchestra had stopped playing now and Laura's words reverberated shrilly around the room. Several clusters of party goers moved unapologetically nearer, not wanting to miss out on any drama. Abi looked at Sam for guidance. The golfer refused to meet her eye. His head was hurting and all he wanted was for everyone in the room to disappear; everyone, that is, but Laura.

Abi sighed. 'We may as well tell her the truth, Sam. She's going to find out sooner or later.'

Laura compressed her lips into a thin line. 'Well?' she said, addressing her husband.

Sam gave Abi a fierce look. 'I don't think this is the right time or place, do you?'

Abi shrugged. 'We've got nothing to be ashamed of.' She opened her sequinned clutch bag, fumbling drunkenly with the clasp. 'Sorry, Laura,' she said as she took out a pack of Marlboro Lights. 'I didn't want you to find out like this. But the fact is' – she paused to light her cigarette – 'Sam and I have been having an affair for the best part of five months.'

A gasp went up from the onlookers, followed by an

outbreak of excited twitterings. Having witnessed what was going on, Keeley broke through the crowd of people who'd gathered around the threesome and marched up to Laura. Marianne and Cindy were close behind her. 'We're here for you, Laura,' Keeley said, squeezing her friend's shoulder. 'If you need us.'

Laura nodded dumbly, too stunned to speak. She turned to Sam. 'Is it true?' she managed to choke out.

Sam reached for his wife's hand. 'Look, sweetheart, why don't we go somewhere more private and I can explain?'

'So it *is* true.' Laura snatched her hand away. 'Don't you "sweetheart" me,' she yelled. 'First you drag us into the newspapers with your filthy dogging – and now this! I've had it with you, Sam. You obviously don't give a toss about the girls and me. All you care about is your own selfish pleasure. Is there anything else you haven't told me? Are you sure you haven't got a whole harem of bunker babes stashed away?'

From the doorway, Jackson watched as Laura tore into her husband. He'd known about Sam's affair with Abi for several months. In fact, there wasn't much that went on at St Benedict's he didn't know about – his contacts kept him well informed. But, realizing he'd have a job explaining to Laura precisely *how* he knew, he'd decided to keep his counsel. He badly wanted to go to Laura's side. If ever she needed him, it was now. If only he didn't feel so dreadfully self-conscious among all these strangers. Although a sizeable crowd had gathered around the golfer, most of the guests were saying their goodbyes and preparing to leave. Soon, they would be filing past him, whispering and pointing. Looking around, Jackson spotted a crumpled papier mâché mask abandoned on a nearby table. It was an ugly thing with slits for eyes and a huge hooked nose. With head bowed, he took the few steps to the table, picked up the mask and slipped it over his head.

Sam rubbed his eyes. This was turning into the longest night of his life. 'There's no one else, I swear it,' he told his wife in a pleading tone. 'Please, Laura, can't we get out of here? We're making an absolute spectacle of ourselves.'

'You should have thought about that before you started fucking Little Miss Golf Buggy over there,' said Laura, looking daggers at Abi, who was casually smoking her cigarette, perfectly confident that at the end of the evening Sam would be leaving with her.

Suddenly, another voice rang out. 'Hey, Sam, aren't you forgetting something?' The golfer scanned the crowd, searching for the face behind the voice. A slender man, hovering behind Laura, in the shadow of an alcove, caught his eye. He was still wearing his mask and dressed incongruously in jeans and a thin cotton jumper.

'Up here,' came the voice again. Sam's gaze switched to the podium. Standing beside the lectern was a mixed-race girl in a waitress uniform. She was very pretty with delicate features and long hair tied in a ponytail. Sam thought she seemed vaguely familiar. For a long moment, she stared at him. 'Don't you remember me?' she said at last.

Abi jabbed a finger towards the podium. 'Oi, waitress

girl. Back off,' she said sharply. 'This has got nothing to do with you.'

'Oh, but it's got everything to do with me,' the girl replied coolly.

All at once, Sam felt a dreadful lurching in the pit of his stomach. It was all coming back to him; he *did* know her. The stag night. She was the girl he'd shagged in the video-conferencing suite.

Laura folded her arms across her chest. 'Come on then,' she said to the girl on the podium. 'Let's hear what you've got to say.'

Elissa thrust out her chin defiantly. 'Sam Bentley slept with me too,' she said. There were more excited murmurings from the crowd. She rubbed her hand across her stomach. 'As a consequence of which, I'm eight weeks pregnant.'

Laura's mouth dropped open.

Sam's expression suggested the incommunicable anguish of someone who has just trapped his fingers in a car door. 'She's lying,' he cried. 'She can't be pregnant. I used a condom.'

At this, Laura swung her arm back and slapped Sam across the face as hard as she could. He touched his hand to his mouth. It came away bloody where Laura's diamond engagement ring had cut his lip.

'You're pathetic, do you know that?' Laura said. She turned to Abi, who had tears rolling down her cheeks, her beautiful face distorted with shock and sadness. 'You're welcome to him, Abi. I just hope you know what an arrogant, egotistical, deceitful pig you're taking on, that's all.' She fixed her husband with a cold stare. 'I'm going

366

home now,' she said calmly, 'to get some sleep. And in the morning I'm leaving you, and I'm taking the girls with me.'

As she turned to go, Sam lunged for her arm. 'Oh no, you're not,' he snarled as he yanked her back towards him.

The man in the mask stepped out of the shadows. 'Take your hands off her.' His voice was quiet but very firm.

Sam glowered at him. 'Do yourself a favour, and piss off – okay?'

The man spoke again. 'I said ... Take. Your hands. Off her.' He tore his mask away and flung it to the ground. Several guests cried out. Others, including Keeley, stepped back in shock. Cindy bit her lip and looked at the ground. She had a very bad feeling.

'Well, look who it is,' said Sam sneeringly. 'The great Jackson West. Come to grace us all with his presence.' He released Laura's arm and took a step towards the interloper. Like many racing drivers, Jackson had a slim frame, and Sam seemed to dwarf him. 'Why don't you crawl back to your Munster mansion, mate? What happens between me and my wife has got fuck all to do with you.'

'That's where you're wrong,' said Laura evenly. She reached out and took Jackson's hand. 'You see, Sam, you're not the only one who's been having an affair.'

Marianne and Keeley gawped at one another. Cindy kept her eyes firmly on the ground. She could hardly bear to watch.

Sam started laughing, but his eyes were hard and cold like chips of ice. 'Oh please,' he said, clutching his stomach stagily. 'You're having it off with that . . . that *creature*?' He leaned towards Laura. 'I knew you were fucking someone else,' he hissed in her face, 'as soon as I found that slutty underwear in your drawer.'

'Don't you dare speak about Jackson like that!' Laura cried. 'He's more of a man than you'll ever be.'

Sam's face twisted into an ugly scowl. 'Oh, sweetheart, you don't know the half of it.'

'What are you talking about?' said Laura, frowning.

She felt Jackson's hand at her elbow. 'Come on, Laura, let's go,' he said. 'He's had far too much to drink. We're not going to get any sense out of him tonight.'

Sam shook a clenched fist in his rival's face. 'My wife's not going anywhere until she's heard the truth about you.'

'Oh for heaven's sake, if you've got something to say, just say it,' said Laura.

Sam picked up a glass of whisky that was lying, half-drunk, on a nearby table and downed it in one. Then he began walking round Jackson in a slow circle, looking him up and down contemptuously as he did so. 'I'm guessing that all the nice ladies and gentlemen standing in this ballroom see you as a pretty tragic figure,' he began. 'And, on the face of it, I suppose you are. You were a sporting hero with the world at your feet, and then you had an horrific car crash, which left you with a face like a melted candle and a bad case of agoraphobia. No wonder you wanted to find yourself a nice quiet spot like Kirkhulme where you wouldn't be bothered and you could live out your days polishing your trophies and pruning your rose bushes.'

Jackson's nostrils flared. He began counting slowly

backwards from thirty, a technique he'd used in his racing days when he was on the starting grid and wanted to block out all the noise and drama around him.

'But that's not all you get up to in that big old house of yours – is it, Jacko, my old son?' Sam stopped pacing and stared at Jackson's face, noting the beads of perspiration that had formed on his top lip. 'Getting worried, are you, mate? And so you should be.'

'Oh for God's sake!' Laura cried. 'Stop playing these ridiculous mind games.' Shoulder-charging Sam out of the way, she took Jackson's hand and began walking towards the door with him.

'He's a drug dealer, Laura.'

Laura stopped in her tracks. 'What did you say?' she said, without turning round.

'He's a drug dealer. One of Cheshire's biggest. He keeps the whole of St Benedict's supplied single-handedly.'

Laura spun to face him. 'You're lying!' she cried. 'You'll say anything to stop me leaving this room with him.' Her hand went to her throat as if she were having difficulty breathing.

Sam shook his head. 'Where do you think he gets his money from? His racing career crashed and burned years ago.'

'Property investments,' Laura spluttered. She turned to her lover. 'Isn't that right, Jackson?'

Jackson opened his mouth to speak, but no words came out.

'It's true,' said Sam. 'Jeff Goodbody told me all about it.'

Laura's hand fell away from Jackson's. 'And what the hell would Jeff know about it?'

'Why, he's the middle man,' said Sam as if it were blindingly obvious. He picked up another abandoned drink — a viscous orange-pink cocktail and knocked it back. 'Jackson imports the drugs and Jeff sells them out of the club shop.' He held out his arms to the guests. 'You can vouch for that, can't you, guys?'

There was a deathly hush. Some people started walking towards the door. 'Jacko's housekeeper acts as courier,' Sam continued blithely. 'After all, nobody would suspect a middle-aged woman in a housecoat of being a drugs mule, now would they?'

At this, the cogs in Cindy's brain began whirring as she remembered the overheard conversation between Jackson and Mrs Driver.

'According to Jeff, Jackson's been in the business for quite a while,' Sam continued. He sounded almost blasé now. 'And when he moved from France, he just transferred the whole operation here — isn't that right, Jacko?'

Jackson held out his arms to Laura. 'I can explain everything,' he began.

Laura's face crumpled. 'You bastard,' she spat. 'You fucking bastard. You know what? You two are as bad as each other.' She threw one last scornful look at Jackson and ran from the room. A moment later, Sam ran after her.

As the remaining guests stood there in stunned silence, Anthony Lanchester, who had watched events unfold from a balcony, appeared on the podium, flanked by two burly security guards. The club's reputation was his number one priority and there was some swift damage limitation to be done. 'Now listen, everyone,' he said, clasping his hands together. 'Most of us – including our Sportsman of the Year – have had rather a lot to drink tonight, and I don't doubt that in the morning, certain people are going to regret saying certain things. The best thing we can do is go home to our beds and forget whatever it is we think we've heard – for our own good and the good of St Benedict's.' He paused to allow the meaning behind his words to sink in. 'All that remains now is for me to thank you all for coming and wish you a safe journey home. I think you'll all agree it's been an evening to remember.'

Twenty-One

Jackson spent nearly half an hour searching for Laura in the clubhouse and grounds. To his dismay, she was nowhere to be found. He wished he'd reacted quicker, that *he'd* gone running after her, instead of Sam. But he'd been overwhelmed by the situation – all those strangers staring at him, knowing his private business. He performed one last sweep of the front lawn, then sank down on the damp grass and buried his head in his hands. It had been a mistake coming to St Benedict's – but he'd been caught up in the moment and excited at the prospect of wresting Laura from Sam's grasp once and for all. As he sat there alone, terrified at the thought that he might have lost Laura for a second time, he cursed Jeff Goodbody out loud. The golf coach would pay for his indiscretion; Jackson would make certain of that. God knows, he hadn't planned to keep the truth about his business interests from Laura forever – just for a few more weeks, until she and the girls were safely installed at Coldcliffe. But now all his best-laid plans lay in ruins and his guts ached with the unfairness of it all. He stared around the silent grounds and shivered. The air was chill and the breeze moved through the amorphous trees like a ghostly hand. It was clear that, like the rest of the dinner guests, Laura and Sam were long gone, and now it was time for him to make his own way home.

As Jackson headed back to his car, he caught sight of a lone figure standing by the stone balustrade on the terrace. His heart leaped in his chest, but then the figure stepped into the yellowy glow of an art deco streetlamp and he realized it wasn't Laura – but Abi Gainsbourg. She waved when she saw him and beckoned him nearer. All he wanted was to be alone with his thoughts, but in the circumstances he couldn't very well ignore her. As he reached the top of the stone steps, he saw that the caddie's face was puffy and streaked with tears.

'Do you know where they are?' she asked. Her voice sounded thick and snotty. 'I called Sam on his mobile, but it's going straight to voicemail.'

Jackson shook his head. 'No. I've looked all over for them. I guess they went home.'

Abi shivered and pulled her fake fur stole more tightly round her shoulders. 'What do you think's going to happen now?'

Jackson shrugged. 'Who knows?' He turned to go, not wanting to get caught up in a post mortem of the evening's events. 'I'm heading off now. See you around.'

He was halfway down the steps when Abi called out to him. 'Hey, I don't suppose there's any chance of a lift, is there?'

He stopped and looked over his shoulder. 'I'm not sure that's such a good idea.'

'Please,' said Abi. 'I don't want to wait out here on my own for a cab. I don't live far; just off the bypass.'

Jackson frowned. 'What about your husband? He was working here tonight, wasn't he? Can't he take you home?'

'He'll be ages yet,' said Abi. A fat tear rolled down her

cheek. 'In any case, I don't want him to see me in this state.'

Jackson sighed. He hated seeing women cry. Against his better judgement, he was going to have to do the decent thing.

In the kitchen, Xavier was sharpening his knives. Professionally speaking, at least, the day had been nothing short of a triumph. His tasting menu was the toast of the gala dinner and, along with the dirty plates, the waiting staff had ferried back compliment after compliment. Meanwhile, his other little business interest had notched up a spectacular success. Earlier in the day, Flight of Fancy, the twenty-five to one outsider, had romped home in the two p.m. at Haydock Park. Not only had the chef's £200 bet netted him a healthy return, he also stood to receive a quarter share in the prize money. At that moment, however, celebration was the last thing on the Frenchman's mind. His wife was cheating on him, but somehow, miraculously, his stricken heart continued to pump blood around his body. Tomorrow, he was going to have it out with her. Understandably, it wasn't something he was looking forward to.

While the porters returned order to the kitchen, Xavier headed outside for a well-deserved cigarette. Rather than smoke his Gauloise beside the stinking dustbins, he wandered out into the grounds and leaned against a tree, his form almost completely concealed by its shadow. As he stood there, enjoying the feel of the night air against his sweat-soaked chef's whites, he caught sight of a couple walking across the lawn. As they passed under a streetlamp, he realized, with a jolt, that the woman was Abi. Although the couple was some thirty or forty feet away, he would have recognized his wife's outline and deportment anywhere. He glanced at his watch. One fifty a.m. the gala dinner had ended nearly an hour ago. Abi had told him she was getting a cab home. She should have been safely tucked up in bed by now. He watched with mounting rage as the man extended an arm and wrapped it round Abi's shoulders, drawing her into his body. She seemed glad of the support, laying her head against his upper arm, as if her neck were too weak to bear it. Locked in this embrace, they made their way to a classic sports car, parked not in the car park, but in a layby off the main drive, as if they'd arrived in a hurry. Only then did the man release Abi. He unlocked the car and helped her into it as if she were a child or an invalid. The car accelerated away, throwing up a shower of gravel in its wake, and Xavier crushed his burning cigarette in the palm of his hand. He didn't feel a thing.

As he drove away, Jackson was feeling panicky and faintly nauseous. Laura, until an hour ago secure and inviolate, was slipping from his grasp. With one hand on the steering wheel, he opened the glove box and removed a box of tissues. 'Here,' he said, handing it to Abi.

'Thanks, Jackson, you've been ever so kind,' Abi said. She removed a tissue and wiped her eyes. 'I'm sorry about crying on your shoulder back there. I'm an emotional wreck. I can't stop thinking about Sam and that waitress. Did you see her? She only looked about twenty.'

'Put your seat belt on,' Jackson commanded. He was

in no mood to talk. They drove in silence for five minutes or so. Jackson knew the route well and he raced down the dark country lanes with his foot hard on the accelerator. The sooner he got Abi home and he could be alone the better.

'Can I ask you something?' Abi suddenly piped up.

'What?'

'Are you really a drug dealer?'

Jackson turned to look at her and in the split second that his eyes left the road, the Aston's front bumper clipped the edge of a high grass verge. The car was going so fast, it immediately started slewing sideways. Demonstrating the lightning reflexes which had made him such a force on the race track, Jackson fought to bring the vehicle under control. But it was useless. In a matter of seconds, the Aston had gone into a spin and was hurtling across the road before it finally came to rest with its bonnet concertinaed against a mature cedar.

For a moment or two, Jackson sat there motionless, dazed by the impact. It was only as he reached down to release his seatbelt that he noticed the shattered windscreen. He turned to Abi. She was slumped against the door, her head lolling on her chest, her own seatbelt hanging unused from its holster. He spoke her name. She didn't reply. He reached across to her and saw that her fur stole was soaked with blood. Pushing it away, he gasped when he saw the hunk of broken glass embedded in her chest. There was no need to listen for a heart beneath.

It was six in the morning before Jackson was finally released from police custody without charge. Physically and emotionally drained, he returned to the sanctuary of Coldcliffe Hall, where he sank into a troubled sleep, tossing between grotesque reality and savage, frightening dreams. The last twenty-four hours had been the worst of his life. A woman was dead, and the repercussions were too dreadful to contemplate.

At midday, he rose and went to the bathroom, where he stood hunched over the sink and stared at his reflection in the mirror. The face that greeted him was even more hideous than usual. His eyes were sunken and his scars seemed angrier than ever against the pale grey of his skin. He was alone in the house, for it was Sunday and Mrs Driver's day off. Usually, he liked having the place to himself, but now he longed for company: anything to stop him dwelling on the twin horrors of losing Laura and the torn artery inside Abi Gainsbourg's chest. Besides which, there was housekeeping to be done: paperwork to be destroyed and contraband to be removed. That way, if any of the gala dinner guests did decide to blab about his little business empire, there would be no evidence to support their claims. After splashing his face with cold water, Jackson went downstairs and fired off a text to Mrs Driver, telling her to come to the house as soon as possible.

Afterwards, he made a cup of strong, scalding tea and carried it from room to room, trying to get a fix on what needed to be done. Twice, he picked up the phone and put it down again without dialling. He desperately wanted to speak to Laura and tell her about Abi's death before she heard it from some other source. The trouble was, he didn't know what to say to her, even if she were willing to listen. Setting his teacup down on the bureau, he squeezed his eyes shut tight, trying to block out the intrusive thoughts that were crowding his brain and threatening to send him half mad.

At twelve forty-five, Jackson put on his swimming trunks and headed out to the pool, having decided that a swim and a relaxing spot of tai chi would help clear his head. It would be his last dip of the summer; tomorrow, the pool was being drained before the leaves started falling. As he walked across the lawn, towel slung over his shoulder, he looked up at the unfamiliar clouds and shuddered. The weather seemed to have turned overnight and there was a distinctly autumnal flavour in the air. When he reached the patio area, he tossed his towel on a steamer chair and kicked off his sandals.

Some twenty feet away, Xavier crouched behind a row of bushy privets, his lanky frame still clad in his soiled chef's whites from the night before. It was less than ten hours since the Frenchman had learned of his wife's death and a powerful cocktail of shock and grief had left him in a heightened state of arousal. From his hiding place, he studied Jackson's semi-naked body intently, noting bitterly that there wasn't a mark on it. Meanwhile, Abi's rapidly cooling corpse lay in the hospital morgue. According to the police, all the evidence pointed to a simple road accident, but the knowledge did nothing to assuage Xavier's pain. Accident or not, Jackson West had killed his wife. The fact was indisputable.

As he watched his perceived love rival perform a series of tai chi poses barefoot beside the pool, fresh tears began to form in Xavier's red-rimmed eyes. Abi had regularly attended tai chi classes in the fitness suite at St Benedict's, and he found himself wondering if this were where she had met Jackson for the first time. As he executed his graceful routine, Jackson appeared utterly impassive. In stark contrast, Xavier felt as if his internal organs had been wrenched out, ground to a rough paste with pestle and mortar and then forcibly reinserted via his rectum. The chef wiped his damp cheeks angrily with the heel of his hand. Without Abi by his side, all his achievements seemed meaningless, even his glittering Michelin star. He knew then that he had sharpened his knives for the very last time.

Over by the pool, Jackson shifted his weight on to his rear leg, drew his hands slowly apart and began to push forward, as if shutting an invisible door. At that moment, Xavier came crashing through the bushes, teeth bared and right hand held aloft. Seconds later, a blood-curdling scream shattered the afternoon calm of Queen's Crescent. On the balcony of Cedar Lodge, a startled Cindy almost dropped her secateurs. Her pruning forgotten, she spun round and scanned the landscape. At once, her eye was drawn to a pair of figures in the gardens of Coldcliffe Hall, though they were too distant to be recognizable. One lay on the ground, unmoving. The other, who was dressed entirely in white, stood over him, seemingly offering little assistance.

Frowning, Cindy cupped her hands round her mouth and called out to them. 'Hey! Is everything all right?'

The figure in white looked up and gazed towards the balcony. As a beam of watery sunlight fought its way through the clouds, Cindy thought she saw something glinting in his hand. After a few seconds, he turned and began walking briskly away. The man on the ground remained motionless. Heart pounding, Cindy ran back into the master bedroom, pausing only to snatch up her mobile from the bedside table, and raced down the stairs two at a time. She wasn't sure what she had just witnessed, but she was intent on finding out.

The moment she arrived at Coldcliffe, Cindy knew something was seriously amiss. The security gate was partially open – the aperture just wide enough to allow a slim adult access. The control panel, mounted on one of the supporting walls, had apparently been forced open and a jumble of wires spilled out of it. A few metres away, a crowbar lay abandoned on the pavement. Cindy fingered her mobile phone anxiously. The vandalism of the gate indicated the presence of an intruder. Perhaps she should call someone – like Kieran, who was only at St Benedict's and could be back home in less than five minutes – or even the police. Suddenly, she heard a loud wail, punctuated by a splash. Without a second thought for her own safety, Cindy picked up the crowbar and slipped through the gate.

She found Jackson sprawled on the lawn, unconscious and barely clinging to life, a nine-inch, triple-riveted professional meat cleaver embedded in his shoulder blade. With one trembling hand, she dialled 999 on her mobile; with the other, she used Jackson's towel to staunch the flow of blood that had turned the grass beneath him scarlet. She was so busy tending to the former racing driver she failed to notice Xavier, floating face down in the pool. But by then it was already too late.

*

Naturally, the entire bloody chain of events was splashed all over the newspapers. It was a tragedy of almost Shakespearean proportions – one of those 'you couldn't make it up' stories that kept the headline writers busy for weeks. Laura's affair with Jackson came out, as did Sam's fling with Abi. The media interest was so intense that Laura, Sam and their young daughters were forced to go into hiding for several months. Sam even missed the German Masters, which showed – perhaps for the first time – the true extent of his dedication to his family.

Xavier's sister Sylvie flew from Paris for the inquest. Her testimony recounted an early morning phone call in which an hysterical Xavier had told her of Abi's death in a car driven by her *amour*, as he put it. He also told his sister, in no uncertain terms, that he planned to exact revenge on the man he mistakenly believed was sleeping with his wife, though no specifics were discussed. Crucially, Sylvie also revealed that her brother had never learned to swim and possessed a morbid fear of water as a result of a childhood boating accident.

Given the evidence before him, the coroner had no choice but to record an open verdict. Although the post mortem revealed that Xavier died by drowning, nobody knew for sure how he came to be in the water in the first place. Medical experts testified that Jackson would have been immobilized by the first blow of the cleaver and therefore incapable of pushing his assailant into the swimming pool. Two alternatives remained: that Xavier, distraught at the loss of Abi and believing Jackson to be dead, then took the tragedy to its logical conclusion by killing himself. Or, that the chef fell into the pool accidentally, perhaps while trying to wash the blood from his hands.

And so the close-knit community of St Benedict's was left to mourn two of its brightest stars; two young lives snuffed out in their prime. Given Xavier's murderous intentions, no representative from the club's management saw fit to attend his funeral; though they did stump up for a modest wreath. Abi, however, was viewed as a perfectly innocent victim, who just happened to be in the wrong vehicle at the wrong time. Soon after her death, the club established an award in her memory. Presented at the annual gala dinner, the Abi Gainsbourg Medal would be awarded to the caddie who had shown service and dedication above and beyond the call of duty. To salve his guilty conscience, Sam Bentley personally paid for the medal to be struck in solid eighteen-carat gold.

As for Jackson – he survived. But the once great racing driver was destined to spend the rest of his life in a wheelchair. The cleaver – capable of slicing through a pig's carcass with a single stroke – had severed his spinal cord, rendering him permanently paraplegic. Although he had full mobility in his upper body, from the waist down he may as well have been dead. There *was* one piece of good news, however: somehow, Jackson's illegal business operation remained hidden from both police and media. Keen to protect the club's reputation – and not wanting to bite the hand that fed them – the members of St Benedict's had stayed resolutely schtum. So at least Jackson was spared the indignity of a criminal charge for drug dealing. But that, needless to say, was cold comfort.

Epilogue

It was the first week of the New Year. A blizzard had struck Kirkhulme overnight and the clubhouse at St Benedict's looked even more picturesque than usual, covered as it was in a glistening rind of snow. In the Ladies' Lounge, Marianne, Keeley and Cindy were drinking Bloody Marys in front of a fragrant cedar-wood fire.

'I shall be so glad when the winter's over,' said Marianne. 'These cold days and long nights are playing havoc with my skin.' She smiled at Keeley. 'But just think: in three days' time, we'll be sunning ourselves on a tropical beach. I can't wait; I don't think I've ever looked forward to a holiday so much.'

'Me neither,' said Keeley. 'Ryan's such a sweetheart. As if paying for the whole trip wasn't generous enough, he's given me two grand to spend on beachwear.' She held up her hand and began counting off her purchases on her fingers. 'I've bought four new bikinis, three swimming cossies, half a dozen sarongs, eight vest tops, five pairs of flip-flops and the same pair of DKNY sandals in three different colour ways.'

'Goodness, what a lot of stuff,' Cindy remarked. 'You're only going for two weeks, aren't you? I shouldn't think you'll even get to wear half of it.'

Keeley shrugged. 'Probably not, but it doesn't hurt to be prepared. In any case, I didn't spend the *whole* two grand.'

'Really? That's not like you, darling,' said Marianne.

'I know, you should've seen Ryan's face when I handed him two hundred quid change. He tried to give it back to me – "Treat yourself in the spa," he said. But I put my hands behind my back and refused to take it.'

Marianne's eyes widened. 'In that case, it *must* be love.'

'Maybe,' said Keeley with a shy smile. 'It's too early to say for sure.' She gave Marianne a gentle nudge with her elbow. 'Anyway, look who's talking. You and Scott are practically joined at the hip these days.'

Marianne's bosom heaved. 'Honestly, girls, I never thought one man was capable of satisfying me – sexually or emotionally – but Scott's proved me quite wrong. In fact, the only down side of our relationship is all the disapproving looks I keep getting from other women.'

'Why – because they disapprove of the age difference?' Cindy asked.

Marianne snorted. 'Heavens no – because they're all sick as dogs. Take it from me, there's an awful lot of frustrated women at St Benedict's now that Scott's kicked the gigoloing into touch.' She closed her eyes and sighed. 'Our sex life is simply stupendous. The first thing I'm going to do when I get him into that beachfront villa is rip his clothes off and beg him to take me roughly from behind.'

Cindy managed a feeble smile. Even now, she still found Marianne's frankness about sexual matters unnerving. 'I'm *sooo* jealous about your trip,' she said, expertly steering the conversation to more wholesome territory. 'I wish *I* was going to the Maldives.'

'It's still not too late to twist your husband's arm,'

Marianne said. 'Think of the fun the six of us could have together.'

'There's no chance of that, honey. Kieran's booked to do a series of golfing masterclasses at the club. I don't know why he's bothering – it's not like we need the money, especially now that my design business is doing so well.' Cindy gave a self-satisfied smile. 'I knew that working for Jackson would get me noticed, but I had no idea things would take off the way they have. But, then again, I didn't anticipate getting a whole heap of extra publicity in the wake of the attack.'

'Well, it's nice to know *someone* profited from that nasty business,' Keeley said cattily. Even now, four months later, she was still smarting because Cindy had known about Laura's affair before she did.

Marianne gave Keeley a warning look. 'Let's not spoil the mood,' she said tightly. 'Not today, of all days. Speaking of which' – she nodded towards the door – 'I think our guest of honour has just arrived.'

Keeley let out a squeal of delight. 'Laura!' she cried as she went running to greet her friend, who had landed at Delchester Airport just twenty-four hours earlier. 'I've missed you so much,' she said, embracing her. 'St Benedict's hasn't been the same without you.' They joined the other women beside the fire.

'It feels as if I've been away for ever,' said Laura as she kissed first Marianne and then Cindy. 'You girls must fill me in on everything that's been happening.'

Marianne put her arm round Laura's shoulders. 'It's wonderful to see you, darling, it really is. How was Miami?'

'Oh you know . . . hot, busy, brash. Still, Sam managed to get plenty of golf in, and the girls loved living right on the beach.'

'You're positively glowing, honey,' said Cindy. 'That extended break has obviously done you the power of good.'

Laura gave her a wry look. 'Yes, it's just a pity Sam and I didn't have any choice in the matter.'

'It was dreadful the way the press hounded you out of your home like that,' said Keeley. She gave a little shudder. 'I'm so glad all that stuff's behind us now.'

There was a long silence as each of the women silently contemplated the ugly chain of events that had left two people dead and a third paralysed for life. In the midst of their reverie, a waiter appeared. 'Ladies? Your table's ready now, if you'd like to follow me.'

Heads turned as the quartet entered the dining room. There were many who believed the golfer's wife would never dare show her face at St Benedict's again. As Laura slid in beside Cindy on the velvet-covered banquette, she tried to ignore the pointed looks and whispers, but it wasn't easy.

'Don't worry about *them*,' whispered Cindy, sensing her friend's discomfort. 'They'll soon find someone else to gossip about.'

Laura smiled tentatively as she buried her head in the brunch menu. 'I see the food's had an overhaul,' she murmured.

'Yeah, they hired a new chef a couple of months ago,' said Keeley. 'But he's not half as good as Xavier.' She bit her knuckle. 'Sorry, that was really insensitive of me.'

Laura let the menu fall away from her face and looked around the table. During her sojourn in Miami, she'd kept in touch with the others by email and the occasional phone call, but the issue of Xavier's attack on Jackson had never been properly discussed. 'Look, girls, I don't want any of you walking on eggshells around me,' she said. 'We all know what happened, and I'm happy to talk about any of it.'

Keeley didn't need a second invitation. 'I just can't believe you were carrying on with Jackson all those weeks and didn't breathe a word to anyone.' She pursed her lips. 'Anyone except *Cindy*, that is.'

Laura's lower lip wobbled as if she might be about to cry. 'Believe me, I wish with all my heart that I'd never started that stupid affair. Then Xavier and Abi would still be alive and Jackson wouldn't be in a wheelchair.'

'You mustn't blame yourself, darling,' said Marianne forcefully. 'It wasn't you driving the car that killed Abi. It wasn't you wielding the hulking great cleaver that sliced through Jackson's spinal cord.'

At this, Cindy winced. 'Do you have to be quite so graphic?'

Marianne sniffed. 'I'm only stating the facts.' She turned back to Laura. 'Have you been in touch with Jackson since the accident?'

'I sent him some flowers when he was in hospital, but we haven't spoken. That was part of my agreement with Sam when he and I decided to make a go of things.' Laura's voice tailed off as Jeremy, the maître d', approached their table, gliding across the floor as if he were mounted on castors.

'Mrs Bentley, how lovely to see you,' he cooed, making an expansive gesture with his arms.

Laura smiled. 'Thank you, Jeremy. It's good to be back.'

'And how is Mr Bentley?'

'Very well, thank you. He's out on the golf course as we speak.'

'Wonderful! And those gorgeous daughters of yours?'

'Looking forward to seeing their friends again, I think.'

'Fabulous!' said Jeremy, beaming like a proud parent at a school play. 'Now, are you ladies ready to order?'

Laura looked around the table. 'Shall we have our usual, girls?' The others nodded.

'Smoked salmon and caviar blinis for four. Excellent choice,' said Jeremy. 'And to drink?'

'We'll have a bottle of Cristal, to celebrate Laura's homecoming,' said Marianne. 'My treat.'

Laura waited until Jeremy had floated off on his cloud of bonhomie before posing her next question. 'So,' she said, twisting a curl round her finger anxiously, 'have any of you seen Jackson since he was discharged from hospital?'

'He's still living at Coldcliffe,' said Marianne. 'He has a full-time carer now – a jolly, big-boned girl with lots of frizzy hair. I sometimes see her pushing him around the village in his wheelchair.'

'And that scary housekeeper of his is still on the scene,' said Keeley. 'I've heard Jackson relies on her more than ever.'

Laura looked down at her lap. 'So he's still dealing?'

Keeley shrugged. 'Let's just say there's been no let up

in supply to the club shop. Ace is the acting manager now, just until they find a replacement for poor old Jeff.'

'What do you mean, "poor old Jeff"?' exclaimed Cindy. 'Sacking's too good for that man. In my opinion, the club should have notified the PGA and had him banned from working at any golf club in the country.'

'What about Jeff's wife?' Laura asked. 'Did she stand by him?'

Marianne shook her head. 'You're joking, aren't you? She filed for divorce last month. Only a fool would stand by a man who'd cheated on her so publicly.' She reached out and squeezed Laura's forearm. 'No offence, darling.'

Laura smiled sadly. 'None taken.'

'Can I ask you something?' said Cindy, moving a silver-plated cruet set out of the way, so she could rest her elbows on the table.

'Sure.'

'I know you had strong feelings for Jackson, but, with hindsight, do you think you really were in love with him – or was it just that he happened to be there when you were going through a tough time with Sam?'

For a long moment Laura didn't answer. Cindy reached a hand across the table. 'I'm sorry, honey. I shouldn't have asked. It's none of my business.'

Laura took a deep breath. 'Don't be silly. You're my friend; you're entitled to ask personal questions. The answer is yes, I did love him. More than I've ever loved any man.' She sighed. 'And, despite everything that's happened, I think I always will.' Her face hardened. 'But he lied to me and I can never forgive him for that.'

'Sam lied too, and you forgave him,' said Keeley quietly.

Laura's jaw tensed. 'I haven't forgiven him either. But Sam's a good provider – and, more importantly, he's the father of my children. Speaking of which –' She hesitated. Jeremy had arrived with the Cristal. Sensing that the group was deep in a private conversation, he moved swiftly, filling their glasses with a practised hand, before placing the bottle in an ice bucket and sliding away.

'You were saying . . . ?' prompted Marianne.

Laura smiled shyly. 'I wanted you girls to be the first to know.' Her hand went to her stomach. 'There's going to be another addition to the Bentley brood. I'm pregnant.'

There was a stunned silence. Keeley was the first to speak. 'Blimey. That's a turn up for the books.'

'Yes, it was a shock for me and Sam too,' said Laura. 'The pregnancy was an accident, but a happy one.'

Keeley reached out to hug her friend. 'Well, if you're happy, I'm happy too.'

Cindy was next in line. 'Congratulations, honey. That's wonderful news,' she said, kissing Laura on the cheek.

'It certainly is,' agreed Marianne. 'So now we have two things to celebrate.'

'What's this one going to be called?' asked Cindy. 'I know, how about Gleneagles?'

'Or Bogey?' said Keeley gleefully. 'You must admit, it does have a certain ring.'

Laura smiled. 'Sorry to disappoint you all, but Sam and I have picked the names already.'

'And?' Marianne said eagerly.

'If it's a boy, we're going to call him Tiger, after –'

Marianne held up a hand. 'I think we can guess.'

'And, if it's another girl, we're going to call her Isabella, after my grandmother.'

'That's pretty,' said Cindy. She gestured to Laura's stomach. 'You're hardly showing at all. When's the baby due?'

'The end of June – which means Sam'll be a dad twice in the space of five months.'

'Ah yes,' said Keeley. 'Elissa. So what's the score there then?'

'Sam's refusing to have anything to do with her until she's had the baby and a DNA test establishes paternity.'

'How would you feel if the baby does turn out to be Sam's?' Cindy asked gently.

'I don't honestly know. I'm trying not to think about it until it happens.'

Marianne smiled sympathetically. 'Whatever the outcome, you know we'll always be here for you, Laura, don't you?'

'Of course she does,' said Keeley, curling an arm round Laura's midriff.

Cindy nodded. 'Any time of day or night. We'll only be a phone call away.'

Laura looked at her friends, unsure which of them she loved the most. 'Thank you,' she said, her eyes filling with unexpected tears. 'That means a lot to me.' She gazed around the dining room, taking in its elegant chandeliers and sumptuous fabrics. 'It's funny,' she said thoughtfully. 'I was dreading coming back to St Benedict's. I thought that after everything that happened last summer it would feel different somehow. But, you know what, it's just the same.'

'St Benedict's never changes,' said Keeley. 'That's why it always feels like coming home.'

Marianne picked up her champagne glass. 'I'd like to propose a toast.'

'To Laura,' said Keeley, raising her glass.

'And little Tiger-Isabella,' added Cindy.

Laura chinked her glass against the others. 'To St Benedict's,' she said proudly. 'And all who sail in her.'

'St Benedict's,' the others chorused.

Laura smiled, happy to be back where she belonged.